A Navy Commander and F-18 pilot with hundreds of aircraft carrier landings, David E. Stevens holds engineering degrees from Cornell and the University of Michigan with graduate work in astrophysics. He test piloted new fighters and received a technical aviation patent. With a Top Secret clearance, Dave managed classified defense programs and served as Strike Operations Officer for the Persian Gulf. He has traveled to over two dozen countries.

Resurrect was a finalist in the Colorado Gold Action/Thriller of the Year competition, 2011.

RESURRECT

David E. Stevens

MONARCH
BOOKS

Oxford, UK & Grand Rapids, Michigan, USA

First published in the UK in 2012 by Monarch Books
(a publishing imprint of Lion Hudson plc)
Wilkinson House, Jordan Hill Road, Oxford OX2 8DR, England
Tel: +44 (0)1865 302750 Fax: +44 (0)1865 302757
Email: monarch@lionhudson.com
www.lionhudson.com

Published in association with Terry Burns, Hartline Literary Agency, 123 Queenston Drive, Pittsburgh, PA 15235 www.hartlineliterary.com

ISBN 978 0 85721 249 8 (print)
ISBN 978 0 85721 341 9 (Kindle)
ISBN 978 0 85721 342 6 (epub)

Distributed by:
UK: Marston Book Services, PO Box 269, Abingdon, Oxon, OX14 4YN
USA: Kregel Publications, PO Box 2607, Grand Rapids, Michigan 49501

The text paper used in this book has been made from wood independently certified as having come from sustainable forests.

British Library Cataloguing Data
A catalogue record for this book is available from the British Library.

Printed and bound by MPG Books

ACKNOWLEDGMENTS

This book wouldn't have been possible without the help and support of so many. My wonderful wife, Lilli, is the ultimate encourager, supporter and subject-matter expert. Terry Burns, one of the top-ranked literary agents and an award-winning western author, is an amazing and patient man who saw something in my rough manuscripts. Tony Collins, and the Lion Hudson team, courageously took on the project and helped polish it. Special thanks to my brilliant and talented editors. Normandie Fischer taught me much, including what I should have learned in English class. Ryan Deken was great at asking "Why this?" and Jenny Ward, somehow, made it all fit perfectly. A special thanks to Fred Miller for his cinematic perspective and phenomenal wisdom, and to Garrett Johnson for his exceptional artistic and technical work.

The accuracy of this story hinges on the expertise of many, from physicist to philosopher, doctor to district attorney, literary agent to secret agent. I want to give a huge thanks to my subject-matter experts who gave generously of their time, talent, and knowledge: Vince Battistone, Ken Bowersox, Winston Broad, Reed DeVries, Joe Dyer, Amy Eisenbeck, Tommy Harper, Jay Jost, Kristi Kyle, John Marshall, Cherry Meadows, Jerry Meadows, Bill Napier, Jim Roberts, Brett Sappington, Dan Smith, Scott Straub, and Joe Veverka. A few remain unnamed, due to the dangerous work they do to keep the world safe.

I also want to thank the many awesome reviewers, authors, friends, and family members who helped me craft a better story. They include: Joe and Linda Baggett, Chris Boblit, Stan Boyd, Jackie Bray, Albert Comulado, Victoria Comulado, Naomi Chuckwuk, Lori Davidson, Lori Derr, Nikki Dutton, Susan Dyer, Lester and Margaret Eisenbeck, Susan Femino, Ken and Lisa Farnham, Tim Goad, Rob Gryger, Lesia Harper, Laura Stevens-Hawkins, Dan Hawkins, Kathy Heard, Chandler Johnson, Christian Johnson, Judy Johnson, Kevin Johnson, Rob King, Leslee Kitchings, Tracy Kuhar, Tim Hendricks, Mike Lee, Sheila Mannion, Nancy Mayhew, Steve McQueen, Gene Mixson, Molly Mueller, Mary Ann Moore, Richard Mustakos, Mike Pasternack, Noelle Pedersen, Lee Person, Cletus Pew, Michelle Pliska, Betsy Smith, Ray Stone, Bart Waggoner and Pat Weiler.

I
RE-ENTRY

1

DEPART

Thirty-foot blue-white blowtorches slashed the twilight, driving the twenty-ton fighter down the runway like an angry rhino on crack. Using small rudder corrections, Commander Josh Logan kept the overpowered F-18 Super Hornet tracking straight. Clumsy and ungainly on the ground, it transformed into an agile and graceful bird of prey as it leaped into the air.

He was delivering the brand-new fighter to a squadron on the West Coast. It was a routine ferry flight, but it felt great to be back in the air and away from his desk.

The 50-million-dollar Hornets, assembled only a few hundred yards away at the Boeing plant, shared St. Louis International Airport with commercial airliners. The air-traffic controllers wanted the fighters out of their crowded airspace as soon as possible. Happy to oblige, Josh pulled the jet into a sixty-degree climb. Smiling, he knew his vertical departure in afterburner dominated the dusk like a comet. He'd loved roller-coasters as a kid. Fighters were just roller-coasters without the track.

As he raised the landing gear, he caught something out of the corner of his eye – a tiny blur of motion accompanied by the slightest of vibrations. He quickly checked his engine instruments – everything looked OK.

The red-tailed hawk tucked its wings and dove, but too late. It struck inside the landing gear bay at 250 miles an hour. The bird expired in an explosion of feathers, the impact creating a hairline fracture in a high-pressure fuel line.

As he rocketed through 10,000 feet, Josh pulled the Hornet out of burner and reduced his rate of climb. Checking his radar, he slewed a cursor on one of the cockpit screens with his throttle-mounted mouse. He realized he was just working on his "office computer" – like everyone else. There were a *few* differences. His office chair was a thinly padded ejection seat, his phone, a mic inside his oxygen mask. Noisier than most offices, his sat a few feet in front of hundreds of twirling titanium turbine blades, shredding air at 70,000 rpm.

Office dress code required a suit – a green fire-resistant flight suit. Over it, he wore a G-suit zipped tightly around his legs and stomach. During hard turns, it inflated, forcing blood back to the brain to prevent blackout. G-suits were sophisticated technology, but he always thought they looked like… green cowboy chaps. He'd never ridden a horse, but strapping into a fighter might not be that different than saddling up a high-strung bronco. They shared the promise of a wild ride, and both were capable of ejecting their riders.

Scanning his engine instruments, Josh saw the rpm sagging on the left engine, but it was within limits.

He checked in with Kansas City Center for his final cruise altitude.

They responded, "Hornet Zero Seven, climb and maintain flight level four seven zero."

Josh repeated the altitude back followed by a "roger." Technically, the correct response was "wilco," meaning, "will comply." Like most pilots, he never used it. Probably just an inherent dislike of being compliant.

As he flew toward the sunset, he realized that if there were such a thing as a perfect life, he had it. The Navy had promoted him early and he'd married an amazing woman. His friends jokingly told him it was all downhill after the honeymoon. Recalling the passion of last night's first anniversary celebration, Josh knew they were wrong.

The only damper had been this morning, when the subject of children had come up yet again. They'd agreed to wait a year. It had been exactly one year. He hadn't said anything, but she could read him like a book. She was ready; he wasn't. She'd been uncharacteristically quiet as he left the house.

To the cockpit he said, "I'm a test pilot. I've flown in combat and landed on carriers." He sighed. But raising kids…

Leveling off at 47,000 feet, he tabled the internal debate and enjoyed the view. His accommodations were Spartan, but unlike many offices, his had a window, and what a window it was. The fighter's bubble canopy gave him a panoramic view with only a centimeter of Plexiglas separating him from the cold, thin, 600-mph air.

Nine miles high, cruising on a thundering twin-turbine Harley, he chased the setting sun across the continent. The sun always won, but, flying close to the speed of sound, he gave it a run for its money. Sunsets, normally lasting fifteen minutes, stretched to an hour. With 80 per cent of the atmosphere below him, he saw a brilliantly compressed sunset with colors that spanned the spectrum. Above him was the dead, dark black of space. Stars stared down, unblinking, having lost their atmosphere-induced twinkle. The black dome ended in a narrow strip of deep iridescent purple. The purple feathered into infinite shades of blue, from the darkest navy, across a band of powdery sky-blue, into a brief gasp of turquoise. Finally, an explosion of brilliant yellows, fluorescent oranges, and deep, rich reds cut the horizon like a rip in the heavens.

He savored the beauty and solitude of extreme altitude, knowing there'd be few of these moments in the years ahead. A thirty-two-year-old Commander, he had one real flying tour left. He'd really miss it… everything but the night carrier landings. Landing a twenty-ton fighter at night, on a moving deck the size of a tennis court, was still the stupidest thing he'd done more than once. Darkness stole any peripheral vision, and with it that indefinable *feel*, leaving nothing but an elaborate video game with a penalty – lose and you die.

A familiar female voice broke his reverie. Bitching Betty – the pilot's nickname for the automated warning system – spoke when the computer detected an emergency requiring immediate action. In her calm, sultry voice, she shared the worst words in her limited vocabulary – "Engine Fire Left. Engine Fire Left."

Josh's first reaction was disbelief, followed by a curse as he slammed the left throttle off. Jabbing the Fire Warning light, he cut fuel flow to the engine. He then punched the fire-extinguisher button, releasing a flood of halon gas. Holding his breath, he waited... and waited.

It seemed an eternity, but it was only seconds before the fire light extinguished. Breathing again, he saw his now single-engine jet was losing airspeed rapidly. He throttled up the remaining engine and pushed the nose into a descent.

Kansas City Center called. "Hornet Zero Seven, we show you descending out of your assigned altitude, say intentions."

"Center, Zero Seven, had a fire. Declaring an emergency. Need to land as soon as possible."

"Hornet Zero Seven, say fuel remaining and souls on board."

Why did they always say, "Souls on board?" It was standard aviation terminology, but it gave him the creeps. "I have plenty of fuel, and it's just me. Need a vector to the nearest field with at least 5,000 feet of runway."

The Center Controller came back quickly. "Closest field is Kansas City, ten degrees right of your nose, seventy miles. You're cleared direct."

He turned to the new heading and scanned his displays. The right engine and hydraulics looked good. He had plenty of fuel, but automatically checked his gauge – 7,000 pounds. Wait... that couldn't be right. He'd had over 8,000 a minute ago! As he watched, the digital indicator dropped to 6,900. It suddenly made sense. Here was the fire's source – a massive fuel leak. He timed the drop and did a quick calculation. He'd be out of fuel in ten minutes. He was pleased he could remember how to multiply. IQ dropped with adrenaline, and he was producing his share.

"Center, Hornet Zero Seven, looks like a major fuel leak caused the fire. I have, maybe, ten minutes left. Need something closer. I'll take *anything* with even 3,000 feet of runway."

The Controller, now matching some of the stress in Josh's voice, said, "Standby, Zero Seven."

Josh edged the throttle up gingerly, increasing his airspeed and descent. He was in a race, stuck between the proverbial rock and a hard place. With his jet hemorrhaging fuel, the last thing he wanted to do was run the remaining engine *hotter*. But it was either burn it or lose it.

"Hornet Zero Seven, there's a small airport on the outskirts of the city, fifty-five miles from your position. It has a 4,000-foot runway."

"I'll take it."

"Hornet Zero Seven, turn right to heading two niner five. Descend at pilot's discretion. We're clearing all traffic between you and the field. Destination weather is broken to overcast with a 1,200-foot ceiling."

He pushed the fighter into a steeper descent, accelerating to 450 knots. It felt more like a dive-bombing run than a landing approach. He refined his heading and scanned his fuel gauge for the umpteenth time. He might have just enough fuel to make it.

He realized that his current job would prevent situations like this in the future. Testing new fighters was just a collateral duty. His real job was program manager for the next generation of robo-fighters, Unmanned Combat Aerial Vehicles or UCAVS.

Center switched him to Approach Control. Doing 400 knots as he checked in, they cleared him to break the 250-knot speed limit below 10,000 feet.

Fifteen miles from the airfield, he descended into the clouds, leaving the sunset of the heavens above for the darkness below. As he transitioned to flying by instruments, Betty, with no apparent concern, said, "Fuel Low. Fuel Low." With adrenaline rising again, he was thankful for his Heads-Up Display. The green flight symbols appeared to float ten feet in front of the windscreen, keeping his eyes out of the cockpit and slashing his workload. The technology was pure magic, referred to by fighter pilots as PFM.

He punched through the bottom of the overcast, leveling off 1,000 feet above the ground. Below the clouds, it was dark, but the Approach Controller had lined him up nicely. He saw the runway lights, seven miles off his nose.

The Approach Controller gave him the tower frequency and added, "Good luck."

He thanked her, switched to the tower, and pulled the throttle back to idle to slow down.

As he checked in, the tower immediately cleared him to land. He didn't even know the name of the airport, but he could tell he was in the middle of suburban sprawl. Under him was an ever-expanding grid of street and house-lights, spread out like an illuminated net as far as he could see. Ahead, he saw the telltale flashing red lights of the crash trucks flanking the runway.

Slowing to 250 knots, he lowered his landing gear and flaps. He was only four miles from the runway. He was going to make it.

As the landing gear came down, he felt an unusual thump, followed by the simultaneous illumination of both engine fire lights. Looking up, he saw an orange reflection in his canopy rear-view mirrors. At the slower speed, the flames were now clearly visible between the fighter's twin tails. Opening the landing-gear doors must have pushed air into the engine bay, reigniting the fuel. His fire extinguisher was empty and the jet could explode at any second. The emergency procedure for this situation was simple – eject. But he was over a populated area and so close to the runway.

He coaxed his fighter. "Come on, baby. We're almost there." The fire trucks would be ready to spray him down if he could just get the fighter on the runway.

Less than a minute from touchdown, he felt the sick sensation of deceleration. He shoved the throttle forward to no effect. He still had 1,000 pounds of fuel! With a terrible sinking feeling in his stomach, he knew the fire had burned through his remaining fuel lines.

Betty casually added, "Engine Right. Engine Right," as his other engine flamed out.

Only two miles from the runway... but it might as well have been 200. Twenty-ton fighters made lousy gliders.

Everything began to move in slow motion. He knew that in fifteen seconds, the beautiful new jet would slam into the ground. The fireball would blow burning metal and graphite across several acres. There were too many lights below. Each was someone's home, someone's life and family. The small airport was in the middle of suburbia. He couldn't eject... not yet.

Scanning the ground, he saw a small, dark area a half mile to his left. No lights meant no houses. The floating green symbol in his HUD projected his flight path, or in this case, his impact point. If he turned, he *might* have just enough height to glide the burning fighter into the dark area. He banked the jet away from the runway. To make sure the wounded Hornet didn't turn or stall, he'd have to get as close as possible before punching out.

With the engines silent, the tower must have determined his intentions. Their last transmission was simply, "Good luck and Godspeed."

As the last engine spooled down, the hydraulic pressure began to falter. The jet responded sluggishly, as if angry with him for heading away from the runway. He had to use exaggerated stick inputs to control the dying fighter.

To slow his descent, he needed to hold the nose up, but the jet began to buffet and shake as it approached stall speed. If the Hornet stalled, it would roll over and tumble to the ground. There were houses on each side, and under his nose was a brightly lit and occupied soccer field. He fought his instinct and pushed the stick forward, increasing his descent rate to maintain flying speed. As he dropped through 200 feet, Betty pointlessly shared, "Altitude. Altitude."

Just a few more seconds.

Red hydraulic fluid sprayed across the wing like blood from a severed artery, as Betty spoke her final words. "Flight Controls. Flight Controls." With no hydraulic pressure, the jet began an uncontrolled roll to the right. Even as he slammed the stick left, he realized the futility. His Hornet had bled out. She was dead.

Letting go of the useless stick, he pulled the yellow-and-black handle between his legs.

An explosive charge immediately blew the giant bubble canopy off the jet. Simultaneously, his shoulder, waist and leg restraints retracted, yanking him firmly against the seat. With the force of a couple sticks of dynamite, the ejection charge detonated. Rattling his skull and compressing his spine, the seat blasted up the rails like an artillery shell. As it cleared the cockpit, its rocket motors ignited, firing him into the night.

The ejection occurred well outside the seat's design envelope. The altitude was too low, the bank angle too high. The rocket-propelled seat tried to right itself as it accelerated from the almost inverted jet. Clipping the top of the forest at over 100 miles an hour, it ripped through the treetops, breaking branches and bones. Sensing extremely low altitude, the seat's simple barometric sensor deployed the parachute. The chute shredded. Its tangled shroud lines caught and slung Josh like a puppet on the end of a string, slamming him against the trees. Finally, his unconscious body slid to the forest floor like a rag doll. Shock constricted his arteries as his heart struggled against the decreasing volume of blood from internal hemorrhaging.

A quarter mile away, a boiling cloud of orange and white flame climbed above the forest, as the fighter followed its pilot into the ground. The young soccer players stopped in their tracks to watch the orange mushroom cloud expand above the treetops. Like a short fireworks finale, rolling thunder echoed through the woods as the artificial sunrise briefly lit the forest.

Josh opened his eyes. He saw the silhouette of treetops against the soft orange glow of the low clouds. The orange cast came from the sprawl of sodium-vapor streetlights surrounding the woods where he lay. He knew the funeral pyre of his late Hornet added a flicker to the glow. A few stars peeked through a hole in the cloud cover. Faintly, he heard sirens in the distance. Otherwise, it was the peaceful quiet of an early spring evening before the crickets awoke. He couldn't move or feel anything. His only sensation was sight and the metallic taste of blood.

He knew he was dying. With surprising calm and clarity, he realized he'd had an incredible life. He'd done things that most only dreamed of.

What was next? His dad was a pragmatic scientist. As a child, Josh had never attended church, but he'd always wondered if humans really were accidental combinations of organic molecules. He didn't see sufficient evidence to believe in God, but knew that lack of proof didn't prove anything.

His vision began to fade. His thoughts went to Kelly. Not just his wife; she was his best friend. He wished he could see her, tell her it would be OK… His thoughts became less distinct. If there were a God and an afterlife… he'd soon find out. As his heart beat its last beat, he thought, at least I get to see the stars one last time…

2

NETHERWORLD

He awoke in pervasive nothingness, his mind floating unmoored. He wanted to open his eyes and move, but didn't know how. It was the panic of waking up in a different bed and, for a moment, having no idea where you were… but it never stopped. He tried to speak into the nothingness. "Is anyone there?" He couldn't hear his own voice in this sensory-deprived netherworld. There was an intellectual fear but no adrenalin. He needed to *feel* something, anything.

Trying to remember how he got here, he suddenly realized he had perfect recall. In fact, it was as if he could access every memory he'd ever had and view them in IMAX. Maybe it was like the total recall of hypnosis, but it really didn't matter how it worked. He couldn't maintain his self, his sanity, in the nothingness. Reviewing his life as if it were a movie, he began to feel more grounded, more relaxed… if only he had some popcorn.

He began with his childhood and realized he was *seeing* it through the eyes of his young self, but *processing* it from an adult's perspective and without the emotion. It was hard not to flinch – figuratively speaking, since he had nothing to flinch – at the many dumb things he did. Watching events that had seemed terribly traumatic at the time, confirmed that tragedy plus time equals comedy.

As a young adult, he'd always thought of himself as a logical creature, but his review was proving him wrong. How many times had he rationalized or justified actions that were neither rational nor justifiable? How often had he built illogical cases in his mind, brick by emotional brick, mortaring them together with anger or fear? From his current perspective, it was pathetically transparent. The childhood saying, "Sticks and stones may break my bones, but words will never hurt," was a lie. The lasting pain was caused by words. Words he heard… and words he spoke. He wished he could go back and undo them.

As he moved forward in time, some events held particular clarity. They were usually turning points or brushes with death, often both. By focusing on them, he found he could immerse himself in them as if he were there.

The aircraft carrier and its escort ships were skirting a typhoon in the South Pacific. Josh's squadron commander asked him to fly the tanker mission that night. His job was to provide extra gas to those struggling to land… meaning he would be the last one back.

The typhoon took an unexpected turn and the weather went from bad to worse. Wind and waves tossed the 100,000-ton carrier like a child's bathtub toy. The recovering jets had to make multiple approaches to land, forcing Josh to give away all his extra fuel.

As the last jets made it aboard, the storm increased in intensity, going from worse to nightmarish. Visibility dropped to almost zero as the sea and sky merged into a violent, visceral pitch-black. Josh had only enough fuel for one approach. If he failed to catch a wire, there would be no tanker for him and no second chance. He'd flameout and eject into the typhoon. With the helicopters grounded, there'd be no way to find him in the forty-foot waves.

With a quick, vague prayer, he flew his best instrument approach through the tortured air. It was like trying to keep a roller-coaster on glide slope. Less than a quarter mile from the ship, he saw absolutely nothing beyond the nose of his fighter. Finally, only seconds to impact and still blind, he had to abort the approach or risk crashing into the ship or sea.

Just as he added power, the ship emerged like an apparition through the thick, oily sheets of rain. He was way too high and too far right. Knowing it was his only chance, he pulled the throttle to idle and slapped the stick hard left, dipping the wing in an attempt to dump lift. The fighter fell like an express elevator. At the same time, the ship's deck, pushed by the giant ocean swells, heaved up to meet it. As he tried desperately to level the wings, his fighter slammed down onto the deck with all the grace of a "Fat Albert" belly flop. The left tire exploded as the Hornet bounced back into the air. Somehow, the tip of the tail hook caught the fourth and final steel cable, ripping the jet violently out of the night. He went from pilot to crash-test dummy in two seconds. Sitting motionless on the flight deck, hands still clenching the stick and throttle, he was pleasantly surprised to be aboard and alive.

Looking back, he realized the death-defying endorphin highs must have muted the memories, allowing him to be lured back into the night sky again and again.

As he continued to review his life, he wasn't sure if minutes or days passed. He saw Kelly, his wife, and followed their one-year marriage. He replayed in detail his last night and morning with her. Finally, he replayed the fire and ejection. It was like watching a movie with a sad ending... but it was his movie. A collage of opposing emotions washed through him. He was proud and embarrassed, peaceful and frustrated, happy and wistful. Surprisingly, he found it easier to accept his failures than his what-ifs. He could have, he should have, done so much more. With that thought, his consciousness dissolved.

A little past midnight, a dark sedan pulled up in front of a small house in suburban St. Louis. A uniformed Navy Captain stepped out. He walked slowly to the front door and rang the doorbell. He waited. The door opened. A pretty, redheaded woman in a bathrobe greeted him with surprise. Calling him by name, she invited him in. Her smile faded as she saw his expression.

Do you know what happened?

Josh was suddenly conscious, remembering everything that had transpired. He still had no physical sensation, no sensory input from his body at all. He realized his world was neither dark nor light, silent nor loud. It just *was*. He sensed the passage of time, but couldn't be sure if it were real or an illusion.

He heard the voice again. *Do you know what happened?*

"Yes... well... no. I waited too long to eject." He still couldn't hear himself speak. "I thought I..."

You were severely injured.

Severely injured was way better than dead. After his life review, he was surprised to be having this conversation. He must be in a hospital. "Where am I?"

You have a decision to make. The doctors cannot save your body, but you can be given a new life, a new mission.

Like laughing at a funeral, he almost asked if he were on a reality TV show. Instead, he said, "Can't *save* my body? What do you mean?"

Ignoring his question, the voice continued calmly. *If you accept, you can never go back to your old life. Those you knew will believe you died in the crash.*

Died? "Who are you?"

Your questions will be answered if you accept, but you must choose.

He didn't doubt his body was on life support, but if that were true, how could he be having this conversation? He couldn't see or feel anything, yet he clearly heard the voice. Actually, he clearly *understood* the voice. Was he really *hearing* it? If this were a dream, it didn't matter, but he couldn't convince himself it was a dream. If it were real... well, the choice was simple. He felt stupid, but had to ask, "I need to know I'm not making some kind of contract that I... I don't understand." What did they want from him?

He almost sensed amusement in the reply.

You will be able to act in any way you believe appropriate.

He had a million questions. It was odd; he should feel sad or frightened, but felt neither. It was as if he were choosing a cell phone plan. "OK."

His consciousness faded.

A flag-draped casket sat on a stand in a cemetery. Arrayed around the casket, in neat rows of folding chairs, were family and close friends. Surrounding them, and filling much of the small cemetery, was a sea of formal white uniforms with colorful ribbons, contrasted by an equal number of dark suits and black dresses.

A Navy color guard silently removed the flag from the casket and slowly, with great ceremony, folded it into a neatly tucked triangle. They handed it to a Navy Captain standing at attention. A large and imposing figure, the Captain wore a formal-dress white uniform with a chestful of medals and ribbons. He took the flag and slowly stepped to the widow's side. Dropping to one knee and speaking to her very softly, he offered her the flag.

As she accepted, four F-18 Hornets approached the cemetery at low altitude. They flew in a tight "V" formation, one fighter to the left of the lead aircraft, and two to the right. Just before they reached the cemetery, the second jet on the right abruptly pulled straight up and away from the other three. The single jet flew off toward the sunset, leaving an obvious hole in the formation. Breaking the solemn silence, the "missing man" formation flew directly over the top of the ceremony. The widow, stoic to this point, looked up with tears streaming down her face.

He woke again, in a world of no sight or sound. He had so many questions. Once again, he asked, "Who are you?"

Who do you think we are?

A ridiculous scene popped into his head. It was the opening sequence of an old TV rerun he'd watched as a kid called *The Six Million Dollar Man*. Almost killed in a crash, the main character was rebuilt as a bionic man. Even forty years later, it was ludicrous. The technology required to run sixty miles an hour still wasn't possible. On the other hand, genetic science had advanced to the point where it *was* possible to clone almost anything. No doubt, that included *human* parts. Many possibilities ran through his mind. He remembered one of his college courses taught by the astronomer, Carl Sagan. Sagan introduced them to Occam's Razor, a principle that dated back to the fourteenth century. It simply stated that, all things being equal, the simplest solution was usually the correct one.

"I'm guessing you're some classified agency with advanced medical technology?"

No response.

He was about to repeat the question, but wasn't sure he wanted confirmation that he was a lab rat. Instead, he asked, "What's your name? What do I call you?"

You may use whatever name you wish.

That didn't help at all. Feeling a little rebellious, he said, "When I was a kid, I pretended to have an *invisible* playmate. I called him

Jesse." A little sarcastically, he added, "You're invisible, so…"

Silence.

He thought it was pretty funny, but changed the subject. "What exactly is your mission or purpose?"

Mankind.

"Ah, yeah, that's great." He was talking to a flippin' fortune cookie. "Could you be more specific?"

You have a lot to learn. First, there are some rules that we must cover.

He thought, here was the fine print.

You can never return to your past life. You will not look as you did. Your friends and family will believe that you are dead and buried.

He'd pushed those thoughts aside, but with Jesse's comment came a flood of emotions. He couldn't see Kelly? Slowly, he said, "I… I have to know my wife's OK."

It has been difficult for her, but she's strong. She's moved on. Pursuing your past will only make it worse for you and for those you knew. Success in your new life may save hers. You must let her go.

Let her go? What did that mean…? He couldn't think about it, not now. With a mental sigh, he said, "OK, what is it that I'm going to be working on?"

What destroys life?

"There you go. Cheer me up by talking about death on a *global* scale. That's easy – *we* destroy life."

Mankind has destroyed the most life?

"Oh… are you talking about natural catastrophes, mass extinctions, stuff like that?"

Yes.

"Yeah, I guess we're amateurs compared to Mother Nature." He paused. "Why are you asking?"

Mankind's climb to civilization has been neither smooth nor steady.

He thought for a moment. "You're telling me this, because we're facing some kind of natural disaster… aren't we?"

Yes.

"Cataclysmic?"

Yes.

"What is it?!"

You will learn soon enough. It's time to begin your transition back.

Before he could object, he felt his consciousness fade once again.

When Josh awoke, he still couldn't see anything, but instead of the absence of sight, there was absence of light. He actually *felt* something, almost as if he were moving. It was odd, but better than feeling nothing. He sensed Jesse's presence.

"So, have you fixed me up?"

Yes.

Impatient, he said, "Why can't I see anything?"

All in time.

He reverted to humor. "Can I run faster and jump higher?"

Yes.

He'd been kidding. "Really?"

Your physical abilities were enhanced.

"Enhanced? What do you mean?"

Your abilities are not unique, but they are rare.

"How rare?"

One in a million.

"How'd you do that?"

It's time for you to return.

"Wait! Return to what? You haven't told me what disaster we're facing, or what I'm supposed to do! Who am I working with?"

You can ask for guidance any time.

"Guidance! What are you talking about?" As his awareness faded, he had an ironic and slightly terrifying thought. Would it not be poetic justice if he were to become some sort of biological UCAV with Jesse as his "controller"?

An ambulance arrived at Kansas City Medical Center. As they rolled a man into the trauma area, the ER doctor asked the paramedic, "What do we got?"

"Male, probably early thirties, found on the side of the road. No obvious signs of trauma. Vitals are stable, good pressure and EKG, pupils equal and reactive, but he's not responsive."

"Who is he?"

"Don't know."

"No ID?"

"No clothes. He was naked as a jaybird."

The ER nurse was already hooking up an IV and drawing blood as the doctor started the exam. Lifting the patient's eyelids, he shined a small flashlight into the pupils. He then looked in the John Doe's mouth, listened to his chest with a stethoscope, and felt carefully around his head and neck. Peeling his gloves off, he said, "Soon as you got the blood, let's get his noggin a CAT scan, stat."

The blood test results arrived as they rolled the John Doe back from Radiology.

Flipping through the lab results, the doctor said, "Hmm." He took his glasses off and rubbed his eyes.

The ER nurse raised her eyebrows. "Anything?"

"Yeah, his blood work's a lot better than mine." He looked up and saw the radiologist who had accompanied the John Doe.

She shook her head. "Sorry, I got nothing on him either. Did a full body scan. He's clean from stem to stern." As she turned to depart, she said, "Let me know what you find, I'm curious."

"Will do."

The doctor took out a pen, went to the foot of the gurney. He ran the pen up the sole of the John Doe's foot, pressing hard.

Frowning, he said to the nurse, "He *shouldn't* be out." He hated giving up a patient without a diagnosis. With a sigh, he shook his head and said, "Send him up to Neuro ICU. Nothing more we can do for him here."

3

AWAKE

A high-pitched hum penetrated his sleep. He was *so* tired. It was just too much effort to swat the mosquito away. He tried to ignore it and stay in his warm, comfortable, half-dream state, but it wouldn't go away. The irritating hum grew louder and became pervasive like the relentless racket of summer cicadas.

Frustrated, he finally opened his eyes – to blurry white squares. The annoying sound began to clarify, becoming a combination of electronic beeps, clicks, and voices. The white squares slowly came into focus as acoustic ceiling tiles. For a terrifying second, he couldn't remember anything, not even who he was. He felt like he was falling and spinning out of control. He closed his eyes tightly.

After a few seconds, the spinning stopped and his memories slowly filtered back. Like streetlights after sunset, they illuminated one by one. He remembered. He remembered everything. He remembered that he no longer had any history, family, or friends.

He opened his eyes. In contrast to his fuzzy emotional state, his senses were razor-sharp. The lights were overly bright, colors artificially vivid. It was as if someone had maxed out the color and brightness settings on a TV. He could read the ridiculously tiny print on the needle-disposal box across the room. He heard several voices outside of what was obviously a hospital room. He not only heard them, he could easily differentiate conversations.

"… his oxygen is 95 per cent, but we still need to watch…"

"… finished prepping the girl in room three for surgery…"

"… pretty comfortable for stilettos, and they were like 50 per cent off…"

His vision and hearing were sensitive, almost overwhelming.

He'd have to get used to it. He propped himself up on his right elbow and immediately felt dizzy and queasy, reminiscent of the alcohol-induced spins that followed a good squadron party. His body responded to his commands, but sluggishly. It felt like the residual effects of a head-to-toe Novocain injection. Lifting his left hand, he saw an IV attached. He carefully turned his hand over, examining it.

"Look familiar?"

Startled, he looked up to see a woman standing in the doorway wearing blue scrubs.

She watched him for a moment and then entered the room, looking concerned.

He realized her comment had been in jest, and he probably looked like a deer-in-the-headlights. Finally, he asked the obvious. "Where am I?" It came out as a raspy whisper.

He saw relief cross her face. "You're in Kansas, Kansas City Medical Center. How are you feeling?"

He was in a public hospital? His voice was still hoarse but getting stronger. "What day is it?"

Pointing at a large digital clock and calendar on the wall to his left, she said, "Monday, March 23rd."

He was relieved. It had only been a few days since the crash. As he looked at the clock and then the calendar, he blinked. No, that couldn't be. He stared at the calendar. It was a few days... *and one year*! What happened? Where was Jesse or his team?

Frowning, he finally looked back at his nurse, really seeing her for the first time. She was attractive, early thirties, tall and athletically slim with dark eyes and blonde hair.

Again, softly, she asked, "How are you feeling?"

"I'm sorry. I feel OK, I guess." He cleared his throat. "I'm just a little..."

"Disoriented?" she finished.

He nodded. As his voice grew stronger, it became stranger. His inflections and accent were the same, but his voice sounded different.

"That's understandable. You've been unconscious for a few days. What's your name?"

That was a good question. For some reason, he was on his own right now. He needed time to figure things out. The best answer was probably closest to the truth. Frowning, he cocked his head to one side and said, "You know, I'm... I'm not sure."

With a professional smile, she said, "Well, I'm your ICU nurse." She spoke slowly, as if he were a child. "My name is Elizabeth. Don't worry, we'll figure out what yours is." She patted him on the shoulder. "Probably just temporary amnesia. I'm going to let your doctor know you're awake. Be right back."

After she left, he wanted to get to the bathroom mirror. Lifting his sheet, he discovered that in addition to the IV, he was tethered with EKG leads and a catheter. He wasn't going anywhere.

His nurse returned almost immediately with a doctor in tow.

"I'm Dr. Tracy Dutton, your Neurologist."

He smiled. "Hi, I guess I'm... not sure."

"How are you feeling?"

"Fine."

"Do you hurt anywhere?"

"No."

"Do you know what happened to you?"

"No." That was the truth.

"Do you know where you are?"

He nodded toward his nurse. "She said I'm in Kansas. How did I get here?"

"A few days ago," the doctor exchanged a quick glance with the nurse, "you were found by the side of the road without any clothes." Continuing, she asked, "Do you know if you're allergic to anything?"

He looked down. That didn't make any sense. Why would they leave him like that? He frowned, shaking his head. Where were they? Where had *he* been for the past year?

Looking back up, he said, "I'm... I'm sorry. What did you say?"

He saw compassion on the nurse's face, as the doctor slowly repeated the question.

He replied, "Allergies? I... I don't know."

With a slight frown the doctor said, "I'm going to check a few things, OK?"

He nodded dumbly.

She shined a penlight into each eye and asked him to watch

her fingertips as they moved. She had him move his hands and feet, squeeze her fingers, and then tapped him on the knee. Pulling up a chair, she asked, "Can you remember anything at all from your past?"

He was hungry. "I like hamburgers."

She smiled. "We'll have food sent up right away."

Trying to avoid more questions, he pointed to his IV. "May I get... unhooked?"

"Now that you're awake, I don't see why not. Elizabeth will take care of that."

She asked a few more questions, made some notes, and left.

Dr. Dutton paused in the hall and spoke quietly to Elizabeth. "He checks out OK, but the amnesia worries me. Keep an eye on him."

Elizabeth nodded. She'd been thinking the same. Returning to his room, she said, "Let's get you mobile." She put on latex gloves and pulled a cart over. "We'll start with the IV."

He nodded and then looked away.

Why were men so squeamish when it came to blood and needles? While he carefully studied the wall, she studied him. He had short, curly, dark hair with unusual, almost red, highlights. A strong jaw gave him a good masculine face, very handsome but approachable.

Finishing with a band-aid on his hand, she said, "That takes care of the IV. Now, we'll remove your EKG leads."

He looked back at her with some relief and smiled. His eyes were gray – no, actually, they were a color she'd never seen. They looked as though someone had mixed all the eye colors in a blender, sort of a steel-gray with flecks of brown, green, and blue mixed in, beautiful and intense.

She opened the top of his gown. As she pulled the EKG leads off his chest, she remembered being surprised that he had no scars. When he arrived, they'd literally checked every square inch of his body for identifying marks. His skin was perfect. It wouldn't have been out of place on a kid, but even little kids had inoculation marks.

"OK, just one more thing, and you'll be free." She knew removing the urinary catheter was going to be uncomfortable and awkward for him. Distracting him, she said, "I don't know if you are... or were, into tech stuff, but everyone's talking about the new app called

Imagine. They're releasing it tomorrow. It's for smart phones, pads, and laptops. It works across every system from Apple to Android, and is supposed to be the ultimate personal digital assistant." She smiled. "The mother of all apps."

Grimacing, with one eye closed, he asked, "What does it do?"

She continued talking casually as she worked. "Everything. It combines GPS, calendar, language translator, video conference, search engine, practically every app ever invented, supposedly, all in one seamless program."

Clenching the bedrail, he whispered, "Expensive?"

"No. They're offering it free, at least for now. I'm sure once we're all addicted and can't live without it, they'll charge for upgrades, like everything else."

As she finished and cleaned him up, she thought he definitely had the body of a professional athlete. He could have been Michelangelo's model for *David*, except he was a bit more buff... in several areas. "OK, we're done."

He nodded without making eye contact.

"I'll put in an order for some food. Other than hamburgers, is there anything else you'd like?"

He shook his head.

Pulling her gloves off, she said, "I'll be right back." Despite her reassurance, amnesia was *not* common, particularly with no sign of trauma. She had watched his face when he'd learned how they'd found him. He'd been genuinely surprised and confused. Trying to imagine what it would be like to lose her identity, her heart went out to him. A young, attractive amnesiac with perfect health, the body of an athlete, and no identifying marks or history. He was the most *interesting* case she'd ever seen.

As she left, Josh let out a soft, "Whew." *That* was uncomfortable. Made more so because she was a beautiful woman about his age. Making sure no one was around, he slid his feet to the floor. Standing up slowly, a wave of vertigo swept through him. He steadied himself against the bed-rail until it passed. Then, carefully, he let go of the rail and stretched. He actually felt remarkably well. The little ache he'd always had in his back, from soccer and karate, wasn't there. His right knee, hurt in a hard skydiving landing, didn't twinge at all. In fact, he felt better than he could remember. He navigated carefully into the small bathroom, closed the door, and went straight to the mirror over the sink.

Someone else stared back. He actually tilted his head and frowned to prove it was really him. He wasn't sure what he'd expected... but not this. They'd *totally* altered his appearance. Only his six-foot-plus height remained. He estimated his age to be early thirties. That worked. His skin was a perfect tan, right between the whitest white guy, and the blackest black guy. He wasn't bad looking before, and, although the face in the mirror was no super-model, he'd definitely traded up.

He pulled his hospital gown off and studied himself in the small mirror. Wow. He'd always played sports, but now he looked like he could be an Olympic athlete. His chest and arms didn't have huge bulging muscles, but they were well developed and proportioned with almost no body fat. If he hadn't seen his face, he'd have said his body belonged to a twenty-year-old. The small mirror only reflected the top half of his body. He stepped back and looked down.

"Oh, my God!" He just stood there, frozen.

He wasn't circumcised anymore. For some reason, this was the biggest shock of all.

There was a knock at the door. A female voice asked, "Are you alright? Do you need help?"

"Ah... no. I'm OK. Everything's fine... in here... thank you."

Still looking at himself in the mirror, he shook his head and whispered to his image, "Ain't *no way* anyone's getting near you with a scalpel now." Continuing his bathroom humor, he glanced down, saying, "Didn't give you one-in-a-million *there*." He shrugged with a half smile. "But it is an upgrade."

Looking back up at his image, he frowned, whispering, "Why would they have reversed...?" He suddenly knew why his lack of circumcision was a shock. The truth sank in. Looking at his hand as he flexed his fingers, he said quietly, "They didn't *enhance* my body... they *replaced* it." He paused. "It's not possible. Even if you can clone a human body, you can't just stuff someone's consciousness into it..." He looked back at himself in the mirror. "Can you?"

The answer was frowning back at him. He sighed. He knew little about medical science. Maybe it was similar to aviation. They flew stealth aircraft *ten years* before the public ever saw one.

Something else occurred to him. Stepping closer to the mirror and leaning forward, he carefully studied the shape of his eyes, nose, and cheekbones. He examined his skin color, hair, and the proportions of his body. He shook his head as if to knock the thought loose, but the evidence was there. *Not only* did he have a new body, he'd *swear* it had a grandparent from every continent! It almost appeared as if he were some sort of… genetic blend, a combination of every race.

Still trying to process the idea, a more disturbing thought struck him. Clearly, Jesse and his team didn't have any ethical issues with cloning a human body. Putting his hospital gown back on, he glanced back in the mirror one more time. "If they're this cavalier about *creation*… how concerned might they be about… *termination?*"

4

IDENTIFY

Elizabeth grabbed a quick lunch in the cafeteria with two other nurses.

Between mouthfuls, Leslee Wong, a young nurse, asked Elizabeth, "So, what do you think? You've spent the most time with him."

"About who?"

"Who?" She raised her eyebrows. "How many mysterious John Does do we have in ICU?"

Casually, she said, "He seems pretty normal."

Leslee added, "And very cute." She frowned. "Think he was abducted by aliens?"

The ICU charge nurse, Lesia Rabb, a beautiful Queen Latifah lookalike, laughed. "More like a brainwashed government agent."

Leslee continued, "My mom doesn't care who I marry, but Dad insists on a nice Chinese guy." Staring at the ceiling, she added, "Bet I could get a guy like this by him."

Receiving several raised eyebrows, she giggled.

Lesia winked at Elizabeth. "Sorry, Leslee, he's clearly a brother, with *some* mixed blood. If no one claims him," she added with a half smile, "I'll take him home and train him."

"You're married," Leslee said with a sincere frown.

Feigning shock, Lesia said, "Oh yeah…"

Elizabeth wasn't surprised they found him attractive. What was surprising was that each assumed he was primarily of their race. She too had simply assumed he was Caucasian with mixed ancestry.

Walking back to the unit with Lesia, Elizabeth said, "He really is a fascinating mixture, isn't he? It adds to the mystery and makes him – I mean, the case – very interesting."

Lesia looked at her with raised eyebrows and a slight smile.

Josh sat up in his bed with his arms crossed, staring at the wall, thinking. He had to figure out what happened. His blended body actually made a weird kind of sense. They improved food crops and livestock by combining different genetic lines, and every race and ethnic group on earth probably developed adaptations to their environment. So... if you were trying to cull the best attributes from the population, maybe you'd pull genes from every race? His old body had been a combination of French, Iroquois Indian, Irish, and German, but now he was sure he was all that and more. He was probably the ultimate mutt. If nothing else, he'd have fun with the forms that ask for ethnic background.

Elizabeth, entering his room, asked, "Remember anything?"

"Nothing new."

As she took his vital signs, she said softly, "John Doe's a bit impersonal. Is there something you'd like us to call you?"

"Uh... *Josh* sounds familiar."

"Josh it is."

Seeing the needle in her hand, he asked, "Think they'll run out of things to test before I run out of blood?"

She shrugged with a smile. "It's possible."

He wasn't going to watch her draw blood, so he studied her. With a cute dimpled smile, she had the proverbial girl-next-door beauty, mixed with exotic, dark eyes. She was about five foot nine, and he was sure she was a natural blonde, yet she had an olive complexion. Although it was hard to tell because she was wearing scrubs, she looked like she had a trim, athletic body with curves in the right places. She also carried herself with confidence, which he always found attractive. As she pulled her gloves off, he saw a wedding ring.

Finishing up, she said, "All the tests so far indicate you're in exceptionally good health." She leaned over conspiratorially. "In fact, better health than most of the hospital staff."

He smiled but his eyes unfocused as he thought, great, he had this enhanced body and he was sitting on *its* butt."

Misinterpreting his expression, she said, "It must be awful to lose your identity."

He raised an eyebrow. "Probably somewhere between losing

your mind and your car keys."

She laughed.

Smiling, he asked, "So what's the staff's theory on me?"

"Oh, you *don't* want to know!"

"I could use some humor right now."

She raised her eyebrows. "You sure?"

"Please."

"Well… let's see. You were in a witness protection program that went bad. You were a troublesome CIA agent whose memory was erased. Hmmm… oh yeah, you're a secret sleeper agent planted by a foreign country."

Laughing, he asked, "How'd they come up with that one?"

"Well, you have a nice mocha complexion," she smiled, "and you're not…" She suddenly appeared uncomfortable. "I mean, you're…" She blushed.

He wanted to help but had no idea where she was going.

Finally, she blurted out, "You're not circumcised."

It was his turn to blush.

Continuing quickly, she said, "You were unconscious for several days. The nursing staff knows what you look like in your birthday suit. You got more attention than usual because of the mystery." Laughing, she added, "They almost drew straws during sponge-bath time."

He realized he'd unconsciously pulled his bed-sheet up around him.

Suppressing a laugh with great effort, she added, "Sorry… TMI." Clearly trying to save him from further embarrassment, she continued, "The other ideas go from being neuralized by the Men In Black, to alien abduction and clone experiments."

Relieved when she moved on, he laughed. Then he stopped laughing. He realized "clone experiments" might actually be correct.

She looked at him curiously. "You OK?"

With complete honesty, he said, "I'm sorry. The ideas really are funny, but I realized I can't be sure that some of them might not be true." Quickly changing the subject, he asked, "What about you, Elizabeth? Where are you from?"

"Oh, we don't need to be talking about me."

"Well… right now, we can't really talk about where I'm from."

She smiled. "I was born in Austin, Texas, the oldest of several brothers and sisters. My childhood was good, if a little boring."

"Why did you go into nursing?"

"I started out as a computer major. My dad had a computer repair business, and I spent hours on his lap learning from him. I loved helping people with their computer problems, but I realized most computer jobs don't interact with people. I like helping people directly, so I tried nursing. Love it."

"Miss computers?"

"No, I still help my friends with them and like to play with the latest tech."

"Kids?"

She looked down and said softly, "No." She paused. "I… I was married for a few months, but he died in a motorcycle accident."

"I'm sorry."

"It's been over a year. I don't think about it much anymore." She paused. "I'd better get on with my rounds."

Not wanting her to leave on that note, he read her nametag, and quickly asked, "Is Edvardsen Scandinavian?"

"Yes, it's my maiden name."

"That would explain the blonde hair, but…"

"Yeah, I know." She laughed. "The skin and eyes don't match. Think I have some relatives from India."

"Well, the combination works beautifully."

She smiled. "Thanks. I need to get back to work. Is there anything I can do for you?"

"You already have."

They locked eyes for a second and then she looked away, saying, "They'll be moving you out of ICU soon, but I'll check in with you before then."

As Elizabeth updated his chart, she thought, he was a nice guy and easy to talk to. The bad news was that there was something seriously wrong with his brain, or… he was hiding something, something bad enough that he'd be willing to give up his identity. In either case, he'd make a lousy romantic interest. She shook her head. Now where did that come from? Probably just Florence Nightingale syndrome... but her intuition told her there was more to him.

As she walked down the hall, she saw Dr. Dutton talking to the hospital administrator, Ned Brockmeyer. Hearing him ask about their John Doe, she joined them.

Dutton was saying, "We ran the entire alphabet soup of tests: CT, MRI, EKG, EEG, et cetera. They all came back normal." She paused. "No, actually, they all came back perfect. He's unusually healthy."

Brockmeyer smiled. "Hope his insurance is equally healthy. Have the police identified him yet?"

Dutton shook her head. "No. His fingerprints haven't turned up anything at all. They're checking DNA."

Brockmeyer frowned. "Great, that means a huge diagnostic bill and no insurance."

Dutton added, "The next step is to bring in a psychiatrist. Severe emotional trauma can also cause amnesia."

"A psychiatrist?" Brockmeyer shook his head sharply. "Absolutely not! That's just more charges we'll never get reimbursed for. He's taking up a bed that could be used by an insured patient."

Elizabeth knew Brockmeyer. Everything came down to profit and loss. Someone once told her that Brockmeyer modeled himself after Donald Trump. Looking down on his comb-over head, all she could think of was a Trump mini-me. Brockmeyer was shorter, balder, and a *lot* less sensitive.

Dutton nodded in agreement. "You're right." She paused. "If he turned out to be some kind of terrorist, the hospital certainly wouldn't be held liable... would we?"

Brockmeyer frowned. "Hmmm." With an exaggerated sigh, he said, "OK, we can have a shrink check him out, but I want you to get Homeland Security involved. If he turns out to be dangerous," he smiled unpleasantly, "it'll be their problem."

Dutton winked at Elizabeth as Brockmeyer scurried off.

Josh devoured the food they brought up. There were no TVs in ICU. He'd already figured out all the controls on the automated bed and was playing with the blood-pressure machine when Elizabeth returned. A welcome diversion, even though he suspected she was just going to draw more blood.

With a smile, she started, "Good news. Since all your tests are negative, they're bringing in a mind specialist."

"A psychiatrist?"

"Well, yeah, but it's Dr. Sheri Lopez!"

He looked at her blankly.

"Sorry. She's a famous psychiatrist, bestselling author, even had her own TV talk show. You don't recognize the name at all?"

"No." He honestly didn't, but he'd never watched much TV.

"She'll be in tomorrow."

He nodded, wondering if a psychiatrist would be able to see through his amnesia claim.

"They're moving you to a regular room in a few hours."

He'd no longer be under Elizabeth's care and probably wouldn't see her again. She was the closest thing he had to a friend. "Thanks for taking care of me."

Smiling warmly, she said, "You were a lot noisier than most of my Neuro patients." She winked. "I'll check in on you after you're relocated."

They moved him to a regular hospital room and found him a bathrobe. Apparently, his new body needed only a few hours of sleep. To catch up on current events, he watched the news networks for hours. Interspersed between the moral and legal tribulations of celebrities, he picked up a little information on the state of the world.

Late that night, after the nurse made her rounds, he decided he'd try to contact Jesse. Jesse indicated they'd given him the ability to communicate. He had no idea how, but with their obviously advanced medical technology, some type of communication implant could be possible. He made sure no one was outside in the hall. Feeling stupid, like someone trying to make a phone call without a phone, he said, "Jesse, can you hear me?" He tried one more time. Then shook his head, realizing how ridiculous it was. He knew no one was going to answer. They'd probably contact him by conventional means when he was out of the hospital, which meant he had to get out as soon as possible.

5

PSYCH

The next morning, a woman in her mid forties entered Josh's room. Since she wasn't wearing hospital scrubs, he assumed it was the psychiatrist, Dr. Lopez. She was petite and professional, with black hair, a healthy tan complexion, and dark penetrating eyes. She wore a stylish sports jacket and silk blouse. Josh suspected her clothes didn't come from Walmart. As she offered her hand, the diamond encrusted Rolex confirmed it.

"Hi, I'm Sheri Lopez."

Josh smiled back. "So far, I'm Josh. Glad to meet you."

She smiled. "Do you think that's really your name?"

She was undoubtedly very capable, and he'd never been a good liar. The best strategy was to stay as close to the truth as possible.

"It feels comfortable." He felt a pang of pain, realizing his real name died with his body.

She was watching his face intently. "Are you OK?"

He nodded. He obviously wasn't good at hiding his emotions either.

"Josh, I've reviewed the medical tests. There's no indication of disease or physical trauma to your brain. In fact, you appear to be exceptionally healthy. There could still be some hidden trauma or drug causing this, but retrograde amnesia also occurs from traumatic emotional events. I'd like to give you some psychological tests and see where that takes us."

"Sure." He had no grounds to say no.

He spent the rest of the day taking written, verbal, and visual tests. Since none of the questions referred to his past, he answered honestly. After she left, he reflected that Lopez was very intelligent, knowledgeable, and confident. It was clear why she was so successful. So why was she involved with a John Doe case?

The next morning, Lopez interviewed Josh's ICU nurse and reviewed the results of the tests. His psychological profile appeared very balanced, although there was a slightly elevated sense of paranoia.

Her cell phone rang. Looking at the number, she shook her head. Speaking of paranoia…

"Hello?"

"What do you have on him?"

She replied, "I'm doing fine. Thanks for asking, and how are you?"

"Sorry," the voice said perfunctorily. "This case bothers me. We can't find anything on him. Do you know how unusual that is?"

"Yes, I do."

"Well?"

She sighed. "He's in perfect health with no identifying marks…"

He interrupted. "Could they have been surgically removed?"

"Even the best surgical techniques leave scars. This guy looks like he's lived in a monastery all his life."

"What about the psychological tests?"

"I was getting to that. I've talked to him for several hours and…"

"What did you talk about?"

"Aside from the usual abnormal psych and personality questions, we talked about the world and me."

"Isn't it unusual to be talking about *yourself* with a patient?"

"If he's an amnesiac, what else can we talk about? Besides, I'm a public personality; anyone can look me up online. I'm trying to build a relationship so he'll open up, or if he's really an amnesiac, it may bring back a memory."

"Is he an amnesiac?"

She paused. "Amnesia that affects basic knowledge of self is usually accompanied by severe brain damage. Complete loss of identity without brain damage is common only in TV dramas. The tests show no brain damage, an exceptionally high IQ, and no neurosis or psychosis." *Unlike you.* "If it's genuine, the most likely cause is severe psychological trauma or intentional brainwashing." She paused. "Maybe you should talk to your friends in the other agencies; see if they're missing someone."

Ignoring the jab, he said, "Bottom line – is he a threat?"

"He's likable enough."

"Is that relevant?"

She rolled her eyes. "Yes, it's very relevant. In simple terms, mean people do mean things. My first impression is that, although guarded, he's got a good heart; someone you'd like to grab a beer with. I'm just giving you my first impression until I know more. I have one last trick to try. I'll let you know how it goes."

"Don't go liking him too much. Oh… have a nice day." *Click.*

She shook her head. Her government contact irritated her because he was a strong, insensitive, task-oriented personality… just like her. She worked hard to control her impatience and dominant personality. He didn't.

As Sheri entered Josh's room, he was leafing through a book.

"Hi, Josh, how are you feeling?"

"Great."

"Any new memories?"

"Sorry, no."

She sat down in the chair next to him. "I've gone through your test results."

Setting the book down, he nodded.

"They suggest you're very intelligent, and emotionally stable." His IQ scores were off the chart. "The only unusual result is an elevated sense of paranoia." She noticed with surprise that the book he set aside was one of hers. She continued, "You appear to be very healthy in every area including most aspects of your memory, except for your identity." She stopped and looked at him closely.

He matched eye contact but said nothing.

"You appear to be as healthy psychologically as you are physically. If you were applying for a high-level federal job, you'd probably be accepted based on these results."

His eyebrows went up slightly. "Sheri, thank you for working with me." He paused. "Going along with my 'elevated sense of paranoia,' am I just an interesting case, or were you asked to check into my situation?"

She should have known that with his intelligence, he'd question why someone of her stature would be on his case. "Josh, you're very perceptive. As they say, just because you're paranoid, it doesn't mean everyone isn't out to get you."

They both smiled.

"In your case, they're not out to get you, but when a man appears out of nowhere, it creates questions." With a half smile, she motioned toward her book sitting on the table. "My area of expertise is mass psychology. I've assisted the government on projects involving public reactions to terrorist acts and mass casualties. Since I live in Kansas City, it was natural for them to give me a call. I'm always curious about unusual cases." She smiled, adding, "You never know when it might make a good book."

He laughed.

She read his body language and knew she was scoring trust points by being honest. "I tell you this because after spending time with you, I don't believe you're a threat."

"Thank you for leveling with me. That means a lot." He looked her in the eye and asked, "If you don't mind my asking, why do you think that?"

"Actually, it's less about psychology than common sense. If I was inserting an agent, the last thing I'd do is leave them naked and unconscious by the side of the road. It draws undue attention." She was sure he knew things he wasn't sharing, but that didn't make him a terrorist. "Plus, after spending time with you, I'm convinced you're a nice guy." She smiled again. "That's a psychiatric term."

Looking down he said, "Thank you."

"There's one thing left. I'd like to try hypnosis."

Josh frowned, squinting his eyes and shaking his head. "Doc... I gotta tell you, hypnosis gives me the creeps. I'd really rather not."

She knew many people felt that way, but they were usually strong "director" personalities, afraid of losing control. He didn't fit that profile. Disappointed, she frowned. "I'm sorry to hear that. I think it could help." She shrugged. "Josh, there's really nothing else

I can do for you."

Cocking his head slightly sideways, he asked, "What's your theory on my situation?"

There was almost a slight sense of amusement, as if he were evaluating *her*. She'd thought of many possibilities, but none fit. "I really don't know. I don't think you just got a bump on your head, but I suspect your situation isn't of your doing." She raised one eyebrow, "Or at least not entirely." She paused. "Based on your remarkable physical condition, *something* happened to you, and I'm very curious to find out what."

She stood up and he stood up with her.

"If you change your mind, I'd be happy to work with you." She gave him her business card.

"I appreciate that, but I doubt I could afford someone of your reputation."

"Don't worry, I'll charge it to the government."

He laughed.

She added, "Seriously, I'd be glad to talk any time. My private cell number's on the back. I'm finished working for the government. Patient/doctor confidentiality would apply."

Unless, she thought, he really turned out to be a threat.

After she left his room, she asked to see his ICU nurse. Elizabeth had come by to check up on him while she was there. She didn't have to be a psychiatrist to notice some attraction.

"Is he OK?"

"Yes, he seems quite sane, very intelligent, and remarkably balanced emotionally, considering his situation."

Elizabeth smiled and nodded. "That means they'll probably release him tomorrow."

"I expect so. Elizabeth, he's squeamish about hypnosis but I really think I can help him if he'll let me. If you get a chance to talk to him... here's my card."

Elizabeth took the card. "Thank you, Dr. Lopez."

"Call me Sheri." She started to leave, then turned back and gave her a meaningful look. "Elizabeth, we really don't know what his situation is... *please* be careful."

As she left the hospital, her phone rang. Looking at the name, she answered, "He wouldn't go for the hypnosis."

"So what do we do next?"

"Nothing. We don't have any grounds."

"So, is he a threat?"

"I doubt it."

"Why, because he's *likable*?"

Controlling her irritation, she said, "Would you insert an agent into this country naked, without identification?"

"No… but I don't like mysteries."

"Then keep him under surveillance."

"Oh, we will. Uh, thanks for your help."

"Whatever."

6

ESTABLISH

Josh was still mulling over the meeting with Lopez when Elizabeth dropped by.

"I hear they're releasing you tomorrow."

He smiled and nodded. "Thanks for finding me that book by Dr. Lopez. You and the rest of the hospital staff have been awesome."

"Yeah, well, you'll also be presented with an awesome bill." She smiled. "But that's where your amnesia might come in handy." She paused. "Do you know what you're going to do?"

Jesse's team should be contacting him soon, but he hadn't expected to wake up in a public hospital. He needed a backup plan. "I guess I'm going to need a job."

She nodded. "I did a little checking around. There's an opening in the hospital... well, hospital grounds maintenance. With your vocabulary you probably have advanced education..."

He interrupted, "I have no known education, skills, or references. Working outside would be a great place to start, in case I turn out to be a lunatic."

She laughed. "You do have references. You were friendly and kind to everyone here. If most of us were in your shoes... well, it speaks a lot for your character."

He smiled as their eyes met.

"Do you have a place to stay?"

He shook his head.

She looked at the floor, fidgeting with her tablet. "Because, I suppose, well, I mean, you're bound to... Uh, look, I have a, uh, guest bedroom in my condo... I mean, just until you get on your feet..." She knocked a plastic cup off his tray table with her tablet. Bending over to pick it up, she dropped her tablet. As she stood up, he saw she was blushing. She suddenly looked very vulnerable and *very* beautiful.

"Wow." He smiled. "That's the best offer I remember getting in my entire life."

It broke the tension and she laughed.

He added, "That's incredibly kind, but I'm sure the hospital staff would warn against it, and they'd be right. I can't even vouch for me."

Holding her tablet tightly against her chest and breaking eye contact, she nodded her head and turned to go. As she left, she said, over her shoulder, "I'll get you that job application."

He'd just turned down an invitation to room with a kind, intelligent, and very attractive woman. He shook his head. It didn't matter what Jesse said, he was still married to Kelly... and he didn't need any distractions.

The next morning Elizabeth knocked on his door and came in with a large white plastic bag and some papers. "The staff brought in some clothes that might fit and here's that job application."

"Wow. Thanks."

As he took the bag and papers, she added, "Already talked to the maintenance department head. You can start tomorrow."

"Tomorrow? That's amazing. How'd you do that?"

"They were already shorthanded and just had someone else quit. I told them we know for sure you don't have a criminal record, and they don't have to hassle with checking references." She smiled. "Besides, he's a friend."

Just then, someone appeared in the doorway. Elizabeth waved him in. "Justin, this is Josh."

Wearing scrubs, Justin was a good-looking, athletic twenty-something. He had streaked blond hair and wore a puka-shell necklace, apparently cultivating a California surfer look. Josh shook his hand as Elizabeth said, "Justin's a nurse too, and he's been looking for a roommate."

Justin said, "Dude, here's the address. Gotta go. Just got off work but have an important appointment."

Elizabeth looked at her watch. "Yeah, I gotta run too."

Josh said, "Elizabeth, you've gone way beyond the call of duty. I don't know how I can ever thank you."

She smiled. "No need." As she left, she said, over her shoulder, "I'll see you around."

An hour later, they brought the release paperwork for Josh to sign. It included an estimate of the bill to date. He went to the bathroom and put on the clothes. Some were obviously new. He suspected Elizabeth, and knew he owed her deeply.

He also owed the hospital deeply. Glancing down at the bill, he said, "Ouch." Then talking to himself in the mirror, he said, "On the bright side, if we can't stop the cataclysm, I'll be debt free soon."

When he came out, a nurse was waiting for him with a wheelchair.

"I won't need that."

"Hospital policy for all patients upon departure," she said flatly.

Despite the nurse's advancing age, she appeared to have a will of iron. Holding his worldly possessions in a white plastic bag, he sucked in his ego and slid into the chair. Pointing forward, he said, softly, "The warrior charges forth to save the world." Under his breath, he added, "In a wheelchair pushed by a woman twice his age."

It was a cold, overcast day but he didn't care. He was outside. His highly attuned senses amplified the sounds, sights, and sensations. He savored the cold breeze on his face, the feel of the sidewalk underfoot, and the simple sounds of the streets. He was back in the real world.

Justin lived in an apartment within walking distance of the hospital. Josh followed Justin's directions, enjoying the walk.

About two miles from the hospital, he found the apartment complex. It was old but appeared to be in good condition and was located in a lively part of the city, with restaurants and clubs nearby.

Josh climbed two flights of stairs and rang the doorbell. A very cute twenty-something woman with short black hair answered.

Josh said, "Sorry. Wrong apartment. I was looking for Justin."

From inside, he heard, "Dude, come on in… I'm on level nine… can't talk. Amber, that's Josh."

Amber invited him in. "He's busy saving the world from brain-sucking aliens in still *another* tournament."

Justin was in a leather recliner, wearing 3D glasses and vigorously working a controller in front of a humongous flat screen.

Amber, looking at him curiously, asked, "So you, like, really have amnesia?"

Josh frowned toward Justin. "Ah, yeah…"

"Wow. That's so crazy. Does it hurt?" She moved closer, unconsciously extending a hand toward him as if to touch a bug.

"Only when people mention it."

She pulled her hand back.

Josh smiled. "I'm kidding. I feel great."

She smiled back with a raised eyebrow. "You look great." Looking back over her shoulder at Justin, she sighed. "Hope you like video games." She shook her head. "I have to go, but it was great to meet you." As she left, she winked. "I'm sure you'll see more of me."

While Justin annihilated aliens, Josh surveyed his new home. The two-bedroom, one-bath apartment was definitely a bachelor pad. Minimum furniture centered on a giant wall TV and an impressive 11.2 sound system.

With a short victory dance, Justin finished the game. About Josh's height, Justin was pretty buff and sported flip-flops, basketball shorts and a T-shirt. "Elizabeth said you're a good guy. Ah, not judging or anything, but you're not gay, are you?"

Josh shook his head.

Justin smiled and gave him a knuckle bump. "Then we're going to have some fun."

Since Jesse or his team hadn't contacted him yet, Josh started work the next day. His job consisted mostly of grounds work. Because it was spring, he did a lot of mowing, mulching, and watering. He actually enjoyed it. If the world didn't end, he might like a garden some day. With his heightened senses, he felt eyes watching him as he worked. It was more than just curious co-workers. He was under observation by someone or some agency.

When he wasn't working, he ran and worked out to discover his new body's capabilities. They were nothing short of amazing. He could not only run faster and longer: his reflexes and recovery were quicker. The hard workouts also helped relieve his growing frustration. He kept expecting someone to contact him, like they did in the spy movies – a meaningful nod or wink – but there was nothing. Maybe they were afraid to contact him while he was being watched, but if that was true, who did Jesse work for? It didn't make sense.

Justin partied most nights and tried to get Josh to go clubbing with him after work. Josh had neither funds nor inclination. He wasn't against having fun, but that wasn't why he was there.

That didn't stop Justin from bringing the club home. He frequently brought back multiple female friends. Justin's heart was in the right place, but he wasn't the master of subtlety, often introducing Josh as his alien-abductee roommate. One night, after a few too many, Justin confided, "Having you as a roommate is almost as effective with women as a puppy."

"Thanks Justin, it's good to finally know my purpose in life."

After a week, the time with Jesse and even his previous life began to feel slightly unreal. It was like waking up after a particularly vivid dream. His memories remained clear, and yet, every morning he shaved someone else's face. What if the face in the mirror was real, but his memories were illusions? With no confirmation of Jesse or his past existence, he began to doubt his sanity.

Josh was sitting on the couch in front of the TV when Justin got home. Justin went straight to the refrigerator, grabbed a beer, and asked, "Want one?"

"No thanks." Staring at the black screen, Josh asked, "Justin, you're a nurse. What are the symptoms of schizophrenia?"

Justin shrugged. "Dude, I'm not a psych nurse." He laughed. "And I barely graduated."

Seeing Josh's expression, he added, "Hey, no problem. Let's look it up." Justin googled it on his phone. "Mayo Clinic says – symptoms include hallucinations and voices, often focused on the perception that the individual is being singled out for harm. They may believe that the government is monitoring every move they make." He paused. "Let's see – it's often accompanied by delusions of grandeur. The delusional conviction of their own importance, power, or knowledge, or that they have a special relationship with a famous person or deity."

Justin looked up at Josh questioningly.

Josh didn't respond, still staring through the blank TV screen.

Justin came over and said, "Dude… I know what will help."

Josh looked up questioningly.

Nodding wisely, Justin said, "We need to get you laid."

Despite himself, Josh couldn't avoid a half smile. "Thanks Justin, appreciate the prescription."

Josh excused himself and went to the bathroom. He splashed water on his face. Occam's Razor said the simplest solution was usually correct. Looking in the mirror, he quietly asked: "Which is more likely? (a) I'm a fighter pilot, brought back from the dead by a voice in my head to save the world from a cataclysm. Or… (b) I'm a fruitcake with raisins for eyes." He sighed and shook his head. "You need help."

As he returned to the living-room, Justin put a shot of tequila in his hand.

Josh downed it without a thought. "Justin, is not being able to recognize yourself also a symptom of schizophrenia?"

Justin frowned. "I don't think so."

"What kind of mental illness causes that?"

Still frowning, Justin said, "I don't know any psychosis that would cause that." Looking serious, he added, "But I've figured out *exactly* what you need."

Josh raised his eyebrows skeptically.

Justin winked. "Amber."

"Amber? I thought she was your girlfriend."

"No, we're just good friends." He smiled. "Well, friends with benefits. I've known her since high school. She totally goes for the tall, dark, crazy types… sorry. Anyway, I bet she'd do you in a heartbeat."

"Thanks." He gave him a half smile. "But I'm in no condition to start a relationship."

"Relationship – who said anything about a relationship?" Seeing Josh's face, he finished, "Yeah, OK. Well, just let me know."

As more days passed, the internal battle grew. After Justin was asleep, Josh went online to the social media sites and tried to look up his wife, Kelly. He found nothing. Then he tried sending a test email to her, but it bounced back: "Undeliverable." Finally, ignoring Jesse's warning, he grabbed Justin's phone and dialed her number. It immediately went to a recording. "You have reached a non-working number…"

He slumped back in the chair. Dropping his hands to his side, he let the phone fall to the floor. His memories and even his appearance could be just another delusion. He was afraid to keep searching for his old identity. It felt like opening the little Russian dolls that nested inside each other. Split one in half, and inside was another identical but smaller doll, and inside that another, and another. He was afraid that inside the last doll… there'd be nothing.

7

INSANITY

It was two weeks after his release from the hospital. He sat alone in his bedroom. The ten-by-ten room was oppressive. Dimly lit by one small fluorescent ceiling fixture, there were no windows or pictures on its off-white walls. The only furniture was the bed he sat on and a cardboard box that served as his bedside table. In front of him was a blank wall with an open closet door. The empty closet reminded him of what he had… nothing. He sat on the edge of the bed in the *Thinking Man* pose, looking at his dim shadow cast onto the apartment-neutral beige carpet.

He was perched on the edge of a greasy, black pool of insanity. It would be so easy just to let go and slip in. He slid off the bed onto his knees. Head in hands, he bent over, elbows resting on his thighs. Softly, he said, "My God, I can't live like this." Louder he said, "Please Jesse, if you're real and can somehow hear me, I need your help!"

Jesse's voice resonated through his mind with the simple statement. *I am here.*

He bolted upright. Jesse sounded the same as when he was in his sensory-deprived netherworld. He sputtered, "Thank God you're talking to me again! I was convinced you were nothing but a delusion!"

Ecstatic to reclaim his sanity, he got up and sat on the bed. He wasn't a poor deluded soul… Or, he thought wryly, his delusions had come back to support him. At this point, he didn't care.

But his relief was short lived. When he was a kid and did something dangerous, as soon as his parents saw he was OK, their relief often turned to anger. So did his. "What if I can't do this?" He was mad. They hadn't bothered to talk to him for weeks! "Or what if I just decide not to do anything?!"

That's your choice.

Testing, he said, "You mean if I just decide to ignore you and party my brains out, like my roommate, you wouldn't pull the plug on me?"

No.

Although he wasn't sure he was really "hearing" Jesse, he perceived the relaxed voice of a patient teacher. He knew he could never sit by and watch the world die, but the rebel in him had to confirm he wasn't just some sort of remote-control, biological UCAV.

His anger evaporated as quickly as it arrived. "I'm sorry, Jesse. This transition is tougher than I thought." It suddenly occurred to him that maybe they left him on his own to give him time to adapt, or test his stability. "So, when do I meet the rest of the team?"

First, you must know the enemy you face.

"Yes! I still have *no* idea why I'm here."

What has destroyed the most life?

"You asked that before." He had since thought about it. "We're not sure what caused *all* the mass extinctions, but we know some occurred because of volcanoes, asteroid impacts, stuff like that, but they're very rare."

Rare?

"Well, we haven't seen any of those types of cataclysms in recorded history." He stopped and laughed. "I guess, by definition, recorded history starts *after* the cataclysm." He paused. "Regardless, we haven't seen anything like that in thousands of years."

On earth.

"On earth?" He was confused. "What do you mean?" Thinking for a moment, he tentatively asked, "Cataclysms on other *planets*?"

Yes.

"Like that comet that hit Jupiter back in the nineties?" He remembered reading that the probability of dying from an asteroid or comet impact was about 40,000 to 1. He remembered being surprised that he was as likely to die from an extraterrestrial impact as he was from a tornado. Ironically, they were also about the same odds as dying in an airplane crash... been there, done that.

"OK, so Jupiter took some hits and comets may be more common than we think. What's your point?"

What would happen if a comet struck earth?

"A comet the size of Shoemaker-Levy?" He had a passion for astronomy, and with his new ability to access his memory, he could call up anything he'd ever read. "Shoemaker-Levy was half the size of the asteroid that they say killed the dinosaurs. But wait... this was a comet, not an asteroid." His mind seemed to operate faster. It was as if, like a computer, they'd upgraded him with a quicker processor and more memory chips. "Comets move at least twice as fast as asteroids, and even though they're less dense, they have greater impact energy. It could kill billions."

How likely do you think an impact is?

A chill went down his spine. "Since you're asking, I'm guessing... not that unlikely?"

You have two years.

"Two years! The earth's going to get hit by a comet in two years?" He stopped. "Why are you telling me this? What am I supposed to do about it?"

Stop it.

"Stop it! How?!"

All in time. First, you must learn.

Still getting over the shock of not being insane, he took a deep breath. He needed time to process all this. Sensing that Jesse was finished with their conversation, he was going to make very sure he knew how to reach him again. "Wait! How do I contact you?"

Talk to me.

He frowned. "Just... talk to you... really?" He was expecting maybe an 800 number. They must have implanted some type of microscopic receiver/transmitter in his auditory canal. One of the black defense programs he'd worked on actually built micro UCAVs. The insect-sized vehicles needed more power than batteries could supply. So, they developed tiny thermoelectric generators powered by a minuscule amount of plutonium. Scaled-down versions of reactors used in deep-space probes, they could supply power for years. He wasn't excited about the thought of having plutonium in his ear.

"So, there will be someone, like, monitoring me all the time?"

Yes.

"Uh… OK." Knowing someone could hear everything he said was a bit creepy. He shook his head, smiling. He might have to stop talking to himself. Then it occurred to him, if they had the technology to implant a communication device, what else might he be carrying. Despite Jesse's assurance, he knew they could have implanted a self-destruct mechanism like UCAVs carried. Click – rogue operative suffers fatal aneurism. He frowned. *Who had* this type of advanced biotechnology? And if they could do all this… why on earth did they need him?

The next day, he received his first check. It wasn't much more than minimum wage, but it allowed him to take care of basic needs.

He never realized how critical an identity was, until he didn't have one. Without a birth certificate or social security number, he was an illegal alien. He came up with some clever stories and made friends with various clerks to get a driver's license and checking account. Since he couldn't use his old last name, he chose "Meadows," the name of a coach who'd taught him many life lessons. One particularly relevant one was – the only thing a person could truly control was his attitude. Happiness didn't depend on others; it was a decision. Josh still struggled with that lesson and thought his new name might be a good reminder.

Where was the rest of the team? It didn't make sense. With the clock ticking down to Armageddon, why would Jesse's organization have him operating by himself? He was painfully aware that Jesse was still nothing more than a voice in his head and there was no evidence to support a comet impact. The definition of schizophrenia continued to haunt him. He'd actually prefer insanity to the reality of humanity's annihilation, but until they put him in a padded cell, he decided to act as if the threat was real. It was all he had.

With his roommate's video games and entertaining, Josh's computer access was limited. He spent most of his free time online at the library. With his faster mind and new photographic memory, he plowed through information, reading everything he could find on comets, physics, orbital mechanics, optics, *and* abnormal psychology. The library's hours and Justin's libido put a limit on his research. He needed help. He remembered Elizabeth was into computers; she might be able to help... Or, maybe, he just wanted a friend, a real friend.

After work, he went up to Neuro ICU, to ask if Elizabeth was busy. One of the nurses pointed him in the right direction.

He met her in the hall. "Hi, Elizabeth. I wanted to thank you properly for all you did for me... for getting me the job. Finally got a paycheck." He shrugged. "Maybe I can buy you lunch... well... I mean, if you're not busy... you know, sometime..."

Before he could stumble through, she said with a half smile, "Sure, my place for dinner, say seven?" She wrote her address and number on a small piece of paper and handed it to him. She said, "Gotta go," turned and left.

Josh smiled his way out of the hospital.

As Elizabeth walked down the hall, Lesia, who'd overheard the conversation, fell in alongside. Elizabeth glanced sideways at her friend.

Lesia said nothing but raised her eyebrows as they walked.

Elizabeth finally said, "I'm curious. Everyone loves a good mystery."

Lesia's expression didn't change.

Elizabeth continued, "It's not like it's a date. I just didn't want him to spend money on an expensive restaurant." Seeing that Lesia wasn't buying it, she stopped and turned to her. "Look, I've been around him enough to know he's a good guy."

Shaking her head, Lesia said, "Honey, *he* doesn't even know if he's a good guy. Even if he is, did it ever occur to you, that whatever happened to him might have been *intentional*, and whoever did it might still be around?"

Elizabeth, looking down, shook her head.

Lesia added, "Elizabeth, it's so good to see you taking an interest in men again. It's *long* overdue. He's cute as a bug, but you know you shouldn't invite him to your place for a first date."

Elizabeth started to protest but saw the "don't even go there" look on Lesia's face.

Nodding in resignation, she said, "So now what?"

Smiling, Lesia took one of her hands. "Sweetie, he already has your address. I'm going to check with Justin and see what Mr. Erection knows about him. I'll also just happen to be in your neighborhood around seven. I'll call. If you don't answer and say, 'Lesia, you're the best,' you'll have extra dinner guests. Remember, I still have a key to your place."

Elizabeth hugged her and said, "You *are* the best."

As Josh got back to his apartment, he realized, as an amnesiac, he'd need something intelligent to talk about over dinner. The headline news on the hospital TV hadn't provided any depth, so he surfed the Internet for current events. He had already found the world was wound tighter than when he left. Dozens of countries were involved in military actions, standoffs, or rising tensions. Terrorism continued to pop up like malignant tumors. Military and police operations surgically excised them, only to have them reappear elsewhere like metastasizing cancer cells. The only tiny bright spot was a strong European Union President from Turkey, who'd successfully rid much of Europe of terrorism. After a of couple hours, he had doubts about whether the human race could survive even without a comet.

He was alone in the apartment, a rare event. He cleared his mind, and using proper radio technique, said, "Jesse, Josh, can you read me, over?" Almost immediately, he received a reply.

Yes.

"I really need to know what my role is." He paused. "But before that, do you have a minute to discuss a more philosophical question?"

He sensed attention.

"There are those that might say a cataclysmic impact is just what's needed to wipe the earth clean of a stupid and dangerous species called man." He added, "I'm not so cavalier, but you can't help but wonder sometimes…"

What is the most powerful force?

He shook his head. Great, back to fortune-cookie answers. "It depends on what you mean by 'force.'"

Silence.

"Well, in physics, the Strong Nuclear Force is hundreds of

times stronger than gravity… guess that's why they call it the Strong Force."

What does it do?

He had to think back to basic physics. "I think it holds atoms together."

Can it organize itself?

"Ah… no."

Can it organize its environment?

No.

Can it replicate?

"No, of course not. You're talking about Life, aren't you?" He thought about it, and then added, "The Strong Force holds atoms together, but *Life* can actually organize atoms. It can grow and reproduce. I think I understand where you're going, but isn't that kind of an apples-to-oranges comparison?"

How many planets in the solar system have life?

"Aside from earth, we don't know. We've sent out unmanned spacecraft for decades to find out."

What have they found?

"Nothing definitive so far. Mars *might* have, or at least had, microbial life. A couple of Jupiter's and Saturn's moons are slim possibilities."

How common is the Strong Nuclear Force?

"It's everywhere."

How common is life?

"If our solar system is any indication, pretty rare."

How common is sentient life?

"Intelligent life? Probably extremely rare. If it exists outside of mankind, maybe one in a billion?"

Life is rare. Sentient life is the most incredibly rare and precious thing in the universe. It should not be dismissed lightly.

It began to dawn on him that Jesse's fortune-cookie replies might be answers to questions he didn't ask, but should have. Before he could respond, Justin came into the apartment accompanied by two beautiful women. At least this time, he had his own rendezvous. As he left, Justin winked and whispered, "Good luck with the ice queen."

8

DINNER

As Elizabeth opened the door, Josh realized he'd never seen her in anything but hospital scrubs. Framed in the doorway was a beautiful woman with blonde shoulder-length hair wearing a white silk blouse and perfect-fitting designer jeans. She *did* have athletic curves in all the right places. "Hi, Elizabeth."

She smiled and said, "You look great in clothes…"

A woman walking down the hall glanced up quickly with raised eyebrows.

Elizabeth stammered, "No, I meant you look good without your coveralls on."

The woman looked straight ahead with a slight smile.

Elizabeth shook her head and said, "Oh, you know what I mean." Laughing, she added, "Come on in."

She showed him around her condominium. Classical music played softly in the background. The furniture was simple but expensive teak, sitting on thick, cream-colored carpet. It was classy but comfortable. The living-room had giant windows and sliding glass doors that opened onto a balcony. The condominium complex was built on a hill, and her fifth-floor home had a breathtaking view of the city lights. The living-room opened onto a large study with several floor-to-ceiling bookcases. A beautiful teak desk held two huge monitors, with an impressive array of computer components hidden underneath.

"Video games?"

"No, I have an Internet business on the side and trade some stocks."

His impression of her went up still another notch.

They spent the next hour enjoying a simple but delicious dinner. He asked her about herself and her job. She told him many funny, and a few sad, stories from her profession. He learned he was dealing with a confident, outgoing, highly intelligent woman. Finally, he asked, "If you had all the time in the world, what would you do for fun?"

"That's easy. I *love* to travel. I want to see the whole world; the more exotic the better. I've been to Canada, Mexico, and the Caribbean, but I've only been to South America and Europe once."

"Why haven't you traveled more?"

She looked pensive. "It's not the cost. For years, I used credit cards to rack up airline miles. I have enough to fly around the world several times." She paused, looking off into space. "I guess you always think you'll have more time. Before I was married, I thought it would be great to travel with my husband. Then, after... well, it's not the same traveling by yourself." Shaking her head sadly, she looked back at him. "That's just an excuse, isn't it?"

Instead of answering, he gently asked, "What happened to your husband?"

She looked down at the table, eyes unfocused. "He went out for a quick motorcycle ride... and I never saw him again." She paused. "The accident was terrible. There was a fire. They had to... identify him... with dental records."

As she spoke, it was apparent her heart was still broken. Her hand was on the table. Without thinking, he gently put his hand over hers. As he did, he suddenly realized – he was witnessing the same anguish his wife might have experienced. He'd been robbed. Robbed of one of the few benefits of death – not being around to worry about those you left behind.

By tacit agreement, they moved to less painful topics.

Finally, she said, "I've never talked this much about myself in my life." Playfully, she added, "Amnesiacs make perfect dates."

He laughed. He also realized he'd just broken a stereotype. There was an inside joke about fighter pilots on first dates. After totally dominating the conversation by talking about flying, the fighter pilot finally smiles benevolently at his date and says, "Well... enough about flying... let's talk about... me."

Elizabeth said, "Now, I want to know how *you* think." She paused. "What do you want to do when you grow up?"

"Save the world."

Her cell phone rang. "I'm sorry, Josh; I really need to take this. Someone was… uh, facing a small crisis and needed to be checked on."

Josh nodded. "Sure."

She answered, "Hi… Yes, fine… Yup." Smiling, she said, "You're the best! Love you, girl. Bye, bye."

Josh said, "She's OK?"

Elizabeth laughed and smiled warmly. "Yes… yes, she's doing great." She continued, "Let's see, where were we? Oh yeah, save the world. Don't we all." She frowned. "But are we worth saving?"

He was surprised to hear her echo his own cynical thoughts. Thinking about his discussion with Jesse, he said, "Elizabeth, I've been brushing up on science. I think I had a knack for it. There's a law of physics that deals with something called entropy. It states that the universe, and everything in it, tends toward disorder over time. Everything will, eventually, run down, burn out, and scatter as time goes on."

She nodded.

"We see a taste of it in our daily lives. Unless we add 'energy' by cleaning and putting stuff away, our home becomes more and more disorganized. Eventually, we have chaos with everything randomly scattered through our house."

"What a relief. I thought it was my housekeeping."

He smiled. "And yet Life creates order out of chaos. It can take matter and energy, and organize it."

She nodded again.

"Take it a step further. Sentient or intelligent life not only organizes *itself*, but it can organize its surroundings. It can create incredible things all around it. It's the only force in the universe that can. Life, kind of, *reverses* chaos… at least temporarily. A wise man said that sentient life is the rarest and most precious force in the universe. I think sometimes, we're too cavalier about our own existence."

She looked very serious and said softly, "Usually, when I think about the universe, I feel very small and insignificant. But when you explain it this way, I realize mankind, despite all our shortcomings, has to be one of the most amazing things in it." She paused. "You know, maybe entropy applies to people too. If we don't constantly add positive energy, people become *dark*, just like the universe."

"I never thought of it that way, but I think you're right."

Then she smiled impishly and added, "Another application of the Second Law."

He frowned. "Pardon me?"

She said, "Entropy... it's the Second Law of Thermodynamics." She winked as she picked up and carefully stacked their plates, taking them to the kitchen.

He shook his head. So much for impressing the little woman. He picked up the glasses and silverware, further reducing entropy.

After putting the dishes in the dishwasher, they moved out onto the balcony. Leaning on the railing, they looked down across the twinkling carpet of city lights. It was a beautiful view on a crisp spring evening. Shivering slightly, Elizabeth stood close. Turning to him, she said, "I really like your view of the world."

Looking down into her eyes, he couldn't help but say, "And I really like the view from here."

She tipped her head up and kissed him. He kissed her back, putting his arms around her. Her scent was subtle but tantalizing. He quickly realized his new body must have a twenty-year-old's hormones. Physically, he felt like he was on a first date.

Unlike his first date, however, he felt remorse. Kelly's face flashed into his mind. He realized that he couldn't simply convince himself that their marriage was no more. He stopped before his hormones got the best of him.

As they separated, he said, "Elizabeth, I... I really should be going." He added, trying to keep it light, "I know I'm still on double-secret probation."

She looked at him carefully, obviously trying to read him. Finally, she said softly, "Yes. I didn't realize it was so late." With that, she went with him to the door. He thanked her for a wonderful dinner, leaned forward, and kissed her on the cheek.

As the door closed, she frowned. It'd been an incredible evening. She was certain he was attracted to her and there was electricity when they kissed, but then he shut down. There was something wrong, something he wasn't telling her.

Sitting on the couch, she thought, Lesia was right, this *was* a date – the first she'd had since her husband died. It wasn't lack of opportunity. Several doctors had asked her out.

She picked up the framed picture of her husband from the side table. As ridiculous as it was, she realized that part of her had been expecting him to walk through the door at any moment, telling her it was all a terrible mistake. Looking at the picture, she shook her head and said, "*He's dead! He's dead. He's never coming back.*"

For some stupid reason she cried. She was angry with herself but couldn't stop. Finally, after almost an hour, it subsided, and with it, her mourning. Setting her husband's picture down, she slowly slid the wedding ring off and laid it carefully in a drawer.

9

CONNECT

When Josh got back to Justin's apartment, he found himself alone, and wanted to continue his discussion with Jesse.

He sensed his presence.

"Sorry for the interruption. Roommate's a good guy but a bit of a slut," he said with some envy. "We were discussing the rarity and uniqueness of sentient life. You made a powerful point. I even used it with Elizabeth." He shook his head, smiling. He wouldn't underestimate her again. "But just because we're unique and rare doesn't make us *good*. I mean, Polio's unique and rare. Mankind's done some pretty awful things."

Is a three-year-old child not worth saving because they hit their sibling?

"Of course they are, but they're children. We're not. We know better. Besides, we don't just destroy ourselves; we excel at driving the life around us to extinction."

Mankind has driven thousands of species to extinction, but natural catastrophes have killed millions more.

He shrugged. "Granted, Mother Nature's a better killer, but I'm not sure that would be an effective defense in a trial."

Mankind is the only life capable of protecting all other life on earth.

Josh stopped, trying to absorb that. The only life capable of protecting all other life? He'd only thought in terms of saving humanity from the comet, but he realized what Jesse said *was* true. They wouldn't just save mankind; they'd save millions of species. It was a different perspective. Still, it was hard not to be cynical. "That may be true, but our track record sucks."

If the species you drove to extinction could speak from the grave, what would they say?

He smiled. "You mean, would they vote us off the island?" He paused. "I guess if we were *really* able to stop an apocalyptic event, we might make up for some past sins."

Life is tenacious. It will find a way under the most extreme conditions, but only if it has time to adapt. Catastrophic change doesn't allow that. Only sentient life can intervene.

That was a powerful statement. Before he could respond, Justin came in with the same two beautiful, but now tipsy, women. Even though he'd just met them earlier that evening, one of them gave him a big hug as if they were old friends, accompanied by an uncomfortably intimate kiss. Frustrated in more ways than one, he retreated to his room.

He had much to think about – not just what Jesse said, but how he said it. Although still sounding like a fortune cookie, he spoke with remarkable wisdom. It was almost as if he had a perspective outside of... No, he didn't want to go there, not yet.

The next morning Elizabeth woke up determined. Her dad had always said she was stubborn as a post. Instead of feeling sorry for herself, she was going to get to the bottom of this mystery. Lesia was right. Even if Josh's situation wasn't his fault, he was probably bad news, but there was only one way to find out. He said he was spending a lot of time on the Internet, presumably to find his identity. His roommate had a computer, but she knew Justin. He'd unsuccessfully invited her to his lair several times. Josh said he was at the library a lot. She smiled, guessing why.

Before she started her shift, she stopped by the maintenance office and asked where Josh was working. They told her he was outside fixing the hospital's lawn-sprinkler system.

Josh was good with his hands and had a gift for understanding systems, but he also had a tendency to get bored with details and rarely read directions. If it hadn't been for the Navy pounding into him the disciplined use of flight checklists, he would've been lost at sea years ago. Sitting on the ground, frowning at the extra parts he had after reassembling the sprinkler, he noticed two legs in hospital scrubs. Looking up, he saw Elizabeth and smiled.

She smiled back and without preamble said, "If you need the Internet to save the world, I have two powerful computers with high-speed access. Can't use both of them at the same time, you're welcome to come over and use one any time you want."

As he stood, he realized that was exactly what he needed. He wasn't sure how much longer he could handle Justin's late-night guests. It wasn't just that he had to frequently retreat to his room or the library; in the small apartment it was hard just to go to the kitchen or bathroom. Several times, late at night, he'd collided with one of Justin's beautiful but scantily clad "friends with benefits." One of them in particular, Amber, frequently forgot even her "scantily." He missed Kelly terribly, and that just aggravated it.

He told her, "That would be fantastic, but I don't want to be a pest."

Grinning, she handed him a key. "I'll let you know when you're a pest."

After Elizabeth started her shift, Lesia came over smiling. "How did it go?"

"We had dinner and talked for hours. Amnesia or not, he's very intelligent and has an amazing insight into things."

Lesia said, "And…?"

Elizabeth raised an eyebrow, smiling. "You mean, did he try to jump my bones?"

Lesia just shrugged.

"No, he was a gentleman." She smiled. "We kissed." She paused and frowned. "But then he suddenly pulled back and said he had to go."

Lesia frowned. "Why are the cute ones always gay?"

Elizabeth laughed, shaking her head. "He's not gay, but he is holding something back." She paused. "I'm going to let him use my computer to help find his identity." Her eyes unfocused as she said, "There's just something about him…"

Lesia laughed. "Oh honey, my first child was the result of that exact same statement, but it's not like you gave him the key to your condo."

Elizabeth's eyes got wide.

Lesia frowned. "Tell me you didn't."

Her silence said it all.

Lesia grabbed both of Elizabeth's hands. "Oh sweetie, what am I going to do with you? You need to be careful. He may not be a sex fiend but that doesn't mean he's not dangerous." Still holding Elizabeth's hands, she looked down. Noticing the missing wedding ring, she softened and smiled. "I can't tell you how good it is to have you back among the living. I'm thankful to him for that, but, baby girl, you need to shop around. Why don't you go out with Bob Hartman? He's the nicest single doc in the hospital, and I know he likes you."

Elizabeth, more to close the conversation, said, "Yeah, maybe I will." She hugged her. "Thanks for looking out for me. You are the best friend anyone could ever have."

Josh spent all his free time using Elizabeth's computer. Slowly he began to realize the magnitude of what they were attempting. He also realized that detecting an undiscovered comet more than two years out was almost impossible. Jesse's organization had access to more than just advanced medical technology. Why they needed him to study the threat independently wasn't clear. All he could think of was that they wanted him to be knowledgeable enough to understand what they were attempting before joining the team.

Studying every idea ever suggested for asteroid and comet deflection, he found many clever and some bizarre concepts. In science, the first task was to define the boundaries of the problem. In this case, it was a new comet, already inbound, on a collision course. The "already inbound" eliminated almost all the ideas due to lack of time. He loved the quote by Sir Arthur Conan Doyle: "Once you eliminate the impossible, whatever remains, no matter how improbable, must be the truth."

An idea formed in his mind. He began to research the programs spawned by the old Strategic Defense Initiative. With the collapse of the Soviet Union, the grand scheme of an impenetrable ballistic-missile shield had slid to the back burner. Josh knew, however, the military were still pursuing several of these classified technologies. Maybe his knowledge about these programs explained Jesse's interest in him.

It was late afternoon. Coming in from her shift, Elizabeth saw Josh working intensely on the computer as usual. She quietly sat down next to him to work on the other computer. After a few minutes, she bit the side of her lip, and without looking up, said, "Josh, you're practically living here, and you're wasting time running back and forth. I have an empty bedroom with an extra bath and could probably use the rent as much as Justin." She turned toward him, looking somewhat defiant.

Josh stopped typing and looked back. "I can't imagine a better arrangement for me, but me living here could put a damper on your social life, and people at work might talk."

"Josh, for goodness' sake, this is the twenty-first century! It's simply a logical arrangement." She paused and added dismissively, "Besides, the people I work with would never question you living here." She turned back to her computer, adding casually, "They already assume we're in a hot, steamy relationship." She tried not to smile as she saw him blush out of the corner of her eye.

It was his last night at Justin's. He was alone in the apartment.

He tried to contact Jesse and quickly sensed his presence. Advanced biotechnology, detecting comets two years out… he needed to know who Jesse really was.

"Jesse, you've been evasive about who you are, and who you represent. I haven't questioned it because you obviously know what you're doing. I'm a breathing example."

Silence.

He knew he also hadn't questioned it because of an underlying anxiety about the answer. He'd try a more oblique approach. "Comet aside, what's your *organization's* purpose? What's your mission statement?" He sensed amusement.

Mankind.

He shook his head. "Yeah, I know. You've said that." He paused. "You obviously have access to amazing technology. Why don't you just use it to help directly?"

When children are learning to walk, do you grab them every time they lose their balance?

"No."

Why not?

"The kid's never going to learn." Josh understood the analogy. "But isn't it a bit late for mankind to learn to *walk*?"

Mankind is still very young.

"In comparison to *what*?" He sensed the conversation was over. Who was he really talking to?

Lesia caught Elizabeth as she started her shift. "How's it going with your mystery date?"

She was afraid to tell Lesia, but she'd find out soon enough. "I… uh… actually I invited him to be a roommate," she finished quickly. "But it's still purely platonic."

With her usual raised eyebrows, Lesia said, "Elizabeth, you're a big girl. I just don't want to see you hurt."

They called a "code" over the intercom, saving her from a response.

After the code, when no one was around, Lesia made a call. Quietly, she said, "Hello, Dr. Lopez?"

10

DISTRACT

It was the second day after Josh moved in and the first that neither of them had to go to work. Needing little sleep, Josh was up early, continuing his research. Around eight, Elizabeth came out of her bedroom and into the kitchen, wearing a short silk bathrobe. Peeking out from underneath was a black negligee that appeared to be woven mostly of air. The robe did its job, properly covering everything, but as she moved, it shifted just enough to make it difficult to concentrate. On top of that, she was barefoot. He liked women in high heels, but for some reason, he always thought women looked particularly sexy barefoot. He wished she didn't keep her condo quite so warm.

She asked, "Do you want some breakfast? I'm going to make some anyway."

Up for several hours, he'd eaten a protein bar. "No, thanks, I'm fine." He tried to angle himself so that she wouldn't be in his direct line of sight.

After a few seconds, she said, "Josh... is there any particular reason the kitchen faucet is disassembled?"

He totally forgot. "Sorry. It was dripping, so I thought I'd fix it. After I took it apart... uh, I realized I needed a couple extra parts." He needed parts because one of the micro springs had shot out and he hadn't been able to find it. Taking things apart to see how they worked was fun, but he had a tendency to lose interest when it came to minor details – like putting them back together.

It occurred to him that he and Elizabeth were opposite personalities, just as he and Kelly had been. Kelly was outgoing, loved people, and lived in the present. She saw the trees but sometimes missed the forest. He, on the other hand, was reserved, task oriented, and lived in the future. He saw the forest but sometimes ran into a tree. Kelly had been his perfect complement: fascinating and frustrating, intriguing and incomprehensible. His secret term of endearment for her was "Kelly-bear," cute as a koala, with the temper and passion of a grizzly. Elizabeth looked nothing like Kelly, but she had that same indefinable… something. Opposites really did attract.

"Ouch!" Elizabeth scared him out of his reverie.

He looked up. "You OK?"

Hopping on one foot, she was trying to look at the bottom of the other foot. Somehow, she made that awkward pose both graceful and sexy.

"Yeah, I'm OK," she said, as she pulled something from the bottom of her foot. Examining it with a frown, she added, "Weird. It looks like a… a tiny metal spring."

Josh quickly looked back at the computer screen.

After pouring herself a cup of coffee, she came over and stood next to him, glancing at his screen.

He once read that Americans had larger "personal bubbles" than other cultures. Elizabeth never got the memo.

She asked, "What are you working on?"

He pointed to the picture on the screen. "It's a diagram of the Oort Cloud at the outskirts of our solar system. It's where dwarf planets and comets hang out."

With her coffee in one hand, she put her other hand on his shoulder and leaned over to look carefully at the screen. As she leaned forward, he couldn't help but glance down the front of her loosely tied bathrobe and suddenly lost all interest in astrophysics.

She caught his glance but pretended not to notice. As she walked back to the kitchen, she knew his eyes were following her. Smiling, she said quietly to herself, "*Bad* girl."

By noon, she was restless and realized Josh hadn't moved from the computer. It was one of those rare, early spring days with crystal-blue skies, summer temperatures, and a gentle breeze.

After another hour, she couldn't stand it. She swept in wearing a jogging suit. "Off the computer! You need to be outside, getting some exercise, vitamin D, and color." Looking at him, she smiled and added, "Well, at least some vitamin D." She got the classic, male, TV-zombie "Uh huh." Inserting her face between him and the monitor, she said, "Go put on your running shoes and shorts. We're going to the park."

He looked surprised but smiled and complied.

They opened the canvas top on her Jeep. For just a few minutes, sitting in the warm sun with the wind in his hair, Josh forgot about the comet and just watched the world go by. They hit a small construction area where they were putting in an entrance to a new mall. The sign said, "Logan Shopping Center." Seeing his old name reminded him of the family he'd lost, bringing him sadly back to reality.

As they arrived at the park, he saw running trails wandered through small lakes, athletic fields, and woods. Brilliant yellow daffodils were everywhere, punctuated by prolific pear trees in full bloom. The white blossoms made them look like giant popcorn balls. Runners, skaters, bikers, and kids filled the park. It was a barely controlled cacophony of sound and colorful chaos. This, he realized, was what he was trying to protect.

Before their run, they stretched against a large oak tree. Elizabeth was exceptionally limber, and could bend herself into impossible but interesting angles. As she touched her toes, he caught a small pin-stripe tattoo on her lower back and admired her truly spectacular empennage. She caught his glance... busted.

They ran on the trail that wound through the park. His new body loped along comfortably. Josh was impressed with Elizabeth's fitness, measured in her ability both to set a fast pace and turn male heads. Nike would have appreciated how she advertised their form-fitting running attire. After three miles, they slowed to a jog.

When Elizabeth caught her breath, she said, "I tried to share some of our conversations with the people I work with, but it didn't go over well. One of the nurses, Leslee Wong, bless her heart..."

Josh started laughing.

Elizabeth frowned. "What's so funny?"

"My memory must be coming back because I remember in the South, right after a 'bless her heart,' usually comes, 'she's a complete idiot.'"

Now Elizabeth laughed. "I would *never* call someone an idiot. I was just going to say she's… optimistically challenged." She shook her head with a smile. "Anyway, 'bless her heart' thinks that ancient humans were noble, modern humans suck, and the universe would be better off without us. Why is human-race bashing so chic nowadays?"

He nodded. "I suspect what we believe to be the decadent collapse of humanity is really just business as usual. Long before reality TV, we had gladiator matches in the Roman Colosseum."

Elizabeth smiled. "They'd probably do human sacrifice on TV today if they could get away with it." She imitated a game-show host. "I'm *sorry*, Bob, that isn't the correct answer… release the lions."

He laughed.

She continued more seriously, "But the Romans didn't wipe out other species or cause global warming."

Josh smiled. "There just weren't enough of 'em." He thought for a moment and then went on. "They say the earth's about 4 billion years old, and man's been around for about a half million. If that's true, let's scale that to human terms. If the earth were 100 years old, mankind would be about five days old."

She nodded thoughtfully.

He asked, "Know what I think?"

"What?"

"I think we give ourselves too much credit as *all-powerful* destroyers. Climate's a good example. For thousands of years the earth's climate drove the rise and fall of civilizations, with ice ages, floods, and droughts. Look at the cradle of civilization in the Middle East. It didn't always look like a desert. Even the Dark Ages were partly due to a mini ice age. *We* didn't cause those climate problems, not back then. It's ironic; for thousands of years the climate's been kicking our butt. Only in the last few decades have we been kicking its butt."

She frowned.

He grinned. "Yeah, I know, the climate may have the last laugh, but the point is, it's our usual arrogance that we believe we're the *bane* of all life on the planet. Yeah, we make radioactive wastes but we forget that we didn't invent uranium. It was always here and radioactive. We just dug it up and concentrated it. Anything we create will eventually be broken down, even if it takes thousands of years. On a geological scale, humanity's presence may look like nothing more than a temporary infection... a minor case of acne on the face of the earth. *And*, it's an infection that, unfortunately for us, can be quickly cleared up with a nuclear war or... a comet impact."

With a half smile, she said, "And this is supposed to make me feel better because...?"

Josh laughed. "Sorry, that's the dark side. On the other hand, we have incredible potential. The industrial revolution is barely 250 years old. We really only discovered we're seriously mucking with the environment seven or eight decades ago. If the earth were 100 years old, then mankind just started soiling its diapers about five minutes ago. We only realized we needed potty training thirty seconds ago!"

Elizabeth giggled. "I like the thought of being a baby, better than being acne."

She had a great laugh.

Looking off into the distance, she said, "So... if, as a civilization, we're still babies... our temper tantrums might look a lot like wars?" She shook her head. "Will we make it to adolescence?"

Josh smiled. "Did your parents think you would?"

She grinned. "No way!" Pointing at the back of her upper left thigh, she said, "I'll have to tell you where I got this scar someday."

He studied it with great scholarly interest. Finally, shifting his eyes back to hers, he said, "There's even more at stake than the human race." He paused. "What do you think would happen if mankind goes gentle into that good night?"

Elizabeth exclaimed excitedly, "You must have read poetry!"

"Ah... maybe." He probably heard it on a TV commercial.

"I'm sorry. It would be very sad if mankind doesn't 'rage against the dying of the light.'"

He smiled. "Yes, but not just for us." He looked at her intently. "Do you realize that we are the only species on the planet that has the ability to save all the other species?"

"From what?"

The sun was setting and an almost full moon was visible on the horizon. Josh stopped and pointed at it. "What do you see?"

"The moon?"

"Yes, and what's on the surface?"

"Green cheese?" she giggled.

He smiled. "More like Swiss cheese."

Still smiling, she said, "Craters?"

"Yes."

"So, you're saying we can save life on earth from an impact like in the movies?"

"Yes."

She smiled and simply said, "Cool!"

He loved the way she accepted a new thought without having to examine it from every angle, as he did. She was extremely intelligent and yet in her ability to believe had an almost childlike innocence.

As they looked at the moon, he detected an "incoming." He'd been watching a soccer game out of the corner of his eye. The teenage players were quite good, but they had accidentally kicked the ball, full force, right at Elizabeth's head. Because of her angle, she was blind to the impending impact. He caught the ball perfectly in his hand, just inches from her head.

She jumped in surprise.

Showing off, he bounced it twice off the side of his foot and kicked it in the air. As it came down, he head-butted it directly into the arms of the surprised teenager running toward them. The teenager smiled and said, "Sorry about that… Hey, wanna play?"

Josh smiled back. "No, but thanks." The teenager, after furtively giving Elizabeth the once over, ran back to the group, who all gave Josh the nod.

Elizabeth said, "Thanks. That would have left a mark. That was quite a compliment they gave you, wanting you to stay and play."

Josh smiled. "I don't think it was *my* form they were interested in."

She laughed.

As they started to walk again, he glanced back. The soccer players' attention was back in the game, but someone else's attention wasn't. A tall man, looking out of place in a sports jacket, looked away as soon as Josh caught his eye.

11

IDENTITY

That evening, Josh sat next to Elizabeth as they both worked on the computers. After several minutes of silence, Elizabeth turned to him, biting the side of her lip. He noticed it was something she did when she was nervous. She'd make a lousy poker player.

"Josh, I don't know what your spiritual beliefs are," she frowned. "I guess you may not either, but I believe there's something much bigger than us out there."

He took his hands off the keyboard and turned toward her. "I do too." He added to himself, and maybe in low earth orbit. Curious, he asked, "What do you believe?"

She looked at him a little defiantly. "I believe in God. I think we all have a purpose in life that we can either choose or ignore. I think mine's to help people. I'm happiest when I do that."

He nodded his head, encouraging her to continue.

She paused. "I think, to whom much is given, much is required."

Under his breath, he said, "Tell me about it."

"What?"

"I said, I think you're right about it."

"Josh, I grew up in church and still go. I guess that makes me," she grinned and imitated a heavy Southern drawl, "one of them there backward eeeevangelical Christians." Suddenly frowning, she continued without the drawl. "I hate that label. The press loves to use it, but if they bothered to study Christianity, they'd realize sharing our beliefs is part of our commission. It's what being a Christian means. They act like anyone who actually tries to share all that 'love your brother, turn the other cheek' junk, must be a fanatic."

Josh added, "A fanatic is just someone who's more excited about something than you are."

She frowned. "But it's more than that. People say they're all for freedom of religion. They say, go ahead, believe whatever you want, but for goodness' sake, don't share it or display it publicly. It might offend someone." She continued with passion. "I understand someone who believes in something can be offended by someone who says *it ain't so*. But how can someone who *doesn't* believe be offended by someone who *does*?"

He frowned. He wasn't sure about her argument, but admired her passion.

She paused. "OK, I think it's safe to say most adults don't believe in the Tooth Fairy, but if I knew you did, I wouldn't be *offended*... I'd be amused."

He smiled.

She continued, "If people don't believe in God, why should they get their panties in a twist about anything religious? They should just be amused and ignore it, like we ignore the Flat Earth Society."

Josh added thoughtfully, "Unless they're not absolutely sure God *doesn't* exist and don't want to be reminded about what it means if they're wrong." He realized he was talking about himself. "Unlike the Tooth Fairy, however, organized religion has had a rather checkered past: the Inquisition, Jihad, et cetera. A lot of conflicts occur because of religion."

She raised her eyebrows. "Do they? If we dig deeper, we usually find conflicts are based on territory, empire building, 'haves' versus 'have nots,' or just plain prejudice. Religion is often used as a convenient justification."

Josh shrugged. "I guess if religious *differences* were the primary driver of conflict, Hindus with multiple gods and Christians with just one should be at each other's throat all the time."

She nodded. "Instead, we see Muslim against Jew, even though they share common history and prophets, not to mention Protestant against Catholic in Northern Ireland." She looked at her phone and said, "Oops. It's way late and I've got an early shift."

As she logged off her computer and headed to bed, she stopped and said, "Sorry." She smiled sheepishly. "Thanks for letting me lecture. You're very easy to talk to."

He smiled back. "Good night, Elizabeth."

Knowing her beliefs were the result of years of religious indoctrination, he was surprised at how good she was at logical debate. He certainly didn't believe what she did, but he almost envied her childlike faith. He'd have to bounce some of this off Jesse. Although Jesse's identity was still a mystery, Josh was certain Jesse had an *advanced* perspective… he just wasn't sure *where* it came from.

Late that night, after Elizabeth was asleep, he sat in his bedroom with the door closed. He'd gotten up enough courage to try cross-examining Jesse again. He called quietly and sensed his attention. "Jesse, I understand your analogy – letting a child learn to walk without catching them – but you wouldn't let them learn in the middle of a freeway. Wouldn't a planet-killing comet kinda fall into that category?"

Yes. That's why you're here.

"What? A minor in Astronomy does *not* qualify me to intervene. That better not be why you chose me!"

Despite your skepticism, you believe in people and your faith is stronger than your fear.

"Faith! What does that have to do with anything?"

Fear is simply belief in a negative outcome that hasn't occurred. Faith is the opposite. It's belief in a positive outcome that has yet to occur. Without that belief, nothing of significance is ever accomplished.

After his talk with Elizabeth, Josh realized he was spring-loaded into the anti-religion mode. Jesse's characterization of "faith" was much broader than Josh's churchy definition had encompassed. "OK, but how is the destruction of our world by a comet going to help mankind learn to walk?"

How do you feel?

He felt frustrated with Jesse's indirect answers. "Why is that relevant?"

Silence.

Sighing, he said, "Overwhelmed, clueless, and inadequate."

How do you feel?

Josh paused. "Afraid."

What else?

It was odd, but there *was* something else. "I feel a… kind of excitement, a positive tension."

What creates happiness?

He had no idea where Jesse was going. "I don't know." He shook his head. "I guess getting something you want?"

Are you happiest after getting it or during the pursuit?

"Well… we should be happy when we get it, but our society is littered with people who reach the top of their game and are miserable."

If you believe you've completed your purpose, you no longer have a reason to live.

"Yeah. We're happiest when we're *pursuing* stuff, aren't we? That explains why I feel excitement, but I don't think you told me all this to help me 'find myself.'"

Do you think societies are so different?

"You lost me."

What was your nation's finest hour?

"I don't know… maybe when everyone pulled together during World War II, or when we landed a man on the moon?" He paused. "You're suggesting that for a society to be happy, it also needs to be pursuing something or have a purpose?"

Yes.

"If that's true, we got a problem. We're usually at our most *purposeful* when we're trying to annihilate each other."

Purpose is often working together to defeat a common enemy.

He felt stupid. "Of course, the comet!" It would certainly give humanity a common goal. He frowned. "But how do you pull humanity together to fight something they can't see until it's too late?"

He sensed the conversation was over. It hadn't helped him figure out who Jesse was, but he was becoming more certain who Jesse wasn't.

It was close to noon and Elizabeth was halfway through her shift.

Lesia said, "Girl, we need to talk."

As they sat down with a cup of coffee in the cafeteria, Lesia said, "He's living with you. Talk to me."

Elizabeth shared what had transpired.

Lesia listened quietly, asking for details at several points. Finally, she sighed. "You said he's spending his time online doing research. What's he studying?"

Elizabeth said slowly, "I guess he's trying to find his identity and figure out what he's going to do with his life."

Lesia raised an eyebrow. "Have you actually seen where he goes online?"

Elizabeth frowned. "Well, no. It's really none of my business."

Lesia gave her the head and finger wag. "*Au contraire*, girl, it's very much your business. He's going to these sites on *your* computer from *your* home." Her face softened as she continued in a gentler voice. "So you got the hots for this guy, who could blame you? But you still don't know anything about him. Honey, you gotta protect yourself. You're a computer geek; find out what he's doing, *carefully*!"

Elizabeth arrived at her condo. She knew Josh's schedule: he wouldn't be home for another couple hours. She looked around unnecessarily and sat down at the computer he used.

12

CONFRONT

It was early evening when Josh got home. As soon as he came in and closed the door, he noticed the silence. The classical music that usually played softly in the background was absent. Elizabeth sat on the couch looking at him intently.

He gave her a questioning look.

She stood up and came toward him. Taking a deep breath, she said, "Look, Josh, I don't want to pry, but you know more about your past than you're letting on."

He felt a knot in his stomach. "Why do you say that?"

She looked a little sad. "I'm not a psychiatrist but I've read up on amnesia. It's usually selective to an event or time. It's hard to believe you have all this knowledge… and don't remember how you got any of it. Dr. Lopez told me you refused hypnosis." She paused. Biting her lip, she said, "I've also seen what you're researching online… US Ballistic Missile Defense, nuclear weapons?" She looked directly into his eyes. "Josh, *who* are you, and what are you doing?" Her voice was a little raspy.

The knot became a pit in his stomach. He hated emotional conflict. "Elizabeth, you're right. I haven't told you everything… but you wouldn't believe me if I did."

She gave him a steely stare. "You might be surprised. Try me."

Looking down, he said, "I… I can't."

"Why?" Her voice cracked.

"I can't explain… it's for your own protection."

"My *protection*? What are you talking about?"

He said, "I'm… I'm sorry. I shouldn't have come here." Shaking his head as if clearing cobwebs, he continued, "I'm putting you at risk. It was a terrible mistake. I'm… so sorry, I'll… I'll leave."

She spun around and went to her bedroom. This wasn't the outcome she wanted, but Lesia was right; he was serious trouble. He had to be some type of spy, and just being with him could make her an accomplice. She needed to report him to Homeland Security.

Listening, she heard him packing his few possessions and then heard the front door close. She stayed in her room, not sure whether to be angry or cry. Even if he wasn't doing something bad, she was *not* going to fall for someone who… who could be killed. Never again… She picked up Sheri Lopez's card.

He left the condo and walked across the parking lot. Then stopped. Sad and angry, he had no idea what he was going to do next. Looking around to make sure no one was near, he said under his breath, "Jesse, I need some guidance. I just royally pissed off the only human being on the planet willing to help me."

He sensed Jesse's attention.

"She knows I'm not being straight with her but I can't tell her the truth. She'll have me committed."

Do you need her?

"Well… yeah. She's… she's all I got. But even if she believed me, I can't involve her. It would put her in danger."

What will happen to her if you fail?

He rarely swore, but let loose a few choice words under his breath. Then sighed, turned around, and went back.

Returning to the condo, he went to her closed bedroom door and knocked gently. Quietly, he asked, "Elizabeth, may I speak to you?"

She opened it tentatively and came out.

"Elizabeth, I care about you and don't want you hurt."

With glassy eyes, she gently shook her head, frowning. "Don't you understand? You *are* hurting me. Stop trying to do my thinking. Let me decide what I do and don't believe." She looked both defiant and vulnerable.

He took a deep breath. "I'm going to explain as much as I can.

Then you can decide if I'm stark raving mad."

She just stared at him.

"If you accept what I tell you, it will change your life and may put you at risk. I'll protect you if I can, but I can't promise any of us will be here a few years from now."

She looked at him questioningly but said nothing.

"The world is facing a cataclysm."

He watched her face as she began to put the puzzle pieces together. Looking at the ceiling, she said quietly, "Those weren't just philosophical discussions. You believe we're going to get hit by an asteroid, don't you?"

Stunned at how quickly her mind worked, he just said, "A comet."

"A comet... how do you know?"

"That's the part that's hard to believe."

Jokingly, she said, "What, you think you're... an alien?"

He smiled. "No, I'm not an alien."

Her eyebrows went up. "An angel?"

He laughed. "No, I'm not *that* deluded. Unfortunately, I'm very human."

Her eyes narrowed as she slowly said, "You believe you're here to... prepare us for the end?"

"No. No, I'm going to do whatever I can to make sure this *isn't* the end."

She put her finger on her lips and slowly turned around. Deep in thought, she walked across the living-room. Stopping in front of the picture window overlooking the city, she stood silently.

He could see her face reflected in the dark windowpane. She was just staring into the night. In the lengthening silence he said, "As a nurse you know schizophrenia is often accompanied by delusions of grandeur."

She said nothing.

The room was painfully quiet. He replayed their conversation in his mind, trying to hear it from her perspective. He realized at best he might earn her pity. She hadn't moved. The only sound in the room was a large decorative clock, loudly ticking off the seconds.

Finally, he realized he had his answer. He picked up his bag and turned to the door. Over his shoulder, he said softly, "I'm... I'm sorry." Turning the door handle, he glanced back. He saw her spin around to face him. She walked toward him purposefully with fire in her eyes. He paused, bracing for the attack.

Stopping directly in front of him, hands on hips, she said loudly, "Josh, I'm attracted to you, but I'm not a child and I'm not stupid!"

There it was. It hurt, but ultimately it was best for her. Trying not to let his emotions show, he repeated softly and genuinely, "I'm so sorry..."

She continued, "What you say is *way* out there!"

He nodded his head in resignation and opened the door. He'd have to start thinking about where to go and what to do if she turned him in.

As he started to leave, she reached in front of him and firmly pushed the door shut. Speaking quickly, she said, "But so is everything else about you. You show up out of nowhere, no fingerprint records, no inoculation marks, not even fillings, for heaven's sake. I've seen every square inch of your body. *No one* can make it to our age without a single scar. Your medical reports say you're the healthiest human I've ever heard of. Your numbers are off the charts. That's not explainable by mental illness." She edged closer. With the slightest of frowns, her eyes searched his face. Staring directly into his eyes as if trying to see inside, she delivered the final blow. "Josh, I know who you are... and who sent you."

His jaw dropped. He barely got out a whispered, "You do?"

Instead of answering, she stepped forward, wrapped her arms around him, and hugged him tightly. "Yes, Josh, I do."

Dropping his bag, he returned her hug. He had no idea what just happened. Could she really know who sent him? No, no... that's wasn't possible... he didn't even know. She seemed totally confident and content with her understanding. He needed to know what she believed but was genuinely afraid to ask. Every endorphin in his body said, "Shut up." He just stood there, frozen in time, gently hugging her.

Elizabeth thought to herself, it was crazy but it actually made sense. Although schizophrenia would've been better; at least it was treatable. As she hugged him, she sighed. Prophets rarely brought good news and it didn't always end well for them… or those around them. While still hugging him, she bit her lip and said quietly, "How can I help?"

He said nothing.

Releasing him, she looked up into his face, and saw his eyes were glassy, as if close to tears. She knew in her heart that she was right.

He finally whispered, "Thank you."

She pulled back, wiping her eyes and said, "OK, what do we need to do?"

Clearing his throat and taking a deep breath, he said softly, "We're on a clock. We have less than two years." Pausing and taking another breath, he added, "I'm trying to work behind the scenes to facilitate the technology required."

All business, Elizabeth said, "What's our first objective?"

Speaking more confidently, he said, "I believe my job is to identify the engineers and scientists who have the expertise and quietly get them working on a solution."

"Why can't we go public?"

He laughed. "Well, I'm pretty sure I could convince the *National Enquirer*."

"You have no proof?"

"And won't until it's too late."

"Why can't the astronomers find it?"

"There are several programs that search the solar system, and they've found most of the *asteroids* that could be a threat, but not comets."

"What's the difference?"

"There are probably around two million asteroids running around between Mars and Jupiter."

She nodded.

"But comets are a completely different animal. There are hundreds of *billions* of cometary objects, and most of them are ten-thousand times farther out than asteroids. Even the closest are outside the orbit of Neptune. The volume of space they can hide in is a trillion times bigger than the asteroid belt."

She frowned, trying to grasp the scale.

He scratched his head and slowly said, "If the asteroid belt was the size of a donut, then the area that comets hang out in would be a sphere one mile wide. And if asteroids were marbles, they'd fill a dump truck. But to hold all the cometary objects, it would take 200 miles of dump trucks parked bumper-to-bumper."

She whistled softly.

He sighed. "Because comets orbit so far out, they reflect almost no sunlight. That means, unlike asteroids, they're pretty much invisible."

"So it takes longer to find them?"

"With current technology, it's really not possible."

She nodded. "OK, so we're not going to see it until it's too late, but how dangerous is it? I mean, is it really like the asteroids in the movies?"

"Worse. Comets can be moving twice as fast as asteroids."

She asked, "But aren't comets made of ice? Won't it melt in the atmosphere?"

"At thirty miles per second, it'll cross the earth's atmosphere in three seconds."

She raised an eyebrow. "No time to melt." Frowning, she asked, "So what happens when it hits?"

"It depends on its size…"

She couldn't help but interrupt, "So size *does* matter."

He smiled. "Unfortunately, yes."

She asked, "What if it was the size of Halley's Comet?"

Staring off into space with little expression, he said, "Halley's comet is about eleven kilometers wide. It would create an explosion of about 200 million megatons."

She frowned.

"That's about the same destructive energy as a full-scale global nuclear war… repeated *every day* for *fifty years*." Eyes unfocused, he continued, "The shockwave and firestorm would incinerate the continents on one side of the planet. Another shockwave would race through the earth's crust, causing earthquakes greater than anything ever experienced. Cities not incinerated or blown away would turn to rubble. Tsunamis a thousand feet tall would sweep the globe.

The explosion and fires would poison the atmosphere and oceans, shrouding the planet in a cloak that would turn day into night for months, if not years. What didn't burn, collapse or suffocate would freeze and starve as the earth entered an ice age. When the smoke finally cleared, the ozone layer might be gone, allowing ultraviolet to sterilize anything that survived."

Looking back at her face, he finished with, "We're not just talking about the end of mankind: we're talking about the end of almost all life on earth."

Into the tense silence, she said, "Well, that sucks."

He laughed.

After Elizabeth went to bed, he spoke quietly to Jesse. He felt his presence immediately. "I patched things up with Elizabeth – thanks. I also read everything I could find on comets, as you suggested. I'm ready to join the team. So, what's the plan? How are we going to stop this thing?"

What are the options?

"I hate it when you answer questions with questions." He paused. "Well, we need experts and resources."

How would you get them?

Clearly, Jesse wasn't going to share what his team was doing, and his questions were beginning to make Josh nervous. "Well, you could do it politically. A world leader could move national resources. Or, you could get an expert who could influence governments. Or, I guess you could try to influence people directly."

Silence.

With a feeling of frustration and foreboding, he continued, "Well, *I'm* obviously not going to get elected to public office with no identity, and I'm not an expert. That leaves influence. But, without credibility or money, there's little chance of getting anyone's attention."

What's influence?

He sighed. "The power to affect the way people think?"

Do you have to influence publicly?

"I don't know. I guess a lot of important decisions are made behind the scenes."

What's required?

Laughing nervously, he said, "I know, I could write a book about our conversations and then start a religious cult." He was certain Jesse was "laughing." There was no sound, just a bright sense of amusement. While Jesse was amused, he figured he might as well ask – "Hey, how about transferring a hundred million dollars into my checking account?"

Silence.

It was worth a try. Probably meant he could forget Occam's Razor and the "simplest solution." More like Sir Arthur Conan Doyle's "whatever remains, no matter how improbable, must be the truth."

He took a deep breath. "Jesse, early on, you asked me who I thought you were." He took another breath and quickly said, "You aren't a government lab or any other agency, are you?" He paused. "I think you're some type of advanced beings from elsewhere, or else-when, here to help us backward savages."

Silence.

"That's it, isn't it?"

That will do for now.

"I knew it!" He actually *didn't* know it and was surprised and a bit frightened. It was a combination of fear of the unknown, and feeling as if he might be representing the human race. It also confirmed his greatest fear. There might not be any "team"… no cavalry, no support, no pension. In fact, he might be it, a team of one… against a 150,000 mph mountain.

13

PARTNER

Josh didn't sleep well.

The next morning, he got up, made a pot of coffee, and went to the computer. It was a comfortable routine. He sat down and stared at the blank screen. Overwhelmed didn't hardly cover it.

Elizabeth came out, poured a cup of coffee, smiled and asked, "So, how do we start?"

Her bright presence and simple question broke the spell. He rubbed his hands together. "I need to put together a team of experts."

She nodded as she came over.

He paused. "This is going to sound a little strange, as the Cheshire Cat said to Alice, but I had a former life. I was a Navy fighter pilot."

"Really?" she said with raised eyebrows.

He thought he heard her mutter, "… fighter pilot prophet…?" He asked her, "What was that?"

Giggling a little, she said, "Never mind." Continuing more seriously, "So who do you need on your team?"

"I'd like to start with some of my old military colleagues…"

"Can you call them?"

"Yes… well… they wouldn't actually… recognize me." He realized his story was going downhill rapidly. "I mean, I don't look like I did… then." His expression was probably like that of a child asking for a third piece of cake.

She nodded thoughtfully as if what he said actually made sense.

Surprised, he pressed on. "Homeland Security may have taken

an interest in me due to my rather odd arrival. I'm sure they've moved on, but accessing some of the military websites might bring… unwelcome attention. I could use your computer expertise."

"What do you need?"

"Can you make sure our visits to certain websites can't be tracked back to your computer?"

She shrugged. "Sure. I can use an IP masking program and make the origin impossible to trace." She slipped into the computer chair. "Took a course in ethical hacking."

He frowned. "*Ethical* hacking?"

Her fingers flew over the keyboard. "Can't stop the bad guys if you don't know how they do what they do. It was fun and I was actually very good at it." After a minute, she said, "OK."

He jumped on the keyboard and called up his program website. After a few attempts, he said, "Dang, they took me out of the military system." He had another idea. He'd try the defense contractors' administrative site. Contractors moved less frequently than military and probably didn't die in crashes quite as often.

He realized with his new photographic memory he could recall absolutely anything from his prior life with perfect clarity, even… his old user names and passwords. "Yes! We're in!" He was lucky. They should have shut down his email account a long time ago. His unexpected demise may have caused his account to slip through the cracks.

Looking on, Elizabeth said, with some concern, "I thought you said you were a fighter pilot. Why are you trying to get into Boeing's website?"

"I was assigned to oversee the development of the next generation of UCAVs, Unmanned Combat Aerial Vehicles."

She looked at him blankly.

"Unmanned robotic fighters."

She raised her eyebrows. "Wouldn't that put you out of a job?"

He smiled. "Yes, it will, but UCAVs can be built smaller and cheaper, and can maneuver faster than a human body can withstand."

She nodded. "They also take the pilots out of harm's way?"

"Yes… although from a State Department perspective, they're

probably less concerned about dead pilots than captured pilots."

"So, are you trying to get classified information?"

"No. You can see this is an unclassified site. It just allows me to send and receive email from inside the system." He smiled. "Despite Hollywood, defense programs never have their seriously classified stuff on a computer connected to the Internet."

"If you're not trying to break in to a classified program, what are you trying to do?"

"I'm not going to break in to one." He gave her a mischievous smile. "I'm going to create one."

She frowned. "I don't understand."

"The system is designed to protect and compartmentalize sensitive information. Classified, or black programs, are 'need to know.' That means no matter how high your clearance, you only have access to information you need for your job. That protects programs if someone talks, but it also means no one can know about all the black programs out there."

Elizabeth, still frowning, said, "Aside from the obvious question of why you would *want* to create a black program; how can you do that?"

"I just need to *read* people into it."

"*Read* into?"

"That's how you bring someone into a black program. They sign a sheet that says they'll have access to classified information, and if they divulge it, they go to jail."

"So you're going to read people into a black program that… doesn't exist."

"Yes."

"What if they ask someone else about it?"

Josh grinned. "That's the beauty. They can't."

"Why?"

"It's a security violation, not to mention bad etiquette, to ask about a black program you're not already a part of."

She frowned. "That's kinda weird."

Josh nodded knowingly. "Welcome to your federal government."

"Are we going to get arrested?"

"I don't think there's a law against *creating* black programs." He shrugged. "At least not yet."

"But how are you going to *create* it?"

Looking serious, he asked, "Do you have Microsoft PowerPoint?"

He worked all day creating the presentation for his new black program. After Elizabeth went to bed, he realized his real challenge was to figure out how to get access to the right people so he could make his pitch. That was a problem. Without an identity, he had no security clearance. Without a clearance, not only didn't he have credibility, he couldn't even get in to see most of them.

He stood up and started pacing. This would be an impossible task even if he had his old identity. It was insanity to believe he could do it with *no* identity. He needed to talk to Jesse but was afraid he'd just get more fortune-cookie answers. As he thought about everything required to make this work, he began to feel overwhelmed again. His mind sputtered, like a car trying to start in too high a gear. He stopped pacing and took a deep breath. Stop looking at the forest and focus on a tree, just the next step. He needed access to people. How could he do that?

He went back to the computer and opened his old account. He found a year of unopened emails. There were thousands. He began to scan them methodically, one by one. Ninety-nine per cent of them were useless even when he was alive. A few helped fill in events that had occurred during his lost year, but he was searching for just one.

Finally, after an hour, there it was. Sent recently, it was a request by Boeing's security department to update his personal information. They updated their access information annually. He thanked the glacial gods of bureaucracy for the gift of red tape. The department responsible appeared to have missed a minor detail... his death. The question was, how could he use this to his advantage? How could he somehow update it to reflect a new name *and* face? His lack of interest in details had gotten him locked out of accounts before by trying too many passwords. He wouldn't risk it. He decided to wait until tomorrow when he could tap Elizabeth's expertise.

It was quiet in the condo, and with his exceptional hearing, he could faintly hear Elizabeth's rhythmic breathing down the hall. She always slept with her door open. He preferred to sleep with his closed. It was an indicator of their personalities. He was private, skeptical, and analytical. She was open, trusting, and giving. That probably explained some of the attraction. He knew her open door wasn't an open invitation; it was just the way she was. She also kicked her covers off as she slept. With her "mostly air" nightgowns and his exceptional night vision, he kept his eyes forward when passing her door... most of the time. He didn't need that dangerously delightful distraction.

Focusing back on the problem at hand, he realized he had a challenge that he saw no way around. He found a comet deflection idea that might work from a physics standpoint, but it was impossible from an engineering perspective. Once again, a dose of discouragement hit him. He had to talk to Jesse.

He started with his usual request for attention by asking very quietly, "Jesse, are you there?" He immediately sensed his presence. "Jesse, I never thanked you for saving my life. I also appreciate my enhanced body. It's truly impressive." He paused and then in a softer voice continued, "Since our last conversation, I've finished my research. There isn't any existing technology that can deflect a comet... not this late in the game. If we had five years, maybe we could develop it, but even then, I don't have the knowledge or experience to run something this big." He sighed. "I'm sorry... you made a mistake in choosing me. I'm not qualified to do this. *Please* take this responsibility away from me."

You have the single most important qualification.

"What, an astronomy minor?"

You were willing to lay down your life for others.

That caught him by surprise. He shook his head. "Sorry to tell you this, but I didn't *intend* to die."

You could have ejected sooner.

"No! No, I couldn't. I had to stay with the jet or people would've died. I had to make sure..."

Yes?

"It... it doesn't matter. It doesn't change the fact that I'm not capable of doing what you've asked."

You do not have the knowledge or experience.

"No kidding. That's what I've been trying to tell you."

So you must enlist those that do.

"Those from my past life, who could've helped, think I'm dead. I can't talk to any of them."

You, and they, have a common friend.

"I don't understand." He felt like a slow child. Then, finally, it dawned on him. "Wait, you mean… me? I can introduce myself as a friend of my past self. I know things about them that only my former self could know." He was talking about himself in the past and present tense at the same time. It sounded seriously schizophrenic. "This is good, but I still need experts beyond my few past friends."

You need leaders of leaders.

"Leaders of leaders? How do I get them?"

You cannot get them but you can inspire them.

"I don't understand."

Leaders of leaders do not require reward or recognition. You must capture their minds and hearts.

"How?"

Communicate with clarity and passion. Show them your belief and your purpose will become theirs. Not everyone will share it, but those who do will multiply you and do what you cannot.

"Like the purpose you've given me." Josh paused. He wasn't sure what power Jesse and his organization actually had but suspected it was substantial. "Can't you just *make* them join our cause?"

Jesse's response was gentle. *We will never interfere with free will.*

He shook his head, thinking wryly, must be like the Prime Directive in *Star Trek*. He still wasn't sure what type of "advanced beings" he was dealing with, but he needed to learn everything he could.

Elizabeth woke up suddenly in the middle of the night. She normally slept very well, but the last two days had been an emotional roller-coaster. Her clock showed a little after three. She heard someone talking quietly. The heating system had gone off and the condo was very quiet. She held her breath and listened intently. Realizing it was just Josh, she relaxed. "… I don't have the knowledge or experience to run something this big. I'm sorry… you made a mistake in choosing me. I'm not qualified to do this. *Please* take this responsibility away from me."

There was a pause. Elizabeth knew she was hearing only one side of a conversation. The heating system came back on and she could hear no more. She was impressed and a little frightened. Either Josh was a prophet with a direct line to the Big Guy… or, he was textbook schizophrenic. She hated to admit it, but she wasn't sure which she preferred, falling in love with a lunatic or an apocalyptic prophet. She should have listened to her mom and dated accountants.

The next morning, she found Josh, as usual, working intently on the computer. She poured herself a cup of coffee and sat quietly, watching him. What was going on inside that head? Almost as if he knew what she was thinking, he suddenly looked up and met her eyes with a half smile.

She raised her coffee cup in question. He nodded.

As she brought him a cup, he said, "Elizabeth, I could really use more of your expertise. I hate to ask, but I need to reestablish my security access at Boeing so I can get in to see the people I need." He paused. "But now we're talking about doing something that could get you in serious trouble."

Still holding her coffee cup, she sat down at the computer. "Where do we need to go?"

He showed her the Boeing website and gave her his username and password.

After studying the site, she said, "There's nothing we can do here. It only allows basic updates. We'll have to talk to someone who can make entries for us on the main server."

Josh raised his eyebrows in question.

She smiled. "Everyone thinks cyber bandits hack into networks by cracking the 128-bit double encryption. It's not impossible, but it would take weeks of super-computer time."

"Then how do they get in?"

She laughed. "The same way every system is cracked… person to person, usually over the phone."

Josh looked skeptical.

"OK, here's an example. You're in the middle of a big project at work. You get a call, apparently, from your IT department. They tell you they have to shut down the network for a software upgrade and it'll be down for hours. Of course, your email and word processor programs are all network based. You can't afford to be down that long. The IT person, trying to be helpful, says they can keep *your* computer up while the rest of the network's down. Of course, to identify your computer on the network, they need your username and password. *Voilà*, they're in!"

Josh nodded. "That makes sense. So, what do we do?"

She winked. "Get me another cup of coffee and my phone. This could take some time."

She called in sick. Using his security-question knowledge and some minor hacking, she convinced a Boeing computer administrator that Josh's identity got confused with someone who died, making his life very complicated. He sat next to her watching and listening nervously.

She asked him multiple security questions from his background, and after several hours of intense work, she finally announced, "Josh Meadows has a Boeing badge and access!"

He jumped up and hugged her, saying, "You totally rock!"

Still in her bathrobe and nightgown, she felt his hands and arms holding her tightly through the thin silk. He suddenly released her, looking distinctly uncomfortable.

She smiled, enjoying his discomfort.

Clearing his throat, he changed the subject. "I'm going to have to go St. Louis…"

Before he could finish, she said, "I have zillions of airline credit-card miles. You can use them, but you can't go looking like…" she waved her hand at him, "… that. I'll need to dress you."

He gave her a half smile and raised eyebrow.

She shook her head. "I mean, get you some real clothes."

"Elizabeth, I…"

She smiled. "Shut up."

II
TEAM

14

CAPTAIN

His success hinged on finding a strong, effective leader to pull a team together, a team that would include high-level scientists and engineers. He needed an insider with credibility. He needed Navy Captain Joe Scupino. Scupino was his first squadron skipper and had led them into combat against sophisticated fighters, but he'd also successfully led aircraft development programs into combat against the General Accounting Office.

Commanding the USS *Gerald R. Ford*, the newest aircraft carrier in the fleet, Scupino had been on the fast track for admiral. Captain of an aircraft carrier was the pinnacle for an aviator, and one of the most sought-after jobs in the Navy. A week after he had taken command, an AMRAAM missile accidentally detonated on the flight deck, destroying three new F-35 aircraft. He had only been the Captain for one week, but the Navy was one of the last bastions of accountability. The old saying about "going down with your ship" still applied. Despite completing an outstanding tour as the *Ford*'s Captain, the fire had eliminated any chance of him becoming an admiral. Promotion competition was too fierce. He could have retired but they had asked him to stay and take over some critical classified programs at Naval Air Systems Command. His office was at NAVAIR headquarters in Patuxent River, Maryland, but he spent most of his time at the contractor facilities where they did the development work. He had satellite offices at the Lockheed Skunk Works in Palmdale, California, and the Boeing Phantom Works in St. Louis… where Josh worked before the crash.

"Captain Scupino? This is Commander Josh Meadows. We haven't met but I worked closely with Josh Logan on a special project before he died."

"Hi, Josh. What can I do for you?"

"Captain, the reason I'm calling is that Josh recommended you for involvement in a very important program, one that I'd like to talk to you about."

"What type of program?"

"We'll have to talk in person."

"OK, but I'm afraid I'm leaving for St. Louis tomorrow."

"St. Louis would be great if you can fit me into your schedule."

"Sure. Can you meet me at the Boeing Phantom Works around noon on Thursday?"

"Yes, sir. I'll see you there."

His next call was to Washington DC. He knew the effort would eventually be global and he'd need international and legal expertise. Carl Casey had been a squadron intel officer with a degree in International Law. They'd been good friends. After Carl's tour was up, he left the Navy and joined the CIA, not an uncommon move for intelligence officers.

After a similar conversation, Carl also agreed to see him. Hanging up, Josh realized he was about to invite a CIA agent into a counterfeit classified program. He smiled. "Oh, what a tangled web we weave."

Josh had a moment of déjà vu as his flight touched down in St. Louis. Thirteen months ago, a happily married Navy test pilot took off from this very runway on a simple delivery mission. He said under his breath, with a half smile, "I'm back... minus one jet and a body."

The Boeing Phantom Works was on the far side of the airport. Walking the two miles around the perimeter helped him conserve his limited funds and settle his nerves. He had good reason to be anxious. He was about to meet someone he knew... wearing a new body. On top of that, Scupino was his only candidate to run the program. Josh did, however, have an advantage. Living in tight quarters on an aircraft carrier for six months, it was impossible not to know your squadron mates – their quirks, their fears, and their dreams.

He arrived at an inconspicuous-looking, windowless, two-story, industrial building. The only thing that hinted at the secrets inside was a tall, barbed-wire-topped fence with a manned guard gate. As the guard checked his ID and cleared him in, he silently thanked Elizabeth.

Going straight to Scupino's office, he knocked on the open door. It was a small office, made even smaller by the occupant. A six-foot-four, muscular, 260-pound, black man with a shaved head rose from his chair. Watching Scupino step carefully around his desk reminded Josh of the classic bull in a china shop. Countering his imposing size were eyes that perpetually smiled, combined with a frequent booming laugh.

As Josh shook his huge hand, he remembered a barbeque at his skipper's house many years ago. Scupino's three-year-old daughter had been perched on his shoulders. With crayons in each hand, she'd been trying to draw on top of his bald head. He never missed a beat, carrying on conversations while handing her different-colored crayons. A patient father translated well into an aircraft-carrier Captain of 5,000 mostly teenage sailors.

After exchanging pleasantries, Scupino brought up Josh's former self. "It was a real blow when we found out about Josh. We're not supposed to have favorite pilots in a squadron – kinda like kids – but we do and he was."

It was surreal hearing someone talk about him as if he wasn't there.

Scupino continued, "I pulled some strings. We flew a missing-man formation over the memorial service. It wasn't hard to arrange, considering what happened."

He knew it was usually only done in fleet squadrons. Josh had flown in a missing-man formation for a fellow pilot who had died in a crash. Just thinking back on it created emotion… but this one had been for *him*. He had to stay on task. Humor helped as he remembered his mom scolding him. "Josh, you'll be late for your own funeral!"

Scupino shook his head. "I was sure he'd make admiral someday."

Josh smiled. "He talked very fondly of his time in your squadron. In fact, he told me he wanted to grow up like you someday." That was a true statement.

Scupino chuckled. "Well, maybe up to the point where I blew admiral."

"We all know what happened," Josh said with vehemence. "That fire was completely outside your control. I… had friends who deployed with you and said you were the best skipper they ever served under."

Scupino, looking a little surprised, said, "Well, thanks Josh, that's good to hear, and that's what's important to me. After the accident investigation was over, that tour turned out to be one of the best of my career. Never been that concerned about promotion as long as I was having fun." With a half smile, he added, "After that fire, I was freed from *ever* having to worry about my career. So, what can I do for you?"

"Captain Scupino, I'm familiar with some of the programs you manage. Bottom line, we believe there may be an intersection between one of your programs and ours. I'd like to read you in, if you're game?"

"OK. Is NAVAIR aware of this?"

Josh remembered Scupino's habit of starting sentences with "OK."

"No, sir, I'm sure Admiral Hendricks doesn't know about this one yet. It's sensitive even for a black program. As you know, we rarely get recognition for anything we work on in the black world anyway."

Scupino shrugged. "In my case, credit doesn't matter. Sure, I'm game. You have my curiosity, but unless it's of strategic importance, I have a pretty full plate."

Josh nodded. "We understand."

Scupino frowned. "OK, that's my other question – who is 'we'? Since you're not in uniform, who are you attached to?"

He could have bought a uniform with the correct insignia and ribbons, but in addition to identifying him as a pilot, some ribbons were what they jokingly referred to as "been there, done thats." They would indicate operations he'd been involved with and places he'd been. He was walking a fine line. He had to be relatable enough that Scupino would accept him as a fellow officer. Distant enough that he wouldn't expect to know the people Josh served with. The F-18 community was too small for him to show up wearing wings.

Josh said, "I miss the simplicity of khakis but I'm on loan to another agency outside the Navy. As I mentioned, it's a bit sensitive."

Scupino smiled. "Yeah, I know." He recited the old joke. "You could tell me but then you'd have to kill me." He paused. "I'd guess your uniform might have included a… Budweiser?… But I won't ask."

Josh raised an eyebrow and smiled back. The Navy SEAL insignia, officially called the Trident, was nicknamed "Budweiser," a corruption of Basic Underwater Demolition/SEAL. With less than 2,500 active SEALS, they were arguably the most elite military team in the world. He felt deceitful by not denying Scupino's assertion but the ambiguity would help mask his background. He quickly moved on. "Here's the paperwork and the usual signing-your-life-away stuff."

Scupino glanced over it briefly, signed it, and handed it back. "OK, what do you got?"

"Sir, what do you know about comets?"

Scupino frowned. "Like Halley's Comet?"

"Yes, sir."

"Probably what everyone knows, they're big snowballs that run around our solar system now and then, putting on pretty displays."

"The team I work with believes they've identified a comet that might be a threat to the earth in a few years."

Scupino frowned, unconsciously clicking his pen. "Wow. Doesn't take a rocket scientist to see what you're thinking. You believe that something we worked on for missile defense might be used on a comet?"

Josh nodded.

"How likely is this… threat?"

"Unfortunately, we believe it's probable."

"How much damage could it do if it hits us?"

"Significant." He was afraid if he told him what "significant" meant, he wouldn't be able to justify keeping the project quiet.

Scupino stopped clicking his pen and sat quietly, staring through his desk. Finally, he said, "I loved flying fighters. I know the 'knights of the air' image is overly romantic, but the parallel's real." He looked up. "I was a history major. Just as the knight's armor, skill and chivalry fell to the new technology of the crossbow, so fighter pilots will bow to the deadly efficiency of UCAVs." He paused. "It's the end of an era, the last of the military warriors to engage in one-on-one aerial combat. I think the last generation of fighter pilots are sitting in elementary school right now." Frowning, he added, "Josh Logan and I worked on some of those programs. I know the work we do is important, but making deadlier, robotic weapon systems, even to save American lives, weighs on you sometimes. Who wouldn't want to work on a project like this?"

Josh just said, "Couldn't agree more."

"Besides, I've always been a closet Trekkie." He paused. "But why is the program classified?"

"Good question." Josh stalled, as he tried to come up with a reason. "Uh, part of it hinges on the use of the advanced strategic defense work. I imagine a lot of it is still sensitive. Part of it may be fear of public reaction."

Scupino frowned. "OK... I guess." He continued, "Well, I'll need to share this with some of our mad scientists. Can you read them into the program?"

"Better yet, we'd like you to take over as the on-site program manager. Then you can take care of the 'read in' paperwork through your organization's existing system. That'll prevent delays and keep control at your level." Josh held his breath.

Scupino raised his eyebrows and smiled. "I *see*. You basically want me to run this thing."

Josh smiled back. "Yes, sir. You've been handpicked from the very highest level." He thought to himself wryly, he'd flown jets as high as 56,000 feet. He could tell from Scupino's body language, he had him.

"It's a lot of responsibility." He grinned. "But I'd be honored."

"Thank you, sir."

Scupino, tapping his pen against his chin and staring past Josh, said, "First, we need technical leads in astrophysics, physics, engineering, and logistics." He paused, looking back at Josh. "This is real? I mean, we're talking serious damage and lives at stake, right?"

Josh said, "I swear; this is as real as it gets and it could potentially be millions of lives."

Scupino nodded. "Then we need the first string, the best and brightest. I know a lot of the players and I'll research the rest. Be prepared, Josh; some of these folks have healthy egos."

With a half smile, Josh said, "That's why we picked you to lead them."

Scupino's booming laugh filled the small room as he shook his head. "OK, we'll get them read in and together for a meeting. How about three weeks from now... By the way, what's the program's name?"

Josh named it on the spot. "Resurrect. Any chance you can get them together sooner?"

"Yeah... I can see the need for speed. Let me see what I can do."

As Josh left, two emotions hit him. For the first time since his return, he had hope. He felt like he'd been carrying the lives of everyone in the world on his back. Now, there were two others sharing his impossible task. The second emotion was triggered by Scupino's comment about the missing-man formation. It was simply a symbolic honor to a fallen comrade, but somehow it made his death real. He was dead to everyone he knew. A chill went down his spine as if someone were walking over his grave. He suddenly realized with horror... that might *actually* be possible.

He returned to the airport for his flight to Washington. Even though he'd been careful with his meager income, he barely had enough to stay in DC overnight. He'd have to return to Kansas City and either earn more or beg it from Elizabeth. He knew it was just his ego but he hated going back and asking her for money.

Fortunately, he had another reason to return – Dr. Sheri Lopez. He needed an expert in media and mass psychology. Thinking of her, he remembered freshman psychology and *Maslow's Hierarchy of Needs*. In a nutshell, it said, before you could worry about the ozone layer, you had to have a full belly. He now had his basic human necessities covered: oxygen, food, shelter, and high-speed Internet. Maslow's next level of need was belonging. He, Elizabeth and Scupino made a team of three. With this, he was able to think beyond immediate needs and consider the bigger picture. He still didn't know if Jesse was from elsewhere, else-when, or some other "else," but he was going to try to tap his knowledge. While waiting for his flight, he would ask Jesse some *deeper* questions. He had found a convenient way to talk to Jesse in public – an old Bluetooth headset Justin had unfortunately taken swimming. After he was through security, he put it in his ear. Smiling, he said, "Jesse, can you hear me now?"

He sensed his presence.

"May I ask some deeper questions, questions about science and philosophy?"

He sensed attention but received no direct response.

He sat down on one of the rows of airport seats outside his gate. "Can you explain the universe?" He now knew when Jesse was amused. This was definitely one of those moments. "Maybe that was a bit too broad." He paused. "Let's see. Is our basic understanding of the universe and its laws correct?"

What do you think?

"No offense, but why can't you just give me a straight answer?"

It wouldn't help.

"Why, because I'm too dumb to understand?" He looked up and saw the man sitting across from him looking at him oddly. Bluetooth aside, he realized his side of the conversation sounded pretty freaky. He smiled at the man, got up, and went for a walk.

Some concepts are outside of your understanding, but that's not why I can't give you the answers.

"Then why?"

Your nature prevents you from accepting them.

"What do you mean?"

You question everything. For you to accept anything, you have to reason it out for yourself.

He laughed. "Mom always called me 'Doubting Thomas.' But I don't think I have a closed mind. I'm willing to accept anything, as long as it's supportable with evidence and logic. I accept you."

Thank you, Josh.

"Sorry, that… didn't come out right." He moved on quickly. "OK,

I think we understand most of the laws the universe operates under. We're getting closer to a Grand Unified Theory that will connect all the forces into one equation. We still have a lot to learn, but I think we have the basics figured out and just need to fill in the details."

What holds the universe together?

"Gravity?"

What is the source of gravity?

"Matter – stars, planets, dust, and gas."

Is that all?

"Uh… no. There's also Dark Matter."

What is Dark Matter?

"Well, apparently, there isn't enough visible matter to create the gravity that holds galaxies together. We've calculated that we only see about 20 per cent of the matter in the universe. Therefore, there has to be another 80 per cent that's invisible. We call it Dark Matter."

What is Dark Matter made of?

"There are several theories… but we're not exactly sure yet."

There was a long silence.

How does Dark Matter affect the universe?

"Well, it should slow the universe's expansion, but a decade ago we discovered the universe isn't just expanding, the expansion appears to be *accelerating*." He paused. "That *is* a bit hard to fathom."

What causes this acceleration?

"Dark Energy."

What is Dark Energy?

"Well, there are several theories… uh… we're not exactly sure what *it* is, either."

Silence.

"OK, they're probably called Dark Matter and Dark Energy because we're in the *dark* about them." He understood why Jesse walked him through this. "I admit parts of our science are not exactly intuitive or fully understood."

Silence.

Josh laughed. "All right, all right! I get the point. I claimed we just needed to fill in the details. *Minor* details, like we don't know what 80 per cent of the universe is made of. Oh yeah, and the universe is being blown apart by an *unknown* force more powerful than gravity."

He paused. "I guess our understanding of the universe kinda sucks." He sighed. "Can you help illuminate my ignorance a little?"

That's enough for now.

"Great." Frustrated, he felt like he knew less than when he started the conversation. He wondered if he and humanity were still in nursery school.

15

INTELLIGENCE

Josh drove his microscopic budget rental car from Dulles International to Langley, Virginia. As he approached the CIA Headquarters, he saw a beautiful SR-71 Blackbird jet perched on a triple pedestal. The sleek, black reconnaissance aircraft had long since been retired but was still, officially, the world's fastest.

He suddenly felt apprehensive and started sweating. Guarding the headquarters entrance, the sinister Blackbird reminded him of Edgar Allen Poe's poem, "The Raven." But his fear wasn't logical. The CIA dealt with external, not internal threats. Trying to lighten his mood, he told himself, "It could be worse. Could be IRS headquarters."

Entering the lobby, he walked across the granite CIA seal seen in so many movies. After checking in with the receptionist, he looked over at the wall of stars. Years ago, Carl had shared with him that each star represented an exceptionally heroic CIA operative killed in the line of duty. There were well over a hundred stars carved into the marble wall. Half remained nameless because their mission, to this day, was too secret to divulge. He suddenly had a new appreciation for their unrecognized sacrifice.

Carl was punctual and met him with a visitor's pass. Once again, he felt strange meeting an old friend who didn't recognize him. He introduced himself and said, "Thank you for seeing me on such short notice."

On the way to his office, Carl said, "You've got my curiosity."

Josh just nodded, following him. He realized that they were about the same height, weight, and hair color. They were also both in excellent physical condition. Outwardly, Carl was a relaxed personality who always carried a slight but perpetual smile, as if constantly amused by the world.

Arriving at his office, Carl said, "Have a seat. So you knew Josh well?"

"Yes, we spent a lot of time together working on black programs." He also knew Carl well. They'd gone on several Western Pacific cruises and had become good friends. Carl was very intelligent and a walking encyclopedia of information on international politics, history and, of course, bad guys and their weapons of choice. He was also conservative, skeptical and a tiny bit paranoid… the perfect intelligence officer. Josh believed that as their program expanded, he'd need Carl's knowledge and insight.

As Josh sat down across from him, he casually scanned the room. Carl had a very neat office and desk. There were no papers sitting on the desktop and his computer screen was blank. As he looked at the only picture on the desk, he suddenly realized he was looking at *his* wife. It was Kelly, wearing a… a wedding gown? Wait! This was a wedding picture of Kelly and… and Carl. His breath caught in his throat as he felt a moment of panic.

Carl noticed his reaction and asked, "Are you all right?"

"Sorry. Think I must have caught a bug," he lied. "It's making me a little lightheaded." He regained his composure and clamped a lid on his emotions. He had a job to do, but he had to know the situation or he wouldn't be able to concentrate. He ventured, "Isn't that… Kelly?"

"Yes. You didn't know? Kelly and I were married about five months ago."

Josh knew the unwritten code. When someone died in the line of duty, the squadron family gathered to help. Although never an expectation or obligation, it wasn't uncommon for a fellow officer to marry the widow of a fallen comrade. Josh didn't know how to feel. "Torn" didn't begin to cover it! His intellectual side understood. His emotional side was horrified. He felt sick to his stomach. All he could do was nod his head.

Carl continued, "A month after the funeral, they had the medal ceremony. That's where I met Kelly again."

A detached part of him realized this was why he couldn't find

Kelly online. The wife of a CIA agent had to keep a lower profile. Trying to focus on something else, Josh asked, "Medal ceremony?"

Carl said, "You weren't there?"

Throwing out a platitude, Josh said, "I couldn't make it physically but was there in spirit." He realized, with dark humor, it was actually the other way around.

Carl continued, "They gave him the Navy Flying Cross posthumously. As I'm sure you heard, he was trying to land his burning jet at an airport surrounded by neighborhoods. There was one tiny area that wasn't developed. They were going to build a new shopping center there. He dropped the jet right into the middle of it." He paused.

Josh was surprised. Carl, the hard-boiled analyst, was actually struggling to hold back *his* emotions.

Switching back to his normal self, Carl continued, "The people who live in the surrounding neighborhoods got the shopping center named after him."

Josh, glad to find a diversion, laughed and said, "He always said he wanted to have a business of his own. He would've found that very funny."

"No doubt." Carl smiled. "Then about seven months ago, Kelly and I were thrown together at a squadron reunion. We started dating shortly after. We've always been good friends. I think Josh would have approved."

Josh swallowed hard. His intellectual side was able to squeeze out, "Yes... he would have wanted her to move on." He needed to focus on why he was here. He decided to tell a story that would let Carl know that he had "known" his former self, and it would also take his mind off Kelly. "Josh told me about the time you two were on the USS *Enterprise*. He said you were in port in Hawaii. You got back to the ship just as the sun was coming up... feeling no pain. Minutes after you hit the rack, they woke both of you. I think he said the squadron officers were scheduled to qualify with pistols at one of the base ranges early that morning?"

Carl started laughing. "I totally forgot about that. Skipper thought we were just hung over. The rest of the pilots knew we were still drunk. They were laughing their butts off. We couldn't have passed a breathalyzer and they put .45 automatics in our hands. The funny part was…"

Josh finished his sentence, "… you both qualified 'Expert.'"

Carl, still laughing, added, "… and the Skipper only qualified as a Marksman!"

Knowing Carl was task-oriented, as soon as the laughing died down, Josh moved on. "Carl, the reason I'm here is that we're working on a critical black program of unprecedented scale. We need your expertise and I trust you, based on Josh's recommendation. He would have contacted you."

"What type of program?"

"Well, as you probably know, we have to read you into it first. I'll level with you; we haven't talked to your chain of command." He knew, by nature, Carl would question everything. If he didn't, he wouldn't have been such an exceptional agent.

Carl frowned.

Josh continued. "Carl, this program has nothing to do with terrorists, foreign troop movements, or weapons of mass destruction. I won't be asking for any classified information."

"Then why do you need me?"

"Because, according to Josh, you're one of the most brilliant analysts he knew, with an exceptional understanding of global politics and international law."

Relaxing a little, he smiled. "International law was my major and I do work in that area, but there are others with more knowledge and experience."

"Maybe, but not that Josh trusted with something this important." He played his ace card. "Captain Scupino is in charge of the program."

Carl's eyes lit up. "The Skipper, huh? Well, I don't see any downside, unless this is going to absorb a lot of time, but I'll have to clear it with my boss."

Josh said, "That's fine, and no, it shouldn't take much time."

There was a pause. Josh pushed on, "Would it be possible to ask while I'm here?"

Carl said, "Guess this is kind of urgent?"

"You'll understand when you see what we're working on."

Carl picked up the phone and punched a button. "Bob, got a second?… Have a Navy type in my office, Commander Josh Meadows. He's a friend of a friend. Wants to read me into a black program to get our agency's perspective on something, is that all right?… No, he said it's just to ask some questions… Yeah, I know if we put any manpower on it, we'll need a charge number." Carl rolled his eyes.

Josh smiled back. Some things never changed.

Carl hung up. "All right."

Josh gave him the paperwork to sign and explained what they were doing.

Half an hour later, Carl's eyes were wide and he said, "This is big. I'm surprised our agency isn't already involved."

Josh shrugged his shoulders. "They probably are at the top, but you know the compartmentalization stuff. Sometimes us Indians need to work directly with each other to get things done."

Carl nodded. "Amen. I'm fascinated but a bit skeptical, since you can't give me the source."

"I don't blame you, I would be too, but be honest; how many times has your agency told us in the military that you couldn't release the source?"

"*Touché.*"

"Carl, I'd share it if I could, but you know those lie detector tests." Josh knew from his friend that lie detectors were often a part of their job, understood but resented.

"So what help do you need from me?"

"As our program expands, we'll need your insight into how to work with other agencies and countries, not to mention personnel clearance and international site issues."

Carl nodded. "Fair enough. I'm excited about participating. The only thing that bothers me is the unidentified source. I understand you can't release it but it just sounds too much like frozen aliens. God knows we've taken enough hits from the public for that. Some people still think we shot Kennedy."

Josh smiled. "You didn't?"

Carl smiled back, rolling his eyes.

"Carl, think about it, if our source is wrong, it won't take long to find out. It would be great if we discover there's no imminent threat. In that case, we spend several hundred million *sooner* than we absolutely had to, *but...* we're ready for a future contingency. On the other hand, if the source is right..."

Carl nodded. "You're absolutely right, there's really no downside." He laughed. "Unless you're from the Government Accounting Office."

Josh grinned.

They shook hands, but as he was about to leave, Carl asked, "By the way, who's handling your program's security?"

Caught off guard, Josh realized he'd never thought about protecting *his* program. He'd been more concerned about others protecting their programs from him. He replied weakly, "We don't really have anyone assigned."

He could see Carl's disapproval. Like a mother scolding a child, Carl said, "You don't have much experience in the Intelligence and Counterintelligence world, do you?"

Josh was honest. "Carl, I got an aerospace engineering degree with a minor in astrophysics, and I've been an operational military officer most of my career. This stuff's new to me, and the people I work for are more of the... big-picture types. That's one of the reasons I came to you."

Carl smiled. "We gotta fix that. There's a contract agent we use who's very good at protecting sensitive, high-value programs and the people in them. Let me see if he's available. He isn't cheap but I imagine your program has plenty of funding."

Josh said, "Thanks, Carl, I appreciate that. If he's available, bring him to next week's team meeting in St. Louis."

Leaving the CIA headquarters building, he tried not to think about Kelly, but the picture on Carl's desk kept reappearing. As he drove past the shadowy Blackbird on the pedestal, Poe's dark poem, "The Raven," came back to haunt him. Lost love mocked by the evil bird's repetitive "nevermore" echoed through his mind.

He blindly followed his phone's GPS to the airport hotel. He checked in, changed clothes and decided to go for a run. He ran and then ran more. Trying to outrun his thoughts, he ran faster and harder. Oblivious to his surroundings or the time, he ran an Olympic pace.

Kelly's face finally faded. He stopped running and looked around, confused. It was getting dark. He must have run for over an hour and had no idea where he was. He wandered aimlessly until he looked up and saw an airliner on approach. He headed in that direction. Somehow, he found the hotel, stumbled to his room, and fell into bed. As his head hit the pillow, he was out.

Because of the nature of his job, Carl shared almost nothing about his work with Kelly, to her great frustration. Since Meadows knew Logan and recognized Kelly in the picture, he thought it would be safe to mention him, and, he had to admit, he was curious.

"Kelly, I met someone today that you probably know. He used to work with Josh in St. Louis – Josh Meadows?"

Kelly frowned, shaking her head. "Doesn't ring a bell."

"Are you sure? He seemed to know Josh very well."

"I'm pretty sure, but maybe if I saw him I'd recognize him."

16

PSYCHOLOGY

Josh slept for ten hours and woke just in time to catch his flight back to Kansas.

Elizabeth picked him up at the airport. As she drove him back to the condo, he shared the results of his meeting with Scupino.

After he finished, she volunteered, "I transferred a thousand into your checking account and got you a credit card."

The only way he could have a credit card was if she co-signed. He was about to object, but stopped, knowing it would be nothing more than male ego noises. He just looked at her, shaking his head. "Thank you, Elizabeth, I really appreciate this and will repay it with interest."

She just smiled and said softly, "With interest."

He watched her out of the corner of his eye. She was everything good about the human race: honest, trusting, positive and confident, beautiful inside and out. He wished, instead of him, Jesse could see her as an example of what mankind could be.

As soon as they got back to the apartment, Elizabeth told him she'd found three more books written by Lopez. With his faster brain, he finished them that afternoon.

Lopez had exceptional insight into the psychology and motivation of large populations. It was such a perfect fit; he couldn't help but wonder if his connection with Lopez was really a coincidence. It had been five weeks since she had examined him at the hospital. He called her that evening. She agreed to meet for lunch the following day.

It turned out they shared a love of Italian food and they met at a small local restaurant she liked. As before, she dressed impeccably in a business suit.

"I was surprised to get your call. You look good and I heard you aren't working at the hospital. I assume you have your memory back?"

"Yes. Dr. Lopez, I can't tell you everything but I can tell you that I used to be a military officer. I was recruited into a special program, and in the process, became a man without an identity." Everything he said was true, if ambiguous.

She nodded. "Sheri, remember? Well, that would explain it better than alien abduction." With a mock frown, she added, "But alien abduction would have made a better book. So how did you end up in a coma?"

"You wouldn't believe it if I told you. Suffice it to say, it was an unintended but direct consequence of what happened to me. I really was in a state of shock when I arrived and did have to reestablish my identity." Also true, but stated in a way that was open to interpretation.

"You showed signs of emotional trauma, but your refusal to try hypnosis didn't make sense for someone trying to find their identity." She paused. "I still don't understand your lack of scars or identifying marks."

"All I can tell you is that my physical condition is a byproduct of what I was working on. I can't say more because of its highly classified nature." Raising his eyebrows, he added, "You may be able to draw your own conclusions." He had no idea what conclusions she'd draw but knew the human brain was good at looking for patterns. He hoped she'd come up with something that would satisfy her. He pushed on. "Sheri, I was very impressed with you at the hospital and have since read your books. You're the best in your field. I'd love to have you join our team."

Looking surprised, she said, "Your team? You have... a team? I... I don't understand."

"We're working on a project of global importance and need an expert in mass psychology. I believe you are that person. I know you already hold a government clearance, and I'd like to read you into a

Top Secret program." He didn't know she had a clearance, but it was a reasonable assumption.

She shook her head. "I gotta tell you, Josh, this isn't at all how I thought this meeting would go. I was expecting to pick up an interesting new patient, or," she smiled mischievously, "at least get asked out on a date." Still smiling, she nodded. "But, yes, I guess I would like to know more."

Josh nodded, adding, "By the way, you understand that you cannot share this with anyone else in the government unless they've been read into this program."

"You mean like my Homeland Security contact?"

He sensed some disdain. "Yes. He hasn't been read in."

"Good."

Josh raised an eyebrow as he handed her the paperwork.

"Just because I'm a psychiatrist, doesn't mean I have to *like* everyone I work with." She read and signed it quickly.

Having finished lunch, Josh looked around and said, "Can we go for a walk?"

As they walked, he ran through the explanation. Lopez got progressively more excited. Finally, she said, "Wow. An apocalyptic comet. I see why you want an expert in mass psychology." She stopped and turned toward him. "Is this for real?"

Josh cocked his head to one side. "Well, another explanation might be schizophrenia accompanied by delusions of grandeur. *But…* a leading psychiatrist diagnosed me as sane."

She laughed out loud. "That's just flat mean. OK, I'll go with non-crazy for now but *only* because my ego's too big to believe I made a mistake."

Josh grinned. "Don't worry; it'll be easy to confirm that I have a team… or at least a bunch of fellow lunatics. Can you meet us in St. Louis in four days?"

With a challenging smile, she said, "I wouldn't miss it."

17

TEAM

Josh flew to St. Louis one day before their first team meeting. They were off to a good start, but that's all it was. They had no plan and no funding.

He found a cheap, third-floor, studio apartment near the airport. Elizabeth transferred another $4,000 into his checking account without him asking. Between deposits, rent, food, and transportation, it was going to go fast, but he had no choice. He had to be there.

The next day – only ten days after their first meeting – Scupino pulled his key experts together. Josh arrived early. He told Scupino he wanted to stay in the background during the meetings. He'd be Scupino's "liaison" with the comet source agency.

Scupino said, "Yeah, I get it. You pass the buck to me and sit back and watch the fun."

Josh smiled. "Absolutely." More seriously, he added, "I have neither the credibility nor the experience to lead this type of team."

Scupino looked at him carefully. "You've been in combat?"

Josh nodded honestly.

Scupino continued, "And you're probably a good leader. You're right. Although you can be young and lead senior people, it takes time to earn their respect and trust."

Josh nodded. "And time is something we don't have."

As he finished, Carl arrived, knocking on Scupino's open door. Grinning, Scupino yanked him in and slapped him on the back. Carl chuckled and pounded him in return. After some mutual good-natured abuse, Carl introduced a man he'd brought with him. "This is Tim Smith. He's one of the best in the world at security. We were extremely fortunate to get him on such short notice."

Smith was medium height, medium build, brown hair, brown eyes, and regular features. He was remarkable in his unremarkableness. Josh realized that this was probably an advantage in his line of work. Although, he wasn't exactly sure what "his line of work" was.

Scupino said, "Tim, it's great to have you on the team."

Seriously and with little emotion, Smith asked Scupino, "Are you really trying to keep a comet from hitting the earth?"

"We have to." He paused. "Tim, forgive me for asking a stupid question but what exactly do you do?"

"You protect the earth. I protect you and your team."

Scupino nodded his head but maintained a slight frown. "Protect us from what? I mean, who'd be opposed to deflecting a comet?"

Smith said, "I don't know."

Carl added, "Tim's like an insurance policy. You hope you never need him, but if you do, and don't have him, it's too late. Whenever you're dealing with high stakes, you attract attention and not always the right kind."

Scupino looked at Josh. Josh shrugged. Scupino said, "OK, what do you need from us?"

"I need the names of everyone involved in the program and permission to talk to them. I know how important the program is and will respect their time but I need access to everyone. I'd also like to attend your major meetings."

Josh and Scupino looked at each other, nodding.

Scupino said, "You've got it." He paused. "You know, if you think about it, you may be on the biggest protection project ever."

Smith nodded but didn't smile.

"How should we introduce you?"

"'Personnel Safety and Security' is appropriate."

Scupino said, "Is there anything else you need?"

"I'd like your key people to create an authentication phrase that can be used if there's any doubt about the authenticity of an order or directive."

Scupino said, "I hate remembering passwords."

Smith shook his head. "It can be a word, a phrase, or even

the punchline of a joke. It would only be used once and only in an emergency. It's not to be shared with anyone but your team leaders."

Carl looked mischievously at Scupino. "Josh said Logan told him the story about us qualifying on the pistol range."

Scupino laughed. "Oh yeah… *that* was a high point in your careers. I'm surprised you could even remember it. We were lucky you didn't shoot yourselves or one of us."

Carl pressed on. "Let's see, my authentication password could be 'Expert.' Yours could be – what was your pistol qualification again? – oh yeah, 'Marksman.'"

Scupino rolled his eyes. He pointed three fingers up, forming a "W," and then turned them sideways into an "E." Doing a good imitation of his teenage daughter, he said, "*Whateverrr.*"

Carl and Josh laughed.

Scupino turned back to Smith. "Anything else?"

Smith looked at Carl, and Carl said, "Ah… yeah, we'll need an account to charge his services to. You can transfer the funds to a CIA account and we'll disburse them to Tim."

Scupino pointed at Josh. "Talk to my accountant."

Josh nodded nervously. "Ah, yes. I don't have that information with me right now but I'll get that to you soon."

On the way to the conference room, Carl told them, "After this one, I won't be able to attend future meetings. I'd rather work on this than anything else, but at my level, the CIA policy is clear. Tim Smith can handle any security questions and I can 'attend' via encrypted conference call if you need me."

They entered the Boeing Phantom Works conference room. A large oval table comfortably sat twelve with another dozen chairs around the perimeter. It only strayed from a conventional meeting-room in that it had no windows and was soundproof and shielded from electronic signals.

Lopez was already there and Josh introduced her to Scupino.

Scupino said, "Dr. Lopez, I've read your books! It's an honor to have you on the team."

"Call me Sheri." Looking pleased, she asked, "Captain Scupino, weren't you the first Commanding Officer of the USS *Ford*?"

Scupino smiled. "I was. Just call me Joe."

Josh had nothing to worry about with these two and their mutual admiration society. Their motivated, outgoing personalities were very similar, but they made a stark physical contrast with Lopez's small hand disappearing into Scupino's bear paw.

Scupino then introduced Josh and Lopez to the lead scientist and engineers. The senior scientist was NASA astrophysicist Dr. Victoria Chandra. Since astronomy was one of his passions, Josh knew who she was. Before joining NASA, she had done postgraduate work under Dr. Joe Veverka, one of the world's leading comet experts. When Josh was an undergraduate, he had heard her speak once as a guest lecturer. Not only was she brilliant, but she had one of the best records for getting unmanned missions to the outer planets successfully. He couldn't imagine anyone more qualified. He even remembered, as a sophomore, having had a bit of a crush on her. She might not fit Hollywood's definition of beauty, but he had always been attracted to strong, intelligent women. Now in her fifties, she remained striking, with long jet-black hair, fine features, and dark intelligent eyes. At almost six foot, she was also quite the contrast to the engineer standing next to her.

Dr. Lee Katori, head of Boeing's Missile Defense Division, looked like the stereotypical image of a Japanese scientist. About sixty, short and slight of build, he had thick, bushy, white hair and wore black horn-rimmed glasses. Also renowned in his field, his reputation was that of a no-nonsense engineer. He'd led many programs, from stealth fighters to tactical lasers.

Katori then introduced them to another engineer from Northrop Grumman. The big aerospace contractors often worked together on large projects. Dr. Garrett Cho had been one of the lead engineers on the Air Force's Airborne Laser. Mounted in a 747, the megawatt laser could take out ballistic missiles in flight. Cho, in his late thirties, wore a Hawaiian shirt and looked like a cross between a sumo wrestler and a California surfer. Big and muscular with wild, blond-highlighted hair, he had a strong handshake and a grin to match.

Scupino started the meeting. "Thank you for coming on such short notice. We all know the basic premise and I'd like to remind everyone that this is a highly classified program. We want open discourse but only among the participants and in controlled areas, such as this. Let's kick it off by understanding the threat. Dr. Chandra, our Chief Scientist, will explain. This isn't a formal meeting, so don't be bashful. We need everyone's ideas."

Chandra stood up, obviously comfortable doing presentations. "Our job is to find a way to prevent a comet from striking the earth. Comets, of course, are the worst-case scenario. They come with higher kinetic energy and detection latency than asteroids."

Scupino held up a hand. "Whoa. Dr. Chandra, can you please translate that into simple pilot terms?"

She smiled. "Sorry. Let's start with what a comet is. We think of them as dirty snowballs composed of rock and ice. While that's usually correct, we can define them more accurately by *where* they come from rather than their composition. Unlike asteroids, comets live in a region outside the solar system called the Oort Cloud and Scattered Disk. That's where Dwarf Planets like Pluto and Eris orbit."

Scupino nodded. "We hear a lot about asteroids. Aren't comets fairly rare?"

"Actually, it's quite the opposite. If you put all the asteroids in the Asteroid Belt together, their combined mass would be less than two per cent of the earth. But if you combined all the cometary debris, it would mass more than *forty* earths."

Cho said, "Holy cow!"

With a slight look of amusement, Chandra continued, "In fact, you've already seen cometary debris. Most meteor showers occur when the earth passes through comet dust trails." Looking more serious, she added, "Unfortunately, because comets are so much further out than asteroids, they're almost impossible to detect until they're inbound. They also move much faster because they have further to fall." Looking at Scupino, she paused. "By 'falling,' I mean they're ten to fifty times 'higher,' or further out of the solar system's gravitational well. Therefore, they carry a much greater punch than asteroids."

"How much more?" Scupino asked.

"When they reach earth, they can be moving two to three times as fast as an asteroid, around forty kilometres per second."

Scupino made a low whistle, and said, "But you'd think they'd be easy to spot with those tails."

"Comets only have tails when they get close to the sun. The tails are just gas, boiled off the ice from the sun's heat. By the time we see a comet's tail, it could be less than a year to impact. On top of that, we're now beginning to believe that comets with very low albedo may be quite common."

With a half smile, Scupino asked, "Comets with low sex drive?"

"Not *libido*." Chandra laughed along with the others. "*Albedo*." Shaking her head, she continued, "Their surface is black, making them extremely difficult to see. By the time we detect one of these dark comets, it's probably too late."

Scupino nodded thoughtfully. "Dr. Chandra, what is... too late?"

She replied immediately, "Comet IRAS-Araki-Alcock. In 1983, a large ten-kilometer-wide dark comet came within five million kilometers of the earth. They spotted it only *two weeks* before its closest approach. Its surface reflectivity was less than *one per cent* – about the same as fresh asphalt – making it practically invisible."

Scupino said, "But since 1983 we have Spaceguard and other programs to help locate these, don't we?"

"Asteroids, yes, but unless a comet has made a recent loop around the sun, we really have no way to detect it."

Scupino said, "Obviously, two weeks is too late, but how much time do we really need?"

"Well... that's what we need to talk about. Surprisingly, it doesn't take much to nudge a comet or asteroid so that it misses us... *if* we catch it early enough."

Scupino said, "I'll bite – what's early enough?"

"Five to ten years." She paused while the team absorbed this. "Most deflection concepts require a couple years to intercept the comet with a spacecraft and mount a small rocket motor or other propulsion mechanism to it. Then, it takes several more years to push it off course. The shorter the time to impact, the more push it takes."

Scupino frowned. "But we won't have five to ten years if it's a new comet and we can't detect it until it's inbound, right?"

"That's correct."

"Well then, can't we just intercept and vaporize it with a nuke?"

Chandra shook her head. "That makes for good movie special effects but it's not as simple as it sounds. In the vacuum of space, *close* isn't good enough. Between the comet's inbound velocity and the rocket's outbound speed, the warhead would close on the comet a hundred times faster than a rifle bullet. Detonate too early and there's little effect. Too late, and the impact destroys the warhead before it can explode. Even if we succeed, we probably just create a bigger problem. Instead of one giant comet, we have a bunch of smaller ones. It's like trading a rifle bullet for a shotgun blast. Even a tiny thirty-meter comet fragment could flatten an area the size of a state. That may be what happened at Tunguska in the 1800s."

Scupino nodded. "Are there any other intercept options?"

"Yes. We can fill a rocket full of nano-particles and release them just before impact. The collision of the tiny particles across the comet's surface should impart their momentum without fragmenting the comet. If we hit it with enough of them, we should be able to change its trajectory."

Scupino nodded. "It sounds like trying to slow down a locomotive by shooting bb's at it."

Chandra shrugged. "Something like that."

Scupino took a deep breath. "Okay, let me summarize. An intercept mission requires five or more years. It won't help with newly discovered comets on a collision course. Nuking a comet is probably a bad idea. So, that leaves shooting rockets filled with nano-particles?"

Chandra nodded. "Nano-particles should work if the comet's small or far enough out that we can hit it with multiple rockets. If it's big or within a year of impact, it would probably require hundreds or thousands of rockets."

"Are there any other options?"

She smiled. "Yes." She paused, looking around the room. "We may be able to hit it with an extremely intense beam of focused energy."

Scupino said, "Vaporize it with a giant laser beam! *That* would be cool."

Cho, the laser expert, laughed. With his booming voice, he said, "That would be totally awesome; unfortunately, we're a long way from Darth Vader's Death Star. There's nothing – even on the drawing board – with a tiny fraction of the power needed."

Katori, smiling, added, "Yeah, but it would be fun to try." Katori and Cho started an animated conversation.

Chandra laughed. "What is it with guys and blowing things up?"

Scupino grinned. "Sorry, we pretty much come out of the womb that way."

She nodded. "I know. I have two sons." Like a kindergarten teacher trying to corral boisterous boys, she said loudly, "As *fun* as I'm sure that would be – and aside from the fact that it's not even remotely possible – there is a simpler, more elegant solution." She paused for effect. As the conversations quieted down she said, "We don't have to *vaporize* it. All we have to do is *nudge* it."

Scupino frowned. "How can a laser *nudge* something?"

"Good question. If we hit it with enough focused energy, we can melt a tiny part of the surface ice or even rock. In a vacuum, liquid goes straight to gas, creating a small gas plume or jet. That jet can impart force, like a little rocket motor. Hit it enough and we can slow the comet down."

Cho added, "I worked on a NASA project to remove space debris from low earth orbit using that technique. Hit the junk with a powerful laser pulse and it creates a tiny plasma jet that slows it down enough to reenter the atmosphere." He shook his head in disgust. "They canceled it because some countries thought we'd use it to take out their satellites."

Scupino frowned. "I see how it might work on a couple pounds of space debris, but a comet?"

Chandra said, "Captain, the earth is a moving target. It orbits the sun at thirty kilometers per second. If we can slow the comet, by just a few minutes, the earth won't be there when it arrives. To do that, however, not only do we have to hit it with an intensely focused beam at extreme distance, we have to keep hitting it continuously for a year or more. The bigger or closer it is, the more energy we have to hit it with."

Scupino said, "Can we do that?"

Chandra nodded to Katori and sat down.

Katori stood up and said, "As you remember, this is the same general problem we were trying to solve with the Ballistic Missile Defense Program. The idea was to burn an ICBM in flight with a laser. As difficult as that is, it's child's play compared to what we're talking about here."

"Why?"

Katori, in turn, nodded to Cho. Cho, leaning forward in his chair, said, "We can hit a one-meter target from a hundred kilometers, but hitting a one-kilometer target from a million kilometers requires ten thousand times the accuracy and energy. It's like trying to etch your name with a laser into a rifle bullet… after it's been fired at you from Washington DC."

Scupino shook his head. "Doesn't sound possible."

Cho smiled. "It's theoretically possible and it's a wicked cool engineering challenge." He paused, shaking his head. "But it ain't gonna be small."

Scupino raised an eyebrow.

Cho added, "The beam collimation – sorry, the accuracy – is directly proportional to the diameter of the beam. This sucker's gonna have to be pretty big." He smiled. "We just need good people and lots of supercomputer time… a blank check wouldn't hurt."

Scupino looked directly at Katori and Cho. "Seriously, can we do this?"

Katori glanced at Cho. "We need to crunch some more numbers and talk to others, but… I think we can."

Nodding excitedly, Cho said, "I know geniuses in the field, who'd give their right arm to play. Throw in a critical deadline and we'll pull in the best and brightest."

Under his breath Josh said, "Be careful what you ask for."

Tim Smith sat quietly, observing the participants. He was what the agency referred to as a "Protector." They jokingly called him 007, but his goal was to be the opposite of James Bond. You couldn't protect anything from the center of a spotlight.

He appreciated Carl getting him the job. Carl knew he had

planned to retire and thought this program would be a good way to go out. He was right and it might even make a tiny interest payment on his past sins.

He'd already started background investigations on everyone on the team. With access to sources very few had, he could find out almost anything, from credit scores to why they visited the principal's office in fifth grade. He would never divulge that information. His job was simply to look for vulnerabilities that the bad guys could exploit. He would investigate everyone, even Scupino. It was his lack of knowledge about his last client that caused the… accident. He'd never let that happen again.

He caught Lopez watching him. He was an expert at noticing people noticing him. It wasn't surprising. As a psychiatrist, she was also a people watcher. She had tried to engage him in conversation before the meeting, but as usual, he'd kept it polite but short. She was a beautiful woman about his age, and he was usually drawn to women with her type of strong, confident personality. Too bad he hadn't met her before. Now, of course, it was too late.

18

FUND

Josh knew that soon, very soon, his team would need real money. He had absolutely no idea where he was going to get the funding. There was no faster way to get unwanted attention than diverting government funds from existing programs. Trying to think positively, he had a flash of illogical insight. He caught Lopez after the meeting and asked her if they could talk privately over dinner.

They found a good Italian restaurant near the airport. While eating delicious butter-and-garlic-infused pasta, Josh asked, "Sheri, how did you become a famous psychiatrist?"

She smiled. "As a child, I was a competitive tomboy. Then I grew up... and nothing changed, except the label. I became a 'highly motivated, task-oriented individual.' For women, they often shorten that to one word that begins with a 'b.'" With a raised eyebrow and half smile, she continued, "I studied psychology, like many, to figure out why I was different. Being competitive, I graduated at the top of my psychiatry class and started a private practice." She shook her head, laughing. "I quickly discovered that I had to work too hard to be sympathetic. I wanted to tell most of my patients to stop whining and deal with it."

Josh nodded. He enjoyed watching her eat, suspecting that she approached life the same way she attacked food – with gusto.

Wiping butter from the corner of her mouth, she continued, "Anyway, that's what took me into psychology of the masses. It was just as fascinating but a lot less messy. My books became best sellers and it catapulted me into the spotlight. I honestly don't care what people think of me, but fame does open doors and I've been able to meet some fascinating people."

Josh said, "That's one of the reasons I wanted to talk to you. In addition to your insight, you're obviously well connected." He paused, frowning slightly. "Sheri, you're the only one on the team that's not part of the government or the military-industrial complex. Speed is of the essence here and some things we have to do can be done better and faster outside the government."

She nodded as she chased the last slippery shrimp around her plate.

"Sheri, can you think of someone in the private sector who might have resources, influence, and a particular passion for our cause?"

She looked up, grinning. "Like a risk-taking billionaire who's into space stuff?"

Josh smiled, nodding.

"Actually, I know just the guy… Edward Brandon."

"You mean, *Sir* Edward Brandon?"

"Yup. He's perfect. He's a brilliant entrepreneur, and he owns the largest private space access company in the world. Brandon's got guts and loves a challenge. He's climbed mountains all over the world, and… he's pretty hot-looking."

Josh gave her a raised eyebrow.

"Yeah, we were a *thing* many years ago. We're still good friends."

Josh frowned. "Isn't he too much of a public figure?"

She gave him a meaningful look. "Josh, not everyone in the public eye is superficial."

"Sorry."

She smiled. "We both know how to keep a secret. I think he's in the US now. I'll call him; see if I can get you two together ASAP."

"That would be awesome. Thank you." Josh paused. "Sheri…"

"Yes?"

"Could you do me another favor?"

"Sure.

"Please don't mention to the rest of the team how we… uh, met. It's not that I'm trying to hide anything but…"

She finished, "Discovering that the source of our comet information didn't know who he was a few months ago, might not instill the greatest confidence in the mission?"

He nodded sheepishly.

She put her hand on his arm and winked. "Don't worry. Your secret's safe with me." Still holding onto his arm, she added, "But, someday, I *really* want to know what happened to you…"

With a half smile he said softly, "Yeah, me too."

On the drive back to his apartment, Sheri called.

"Just got off the phone with Brandon. Told him he had to see you. It was a major secret I couldn't discuss over the phone. That just made him curious. Can you be in New York City a week from today?"

"Absolutely!"

"I'll text you the details."

"Sheri, *you* are amazing!"

She laughed. "I know."

Josh returned to his apartment. He normally avoided talking about anything program-related over the phone, but it had been an incredible day. He was so excited; he had to share it with someone.

He called Elizabeth. Being careful not to talk details, he said, "The meeting went *extremely* well, with a cast of incredible people! I'll fill you in when I see you. On top of everything else, I just had a fantastic dinner with Lopez and she arranged for me to meet with Sir Edward Brandon!"

"Sir Edward Brandon? That's great."

"It really is! This could be just what we need. Sheri knows everyone. I don't know what I'd do without her. She's an absolutely *amazing* woman!"

Very softly, Elizabeth said, "Yes… yes, she is."

Thinking of all the work he needed to do before the meeting, he said, "Well, I better go. I'm scrambling to get my cost estimates together before I meet Brandon, but I just wanted to share that."

She didn't say anything.

"I'm sorry, Elizabeth… how are you doing?"

"I'm doing fine, thanks… I… I better let you go."

As he hung up, he paused. She hadn't sounded as excited as he thought she would. There was something wrong, but he didn't have time to worry about it right now. He needed to schedule a flight and prepare for the meeting.

At the Northrop Grumman lab in Redondo Beach, California, the top-secret program briefing began. Dr. Jackie Jones saw that the young engineer giving the brief was clearly nervous. It was his first time to brief the billion-dollar spy-satellite program's status to her, his corporate manager and vice president. This next generation of satellites would use pulsed laser illumination, similar to a camera's flash. If it worked, it would help them capture extreme high-resolution pictures and even video. Their goal was nothing less than facial recognition from orbit, and they had the most brilliant laser physicists and engineers working for them. If they couldn't pull it off, no one could.

Jones listened to the brief intently. After the young engineer finished, she said, "Conner, you did a great job, but where's Dr. Cho?"

"I think he's in St. Louis. They called him in on some special project. He said he'd probably be back in a week or two."

With surprise, Jones said, "A *week* or two?"

19

QUESTION

It was only a week since the first team meeting. They'd added several more players. Chandra introduced everyone to Dr. Drake Wooldridge, an astrophysicist and professor at Berkeley who specialized in comets. In his early forties, Wooldridge was tall and slim with a neatly trimmed beard and reading glasses perched on the end of his nose. He looked like a professor, except for his clothes. He wore an expensive, custom-made suit.

Josh sensed an underlying excitement and an air of expectancy from the group. Scupino started the meeting by turning it over to Lee Katori, calling him the Chief Engineer.

Despite his diminutive size, Katori had a strong voice. "Working with Dr. Chandra and her staff, we've got a better feel for the power and accuracy needed. We'll be handling energies that we've never had to control before and with a huge increase in accuracy. This isn't cutting-edge technology; it's bleeding-edge."

"All right." Scupino smiled. "You've done the proper disclaimers. Can we do it?"

Katori and Cho exchanged grins. Katori, looking like a three-year-old with candy, said, "Yes, by God, I really think it's possible!" Then the engineer returned. "But it would help to know where we're going to build this."

Scupino nodded. "Excellent." He turned to Chandra. "So, where do we put this thing?"

Chandra leaned back in her chair. "Well, we have a two-body problem. Not only is the comet moving; so are we. The perfect solution would be to put it in space, preferably at an orbital Lagrangian point.

That way we'd have a stable platform that we could point in any direction."

Scupino asked, "How long would it take to build this type of space-based projector?"

Katori said, "Well, in space, the energy source is the biggest issue. We need thousands of times more power than what even the biggest solar arrays can provide. It'll have to be nuclear. Since there are no space-based nuclear reactors of that size, we'd have to scale up an existing design."

Scupino said, "That's going to be a lot of weight."

Katori nodded, looking down at his tablet computer. "To boost these components into orbit will take the biggest rockets out there. Even if we commandeer all of the world's heavy-lift capability, it'll still take a couple years."

Josh spoke for the first time, saying quietly, "We don't have that long."

All eyes turned toward him, and Chandra asked, "What do you mean?"

Josh realized it was time to make a statement that he couldn't back up. "What I'm about to tell you is *highly* classified and must *never* leave this room." He paused. "We believe we may have less than two years to a possible comet impact."

Dr. Drake Wooldridge stood up. "How can that be? There are no known comets on an intercept course with earth."

Josh said softly, "No known."

Wooldridge continued but turned to Scupino. "Captain Scupino, I think I speak on behalf of all of us, when I say how excited we are to be part of this project, but I'm an astrophysicist; comets are my specialty. I have access to the biggest and best observatories in the world, and I have extensive connections to the amateur astronomy network. I'm sure I'd know about this kind of threat within hours!"

Josh couldn't afford to alienate his astrophysicists by challenging their expertise. "Dr. Wooldridge, you and Dr. Chandra are renowned in your field and we're honored to have you on the team." He needed, first, to establish some credibility. "You're familiar with the Shiva Hypothesis?"

Wooldridge nodded. "Yes, of course."

Scupino said, "I'm not."

Josh nodded to Wooldridge. "Dr. Wooldridge, would you mind explaining it. You understand it a lot better than I."

Wooldridge automatically went into lecture mode. "The Shiva Hypothesis suggests that there is a periodicity to mass extinctions, many of which are attributed to extraterrestrial impacts. The cycle appears to coincide with the time our solar system crosses the galactic plane."

Scupino said, "Dr. Wooldridge, can you dumb that down a bit?"

Looking a little irritated, he said, "I'll try." He paused. "The sun is one of hundreds of billions of stars in our Milky Way galaxy. You've seen pictures. Our galaxy is shaped like a Frisbee. All the stars, including our sun, rotate around the center of the galaxy every 200 million years or so. However, our sun's orbit isn't perfectly flat. As we go around, the sun bobs up and down a little... kind of like a wooden horse on a merry-go-round. We cross the Frisbee's disc, or galactic plane, every 36 million years or so as we go around."

Glancing at Chandra, he continued, "They named the Shiva Hypothesis after the Hindu God Shiva, the god of destruction and regeneration. The theory suggests that every time our solar system passes through the galactic plane, the greater density of stars, dust and gas tugs on our solar system, similar to how the moon pulls on the oceans to create tides. This disturbs the orbits of the asteroids and comets, some of which fall in toward the sun. There *appears* to be a correlation between major impacts and our sun crossing the Milky Way's galactic plane. It's an interesting hypothesis but by no means conclusive."

Scupino looked thoughtful. "You said that the cycle is every 36 million years or so."

Wooldridge nodded.

"Well, if I remember correctly, they say the asteroid that killed the dinosaurs was over 60 million years ago."

Josh threw in, "Chesapeake Bay."

Wooldridge and Chandra looked at Josh with some surprise.

Frowning, Wooldridge said, "Yes, during oil exploration in the nineties, an eighty-five-mile-wide crater was found at the bottom of the Chesapeake. Although not as big as the one that killed the dinosaurs, it probably destroyed all life on the East coast and created tsunamis that crested the Blue Ridge Mountains. In fact, it created the Chesapeake Bay. It was dated to about 35 million years ago."

Scupino frowned. "When was the last galactic crossing?"

Wooldridge said, "About two million years ago."

Scupino said, "Then we're OK. We're still here. No impact or mass extinctions."

Josh said quietly, "Not yet."

Wooldridge nodded reluctantly. "The mass extinctions didn't happen right on the crossing date. They were within a few million years. The gravitational perturbations can send comets plunging into the inner solar system, but depending on how far they are from the sun, the in-fall time could be anywhere from two years to four million years." He paused. "I agree comets are a serious threat. What I don't understand," he glanced quickly at Josh, "is how anyone could *possibly* know about an unknown comet two years out."

Josh said quietly, "The information I have came from… another source. One that's so highly classified, I can't share it with you at this time. I'm sorry. I would love nothing more than to give you the background. All I can say right now is that we believe our information is… reliable." He paused. "I wish it weren't."

Wooldridge, with obvious disdain, said, "What are we talking… aliens?"

There was nervous laughter around the room.

Josh gently shook his head. "I'm sorry. I can't say where the information came from."

Wooldridge started to say something, and then stopped.

Josh knew his refusal to explain would force them to draw their own conclusions. They'd probably run the gamut from super-sensitive military space hardware to aliens at Roswell. As brilliant and logical as these people were, they were still people, emotionally driven like everyone else. Most of them were just excited to be involved with an important purpose. "Dr. Wooldridge, when we can release the source, I promise that you and Dr. Chandra will be the first to be notified."

Wooldridge looked a little uncertain, but sat down.

There was a loud buzz of conversations around the table.

Scupino brought them back. "OK, folks, let's focus." Josh admired Scupino's ability to roll with the punches. As things quieted down, Scupino said, "If we're talking two years, boosting a nuclear reactor into orbit will be a challenge."

Chandra added quietly, "It's not two years."

Scupino said, "Pardon me?"

Chandra said, "That's time to impact. We need time to deflect it. Depending on its size and the power of the beam, we'll need to hit it continuously for at least a year. That means we have to be up and operating a year from now."

Scupino whistled. "In that case, no matter how much money we throw at this, even the world's gross national product, we don't have the infrastructure to put up a space-based system. It hinges on too many undeveloped capabilities, any one of which could stop us in our tracks." There was silence in the room.

Into the silence, Scupino said quietly and with the slightest of smiles, "Dr. Chandra, you've already thought of another way."

Josh knew that Scupino played the dumb history major to make people feel comfortable or force them to explain things clearly. In fact, he was very intelligent and knowledgeable about US space and defense capabilities. He was also very good at reading people.

Chandra and Katori exchanged a conspiratorial glance.

She said, "The system has to be ground-based. That massively reduces the logistics-and-power issue. *However*, it creates two other challenges. The first is that we'll need more power and beam correction."

Scupino said, "I understand punching a beam through the atmosphere takes more power, but correction?"

"Yes." She pulled glasses out of her pocket and held them up. "It's like wearing glasses for astigmatism. The atmosphere isn't uniform, that's why stars appear to twinkle. We'll need the clearest, driest air possible, and even then, we'll need to apply an 'optical correction' to the beam."

"Clear, dry air... like on mountaintops where observatories are located?"

"Yes, but that brings us to our second challenge... the earth rotates. If we put this thing on any existing observatory mountain, half the time, the comet would be on the wrong side of the earth. We'd have to wait until we came around again to continue firing."

Scupino said, "Since we may not get enough funding to stop the earth from rotating, what are you suggesting?"

Chandra smiled. "We need to put the beam projectors on the earth's Poles."

Several conversations started around the table. Scupino held up a hand. When the room quieted down, he said, "Explain."

Chandra continued, "We need as much time as possible with an unobstructed shot at the comet. From the North and South Poles we can swivel the beam as the earth rotates and fire it twenty-four hours a day. The Poles also happen to have the driest, most stable air and the least amount of rainfall."

Scupino asked, "Are we talking both Poles?"

Chandra said, "That would be optimal but let's start with one site. It'd be easier to build it on land at the South Pole." She looked directly at Josh. "Unless our source suggests the comet's coming in from above the solar equatorial plane? If that's the case, we'd have to use some type of vessel at the North Pole."

Scupino looked at Josh with raised eyebrows.

Without even questioning Jesse, he suddenly knew the comet was coming in with a slight bias towards the Southern Hemisphere. Josh said, "South Pole."

Major Judy Crowley, an Air Force engineer and MIT grad, said, "You have no power there. You'd need a nuclear reactor."

Chandra nodded. "Yup."

Scupino added, "Easier than putting it in orbit."

Crowley continued, "But we don't own the South Pole. How would we get permission to put a reactor there?"

Chandra smiled at Scupino and Josh. "Not my problem."

More conversations started around the room. Scupino leaned back and whispered to Josh, "Guess I see now why this thing's classified."

Josh nodded and said into Scupino's ear, "I'll talk to Carl about how to set up an operation at the South Pole."

The meeting continued for another hour as they discussed

details. Scupino finally wrapped it up.

Grinning, Cho faked a yawn. "Monster lasers, nukes at the South Pole. Hope we have something more interesting to work on soon."

Scupino finished with, "OK, folks, great job! I feel good about our progress." Glancing at Josh, he added, "I've been promised we'll have funding authorization ASAP. Let's start making this happen. Dr. Chandra, Dr. Katori, please give me preliminary schedule and cost estimates as soon as you can, so we can work up a budget. Gentlemen and ladies, we don't have the authority to pull you off other projects, but I'm sure we'll be able to cut through the red tape soon. Off the record, I'd ask you to make this your number-one priority. Don't want to sound melodramatic, but it's possible that millions of lives may be in our hands, and this may go down in history as the most important engineering project ever attempted."

Josh soberly continued Scupino's statement under his breath, "And if we fail, we just go *down* in history." With notification that a comet was going to hit the world in two years, he expected the mood to be somber. Instead, the atmosphere was more like a good Christmas party. Jesse was right, purpose was critical to happiness.

As he was about to leave, Scupino asked to see him, Chandra, Lopez, Katori and Wooldridge in his office.

They went in and sat down as he closed the door. Scupino, very serious, said, "Dr. Wooldridge?"

Looking a little constipated, Wooldridge said, "Where's the data on this comet? I want to see its coordinates."

Josh asked quietly, "Could you see a dark comet two years out?"

"Of course not! That's my point."

Scupino, looking thoughtful, said, "Please forgive my ignorance, I'm still processing all this." He paused. "I keep thinking I'm missing something. Dr. Wooldridge, I understand your skepticism about the source of the comet information." He shook his head. "But it seems to me, the bigger question is why, if all that you've said is true, hasn't someone already been working on a contingency plan for a comet threat?" He paused again. "It feels a little like the old nuclear doctrine of Mutual Assured Destruction."

Wooldridge looked at him questioningly. In a gentler voice Scupino continued, "We knew that both the US and the Soviet Union had enough nuclear warheads that a war between us might end civilization. As long as both sides knew a war was unwinnable, neither would dare attack. Instead of trying to *fix* the problem, we chose to maintain a delicate balance of destruction, and keep our fingers crossed. The acronym for Mutual Assured Destruction was appropriate."

He stopped and looked directly at Wooldridge and Chandra. "Am I to understand that even though we've known we could be blindsided by an unknown comet, killing millions, possibly billons, within months of detection, no agency has a plan to counter it?"

"The probability was considered low," Wooldridge said defensively.

Scupino shot back, "How do you know that? Chandra said that, unlike asteroids, we can't detect most comets until they're inbound!"

Wooldridge said, "We believe comets that enter the inner solar system are rare."

"Rare? I've been doing a little reading of my own. They now believe the rings of Jupiter and Saturn can only exist if they're constantly restocked with ice and rock from comet collisions. If that wasn't enough, in 1994, we actually witnessed comet Shoemaker-Levy slam into Jupiter. If it had hit us instead, we'd all be toast."

Wooldridge said, "Jupiter's further out and has a much stronger gravitational field."

Scupino smiled. "You could have convinced me they only hit Jupiter, until Dr. Chandra told us about the Araki-Alcock comet. Twice the size of Shoemaker-Levy, it almost nailed us and we didn't see it until it was a few weeks out." He paused. "I may be a history major but I do understand probability. How many other dark comets may have zipped by unseen? Dr. Wooldridge, I'm sorry, I may be preaching to the choir here, but this doesn't make sense to me."

Chandra added, "It's worse than that. One of the world's most brilliant astrophysicists, Dr. Bill Napier, wrote a compelling paper that suggests the probability of comet impacts may be hundreds of times higher than originally predicted."

Wooldridge looked resigned. "It's been more of a question of budgets."

Scupino shook his head and continued in the quiet voice of a teacher. "When I was a young squadron safety officer, I had to take a course in Risk Management. It was really boring, but one thing stuck with me. When you're evaluating how much time and money to put into risk mitigation, you look at two things. How likely is it to happen, and how severe are the consequences if it does?" He paused. "Apparently, even a small comet carries more destructive power than all the nuclear warheads in the world combined. With that type of consequence, even with low probability, it's insane not to do *some* risk mitigation. There are hundreds of giant visible craters on earth, and you said we've been *aware* of a possible cycle of impact-related mass extinctions. I don't know what your belief system is, but I can't help but wonder if the Jupiter impact and the Alcock comet were warning shots fired across our bow."

Josh noticed Lopez gently nodding in agreement. Lopez caught Scupino's eye and said, "May I?"

"Please."

Wooldridge looked relieved.

Lopez started out slowly. "The problem is belief. It's hard for the mind to accept anything without personal experience. In the US, the largest killer of anyone under forty-five is car crashes. They kill 35,000 a year. After hundreds of studies, we know that seatbelts could prevent almost half these deaths. The odd thing is that surveys show almost everyone is aware of this. Yet 10,000 unbelted people die every year. The problem is that unless you, or someone you know, cracked a windshield with your head, it's just not real. We understand logically but not emotionally."

Scupino nodded, looking back at Wooldridge. "I do understand it's hard to work without a concrete source, but this is something that should have been done decades ago. At this point, I don't care if Josh's source is Mork from the planet Ork."

They all nodded with half smiles.

Scupino smiled. "I'm sorry. I'll get off my soapbox. I honestly can't imagine a more brilliant team, or a program with greater potential to help mankind. It's truly my honor to be able to work with you." He paused, looking at each of them. "Let's make this happen."

As the meeting broke up, Wooldridge came over to Josh. "I'm not only a tenured professor at Berkeley, I went there as an undergraduate." He looked down his long nose at Josh. "Do you have a college degree?"

Momentarily forgetting his need for concealment, Josh said, "Cornell."

Wooldridge, looking constipated again, said, "Well… at least it wasn't a *state* school, like…" He waved his hand vaguely in the direction of the others.

Chandra's University of Texas was highly ranked in astrophysics, but Josh knew Wooldridge was simply retreating into the security of his academic credentials. Giving him his due, Josh said, "Berkeley is unquestionably one of the best schools in the world in astrophysics."

"Actually, Berkeley is *the* best in the world."

Josh nodded, "Yes, of course, and I can't tell you how fortunate we are to have someone of your stature on this team. It's truly an honor."

Wooldridge finally smiled. "Glad to be able to offer my expertise."

Josh remembered Scupino's comment about "healthy egos." Still, he was very pleased with the meeting. As the meeting broke up, Josh said softly to himself, "Only two minor details left. Build a secret base at the South Pole and find a few hundred million to fund it." He smiled. "Delusions of grandeur, huh?"

Smith had finished his preliminary background investigation on everyone except Meadows. So far, he'd found absolutely nothing on him, which was virtually impossible. Of course, the CIA and other agencies could erase identities. He smiled, thinking about his own real name, Allen Jackson. Like him, Meadows had to be some type of operative with the military or another agency. Normally, there was a professional courtesy extended between covert operatives. He should have dropped the investigation, but he couldn't. Something didn't add up. He'd noticed how Scupino sometimes deferred to Meadows. Clearly, he was more than a liaison.

Smith sighed. After the accident, he had promised himself he'd never work for anyone again without knowing their background. He would do it carefully and quietly, but he *would* find out who Meadows was and who he worked for.

20

BRANDON

Sir Edward Brandon would be leaving New York to open his new launch facility in Ecuador. Sheri had managed to schedule Josh to see Brandon at 5:00 p.m., just before Brandon departed. To make sure he'd have plenty of time to get to his Manhattan office, Josh took the earliest morning flight.

As he arrived at the airport, he discovered there were major delays due to a line of heavy June thunderstorms pounding the East Coast. His 7:30 a.m. flight finally left at 12:30 p.m. He would still make it but his margin was gone.

It was a rough flight with a lot of turbulence. He felt sorry for the woman sitting next to him. She was clenching the armrest and sweating profusely. He told her he was a pilot and tried to set her at ease by explaining that the pilots would never take them through truly dangerous weather. The rough air was just from the periphery of the storms. It seemed to help. Then the pilot, in a relaxed Texas drawl, announced they'd be stuck in a holding pattern for thirty minutes. He also said they might have to go elsewhere if the weather didn't improve.

Now Josh began to sweat and clench the armrest. He needed this meeting. The scientists and engineers couldn't keep charging their time to other programs without raising suspicion. On top of that, they needed to buy real pieces of hardware, not to mention building a base in Antarctica. He'd used up all of Elizabeth's free airline miles and had to max out his credit card just to pay for this flight.

He glanced over and realized the woman next to him was watching him closely.

With large eyes, she asked, "Are we going to die?"

He took a deep breath and smiled, confessing his nervousness was simply because he had a critical meeting in New York.

Relieved, she said, "I understand. I do meetings all over the country. Why don't you just text them your situation using the airline's Wi-Fi?"

Of course! He thanked her and texted Sheri. She said she'd call Brandon.

Thirty minutes later the pilot updated them. "I'm sorry, folks, if we don't get cleared for an approach in a few minutes, we're gonna have to divert to Philadelphia due to fuel."

Sheri texted him back that the best they could do was delay the meeting till 5:30 p.m. Brandon had to leave no later than 6:00 to catch his flight. Josh looked at his watch: if they didn't start their approach now, he'd never make it. He couldn't pretend to use his Bluetooth headset to talk to Jesse on the plane, so he closed his eyes and sat very still. He had no idea if Jesse could "hear" him inside an aircraft at altitude, but it was worth a try. He tried to sub-vocalize his request for help. He even tried picturing himself successfully making the meeting, symbolically crossing the finish line in a sprint. He felt silly, but had absolutely nothing else constructive to do. After replaying the picture in his mind a few times, he took another deep breath and made a conscious effort to stop producing adrenaline. He opened his eyes, feeling better.

The pilot came up and said, "I'm sorry, folks, looks like we're going to have to divert to…" There was a pause. The passengers looked at each other and the woman next to him asked, "You think he forgot where we're going?"

Before Josh could respond, the pilot said, "Just got cleared for the approach. Should be landin' at JFK in about fifteen minutes. Maybe a little bumpy. Make sure your belts are cinched tight."

The approach was rough in heavy rain and winds, but they landed with only a few bounces. As soon as the airplane hit the gate, Josh was out and running through the airport. Checking the time, he realized he'd have to take a cab. After paying the fare and tip, he'd be down to his last few dollars. He appreciated the irony. He was here because he needed hundreds of millions, but he'd have to take a bus back to the airport.

He burst out of the terminal into a heavy downpour punctuated by lightning and thunder. He was able to grab a cab quickly but as they entered Manhattan, they hit a huge traffic jam. Sitting in gridlock, he Google-mapped the destination on his phone. He was only three miles away. It was 5:15. No way he'd make it if he stayed with the cab. Giving the driver the last of his cash, he jumped out into the deluge and started running. He ran hard, doing four-minute miles through the blowing sheets of rain. He dodged cars like a running back and reached the building at 5:27. Just like the sprinter he'd pictured in his mind, he thought wryly. He'd have to be more careful about how he imagined outcomes.

He looked like he'd walked out of a swimming pool. Squeaking with each step, he went straight to the lobby information desk and showed his ID. The receptionist said, "Raining, huh?"

Josh was still breathing hard. "Is it? I didn't notice."

Looking at him strangely, the receptionist directed him to the elevator.

Brandon's office was, of course, at the top. Alone in the elevator, Josh caught his breath, closed his eyes and focused on what *must* happen. It was difficult. He was used to planning for the worst-case scenario and having a backup plan. He had no backup plan.

As he stepped out of the elevator, he was breathing more normally and saw the clock behind Brandon's receptionist – exactly 5:30.

She raised her eyebrows at his appearance.

He shrugged. "Water-balloon fight in the lobby."

She grinned. Pointing toward a large, ornate entrance, she said, "He'll see you now, Commander Meadows." She winked and said, "I'll get you a towel."

He thanked her and went into the office. As he entered, he had a breathtaking view through floor-to-ceiling windows of a lightning-illuminated Manhattan. Beautiful, dark cherry-wood covered the walls and ceiling, with a rich maroon carpet underfoot. Books completely dominated one wall. The office was an interesting mixture of old world and new technology: he saw multiple large monitors sitting on Brandon's massive cherry desk.

Behind it stood Sir Edward Brandon, looking just like the

tabloid pictures. "Good to meet you, Commander Meadows."

For some reason he wanted to say, "Bond, James Bond." Instead, still dripping, he said, "Do you need any of your plants watered?"

Smiling, Brandon came around his desk as the receptionist came back with a large towel. Wiping his face and hands, Josh offered one relatively dry hand. "It's Josh, and it's an honor to meet you, Sir Edward."

He'd never shaken the hand of a multi-billionaire before, much less a knight. Brandon was a little taller than Josh. In his early fifties, he was obviously in exceptional physical condition. He had a square tan jaw, white teeth, and a beard that matched his wild mop of blond hair. Josh continued, "I admire what you've accomplished, both in the business world and your record-setting adventures." He had read about Brandon's exploits, not all of which had succeeded, but that never appeared to stop him. He wasn't just a self-made billionaire; he was truly an adventurer, a man's man.

Brandon said, "Thank you, but my real interest is space."

"Yes, I know. That's why I'm here."

Brandon's eyebrows went up. "If you don't mind my asking, whom do you represent? I did a little checking after Sheri set this up. To be honest, my people couldn't find anything on you at all. That's extremely unusual but it also increased my curiosity."

"Sir Edward. I *am* a naval officer but I'm… *on loan*… to another agency, one that I am not at liberty to discuss right now."

Brandon gave a slight nod.

Josh continued, "I know your time is valuable but I believe we have something you will find very interesting. Before I share it, do you mind telling me a little bit about what you're passionate about, your long-term goals?" Josh knew he could use words like "passion" with successful people like Brandon.

Brandon started laughing. "So you haven't read the tabloids?"

Josh smiled. "I wanted to hear what your vision really is and see if that intersects with our project." He needed to know more about what made Brandon tick. The best way to learn about someone, and build a relationship, was to ask them about themselves.

Brandon looked carefully at Josh, as if assessing his seriousness, and then motioned him to a seat. He perched on the edge of his desk, and smiling, shared some of his long-term business and humanitarian goals.

After fifteen minutes, Josh thought they would be a good fit… *if* he could convince him. "Sir, I appreciate what you are trying to do more than you know. If I share something with you, will you promise not to divulge it to anyone?"

"Yes, and call me Edward."

Josh pulled out the damp folder with the security paperwork in it. Trying to get Brandon a security clearance would draw too much attention to their program. Since Brandon would never attend meetings at Boeing, no one but Josh would know that he didn't have a clearance. Accurately, Josh said, "This is just a formality. I know you're a man of your word."

As Brandon read over the paperwork, pen in hand, Josh continued, "With knowledge comes responsibility, and with great knowledge comes great responsibility. What I tell you today may change the course of your business and life. I don't do it lightly." Josh knew that people like Brandon responded to challenge and adventure. Security and even safety were often secondary considerations.

Brandon signed the paper and handed it back.

Josh asked, "Is this office secure from electronic eavesdropping?"

Brandon pressed a button on his desk and said, "It's as secure as our current technology can make it."

A half hour later, Brandon was excitedly nodding his head. "This has so many implications. We're not alone, are we?"

Josh, thinking of Jesse, realized he was almost certainly right.

Brandon continued, "But then why…?"

"I'm sorry," Josh interjected. "I've said more than I should. The question is – can you help us? We're asking you to convert your mission and resources from commercial space access, to protecting the earth from a comet. As if that's not enough, you'll have to do it in total secrecy for a while. I can't even guarantee you'll be fully compensated."

"If what you say is true, it's a pretty simple decision, since the alternative is the death of millions or billions, including my family." He paused. "I've always felt that I had a more important mission waiting for me and this, as corny as it sounds, feels right." He looked back at Josh meaningfully. "*If* I were convinced this was real, I'd have no problem committing my business and personal wealth, but there are a couple of things that don't make sense. First of all, why do you need my help? Surely the US government has sufficient resources."

Josh asked, "What do you think will happen when this goes public?"

"Maybe wars will stop and we'll all work together."

"And maybe the world's stock markets will collapse overnight."

Brandon looked out the window toward the skyline and nodded. "Yes, that's possible."

"Only a handful of people know about this. Part of the problem is that the information isn't credible without the source, and the source could be as earth-shaking as the comet. We're stuck between the proverbial rock and a hard place. As we speak, experts are trying to figure out how to introduce this to the public without causing panic or economic collapse."

Brandon nodded. "Of course, that's why Sheri Lopez is involved."

Josh nodded. "Plus, no matter how many resources the government brings to bear, you know they can never act as quickly as private industry. We're trying to put a nuclear reactor and a giant energy-beam projector at the South Pole…"

Brandon interrupted, "And if *Commander* Meadows and the US military are tied to a project involving a giant laser beam in Antarctica…"

Josh finished, "It could create serious international confrontation. By keeping the funding source private for the Antarctic operation, we have a better chance of maintaining our cover story."

Brandon nodded. "I guess that makes sense." He paused. "So – hypothetically – what would you need from me?"

"Your Antarctic expertise and several hundred million dollars to start building the polar base."

"Josh, I've climbed Antarctic mountains. You've picked one of the toughest places on earth to build something."

Josh shrugged. "No choice."

"If I fund this, am I going to be the fall guy if the US denies involvement?"

Josh shrugged again. "Probably." Then he added, "But even if the comet information is wrong, I think history will probably treat us well for building the first planetary defense system."

"No offense, Josh, but I would've expected a higher-ranking government official, like maybe the President, to have made this request."

Josh smiled. "No offense taken, but you can see the risk involved with a high-ranking official talking to you directly. Because of the incredible sensitivity, very few in the government are aware... even at the highest levels."

Brandon said wryly, "Makes it a bit difficult to confirm..."

Josh had an idea. "Do you know who Dr Victoria Chandra is?"

"Chandra? Yes, of course. Everyone in the space community knows her or her reputation."

"Dr. Chandra is our chief scientist."

Brandon nodded slowly. Then he stared out the window as he gently drummed his fingers on the desk. After several moments, he turned back to Josh and blew out a lungful of air. "Josh, can you give me a minute? I need to make a quick call."

"Of course." Josh stepped outside his office, and tried not to pace while picturing a positive outcome.

Within a minute, Brandon came out and asked Josh to follow him. They got on the elevator and on the way down, Brandon said, "OK, I've scheduled a face-to-face meeting with Dr. Chandra. If this checks out, I have two hard requirements. I want to be part of the Antarctic operation, and I want Christoff Bobinski on your leadership team."

Josh nodded his head. "We need your expertise in Antarctica. You'll have full access there." He frowned. "But who's Christoff Bobinski?"

"He's one of my most trusted business partners and he is to extreme construction what Red Adair was to oil well firefighting. He's an absolute wizard in Arctic building projects. You need him."

Josh said, "We can use all the help we can get. I'll run him through our system and we'll figure out how to get him cleared into the project."

Brandon added, "By the way, I *am* going to get some serious tax breaks with this project, aren't I?"

Josh shrugged. "Doubtful. IRS hasn't been read into the program."

Brandon laughed. "Josh, you're not a very good salesman. I'm taking you to my comptroller where you can work the account details so that we'll be ready to hook your system to ours. By the way, *do not* tell my comptroller that there are no tax breaks; she'll have a nervous breakdown."

They arrived at his comptroller's office and Brandon quickly introduced them. Then he said, "I have to go."

As he was leaving, Josh looked at the time and said, "I'm sorry. I made you miss your flight."

Looking back over his shoulder, Brandon winked. "Josh, I can't miss my flight. I own the airline."

Brandon's comptroller looked like his grandmother. He sheepishly confessed he had little understanding of how government accounting worked. She smiled and assured him that she'd worked with the government and knew what to do. All she needed was a point of contact. He promised he'd get all the information she needed as soon as he returned to St. Louis.

As he was about to leave, she handed him what looked like a credit card and a Post-it with a handwritten number. She said, "Sir Edward told me to set up a petty-cash fund for quick-response needs until we get the final clearance." Looking a little stern, she added, "You can use it as a debit or credit card for whatever you need, but there's only $100,000 in the account." Smiling again, she said, "If you lose it or need the funds replenished, just give me a call."

Like a boy given a puppy by his grandmother, he thanked her profusely and promised he'd be careful with it.

Elated, he did a football touchdown dance in the elevator. This was exactly the outcome he had pictured, except for the *petty*-cash fund. He'd just been hoping for a bus fare. He also realized he could pay Elizabeth back. As silly as that was in the scheme of things, it bothered him to borrow money from her. What he really wanted to do was treat her to a fancy dinner as soon as he got back to Kansas

City and buy her a nice gift. He'd be careful with his funds, but he owed her that. None of this would have been possible without her.

As he got back to the airport, Josh called Carl. "Carl, can you do me a favor? I need to have an individual checked out before inviting him on the team."

Carl said, "Sure. Where are you now?"

"New York City."

There was a pause. "Can you stop by DC on the way back?"

Josh understood. They really couldn't talk about sensitive information over the phone and Carl hadn't been able to attend the meetings in person. "Sure, I'll change my flight and can be there tomorrow morning."

"Great. If we don't have to talk details, let's grab lunch at J. Gilbert's around twelve. Do you know where that is?"

"No, but I'm sure I can google it. See you there."

Josh used his new charge card to change his flight to DC. He could fly first class now, but wouldn't. He wasn't against having nice things or bothered by people who did. If things worked out, he planned to have some fun, but not now, not yet. He would continue living at his current level, not just to be a good steward of the funds, but because he didn't need distractions. He knew distractions came in many shapes, but the most dangerous had two legs.

21

REUNION

J. Gilbert's was an elegant steakhouse with rich, dark wood, brick walls and soft lighting. Before Brandon, even buying a hamburger here would have been a financial stress for him.

Josh saw Carl sitting at a table next to the wall. What was it with intelligence agents? They always preferred having their back to the wall.

After joining him and ordering drinks, Carl said softly, "I've been thinking about the site. As you know, no one owns the South Pole. There was a treaty created in the late 1950s – now signed by over forty countries including the US. Basically, it set aside Antarctica as a scientific preserve, established freedom of scientific investigation, and banned all military activity on the continent."

Josh had looked this up as well.

Carl continued, "Our program would certainly qualify with both the letter *and* the spirit of the law…"

Josh said, "But?"

"But, trying to get forty countries to agree on anything is next to impossible, and certainly not in the time we have." Carl smiled. "This is one of those rare times when I think history will vindicate us for being sneaky."

Josh whispered, "What type of story would raise the fewest eyebrows?"

"This may sound funny coming from our agency, but honesty is the best policy." He winked. "It reduces the number of lies you have to remember."

Josh nodded. "Roger that."

Carl asked, "What will the equipment look like?"

"Not really sure, but it will be very big with a large optical telescope for tracking."

"Hmm, off of the top of my head, I'd go with an astrophysics project." He paused. "Which, come to think of it, it is."

Josh smiled. "Sounds good."

After their drinks arrived, Carl said, "So who do we need to check on?"

"He's an arctic construction expert, but he's a naturalized American citizen."

"Where's he from?"

"I'm afraid it's Russia. His name is Christoff Bobinski."

Carl said, "Actually, Russians are usually fairly easy to check on. Tim can run the background check. That's one of his specialties."

"I'm sorry, Carl. I should have run it through him; it never even occurred to me to ask. I'm embarrassed to say this, but I forget he's there. He's like a shadow."

Carl smiled. "Being invisible is another one of his specialties. If you were aware of him, he wouldn't be as effective."

Josh nodded. "We're also considering working with Edward Brandon."

He raised his eyebrows. "*Sir* Edward Brandon?"

"Yes."

Carl smiled. "Well, he is a space entrepreneur."

Josh added, "And he owns construction companies and has Antarctic experience. In fact, Bobinski was his idea. I know he's not an American citizen but if we can't trust someone knighted by the Queen of England…"

Carl nodded. "You're right and this could actually be beneficial. It wouldn't seem odd if he was supporting a space-science project in Antarctica." He paused. "Josh, is there any way we could route some of the government funds through him to make it look like *he's* funding the Antarctic part of the program?"

Josh nodded seriously. "We might be able to do that."

Carl smiled. "Great. Then I don't see a problem."

He was congratulating himself when Carl looked up over Josh's head and said, "Hi, Kelly." To Josh he said, "Hope you don't mind. I invited my wife. We eat here often and thought you guys might like to meet, having known Josh Logan so well."

Time slowed down as he turned around. It was like the slow motion before a catastrophic car crash. Their eyes met as he stood. Adrenaline flooded his bloodstream, creating a flash of anxiety that almost made his knees buckle. She looked exactly as he remembered her, down to her clothes and hairstyle. Kelly was an incredibly cute, fair-skinned redhead with a light dusting of freckles. She had beautiful, intense, green eyes that matched her passionate personality. They could stare a hole right through you when angry. Caught between conflicting compulsions of fight or flight, he wanted to run away, and hold her.

She offered her hand.

Speechless, he took it, as Carl said, "Kelly, this is Josh Meadows."

Looking directly into his eyes, she said, "Hi Josh. Glad to meet you. Carl tells me you knew Josh Logan?"

Josh nodded, managing to get out a "Glad to meet you." Even in his state of shock, he thought that this was just like her, always to the point. Just when he thought it couldn't get any worse, he caught her scent. She was wearing the same perfume, light but unmistakable. It threatened to send him into a memory spiral. Clearing his throat to give him a few precious seconds, he said, "Yes, we worked on some programs together."

"I'm sorry, I don't remember him talking about you, but I know he worked on a lot of those secret squirrel things." She kissed Carl as she sat next to him.

As Josh sat back down, he thought, this can't be happening. He *knew* about Carl and Kelly, but this... this face-to-face reality... He felt like he was suffocating. With huge effort, he tried to compartmentalize his emotions and maintain his composure. His intellect resurfaced and he suddenly had a thought. Maybe this surprise meeting was exactly that, but Carl was a brilliant strategist and skeptical by nature. This might be a test, a test to see if he really knew Josh Logan. Good! He needed a challenge to deal with, anything to keep his mind off... them. He had to tread carefully but he had an advantage. He knew as much about Kelly as any man could ever know about a woman.

Before he could formulate a plan, Kelly asked, "Are you married, or do you have any kids?"

Josh said, "No."

"*Were* you married?"

"Yes. Yes, I was. She..." he stumbled, "... remarried."

"I'm sorry. It wasn't that long ago, was it?"

"Uh... no." This had to be the oddest conversation in history. He knew she would ask questions relentlessly. It was just what she did. He had to change the subject, if only to maintain his sanity. An idea struck him. Before she could ask her next question, he said, "Kelly, Josh told me a funny story once. You'll have to tell me if it was really true."

She finally looked a bit nervous.

"He said you were at a local lake with your ski boat. You did the romantic thing with champagne at sunset. Then you dropped him off at the dock so he could get the truck and boat trailer. While he was getting the trailer, he said you took the boat out for one last high-speed spin."

He saw her eyes widen with recognition. "Oh no, he told you *that*?" Smiling, she hung her head dramatically. "Go ahead."

He knew she liked being the central character in a story, and Carl was enjoying her embarrassment.

"He said he heard you racing off into the night near the shoreline. It was getting dark, and... wasn't the water level in the lake lower than usual?"

She nodded guiltily.

"If I remember correctly, he said that as he brought the car down the ramp with the trailer, he heard an outboard motor running at full speed. Then he heard a cough, stutter, and silence."

Kelly shook her head. "I didn't know the water was only a few inches deep near the island."

Smiling, Carl added, "Oops."

Josh continued, "He said, in the dark he heard a distant, rhythmic splashing sound. He yelled your name but got no answer. He got worried, jumped in, and swam out a couple hundred yards."

Kelly smiled and shook her head.

"As he got closer, he said he could make out the outline of the boat and you swimming in front of it. You were trying to pull the boat in with a rope?"

Kelly protested, "I had to, there was only one paddle. I kept going around in circles."

Carl started laughing.

She added, "He almost drowned laughing at me, so I helped him, by pushing his head under. I was *so* mad!" Kelly's eyes flashed, and then she started laughing.

He couldn't help but think how much he missed those laser-green eyes.

Rolling them, she said, "I *can't believe* he shared that with you! So your only impression of me is an airhead sailor with a bad temper!"

"No, no, I'm sorry. He told me awesome things about you. This was just one of those stories that kinda sticks with you."

Kelly said, "Yeah, he was always a great storyteller... like you." She cocked her head to one side. "It's weird, but as you told that story, I *so* heard him. You told it almost exactly like he would have."

Carl nodded. "She's right. You really could be his brother, with your speech patterns."

Josh realized a new voice-box didn't change his inflection or idioms. He'd have to be more careful. Truthfully, he said, "That's probably because we both grew up in Northern Virginia."

Carl and Kelly both nodded, accepting his explanation.

They went on to talk about military life, having to move frequently and all the other things that go with being in the Navy. Kelly told him the story about how she and Carl had gotten together at the squadron reunion. Dating long distance, they were married two months later and she moved to Washington DC. Then Kelly said, "Of course, those carefree days are behind us now, with the baby."

Josh coughed, almost spitting out his water, "Baby?"

She frowned at Carl. "Carl didn't tell you?"

Carl shrugged awkwardly.

She continued, "We have a beautiful, bouncing baby girl." Like any proud mother, Kelly immediately pulled up pictures on her phone.

Carl added, "She's already got her mother's temper."

Kelly smiled, shaking her head. "She's just strong."

Josh looked carefully at the pictures and saw a beautiful, red-haired baby girl. Softly, he asked, "How old is she?"

"Let's see, Caitlin will be seven months old next week. It's hard to believe…"

Seven months? Something snapped in him. There was a flash and time stopped. For a moment, there were two of him.

Then, he stood up abruptly, knocking his chair over backwards, and rushed to Kelly's side of the table.

Startled, she pushed her chair back. He grabbed her arms just above the elbow and pulled her out of her chair. "Kelly-bear, it's me! It's Josh! I'm alive!" He could see the look of surprise and shock on her face. In slow motion, he saw Carl standing up out of the corner of his eye and sensed everyone in the restaurant turning toward them. Kelly's eyes were wide as she stared intently into his.

Then her face turned from surprise to anguish and fear. Backing up slowly, she started shaking her head and sobbing, "No, no…" She looked away from him and swept her hands up between them, breaking his grasp. Her face continued to morph into terrible agony.

He started to move toward her but felt Carl's hand in the middle of his chest.

With a look of unadulterated hate, Carl yelled, "What the hell are you doing? Get away from my wife!" He shoved Josh back against the table, almost knocking him down, as Kelly ran from the restaurant.

Suddenly, his perspective flashed forward in time. Like a movie trailer, he saw himself running. He was a fugitive. His program crumbling around him, fire everywhere. Then, another flash.

He found himself sitting in his chair at the restaurant, muscles tensed to stand.

"… seven months old next week. It's hard to believe she's already that old, but time flies faster when you're changing diapers." She finished with a smile.

Josh took a cautious breath and tried to relax his calf muscles.

Kelly suddenly tipped her head sideways and said, "Whoa. I just had a total déjà vu moment, like this already happened." She laughed. "I get those all the time, do you?"

He just nodded dumbly, still looking at the picture on Kelly's phone. Finally, he managed to squeeze out, "She's beautiful, just like her mom." Sitting back, he added, "Excuse me, boy's room. Be right back."

As he got up, he heard Kelly whispering to Carl, "I was wrong. I'm pretty sure I *have* met him before."

Inside one of the men's-room stalls, he just stood there leaning against the wall, trying to breathe. It was the same feeling he had after narrowly avoiding a midair collision with another fighter. He did the math again as his overworked adrenal glands quieted. It had to be. Caitlin was his daughter. He shook his head and said softly, "A daughter… I have a daughter."

It also dawned on him that Carl had asked a very pregnant Kelly to marry him. Josh realized he'd been harboring an illogical resentment toward Carl. This… this changed things. Carl had done something few men would have done. He felt genuine warmth for his old friend again. He sighed. "Thanks, Carl."

Shredded by so many emotions, he just had to hold it together a little longer. He latched on to something to help him focus. He had a daughter… a daughter who was going to die in twenty months unless he succeeded.

He went to the sink and splashed water on his face. Wiping it off, he took a deep breath and returned. As he sat back down at the table, he said, "I realized I never congratulated you on your marriage or daughter."

Kelly smiled. "Josh and I never talked about what would happen if one of us weren't here anymore, but," she paused, "I think he would have approved."

He saw her eyes get a little glassy but she was a strong woman. No tears and she never let her voice inflection change. He appreciated that strength now. He glanced at Carl and then looked her directly in the eyes. Slowly but with strength, he said, "I am absolutely certain that Josh wouldn't have wanted it any other way."

She had just met this man, but his words went straight to her heart. She thanked him and excused herself. Once inside the women's room, she cried. She muttered softly to herself, "What's wrong with me? I'm past this!" Why did the approval of someone she hardly knew have such an impact? It had to be hormones… but he just seemed so… so familiar. She got it together and returned. Shifting back into her comfortable cross-examination mode, she said, "So you're not married now. Anyone in the wings?"

Carl shook his head. "She just meets you and she's already weighing you to decide who she'll introduce you to."

Josh, looking a little uncertain, said, "Uh, actually… there is someone." He paused. "She's a nurse in Kansas City but I don't know if my *occupation* will ultimately work for her."

Kelly laughed. "Military officers and nurses; it's such a cliché. Well, she's in for a wild ride, but if she's got any guts, she won't let you get away. Course, she must be a saint if she's hanging with someone like *you*." She wouldn't normally tease someone this early, but for some reason, she felt very comfortable with him.

They finished lunch, but she noticed Josh just pushed his food around the plate.

Finally, looking at his phone, Josh said, "I'm sorry, but I really have to go. Kelly, it was great to… to meet you."

They all stood up and Carl shook Josh's hand saying, "I'll get back to you on that security check."

Josh nodded.

Before Josh could offer his hand, Kelly hugged him. She was a hugger by nature. She felt him tense and then relax, politely patting her on the back.

After he left, she saw Carl looking carefully at her. "You OK?"

Kelly smiled. "Yes. Actually… I'm great." She paused and then shook her head gently. "I don't know why… but for some reason I feel like a weight's been lifted off my shoulders." Then she looked back at Carl with a hint of mischief. "And if Josh's current girlfriend doesn't work out, I know just who to introduce him to… *but* he's going to have to get over his ex first."

"His ex? What are you talking about?"

Looking incredulous, she asked, "Didn't you see his body language when I asked about his previous marriage?" She shook her head. "He's *totally* not over her!"

Carl frowned. "You deduced that from his *body* language?"

"Well, yeah! Wasn't it obvious? He looked like a kicked puppy."

Carl, frowning and smiling at the same time, said, "You're *sure* you don't want a job with the agency?"

She rolled her eyes but grinned. She was going to have to meet this girlfriend of his and find out what the real story was.

Josh drove to his hotel completely numb. He went to his room and threw his briefcase on the bed. Standing motionless, he replayed in his mind all that transpired. Kelly kissing Carl… one of the hardest things he'd ever had to witness. He had fought himself the entire time. Then, the alternate-reality confrontation with Kelly. It was like a bucket of ice-water in the face. He still didn't know what had happened but it was painfully real. Could Jesse have orchestrated it, or was it just a capability of his enhanced body?

When Jesse first told him his old life was gone, he understood… but not really, not emotionally. Then when Scupino told of the missing-man formation, it began to sink in. *He* was the missing man. His death became real, but even then, it was just *him*.

When he saw the wedding picture on Carl's desk, he had run away from the thought… literally. He finally understood. He simply said, "I've lost her."

He ran a hand through his hair. "No!" He slammed his fist on the desk, knocking the lamp off. He wanted to scream at Jesse, rage against the mind-numbing unfairness… but he was exhausted, emotionally desiccated. His whole body sighed as he dropped into the desk chair.

Head in hands, he stared at nothing. When Elizabeth told him how her husband died, he knew she had no closure and felt sorry for her. He'd been oblivious to the fact that he had the exact same problem… the loss of his wife… and now his child. His anger and indignation deflated into despair. He could never tell Kelly the truth, even if the world wasn't hanging in the balance. She'd been through the grief and mourning. She *had* closure and pulled her life back together with a new husband. If somehow she believed him – he remembered her face in his alternate reality – it would rip her apart. It would be monumentally selfish and hurtful. He must, he would, remain silent. "Kelly," he said with anguish and then softer, "Caitlin…"

When he was a child, his dad told him men don't cry. He cried. Then he slept.

22

LOGISTICS

Josh sat in Scupino's office with Smith. He told them about Sir Edward Brandon and Christoff Bobinski.

Scupino looked skeptical. "Isn't *Sir* Edward too much of a public figure? He'll draw the press like a lightning rod."

Josh said, "Maybe, but Lopez is a celebrity too. Along with Brandon's Antarctic expertise and construction companies, Carl suggested we use him to 'launder' our program's money through his companies. That should provide some insulation."

Smith nodded.

Scupino said, "That's good but I'm still uncomfortable having him around our team."

Josh knew that without an official clearance, he couldn't get Brandon into the building, much less into their meetings. "You're right. We wouldn't have him attend any of our regular meetings. The only place we'd see him would be in Antarctica, which would help support our cover story."

Scupino smiled, nodding. "Probably not a lot of paparazzi there. I assume you're taking care of his clearance and how to route the money through him?"

"Yes, sir."

Scupino asked Smith, "What about Bobinski?"

Smith said, "We've checked him out. It wasn't hard. He's a colorful character but appears to be the best in his field."

Scupino asked, "Is he a security risk?"

Briefly locking eyes with Josh, Smith said, "We're all security risks. It just requires the right situation or leverage. Bobinski became a naturalized US citizen during the Soviet days to escape the

Communist regime and because he's a born entrepreneur. He spends a lot of time in Russia and still has a love for his former country. He also has connections with Russian organized crime."

Josh and Scupino looked at each other with raised eyebrows. Scupino said what Josh was thinking. "So, he *is* a risk?"

Smith said, "This may sound strange, but it's the people who don't believe in something that worry us. What we're doing here will help both the US and Russia. I don't see any conflict of interest."

Scupino asked, "What about his connections with the Russian mob?"

Smith said, "It would be surprising if he didn't have connections. When the Soviet Union collapsed, it was like the US during Prohibition. To get anything done, you had to work with the shadier elements. Since then, the Russian government has clamped down considerably, but organized crime is still an economic reality in some areas."

Scupino said, "So what are you saying?"

"Bobinski is tough and doesn't suffer fools patiently, but he has character and even those who don't like him respect him. He's already a multi-millionaire, so he doesn't need the job. He has no obvious vices aside from a love of a good party and Russian women, and he really doesn't care what other people think of him."

Scupino said, "I like him already."

Smith continued, "In other words, he's not a good blackmail target. We also discovered that he once worked on a US government project that required a basic security clearance. It shouldn't be too hard to update it to a higher level. Carl can help expedite that."

Josh finally asked, "Would *you* trust him?"

Smith said, "Yes." Looking off into space, he added softly, "But I've been wrong before."

Elizabeth hadn't seen or heard from Josh since he left for New York two weeks ago. Coming home from work, she was surprised to find a letter from him. She opened it quickly. Inside was a check for $12,000, and a note. *"Here's the $5,000 you loaned me plus interest and reimbursement for the airline miles. Thank you for everything! I couldn't have done it without you. Josh"*

She sat down and said quietly to herself, "That's it? Thanks for everything?" With a funding source, he didn't need her support anymore. There was nothing she could contribute to the cause. She had thought – or maybe just hoped – there was more between them. Part of her was hurt and angry with Josh. Still another part was angry with herself for being angry. She knew what was at stake. Her feelings were irrelevant. With a half smile, she shook her head and said, "What kind of idiot dates a prophet?" She sighed and dropped the letter in the trash.

Dr. Jackie Jones got Cho's voicemail for the third time. She tried Cho's deputy but got the same response. Finally, she called Conner, the young engineer who did the last program briefing.

Without preamble, she jumped in. "Conner, where the heck is Dr. Cho? We've got a major program status meeting for the National Reconnaissance Office coming up, and I'm looking at some serious schedule slips. He hasn't returned my emails or calls in over a week."

"Sorry, Dr. Jones. He's been gone. He's working on that other program, but I'm putting together the technical and schedule status for you."

"What *is* this other program?"

"I'm sorry, ma'am; I'm not read into it. All I know is that it's very sensitive and he has half the lab involved, but no one's talking."

Jones bit down on her first response, forcing herself to acknowledge it wasn't Conner's fault. "When you talk to Dr. Cho, please have him call me *as soon* as possible."

"Yes, ma'am. Would you like to see the charts I'm putting together?"

Jones sighed softly. "Sure, Conner, that would be great." As she hung up, she said quietly, "What on earth could preempt *us*?"

It was the end of July, one of the hottest days of the year in St. Louis. Insulated from the sweltering heat and humidity, there were almost two dozen people in the cool conference room. All wore special program badges. Seeing the "Resurrect" name on the badges, Josh smiled. He probably shouldn't have named it that, but the participants probably assumed it was resurrection of the technology from the old Strategic Defense Initiative.

There was a positive tension in the room, similar to the first flight of a new fighter. Scupino sat at one end of the table with Chandra on his right and Katori on his left. Lopez, Wooldridge, and Cho usually sat in the first tier, spaced around the table. Generally, the second tier was for the more junior personnel. Josh always sat in the second tier near Scupino, trying to keep a low profile. He noticed that Tim Smith also sat in the second tier but never in the same place twice.

Scupino started the meeting. "I'd like everyone to welcome our two new logistics teammates." He pointed to two men sitting at the table to the left of Katori. "This is Dr. Winston Shepherd and Mr. Christoff Bobinski. Dr. Shepherd has several degrees and government certifications in logistics and support. Mr. Bobinski is world renowned in industrial construction, particularly under extreme conditions. Gentlemen, welcome to the team."

There were nods from around the table. Dr. Shepherd was a slightly overweight medium-height man in his fifties, with a hawkish nose and thin black hair combed carefully over a large bald spot. Bobinski was similar in age but looked more like Sean Connery in *The Hunt for Red October*, complete with gray beard.

Josh couldn't help but think, "What a strange and eclectic team to save the world!"

Scupino kicked it off. "So where and how are we going to site this thing?"

Katori said, "We believe we've found the perfect location. Mount Howe is the closest exposed bedrock to the geographic South Pole. This site will allow us to build on solid ground instead of snow pack. That's good since we have to align the beam to within a gnat's eyelash, and we're powering it with a nuclear reactor which generates a lot of heat."

Scupino asked, "Don't we need to be right at the South Pole for the beam to swivel as the earth rotates?" He smiled at Chandra. "See, I've been paying attention."

Chandra grinned back. "Normally, yes, but it's only 300 kilometers from the Pole and the top of Mount Howe is almost 9,000 feet above sea level. That height compensates for not being right at the Pole. The mountain top, combined with the flattening of the atmosphere at the Poles, also means there's 40 per cent less air to get the beam through."

Katori continued, "There's also a major logistics advantage. Turns out, they evaluated Mount Howe back in '89 as a potential airfield to support the South Pole base. A flat plain of smooth, blue ice surrounds the mountain. That means, with some surface prep, conventional wheeled aircraft can land there."

Scupino frowned.

Major Crowley jumped in. "At the South Pole base they have to use special C-130s with skis. Being able to use large conventional cargo jets, like C-5s, vastly simplifies our construction logistics. The only reason they scrapped the idea was that it was too far to the South Pole."

"That's great. What about security?"

Josh said, "With the Antarctic Treaty, there's no way we'll get permission to put a nuclear reactor there without UN debate. Our international expert," Josh didn't use Carl's name, "has been working with Dr. Lopez and Dr. Chandra on a cover story." He nodded at them.

Chandra said, "Mount Howe would be a great location for an astronomical observatory for the same reason we want it."

Scupino asked, "So a new observatory is our cover story?"

Chandra laughed. "No, it would draw too much attention. Hundreds of astronomers would be fighting for observing time before it's even built."

Lopez added, "The cover story will probably be an ozone-layer study. It's a little thin," she smiled, "like the ozone layer, but it should give us some time." She shook her head. "We're not going to keep this under wraps long. There are too many people involved and we'll be moving heavy equipment."

Scupino nodded. "Where are we going to stage out of?"

Katori said, "The Falklands."

"Why?"

"Four reasons. It's one of the closest airfields to the South Pole. It's a stable satellite country of the UK. The islands are very isolated with a population of only 3,000, yet they have a big commercial/

military airfield able to support large cargo jets. Finally, we have a stroke of good luck. Turns out, we have some Boeing people already there."

Scupino raised his eyebrows. "Really?"

Katori continued, "The Australians have a Super Hornet squadron deployed to the Falklands right now."

Josh leaned forward and asked, "What are they doing *there*?"

Scupino, finally in his area of expertise, said, "Despite losing the Falklands War, Argentina still claims that the Falklands are rightfully hers, and recently purchased advanced Russian fighters. I'm guessing the UK made an *arrangement* with the Australians. I'll bet they're funding the deployment of the Super Hornets under the guise of a joint training exercise. It's a clear message to thwart any renewed Argentine interest in the islands."

Katori shrugged. "And as usual, we have Boeing technical reps assigned to support our foreign military sales contracts for the Super Hornets. Two of them are there now. They can easily run our staging office without drawing attention."

Scupino said, "Excellent. Let's look at the timeline."

Katori said, "It's going to be extremely tight. We have to have the facility on top of Mount Howe, ready to receive the energy-beam projector in eight months. We also have to have an operating nuclear reactor by then. Fortunately, the Antarctic summer, with six months of daylight, begins in a few weeks."

Dr. Shepherd, who had been frowning the whole time, finally pulled his glasses off and said, "This is absurd. There's no way we can get a nuclear-powered base on top of a mountain in Antarctica, in eight months. It will take a couple years, minimum."

There was a tense silence. Katori looked from Shepherd to Scupino. Scupino looked at Christoff Bobinski. "Mr. Bobinski, what do you think?"

With a heavy Russian accent he asked, "What are budget constraints?"

Scupino raised his eyebrows and looked directly at Josh.

Josh had watched Bobinski while Shepherd spoke and had noticed an almost imperceptible smile on his face. "None."

Shepherd inserted, "It doesn't matter what the budget is; you have to scrape a runway, build an access road up the mountain, and put a large facility on top. How are you going to do that in Antarctica?"

Scupino then looked at Bobinski with raised eyebrows, clearly giving him permission to speak.

Bobinski simply said, "D7E electric diesel hybrid bulldozers."

Shepherd asked, "How're you going to get them there?"

"One C-17 can carry two of them."

"How're you going to keep them from freezing up? The temperature there gets down to fifty degrees below zero."

Scupino leaned over and whispered to Josh, "Fahrenheit or Celsius?"

Josh whispered back, "At that temperature it doesn't matter."

Bobinski said, "Bulldozers will never be turned off."

Shepherd continued to argue, "There just isn't enough time."

Bobinski said, "We'll use the six months of daylight. Since the sun and bulldozers will be up twenty-four hours, so will we."

Shepherd said, "What about blizzards and white-out conditions?"

Chandra jumped in. "Antarctica actually only gets about an inch of precipitation a year. The blizzards are mostly ground snow blown around by high winds. Antarctica is more like a desert with sandstorms than a winter wonderland. With the energy-beam projector on the mountaintop, it will also be above most of the blowing snow."

Shepherd added, "Where are you going to get enough C-17s?"

Katori laughed. "Dr. Shepherd, you're sitting in a Boeing conference room. We make 'em here."

Shepherd finally stopped arguing and shook his head.

Scupino wrapped up the meeting with more assignments.

Josh thought it was progressing beautifully but he knew the real technical and logistics challenges were ahead. Oddly, one of the things he was most concerned with didn't involve the program. He hadn't been able to reach Elizabeth. He really wanted to see her, particularly after the Kelly catharsis. He'd called several times but always got her voicemail. Still trying to keep a low profile, he hadn't left messages or text.

Smith had finished comprehensive background checks on all the program personnel. No major surprises, but there were a couple individuals that deserved extra scrutiny. Scupino had checked out perfectly. He was everything you saw and more, a man of character. Meadows was another matter. He still found almost nothing on him, even after he had called in favors from other intelligence contacts. He wouldn't stop searching but it was time to let Scupino, as the team leader, know what he knew. Maybe Scupino could clear it up.

Regardless, he wouldn't forget what his primary motivation was – money. This was a very lucrative contract and he needed the money to complete his plan.

Smith stayed behind after the meeting. Speaking quietly, he said, "Captain Scupino, I've finished my background checks on the team personnel."

Frowning, Scupino said, "I thought everyone had to have a background check to get a security clearance."

"They do, but those checks are cursory and often out of date. I dig a lot deeper."

Smiling, Scupino said, "I hope you're not going to tell me that Cho likes to paint his toenails."

Smith actually smiled. "No sir, but if he did, it wouldn't matter because he's an extrovert. He'd be the first to tell you about it. I only look for things that could be used to blackmail or entice."

Scupino sighed. "And?"

"It's a solid team. There are only two individuals that are of some concern. One, because of his financial situation. The other, because I can't find any background information on him. He's what we refer to in the intelligence community as a non-person."

Scupino frowned. "Who are you talking about?"

Smith said, "Can we discuss this in your office?"

23

ANTARCTICA

It was the end of August. Things were moving fast and in several locations. They were sending a team in a C-17 to survey their South Pole site. Scupino told Josh that he would visit Los Alamos and shepherd the laser work, so Josh could go play in the snow.

With all the activity, it was probably good that he was no longer involved with Elizabeth. He'd finally left her a voicemail, asking if she was all right. By text, he'd received a simple reply, "I'm fine." He remembered her telling him that her parents took in strays all the time. It occurred to him that their relationship might have been nothing more than that. Maybe she was just a Good Samaritan like her parents and had moved on once she knew he didn't need her help anymore. Still, he had to admit it hurt, but he needed to keep his focus on the mission.

Josh met briefly with Scupino, Katori, Smith, and Lopez.

Smith said, "We'll need a cover story for the Antarctic logistics flights."

Scupino smiled. "It's common knowledge that the Australians are interested in upgrading their Super Hornets' phased-array radar."

Katori jumped in, "It wouldn't be unusual for Boeing to send a team to install the new radar so they could test it under real-world conditions before buying. Since radar technology is highly classified, it would explain Boeing Phantom Works' involvement and the logistics flights."

Smith and Lopez both nodded.

Scupino, still smiling, said, "This covert stuff's kind of fun."

They wrapped up the meeting. As they were walking to the

parking lot, Lopez casually asked Josh, "How's Elizabeth?"

Josh frowned. "I think she's fine. I haven't talked to her in a couple of months."

She stopped and turned to him. "I thought you two were kind of an item?"

He smiled to cover his hurt, "No, she's just an incredibly kind and generous person. Now that we're off and running, she's gotten back to her regular life."

"Really?"

Not wanting to talk about it, he changed the subject. He needed Lopez's help on when and how to introduce this to the public, and he didn't want to share it with the rest of the team yet. "Sheri, when I get back from the Pole, there are some things I'd like to talk to you about... privately."

Smiling, she said, "Let's have dinner when you get back." She winked and left.

They flew to Antarctica in a Boeing C-17 ER Globemaster. The "ER" stood for Extended Range. In addition to the extra tanks, they'd also installed a giant fuel bladder in the cargo area.

Their mission was to survey the proposed site and set up a base camp. The team consisted of Josh, Katori, Bobinski, and two of Bobinski's people: a civil engineer, and a construction expert. They also had two Boeing flight crews, an Air Force Loadmaster, and a medic. Unlike the old days when military transports had nothing but uncomfortable web-seats, this one had a few regular airline seats. The only thing missing was sound insulation, windows, and a flight attendant.

They stopped in Fort Meyers, Florida to pick up Sir Edward Brandon and load equipment. To keep a low profile, they used Private Sky Aviation, a trusted company that had hosted other classified government flights. The C-17 was quickly loaded with two snowcats, several snowmobiles, a large, portable Quonset hut, and several boxes of equipment. After Brandon joined them, they flew directly to Antarctica with a short refueling stop in the Falklands.

Josh used the 8,500-mile flight to catch up on his reading. With his reduced need for sleep and ability to speed-read, he could finish a dozen books during the flight. On his e-book reader he'd downloaded a wide range of titles including astrophysics, quantum mechanics, cosmology, anthropology, psychology, and sociology. He had biographies of famous leaders, and books on Antarctica, cold-weather survival and mountain climbing. After his conversations with Elizabeth and Jesse, he'd also downloaded the Bible, the Qur'an, the Jewish Tanakh, the Hindu Vedas, and the Buddhist Tripitaka. Like the cutting-edge physics books, he suspected the religious texts would take more time. His photographic memory and speed-reading only went so far. He still needed time to process what he read.

He finished the fourth book of the flight. It was on quantum mechanics and required some thought. He decided he needed a break. The loud drone of the C-17's turbofan engines was like pink noise, and looking around, he saw all his fellow passengers were asleep. Knowing that no one could hear him over the engines, he called Jesse.

He sensed Jesse's presence immediately. He was no longer surprised that his communication link worked inside an aircraft over the Atlantic. It just confirmed Jesse's advanced technology. "Jesse, I've been thinking a lot about what you said. I understand that we know a lot less than I thought. Can you help me at least try to understand more?"

Do you want to discuss science, art, or religion?

That was an odd question. "Why would we want to talk about art? I mean, it's fun and all but… well, you know. As for religion, I'm going to start reading more of the ancient religious texts, but isn't religion mostly just historical stories, moral philosophies and some superstitions propagated over time?"

It's a continuum of understanding. Science is that which you can do, and you understand why and how. Art is that which you can do without necessarily understanding how. Religion is that which you cannot easily do nor understand.

"You lost me."

Are all aspects of medicine understood?

He thought for a moment. "I guess if someone has a known bacterial infection, we can prescribe a specific antibiotic that cures it immediately; so that would be science. Then you have things like acupuncture. It appears to work but we really don't understand how it works; so that would be art?" He paused. "We also have people with illnesses beyond our current ability to treat, but somehow some of them heal miraculously. Would that be the spiritual end of the continuum, or religion?"

Yes.

"That's a new perspective for me, but my confidence is still in science. Can we start there?"

He sensed approval.

After a few seconds, he realized Jesse wasn't going to lecture. He decided to start at the very center of science, specifically, a paradox that had haunted physics for decades. "Quantum mechanics is at the heart of physics, but when you follow it to its ultimate conclusion, the results border on the mystical. A famous scientist, Niels Bohr, once said, 'Anyone who is not shocked by quantum mechanics has not understood it.' Can you clear it up for me?"

He sensed attention.

"OK, quantum mechanics says that at the subatomic level weird things happen. Particles act like both particles and waves, and can be in two different places at the same time. There's a thought experiment called 'Schrödinger's Cat' that illustrates the paradox. It goes something like this. Put a cat in a sealed box with a subatomic particle detector attached to a vial of poison gas. The detector is very sensitive and can detect a particle's presence. The odds are fifty-fifty the particle will appear. If it detects the particle, it releases gas into the box and the cat dies. I suspect Schrödinger didn't like cats. If it doesn't detect it, the vial stays sealed and the cat lives.

"Here's where it gets weird. Quantum mechanics suggests that a subatomic particle can be both over here and over there, until observed. Only by being observed, is the particle locked into one location." He paused, shaking his head. "If you follow this to its conclusion, it means that until someone observes the particle detector's results… the cat is both dead *and* alive. That's absurd! It suggests that *reality isn't real* until an observer observes it." He paused. "The only other way around the paradox is to believe that there are multiple universes being created all the time. In one universe, the cat's dead, but another universe splits off, where the cat's alive. Neither explanation makes sense."

Then why do they believe it?

"Seventy years of experimental results confirm that quantum mechanics works, and many technologies we use require it. In fact, without it, our Blaster wouldn't operate."

Yes?

"Niels Bohr summed it up, 'Nothing is real until it's observed.' That can't be the right interpretation!"

The interpretation, although incomplete, is correct.

Surprised, he blurted out, "That totally sucks!" He didn't expect Jesse to support science's ridiculous interpretation. He shook his head. "So, the stupid philosophical question, 'If a tree falls in the forest and no one hears it, does it make a sound?'... might not be so stupid." He stopped and thought for a moment. "OK, let's take it a step further. If an *observer* is required to *lock in* the outcome... why couldn't they *influence* that outcome? I mean, the whole idea of needing an observer to anchor things into reality is crazy, but if you accept that, it isn't a big leap to think the observer might actually be able to manipulate that outcome."

The Loadmaster came by with box lunches, waking up the passengers and ending Josh's conversation. As she was passing them out, she was humming "How now brown cow." Someone told him that their future base had been nicknamed "Brown Cow." He couldn't figure out how they'd come up with that name, until now. Since Mount Howe was the only landmark, it almost made sense.

Fueled by a dry ham sandwich, apple, and cookie, he decided to tackle another book. He started reading a book on cosmology but then stopped. Thinking about his conversation and quantum mechanics' almost supernatural conclusions, he decided to take a stab at some of the religious books.

He was well into them, when he noticed everyone was asleep again. "Jesse, are you still there?"

Yes.

"OK, quantum mechanics says the observer locks the outcome, but it doesn't say anything about the observer *influencing* that outcome. However, I've found that idea in a number of non-science books, including some very old ones like the Bible. You're going to think I'm an idiot, but I can't help but wonder if it's possible to reconcile quantum mechanics with… well, what I believed was nothing but silly religious beliefs. It's almost as if the further our understanding of the universe goes, the stranger it gets, and the closer it gets to… weird spiritual stuff."

Yes?

"You know, Jesse, I appreciate you helping me think through this, but you kinda stink at answering questions. How about just this once saving us some time and giving me the answer?" He sensed amusement.

The answer is not intuitive. You are doing well. That will be enough for now.

"That's all right, my brain hurts." He felt like he was on the verge of understanding something very important. It was frustrating. The puzzle pieces were there. He just didn't know how to assemble them.

24

MOUNT HOWE

Josh and the others crowded into the cockpit as the C-17 approached Mount Howe. It was mid September, the end of the long, dark Antarctic winter. The sun lit only the mountaintops, with a twilight shadow on the surrounding, featureless, white plain.

As they circled, Oleg, one of Bobinski's men, snapped hundreds of pictures of the ridgeline using a telephoto lens. They were looking for the optimal site at the top and a way to get to it with heavy equipment. Bobinski asked the pilot to circle one more time and go lower.

She was an Air Force test pilot assigned to Boeing. "No problem, I'll go as low as you want, but we'll have to land soon to have enough fuel to make it back."

The landing was rough, as if they were setting down on a cobblestone street. They had brought equipment to change tires if needed. The aircraft finally bumped to a stop and the pilot shut the engines down. She kept the auxiliary turbine running to supply power and heat for the aircraft.

After everyone bundled up in Antarctic gear, they lowered the C-17's giant ramp. Brandon was the first off. As Josh's foot hit the ice, Brandon yelled over the turbine whine, "Welcome to the bottom of the world!"

Josh, feeling a little like the Michelin man, nodded. Their clothing was the best money could buy. It kept his body warm in the twenty-five-below-zero temperature, but his face was partly exposed. Even without much wind, his cheeks stung and his eyes watered, with tears quickly freezing to his face.

Brandon, watching him, smiled. "It's actually spring-like

temperatures for Antarctica."

After adjusting to breathing icicles, the next thing that struck Josh was the eerie twilight. It was the dawn before sunrise with just enough light to read. But it was a perpetual sunrise, with the direction of the sunrise glow rotating slowly around the horizon like the hour hand of a clock.

In the sky to the south, he saw the greenish glow of a faint aurora borealis. Correcting himself, he realized he was in the Southern Hemisphere and said softly to himself, "aurora australis." He'd always been fascinated by them. High-energy particles captured from the sun spiraled down the earth's magnetic pole like water going down a drain. As the particles dove through the atmosphere, they collided with the air. The ghostly green glow was the oxygen molecules' funeral pyre. The crash zone of particles formed a giant circle, 2,000 miles in diameter, centered on the magnetic pole. The aurora, always present, was usually only visible in darkness or when the sun was angrily energetic.

Antarctica was alien enough without the twilight and ghostly glow. As he looked at the horizon and slowly turned, he saw vast plains stretching into the distance until they merged with the gray horizon. He continued to turn until he saw the mountain ridgeline. It jutted out of the plain like a dull circular-saw blade cutting up through a piece of white plywood. Hundred-foot-tall snowdrifts looked like white caulk liberally applied to seal the ridgeline to the icy plain. The mountaintop was the only part high enough to receive direct sunlight. With the sun at his back, the mountaintop looked like a sculpture lit by a spotlight, majestic and surreal.

Looking down, he kicked a layer of dry, loose snow from the underlying ice sheet. He was standing on what looked like a beautiful blue lake, complete with wind ripples frozen in place. The "ripples" stuck up several inches, explaining the rough landing.

Bobinski saw Josh looking down at the ice and joined him. Josh reminded him of the young KGB agents and political officers of the Soviet days. They wielded unchecked power and were universally feared and despised. He had noticed how Scupino sometimes deferred to this man. He suspected he was CIA... too close to KGB.

As Josh kicked the snow off the ice, Bobinski yelled, "Zamboni!"

Josh said, "Pardon me?"

Bobinski came closer and said, "Do you ice skate?"

"Badly. Yes, I know what a Zamboni is." The ice resurfacer was used on rinks everywhere.

Bobinski said, "We use specially built Zamboni on steroids!"

Josh smiled, obviously trying to picture it.

Bobinski continued, "It will scrape ice and fill with hot water until smooth. We create any size runway. Will last for years because of temperature."

"You've done this before?"

"Siberia is not so different." He paused and looked directly at Josh. "Why are you here?"

Josh smiled. "You mean I'm about as useful as a bikini in Siberia?"

Bobinski cocked his head sideways. "Bikini we find use for."

Josh stopped smiling. "Mr. Bobinski, I'm not a spy. I'm actually one of the architects of this program, and I like to imagine I'm smart enough to know where I'm incompetent. I'm here to learn. I may ask questions because it affects other parts of the program, but you're in charge here and have the final say on site decisions."

Bobinski shrugged his shoulders. He liked what Josh said, but talk was cheap. It was hard to overcome suspicions after working with so many that looked and sounded like him.

Bobinski's men slowly drove the snowcats, loaded with supplies, down the C-17 ramp. They were bright orange and looked like large, jacked-up SUVs running on tank tracks.

Before they climbed aboard, Bobinski said, "First we find location for base camp at foot of mountain. It must be big enough area to house workers, fuel depot and communication center. Then we study photographs and choose gentlest path to top."

The ridgeline had a series of small rounded peaks. They drove to the spot directly under the highest peak, Mount Howe, but the giant snowdrifts obscured the bedrock. Bobinski shook his head and directed them to drive parallel to the ridgeline until they found an area of exposed bedrock. It looked like a gentle ski slope of volcanic gravel, but its angle and location allowed the prevailing winds to scour it, keeping it free of snow.

They stopped and got out. Bobinski gave orders to his two engineers, Oleg and Sergei. Brandon, who'd been scanning the ridgeline with powerful binoculars, handed them to Bobinski and suggested a possible ascent point.

Josh joined them. Pointing to the area where Bobinski's men were working, he asked, "Why this site?" He had lifted his goggles so Bobinski could see his face.

Studying him closely to see if he was being micromanaged, Bobinski replied, "We need to be on bedrock close to the mountain peak in case we need to run power lines up."

Josh nodded. "Power lines?"

Bobinski said, "Don't know if we can get reactors to top. Might put reactors down here and run power up with cables."

Josh nodded again and just said, "OK."

Sergei and Oleg set up the foundation perimeter, as the rest of them pulled out the parts for their new home. A sophisticated, partly inflatable Quonset hut, it was anchored to the ground by steel cables. Carbon-graphite ribs, lightweight polymer panels, and a double-layered inflatable skin allowed for rapid assembly. The structure was large, about five by ten meters, but with all of them working together, it went up quickly, despite the steady, subzero wind.

Bobinski noticed that Josh worked hard and quietly took orders from his men. After several snowcat runs back to the C-17, they had installed generators, satellite communication dishes, and a small weather station. Inside, they put in heaters, folding tables and chairs, a small galley, laptop computers, communication equipment, and sleeping bags. It was a full day's work.

After they finished, they went inside.

Bobinski said, "Time to eat and get sleep. Tackle mountain tomorrow." They voraciously ate military pre-packaged field rations and climbed into their sleeping bags.

Josh was the first awake the next morning but had still managed to finish reading two more books before he fell asleep. He read a book on mountain climbing and a Lincoln biography. He wasn't sure which might be more relevant to his current situation.

After another hearty breakfast of military field rations and hot coffee, they sat around a laptop looking at photographs taken from the C-17. Bobinski and his team correlated the pictures into a 3-D representation of the mountain. Usually they used English, but when Bobinski's men got excited, they shifted to Russian. Bobinski would bring them back to English and explain anything that transpired. Finally, Bobinski, stroking his beard and speaking primarily to Brandon, said, "Best path up mountain is obvious from radar mapping and pictures, but may have dangerous areas."

Brandon, pointing at a picture on the screen, said, "Should be able to take the snowcat to here, maybe a little further. Then proceed on foot. There may be some loose slopes and small crevasses. The only way to be sure is to take a look."

Bobinski nodded, and turned to Josh. "We take both snowcats up mountain. You can come along if you stay out of way and help with equipment."

Josh smiled and nodded.

Wedged in the backseat of the second snowcat, Josh sat between boxes of climbing and survey gear. Oleg was driving with Katori in the passenger's seat. The snowcats trundled off along the plain in the shadow of the mountain.

The C-17 and base camp were on a plateau 8,000 feet above sea level. That meant they only had to climb about 1,700 feet to get to the top of Mount Howe. But first, they had to drive several miles to find a slope gentle enough to start their ascent. The snowcat's suspension allowed the tall cab to sway continuously as they climbed. Noticing that Katori looked a little green, Josh was glad his new body wasn't susceptible to motion sickness.

They were halfway up the mountain when they hit an impasse. The mountain ridgeline was 600 feet wide at the top, dropping off progressively to vertical cliffs on both sides. There were also large ripples in the ridgeline, as if someone had tried to compress it along its length. They hit one of the ripples that had split open, creating a small rocky crevasse. It was too wide for the snowcats to traverse. Everyone got out.

Brandon took over. He'd already interviewed everyone to determine their physical fitness and climbing experience. Although

Josh won in the fitness department, he'd never climbed before. Brandon chose Bobinski, Oleg, and Josh, leaving Katori and Sergei behind with the snowcats.

Brandon had already given them a climbing-safety brief at the base camp, but here at the top, he reviewed it. "We shouldn't have to do any exotic climbing, but we'll have to cross a couple of small crevasses. The slope shouldn't be steep, but the combination of loose rock, high altitude, and extreme cold is always dangerous." He smiled, obviously enjoying himself. "We're going where no one has been before! If you have any problems or questions, stop and ask. Don't be stoic."

Brandon helped Josh and Oleg into their climbing harnesses, roping them all together with forty feet of separation. Then he showed them how to assemble and install a small metal footbridge across the crevasse. "Bridge" was an optimistic term. It looked more like a cheap aluminum ladder dropped across the gap and anchored to the rock. Josh, knowing they'd invited him along as a Sherpa, picked up the heaviest pack containing bridge parts and survey equipment.

The first test was crossing the bridge laden with the packs. With no fear of heights, Josh looked down as he crossed. It wasn't that deep compared to the cliff to his left and right, just deep enough to kill you.

After Brandon led them across, he took the lead and put Bobinski, who had mountain-climbing experience, at the back. Josh and Oleg were in the middle.

They moved carefully up the slope until they hit a second crevasse, where they put up another bridge. On the other side, they took a break. Brandon and Bobinski, who had been practicing and working out, were breathing hard. Even Oleg, a long-distance runner, was struggling. Barely winded, Josh loved his new body.

Brandon tapped Josh on the shoulder. Josh turned to see him pointing silently at the sky near the horizon. The aurora had brightened considerably, with soft, undulating curtains of green fire. It was beautiful.

After a short rest, they continued their climb uneventfully. Finally, almost at the top, they stood on a gentle dome of what appeared to be mostly exposed granite. On one side of the dome was a level rock shelf, naturally carved out of the mountain. Bobinski and Oleg pulled cameras and survey equipment out of the packs and started taking pictures and elevation readings. With nothing to do, Brandon disconnected himself and Josh from Bobinski and Oleg. The two of them climbed the last few dozen meters to the very top of the mountain.

As they reached the summit, they were initially facing back toward Bobinski and Oleg, and looking directly into the perpetual sunrise. The tiny C-17 looked like a toy on the plain 1,700 feet below. Josh felt like he was standing on an island. An island of orange, sunset-colored rock surrounded by an ocean of shadow. The plain blended into the sky at the horizon, making it difficult to tell where the earth stopped and the heavens began. It was like something out of a dream.

Brandon said, "Do you realize we're the first to ever stand on top of this mountain? We're at the top… of the bottom of the world."

Josh nodded, thinking there had to be a country song in there somewhere.

They both slowly turned around until the sun was at their backs and they faced the geographic South Pole.

As a ghostly green glow illuminated their faces, Brandon said, "Oh my God!"

During the final climb, the ridgeline hid most of the light-show. Now, standing on the peak, they saw an incredibly energetic aurora. Two 100-mile-high, luminous, gossamer curtains slowly rippled toward each other as if blowing in a gentle breeze. Beautiful, bright white and ghostly green, they blended into a rich translucent red at the top. At the bottom of each curtain was a narrow band of rich purple, as if a cosmic interior designer added a royal fringe. It was a spellbinding and alien vista.

They both stood transfixed for many minutes. Then, Brandon pointed at a star barely visible through the aurora. "Isn't that Jupiter?"

It was the brightest star on the horizon, but still barely visible in the twilight. Josh nodded.

Brandon whispered, "It's passing the orbit of Jupiter right now, isn't it?" Without waiting for a reply, he looked up, adding,

"It's inconceivable that a mountain – a mountain bigger than we're standing on – could fall from the sky." Brandon paused. Then looking back at the aurora, he added, "I feel like a tiny ant on a giant stage… looking up at the bottom of huge theatrical curtains closing after a performance."

Josh, echoing his thoughts, said softly, "I hope it's not the final act."

As they pondered the sheer scale, they saw the two colossal curtains of tortured particles finally meet, becoming one. It was an incredible crescendo. The sky vibrated with a riot of glacially slow, roiling sheets of color. Slowly twisting and turning, they looked as if someone was gently shaking giant curtains from above. Josh stared, awestruck. It was the most beautiful thing he'd ever seen in his life.

Without looking away, Brandon whispered, "Makes it kind of hard not to believe in God."

Interrupting their contemplation, Bobinski yelled up from below.

25

FREEFALL

Josh and Brandon climbed back down quickly and found Bobinski standing on the natural rock shelf, exclaiming, "This is perfect foundation for beam projector and control room."

They gathered and repacked their equipment and started down the mountain, frequently glancing up into the sky. With a downhill traverse, and no more bridge parts to shoulder, the trip went quickly. They crossed the last bridge and reached the snowcats. Disconnecting the rope from their climbing harnesses, they gathered the equipment to load into the cats. Josh stood next to the metal bridge and finished coiling their climbing rope into a bag. Holding the end of the rope with the large metal carabiner clip, he smiled, thinking that yesterday, he didn't know what a carabiner was. He'd only seen them used as key chains.

Looking up, he saw Oleg, free of his tether, venturing toward the edge of the ridgeline. With camera in hand, he was obviously trying to get a picture of the C-17 below with the aurora in the background. Then Oleg, looking through his camera's LCD, stepped on a large patch of ice. As in a Charlie Chaplin movie, his arms began to windmill rapidly, but despite his comical contortions, gravity was winning.

Brandon and Bobinski, standing next to the snowcats, watched the antics with amusement. Oleg finally landed on his back, still clutching his camera.

Assessing the situation, Josh's mind suddenly went into overdrive. His brain instantly projected the outcome and courses of action. He was the closest but still about 100 feet from Oleg. Taking the end of the rope he was holding, he tore his gloves off and quickly clipped it around one of the bridge's metal struts. Reaching into the rope bag, he snatched the other end of the rope and ran toward Oleg.

Oleg had fallen on a part of the ice sheet that wrapped the edge of the ridgeline like a frozen waterfall. The slope got progressively steeper for thirty feet, and then dropped off vertically to the plain, 1,700 feet below. Oleg slid on his backpack toward the edge.

Brandon and Bobinski's expressions changed as they realized what was happening.

Josh was sprinting with the climbing rope uncoiling out of the bag behind him. With his freezing hands, he clipped the end of the rope to his harness. It was too long but he didn't have time to fix that.

He saw Brandon running toward the metal bridge with Bobinski following.

Oleg's arms and legs flailed as he clawed at the ice, trying to right himself, but his heavy gloves prevented him from getting purchase. He was like an upside-down turtle being used as a hockey puck.

Josh ran as fast as he could, but it wasn't fast enough. Oleg passed the point of no return and was about to go over the cliff. With all his strength, Josh launched himself into a dive calculated to intercept Oleg.

A detached part of him asked what he thought he was doing. If the bridge didn't hold, they were both dead. What would become of humanity's battle? Oleg's torso slid over the edge as Josh slammed into him, grabbing his backpack and coat. The impact accelerated both of them over the cliff into freefall. Oleg screamed, clinging to Josh. Their momentum propelled them away from the cliff in an inverted bear hug. Josh was upside down, Oleg, right side up, their heads pressed into each other's chests.

They fell forever, or so it seemed with Josh's hyperactive time-sense.

A hundred feet down, the rope suddenly reached its end, brutally jerking them to a stop like ragdolls on the end of a rope. Josh's harness cut into his torso as Oleg's weight almost pulled his arms from their sockets. As the metal bridge above clanged and shrieked against the rock like fingernails on a chalkboard, their bear hug broke and Oleg slid toward his death. At the last second, Josh caught him by his wrists. If he hadn't shed his gloves, Oleg would be gone.

They looked like a circus trapeze act. Josh hung upside down, holding Oleg by the wrists. As if that wasn't bad enough, he glanced quickly back at the face of the mountain – *not good!* His dive for Oleg pushed them far away from the cliff face. Now, their trapeze was rapidly swinging back toward the rock wall. Josh quickly calculated three things. There was nothing on the smooth cliff to hang on to. The impact with the rock wall was going to hurt, and in their current configuration, even if they survived the impact, they'd never hold onto each other. Using all his strength, he pulled Oleg back up into a bear hug. Twisting his torso so that he'd be between the cliff and Oleg, he knew exactly how Wile E. Coyote felt.

Josh slammed into the cliff back first. Air exploded from his lungs as Oleg's head broke his ribs. It felt like falling on your back from a tall ladder onto concrete… with someone landing on top of you. Even worse, the bridge slid again, slipping them another foot. He was supporting the weight of two men. His harness squeezed his broken ribs, making it impossible to breathe. Stunned and fighting for air, he managed a quick plea to Jesse.

Josh could only whisper. He told Oleg to climb up his body and grab the rope. Frozen with fear, Oleg stuck to him like Velcro. Josh knew he'd lose consciousness if Oleg couldn't transfer his weight to the rope. With the last of his air, he whispered, "Oleg… bridge could fall any time… climb… now!"

Oleg finally looked up and pulled his gloves off. Slowly disentangling himself from the bear hug, he began to climb, using Josh's body as a ladder. Like a boa constrictor, Josh's harness squeezed him tighter. His vision faded. Oleg finally grabbed the rope, taking some pressure off and allowing Josh a shallow, painful breath. Then Oleg lost his grip, falling back on Josh and kicking him in the side. With broken ribs pushed against his lungs, he would have screamed if he had the breath. With no air, Josh's consciousness finally slipped away, bringing relief from the searing pain.

Brandon and Bobinski had reached the bridge and gotten their weight on it just as the rope went taut. Brandon took control. He yelled to Sergei to connect two more ropes to the snowcat and throw them over the side. Then he motioned to Katori to switch places with him. As Katori added his weight to the bridge, Brandon ran to the snowcat. He clipped the new rope to his harness and slid across the ice to the cliff edge. Leaning over, he was surprised to see Josh *and* Oleg hanging 100 feet below. He couldn't believe anyone could hold onto a 200-pound man at the end of a 100-foot fall… much less survive. He yelled down, "Are you all right?"

Oleg yelled back, "*Dah*… not sure about Meadows!"

Brandon took the end of the new rope and clipped its carabiner around the rope holding Josh and Oleg. Sliding it down toward them, he yelled, "Unclip the rope I'm sending down and attach it to your harness! We'll pull you up!" He knew Oleg didn't have the ability to tie it to Josh. He needed to get Oleg's weight off the original rope before the bridge gave out.

He could see Oleg using Josh's body as a shelf while he fumbled with the carabiner with freezing hands. Finally, Oleg clipped the new rope to his harness. Brandon motioned Sergei to back the snowcat slowly away from the cliff. "Oleg, use your arms and legs to keep yourself off the cliff face as we pull you up!" He could see Josh hanging limp in his harness.

They all heard the metallic groan of the bridge as the rope bent the strut it was tied to. Still perched at the edge of the cliff, Brandon yanked his gloves off. Grabbing the second rope attached to the snowcat, he tied it around the rope holding Josh, using a special Prusik knot. Tied correctly, it wouldn't allow the bridge rope to slide through it. But before he could finish, the strut snapped, ripping the unfinished knot from his hand and over the edge.

He saw Josh fall and held his breath as the rope slid by him. Finally, it went taut as his incomplete knot grabbed and held.

Just then, Oleg's head appeared and Brandon told Sergei to stop the snowcat. Oleg scrambled up over the ice slope to a level area.

Brandon once again motioned Sergei to back the snowcat, as he yelled down to Josh, "Can you hear me? We're pulling you up! Try to fend yourself off the cliff!"

Josh woke up as his head banged sharply against rock. He opened his eyes and found himself hanging upside down. The view of the 1,700-foot drop was breathtaking… literally. He wasn't sure he wanted to be awake. As he scraped against the cliff, he was pleased to see he was moving in the right direction for a change. He slowly and painfully righted himself so that he was looking up instead of down. With broken ribs and freezing hands, he used his legs to reduce "cliff rash."

After what seemed like hours but was actually minutes, he reached the top.

Brandon yelled to Sergei to slow the snowcat to a crawl and then stop. Grabbing Josh's arms, Brandon and Bobinski carefully pulled him up over the edge and beyond the ice sheet.

As soon as he was on relatively level ground, he rolled over on his side into a fetal position with his arms wrapped around his chest. Brandon and Bobinski leaned over him. He felt Bobinski gently disconnect the rope from his harness and put his own gloves on Josh's frozen hands. Then he felt them wrap something around his head. Brandon, trying to ascertain Josh's condition, held up three fingers and asked, "How many fingers do you see?"

"Three."

"Do you know where you are?"

"Disney World?"

Brandon smiled and shook his head. "I can give you something for the pain. Are you allergic to anything?"

"Yes."

Brandon leaned closer.

Josh whispered, "Gravity."

Brandon and Bobinski both started laughing. Bobinski said in a conspiratorial tone, "Once we get you off mountain, I have special drink that will help with pain."

Brandon put a pill in Josh's mouth and gave him some water, "We have to get you down. Can you walk to the snowcat?"

Josh nodded, grimacing. Slowly he rolled onto his stomach, trying to get his knees under him. Bobinski and Brandon, taking his arms, helped him stand.

Josh grunted.

Brandon warned, "He may have internal injuries; be careful lifting him."

Josh shuffled like a little old man with Brandon and Bobinski supporting him on each side.

They gently helped him up into the snowcat. Bobinski drove. Brandon and Oleg sat on each side of Josh in the back. Bobinski radioed ahead to have the medic standing by and prepare to leave. Josh grunted, "We don't need to leave. Mission is priority. I'll be fine."

Bobinski said, "*Nyet*. I make decisions here, remember?"

26

MEDIC

There was no privacy in the Quonset hut. Everyone gathered around. Josh watched their faces, as the Air Force medic cut his shirt off. Their flinches and grimaces didn't instill a lot of confidence. Looking down at himself, he saw huge red and purple bruises wrapping around his torso. He also had a deeper, head-shaped bruise over his ribcage and knew his head was bleeding. The medic began a thorough examination. He palpated his chest, listened to his lungs with a stethoscope, and checked him for concussion.

After asking him a few questions, he finally told Josh and the rest of the team gathered around, "I have good news and bad news. The good news is, you're going to live and don't need immediate hospitalization. The bad news is that you don't need hospitalization because there's no real treatment for broken ribs… oh, and your back looks worse than your front."

Josh, seeing the guilt on Oleg's face, winked at him and said, "I was really just trying to get out of carrying those dang bridge parts."

Oleg smiled and Bobinski laughed. "You're officially off active duty list. I prescribe old Russian cure." He reached into his pack and pulled out a bottle of Jack Daniels.

Josh looked at Bobinski with raised eyebrows, and Brandon said, "You're kidding!"

Smiling, Bobinski opened the bottle. "Only *real* American cultural contribution to world."

In a lot of pain, Josh wasn't about to turn down a shot of Jack. He started to stand but the medic said, "Not so fast. I still need to stitch up the holes in your head."

Brandon couldn't resist. "He jumped off a cliff. You don't have enough silk to stitch up the holes in his head."

They laughed as Bobinski toasted, "To holes in head!" and they "clinked" plastic cups and drank in one swallow.

The medic, pointing at the bottle, said, "Go easy on that."

Bobinski said, "Of course," as he poured them another shot.

Despite the pain, Josh couldn't help but smile. Take a Russian industrialist, Russian and American engineers, an American Navy pilot, and a British knighted billionaire. Throw them together into a death-defying adventure, and background, education, and culture evaporate. You end up with a bunch of boys, laughing and scratching. New comrades in arms, they stayed up, sipping Jack and sharing increasingly exaggerated tales.

Mission complete, they flew back the next day. Josh, wanting to maintain a low profile, made all of them promise to play down his role in the rescue. He was relieved when they all agreed. Tired and still in pain, he slept most of the trip.

Scupino met the C-17 as it arrived in St. Louis. As Josh walked stiffly in from the flight line, Scupino came up to him and said, "I'd give you a big hug and kiss if you hadn't busted your ribs."

Josh frowned at Scupino. "Who else knows?"

Scupino, obviously enjoying himself, said, "Oh, just me… and everyone on the team."

Josh frowned as Scupino smiled. "Relax, Josh. News like this travels faster than Facebook, and it's great for team *esprit de corps*." He laughed. "You'd be on YouTube by now if Oleg hadn't dropped his camera over the cliff."

Josh said, "It wasn't that big of a deal."

Scupino looked serious. "Yes, Josh, it was. I'm very proud of you and it's exactly the type of action that helps pull a team together against overwhelming odds. I'd put you in for the Navy Cross, if I knew who the heck you worked for."

Josh shook his head.

Scupino said, "Look, Josh, you put this program in my lap. As the Program Manager, I am recognizing your act on behalf of the entire team." He smiled again and added, "*And*, as a Navy Captain,

I'm ordering you – Commander – to sit quietly while we sing your praises. Is that understood?"

Josh finally gave a half smile. "Yes, sir."

Josh didn't look forward to attending the team meeting the next day. He waited until just before it started and tried to slip in quietly, but as soon as they spotted him, they gave him a standing ovation. He was good at a lot of things; this wasn't one of them. He just shook his head and slipped into his seat. So much for a low profile.

Smiling, Scupino said, "Josh's more comfortable hanging upside down from a cliff than being recognized."

The group laughed, and Josh, trying to be a good sport, nodded.

Scupino continued, "Seriously, the entire survey team did an outstanding job. Josh's act of courage may never be recognized outside of this group, but *we* will know and appreciate having served with men and women like him." Again, there was a strong round of applause.

Finally, to Josh's relief, Scupino said, "Now we have to get back to saving the other seven billion. Mr. Bobinski, can you give us your evaluation of the site, please?"

Bobinski leaned forward and cleared his throat. "Site is suitable, but there are challenges. We surveyed location for runway, base and the beam site at top of mountain. We can put in 20,000-foot runway that will allow us to land," he smiled, "more *delicate* American cargo jets." There were good-natured groans from the Boeing engineers.

Bobinski continued, "But cutting road to top of mountain will be difficult. Requires building bridges over crevasse, cutting road last two kilometers, and flattening mountaintop so Blaster can rotate and stay locked on comet as earth turns." Bobinski paused. "Even with best equipment and men, road will take too much time and creates schedule uncertainty."

Shepherd jumped in with satisfaction. "As I originally stated, it cannot be done in less than a year."

Josh and Scupino had agreed that Shepherd was a bureaucrat who always found reasons things couldn't be done, but it was good to have a devil's advocate asking the tough questions. It kept them honest.

Scupino gave Bobinski a small wink that Shepherd couldn't see.

Bobinski continued in a calm voice, "To make sure we stay on timeline, we build road at same time we are lifting observatory components to top."

Shepherd looked at Bobinski suspiciously. "What do you mean... lifting?"

Josh thought, Bobinski couldn't have paid someone to be a better straight man.

Bobinski continued, "We use H-60 helicopters to lift components to mountaintop, where we assemble them."

Smiling, Scupino added, "Some assembly required."

Bobinski continued, "Prefer good Russian-built helicopter, but H-60 is already designed to fit inside C-17... and Sikorsky was, of course, Russian."

Shepherd whined, "You can't be serious. There's no way helicopters can lift heavy equipment to the top of that mountain."

Without missing a beat, Bobinski continued, "S model H-60 can lift 4,000 kilos and has 12,000-foot service ceiling. Payload is reduced by altitude, but cold, dry air increases turbine power output."

"What about the reactors? There's no way you're going to lift those things up the mountain with their lead shielding," Shepherd said with a smirk.

"Don't have to. Reactors stay at base of mountain. Will run power lines to top."

Scupino, without even looking at Shepherd, asked, "When do you need the helicopters?"

Bobinski said, "Antarctic summer starts in one week. We have six months to complete. Need helicopters yesterday."

They all looked at Shepherd to see if he had a rebuttal.

Shepherd just frowned, shaking his head.

Scupino said, "OK, who has contacts at Sikorsky?"

Major Judy Crowley raised her hand.

"Great. Major Crowley, your mission is to beg, borrow, or steal two H-60s. If you run into problems, let me know. We'll shake some trees."

Crowley smiled and nodded.

Scupino continued, "Chris, is there anything else you need now?"

Bobinski smiled. "*Nyet*. If I need it, I buy it."

Scupino caught Smith as they were leaving and with a grin asked, "You think Josh needs a keeper?"

Smith retorted, "I'm not happy with Bobinski or Brandon, and Meadows' act put himself and the program at risk."

Obviously realizing his humor had fallen flat, Scupino quickly excused himself.

Smith had interviewed the entire expedition team. Oleg was just inexperienced. Bobinski and Brandon, correctly, blamed themselves for not keeping a closer eye on Oleg. Ultimately, however, he knew the fault was his. It was his job to protect the team and he wasn't there when he should have been. He wouldn't make that mistake again.

Although still frustrated with the lack of background information, Smith grudgingly admired what Meadows had done, both intent and execution. He knew it wasn't a grandstand move, because each of the eyewitnesses laughed, recounting Meadows' attempt to keep it quiet. He couldn't help but think Meadows might actually make a good protector, but that wouldn't stop him from finding out who he really was.

III
CHALLENGE

27

BIG BANG

With only a year and a half to impact, Josh knew it was time, probably past time, to figure out when and how to introduce this to the public. He needed to talk to Lopez... but privately. Broaching any of this at a team meeting might raise awkward questions, such as why this team was making public-notification decisions instead of, say... the White House.

Lopez was back in Kansas City recording a TV special. He called her. She told him she'd be finished tomorrow, and they could meet for dinner.

With his need to get back and forth between Kansas City and St. Louis, not to mention his broken ribs, he decided this would be a good time to get a car. He loved performance cars, but ended up buying a two-year-old Ford sedan. He just needed reliable transportation that wouldn't draw attention. Of course, he did manage to find a Ford with a high-performance package. Using cash from Brandon's account, it only took a few minutes to close the deal.

Sliding gingerly behind the wheel, he tried not to bump his ribs. It only hurt when he moved, breathed, or sat still. He hadn't seen a doctor and wouldn't.

He actually enjoyed driving, particularly this time of year when the leaves were starting to change color. It also gave him time to think and it was the first time since Antarctica he had an opportunity to talk to Jesse.

Established on the freeway, he asked, "Jesse, can you talk?"

He immediately sensed his presence.

"If I may, I'd like to continue our conversation. I've been thinking a lot about what you said and its implications." He paused. "If an observer not only locks-in outcomes, but could actually influence them… then, our lives, the world, maybe even the universe, could be controlled by the sentient life in it."

Yes?

"That seems awfully *bio-centric*. Puny bags of protoplasm, created by the universe's accidental mixing of molecules, suddenly start ordering the universe around?"

How did the universe start?

"You're asking me?" He paused. "We think it started with the Big Bang."

How did the Big Bang begin?

"It started from a tiny point, an infinitely small, infinitely dense – all the mass in the universe – point. They call it a singularity."

What is a singularity?

"I don't know. I think 'singularity' is really just a cool scientific term that means – everything we know breaks down and we got no flippin' idea what's going on."

What part of science applies to singularities?

"Well, it's an infinitely tiny point, so quantum mechanics would clearly apply."

Where does quantum mechanics say the singularity came from?

"Well, at the quantum level, not only can particles be in two places at the same time, they can also pop in and out of existence. I guess it just kind of… popped into existence."

When the singularity appeared, what was the state of the universe?

"I'm not sure what you're asking." He paused, a little frustrated. "I mean, at the very beginning there was nothing. Then, there was a singularity."

Silence.

"OK, I guess there were *two* states… *nothingness* and *the singularity*." He thought for a moment. "But according to quantum mechanics, *both* would exist simultaneously until…" He stopped. "Wait! With no *observer*, the singularity couldn't have been *locked* into reality. There'd be no Big Bang. See, there's a paradox."

How do you know there was no observer?

"Because nothing existed before the Big Bang!"

How do you know that?

"Hmm." He paused again. "Good point. The most fundamental law of physics says it's impossible to know what was before a singularity." He began to absorb the implications and had a flash of insight. He started laughing and grabbed his side in pain. Swerving, his tires ran over the rumble strips on the edge of the road. He pulled back into the lane, slowed to the speed limit, and put the cruise control on so he could think it through.

At the subatomic level, quantum mechanics says no state is set and nothing is real until an observer observes it. The Big Bang started at the subatomic level. Wouldn't it be hysterically funny if quantum mechanics required an observer to start the universe? What if... instead of *sentient life* being the result of random combinations of inanimate matter... *inanimate matter* was the result of sentient life?

That brought up a whole slew of new questions. Obviously, believing that *life* was responsible for the universe, instead of the other way around, was crazy and *totally* bio-centric. Josh shook his head. But was that really any weirder than the current explanation of the origin of singularities and the universe? He drove on to Kansas City pondering the idea and its implications. Fascinating and foreign, it was like swishing a new flavor around in his mouth. Instead of mind created by the universe, the universe created by mind...

It was late afternoon as he hit Kansas City. He called Lopez. She had just wrapped up her video shoot and invited him to her house for dinner. That was good, since Lopez's celebrity status meant that fans sometimes interrupted the restaurant meetings. She also promised a new Italian recipe. Despite his pain, Josh looked forward to dinner. Lopez didn't do anything halfway, and he suspected she was an exceptional chef. He told her he'd check into his hotel and then come over. In her usual direct manner, she said, "Food's mostly done. Don't worry about the hotel. Come on over."

28

LITTLE BANG

Josh was impressed. Sheri's house was an imposing but elegant brick home in the best part of town. She met him at the large ornate doors wearing a chef's apron. Mouth-watering aromas of garlic and fresh bread wafted through the air as she invited him in. On the way to the kitchen, he saw a beautifully decorated home with marble floors, cathedral ceilings, and crystal chandeliers. It looked immaculate... until they passed the study. He knew she was an author and surmised that the study and its explosion of papers were off limits to her housekeeper. As they walked by, he nodded toward it and casually asked, "Suicide bomber?"

She laughed.

The kitchen was huge and equally impressive. Beautiful granite countertops and expensive cherry cabinets contrasted the large, commercial gas stove and subzero freezer. This was a cook's kitchen. There was a formal dining-room, but the kitchen had a large island with a wrap-around granite bar. It made sense since most eating and parties ended up in the kitchen anyway.

Sheri handed him a glass of Chianti and put him to work cutting tomatoes for the salad. Pulling the lasagna out of the oven, she set it on the bar to cool. As she added the tomatoes to the salad, she asked, "How are you feeling? How are your ribs?"

Dismissively, he said, "They're fine."

She gave him a "Yeah, right" look, and topped off his wine glass.

She took the garlic bread out of the oven and pronounced the lasagna ready. Putting plates and silverware out, she motioned him to sit at one of the bar stools.

Lopez always wore tailored business suits or sports jackets, but as she pulled off her chef's apron, Josh saw a different side. Her clothes, while still elegant, were casual and much more feminine, *and* she was barefoot. He realized that in the hospital, he viewed her as an obstacle to overcome. Then, later, saw her as a potential ally to recruit. Now, seeing her in a silk blouse and form-fitting skirt, he realized Sheri was a very attractive woman. Opposite to Elizabeth in almost every way, Sheri was dark, more petite, and voluptuously curvy. Their personalities were also very different. Elizabeth was people oriented. Sheri, definitely task oriented, as was he. That similarity explained why he felt comfortable around her. Nevertheless, Sheri really was beautiful. As she sat down next to him, her loosely buttoned top drew his eyes. Suffice it to say, he'd need to keep his eyes above her impressive cleavage and cut himself off after his second glass of wine.

She caught his glance.

He quickly focused on his lasagna. As Josh expected, she was a phenomenal chef.

After several minutes of concerted eating, punctuated by compliments to the chef, Sheri started the conversation. "Josh, what's the story on Tim Smith?"

Wiping delicious tomato sauce and cheese from his face, he said, "He's supposed to be one of the best security specialists the CIA has. Why?"

"Yes, I've heard he's extremely competent. I've talked to him a few times. With his job, he has to remain detached… but there's something else there." She shook her head. "Josh, I'm not trying to be nosy." She paused. "But his *affect* is flat. He almost exhibits symptoms of…" She stopped and looked back at him. "I don't want to jump to conclusions. Can you tell me anything about his background?"

Josh asked, "Are you concerned about *him*, or his ability to carry out his job?"

"As a psychiatrist, I have to say our mental health affects everything we do."

Josh realized that Smith's job was to protect and monitor the team, but who was monitoring him? Sheri was the most qualified and might be able to help him. "Carl did give us some background.

Obviously, we want to hold this in the strictest of confidence."

She nodded.

"Carl said Tim was one of the CIA's best field agents. His specialty has always been protection. He has a natural instinct and passion for it. When you think of protection, you don't usually think about killing people, but I guess it's like an offensive tackle protecting the quarterback. I gathered from Carl that Tim can be quite deadly. In order to protect, he's had to kill a number of assassins and terrorists over the years." He paused. "About a year ago he was involved in an operation in Turkey. They assigned him to protect a European Union Commissioner under a terrorist death threat. The man he was protecting was married and neglected to tell Tim that he was involved in an affair. Evidently, the Commissioner's mistress tried to sneak into the house late one night. Dressed in black, she came in through a window, carrying something that looked like a gun. Tim shot and killed her." He shook his head. "Tim was exonerated by the agency and the entire event was hushed up."

Sheri frowned but said nothing.

"Carl said he's as effective as he ever was, but, understandably, his heart isn't in it anymore. He told Carl he was going to retire. They're friends and Carl asked him to do this final job. Considering the nature of our mission, Carl thought it would be good for Tim and allow him to retire on a high note."

Sheri softly repeated, "Retire…"

Josh asked, "Does that help?"

She sighed. "Yes… unfortunately, it does."

Frowning, Josh said, "Sheri, I don't mean to sound insensitive, but with what we have at stake, do you think his condition could endanger the program?"

She shook her head. "I'm not sure." She paused. "Everyone faces tragedies in different ways. I'll try and talk to him."

As Josh finished his second helping of lasagna, Sheri changed the subject. "OK, Josh, what can I help *you* with?" With an impish smile, she added, "Relationships? *Fear of Flying*?"

Josh's eyebrows went up with concern, until he realized she was referring to the novel. He smiled. "Is there anyone who doesn't struggle with relationships?"

"Yeah, dead people."

He laughed, thinking, that wasn't true. He said, "Actually, I need your brain."

Smiling, she said, "Just my brain?" Then quickly added, "Yes, of course, what do you need?"

After a quick double take, he said, "How do we prepare the public for the inevitable discovery of a planet-killing comet?"

She nodded. "I've been thinking about that a lot. I believe we need to leak the information slowly. I have an idea but I need to talk to Brandon first. Give me a week and I'll give you a plan."

Josh nodded. "You've got it."

She moved their empty plates to the sink and topped off their wine glasses. Then she turned to him and said, "Now, off with your shirt. Let me take a look at those ribs."

He said with surprise, "You're a psychiatrist."

Sarcastically, she said, "Josh, *hello*. Psychiatrists have to go to medical school, too. I can handle broken ribs."

Josh thought, no possible way! Doctor or no doctor, Sheri Lopez was looking way too hot and he had two glasses of wine onboard. With her hands on him... well, he wasn't sure he trusted himself and didn't need any more complications, particularly after Kelly and... Elizabeth. Seeing that she wasn't backing down, he told her the truth.

"Sheri, I'm sorry. I didn't mean to offend. The real reason is... me. Unfortunately, you are looking like *waaay* gorgeous. I don't drink much and haven't been with..." He shook his head. "I don't mean to be crass but you're starting to look like dessert," he finished with a sheepish smile.

She smiled back warmly. "Thank you, Josh, for being honest and thank you for the compliment."

Josh's phone rang. Saved by the bell. "Sheri, this is Scupino. He doesn't usually call unless it's important. I'm sorry; do you mind if I take this?"

"Of course not."

He stood up and walked around her living-room as he talked.

Sheri smiled to herself. Dessert? She'd been thinking the same thing. His confession only made him that much more endearing, but it wasn't just his earnestness. He seemed like a tragic Greek hero – throwing himself over a cliff to save another, yet carrying a profound sadness. She had no idea what happened to him, but knew instinctively, and professionally, he'd faced death and carried a secret. She thought wryly, he was a psychiatrist's dream! That, mixed with a great bod and a couple glasses of wine… She didn't need his confession to confirm that he was attracted to her, but there was something holding him back. It was just another challenge and she loved challenges. With a sly smile, she said under her breath, "We *are* going to play doctor… one way or another."

As he returned and sat down, she asked, "Everything OK?"

He looked a little surprised. "Scupino just called to check up on me. He asked if I had had my ribs looked at." Josh winked at her. "I told him I'm seeing a doctor."

With a disgusted smile, she shook her head. "Josh, he's right. You really need to let someone look at them."

He shrugged. "That's the least of my problems."

She had an idea. "Josh, may I ask you a personal question?"

"Yeah… I guess."

Watching him closely, she asked, "When was the last time you talked to Elizabeth?"

He looked down. "June 10th."

Bingo! She caught the flicker of pain across his face. It said it all. Here was one of his *internal* contusions. Some of her colleagues looked down on psychiatry, but diagnosing and treating *this* type of injury was often harder than fixing broken bones. Using the classic listening technique, she repeated, "June 10th?"

He nodded. "It was right after you set up the meeting with Brandon."

She tapped her finger to her lips and said slowly, "Right after… *we* had dinner." Uh oh. She realized that it was probably good she put on the brakes. Indulging in "dessert" might have added serious complications for him. "Josh, did you try to contact her after that?"

"Yeah, I sent her a check in the mail about a week later."

"A check?"

"Yeah, paying her back for some money she loaned me while I was reestablishing my identity."

"You wrote a note with it?"

"Of course, I thanked her for everything."

"You *thanked* her for everything."

He nodded.

"That was it? That was all it said?"

Looking worried, he said slowly, "Yes…"

"Josh, have you called her?"

"Several times, but she never answered."

"Did you leave messages?"

"No, except for the last time. A couple weeks ago, I finally left a message asking if she was all right. She texted me back."

Sheri raised her eyebrows in question.

"She said she was fine."

"She said… *fine*?" She couldn't help but give him the "flinch" look. The one you give someone who just missed the nail with the hammer and hit their thumb.

He sighed. "*Fine* doesn't mean fine, does it?"

She shook her head and said softly, "Josh, may I make an observation?"

"Please."

"When you were in the hospital, I gave you a comprehensive battery of mental and psychological tests. You have some amazing abilities."

He shook his head and was about to object, but she held up her hand.

"Your IQ is at the top of the measurable scale, and you have a photographic memory, don't you?"

He nodded.

"But as a psychiatrist, the thing that impresses me the most is your EQ or Emotional Quotient. You have outstanding people skills. As a celebrity, I've had the opportunity to work with people who have exceptional talents, but I've rarely come across someone with all of this in one," she winked, "rather impressive body. Do you have any idea how rare it is to have your IQ *and* EQ?" She smiled. "Particularly, in a man?"

He laughed. "You're building me up because you're about to say I'm totally clueless with regard to Elizabeth."

"See? You're very perceptive and absolutely right. You're a complete blockhead with regard to Elizabeth, and I think you totally missed the boat." Gently squeezing his arm, she added, "Don't be too hard on yourself, you're only human." Only partly joking, she added, "You *are* human... right?"

"Yeah, but your assessment of my EQ must be wrong."

"Not at all. You're exceptional at reading everyone, except yourself. Don't feel bad, no one can. If they could, I wouldn't have a job."

"But I obviously can't read Elizabeth either."

Laughing, she said, "Part of it is simply that you have a handicap... you're male." More seriously, she added, "Your real challenge is that you're emotionally attached. You're too close. It's like trying to read yourself."

He frowned, shaking his head.

"Josh, it's like looking outside through a window at night. You can see outside clearly... until you turn a light on inside the room. *That light is like emotion.* Once it's on you can't easily see outside anymore. In fact, the only thing you can see clearly... is your own reflection."

He nodded, obviously deep in thought.

She had an idea. Originally, she planned to let him stay at her house – one way or another – but not now. Looking at her watch, she said, "I didn't realize how late it was. Josh, you need sleep to heal. Can we talk more tomorrow?"

He nodded, looking a little surprised at the sudden transition.

She asked, "You're staying in Kansas City tonight, right?"

"The airport Holiday Inn Express."

"Great, I'll call you tomorrow morning."

Standing up, he thanked her for dinner.

As she walked him to the door, he moved slowly, obviously in significant pain. Poor guy, hurting inside and out, and she might have had something to do with the *inside* hurt. She knew what she had to do.

29

REUNITE

There was a knock on his hotel room door. Josh put his e-book reader down and frowned. It was after eleven o'clock. There was only one person who knew he was here.

He opened the door expecting Sheri, and found Elizabeth. Stunned, he just stood there.

Finally, raising her eyebrows and gesturing inside, she asked, "May I come in?"

"I'm sorry. Of course… of course!"

As she entered, she held up a small black bag. "I'm here on business. I heard about your *accident* at the Pole."

"How did you know about that?"

Looking serious, she said, "YouTube."

"YouTube?!"

Finally smiling, she said, "I'm kidding. Sheri called me. She said you refused to let her examine you and knew you wouldn't see a doctor."

He knew his guilty look confirmed it.

She went straight to the bathroom sink and started washing her hands. "So, let's get that shirt off and have a look."

"That won't be necessary."

Talking over her shoulder, she said without humor, "Josh, that's a direct order from your medical support team. Do we need to get Scupino involved?"

He frowned but started unbuttoning his shirt. As she came out of the bathroom, she saw him struggling and helped him pull the sleeves over his hands.

She shook her head as she saw his torso. "You look like you've been playing dodge ball with pipe wrenches."

He couldn't help but smile.

She opened her bag and put her stethoscope on. Frowning as she looked at his neck and head, she said, "Didn't they put any bandages on these lacerations?"

"Yeah, but I took them off to take a shower and…"

She finished, "You couldn't get them back on *by yourself*."

He shrugged.

She pointed at the giant black-and-purple bruise over the left side of his ribcage. "Let me guess, that's a likeness of Oleg?"

He laughed, followed by an "Ouch."

She shook her head. "All right, this may hurt a bit but I need to feel your ribs to see how they're healing. Sit down in that chair." She leaned over and gently ran her hands across his chest, sliding them over his ribcage and pushing in lightly.

It did hurt.

Nodding, she said, "It's your two middle ribs. They're the ones most likely to break." She warmed her stethoscope and told him to breathe deeply. She listened in several places on his chest and then went behind him to put it on his back. She whistled softly. "Yeah, that's going to leave a scar or two."

She didn't sound that sympathetic.

Pulling two pill bottles and some ointment out of her bag, she said, "Your lungs are clear and your ribs seem to be healing well. We could wrap your chest but that tends to restrict your breathing and can increase the chance of pneumonia. I'll put some antibiotic ointment on the lacerations." She went to the sink. "You have some major hematomas. I'll massage the tissue around the bruised areas to improve blood flow." She came back with six pills and a glass of water.

"What are these?"

"Just prescription-strength ibuprofen for the pain, and melatonin."

"Melatonin?"

"It's something your body produces to help you sleep. It's an antioxidant and it's good for you. Doesn't matter how tough you are, you need sleep to heal."

It *had* been difficult sleeping lately, for several reasons. One of them was standing in front of him. He gulped the pills down, saying, "Pills don't have much effect on me."

Moving behind him, she rubbed the ointment into the cuts on the back of his head and neck. It stung a little. Then she started to massage his shoulders, where his body took a lot of the impact.

"You're very tense," she said. "If we're going to promote circulation, you're going to have to relax a little."

It hurt at first, but the awesome sensation of her hands quickly overshadowed the pain. "Elizabeth, I need to tell you something."

He heard, "Uh huh," from behind him.

"I think I owe you an apology. There may have been a... a miscommunication."

She didn't respond.

"Sheri helped me understand that it's probably my fault."

He couldn't see her face and she still said nothing.

"I just learned that *fine* doesn't mean fine."

He heard her stifle a laugh.

Frowning, he said, "Sending that check without talking to you first was probably dumb." The massage pressure suddenly increased. "Ouch."

The pressure eased. "Apology accepted. Now shut up and relax."

He closed his eyes. His pain diminished. His *body* didn't hurt as much either. He forgot how good a massage could feel. It wasn't sexual; it was just incredibly relaxing and comforting.

She slowly moved around to face him and worked on his shoulders from the front. A detached part of him realized that this was the first time this body had ever experienced any significant human touch. After several minutes, she worked on his upper arms and then slowly worked across his chest. Moving around his side and down his chest, she gently massaged his stomach. His eyes opened. The massage was no longer increasing circulation just to his bruises. He reached out and gently touched her waist, and then suddenly remembered. "Oh! I forgot. I have something for you!"

She looked a little surprised as he stood up and went over to his suitcase. He said, "It was a present I was going to send with the check, but I decided to wait and give it to you in person." He shook his head. "Not such a brilliant plan in retrospect." As he opened his suitcase, he saw her pick up his e-book reader.

Sitting on the edge of the bed, her face illuminated by the reader, she said, "Have you read all these?"

Rummaging through his bag, he said, "All but two."

"There are over a *hundred* books in here… on a huge range of topics!" Frowning and giggling, she said, "You read a book on Cosmetology?"

He looked up, laughing. "*Cosmology.*"

"Oh."

He frowned. He was sure he had put it in here somewhere…

Obviously reading from the cosmology book, she said, "Big Bang… that sounds interesting."

He found it! Pulling the small box from his bag, he said, "Ah, yeah, it is. The theory on how the universe expanded from an infinitely dense and tiny point."

Under her breath, he heard her say, "Speaking of infinitely dense…"

"What?" He looked up. She'd been rolling her eyes but quickly smiled at him. "Uh… I mean, how do they know the universe came from an infinitely dense… point?"

Setting the little box on the desk, he said, "They just looked at where the universe is now, and kind of rolled it back in time. It's like playing a movie backwards. Ultimately, the universe, and the Big Bang explosion that created it, ends up collapsing into a tiny dot called a singularity."

"What's a singularity?"

Déjà vu, but he was better prepared this time. "Some say it's a hole in space and time. I'd say, more accurately, it's a hole in our knowledge."

Frowning, she asked, "What was before the Big Bang?"

Weird. Almost the exact same questions. "Why the sudden interest?"

"Just curious," she said casually.

"Well, before the Big Bang there was nothing, not even time or space, but we really can't know for sure."

She stood up, setting the e-book reader down. "Let me

summarize. The universe started from absolutely nothing, blew up in a flash, and they don't know what was before it or what started it."

"Uh… yeah, basically."

"Cool," she said with casual confidence. "Then I do understand."

Looking surprised, he said, "You do?"

"Duh. The earth was without form and void, and darkness was on the face of the deep. And God said, 'Let there be light;' and there was light."

He smiled, shaking his head. Of course, she would bring it back to her simple religious beliefs. Then a thought struck him. Before the Big Bang there was no matter, no energy, nothing – versus – "without form and void, and darkness was on the face of the deep." Then, the singularity exploded in a blast of pure energy – versus – "Let there be light"… Light *is* energy. He realized his physics description wasn't a heck of a lot different, or even more informative, than Elizabeth's biblical one. Obviously, he preferred the science version, but… it was interesting in light of his conversation with Jesse about the need for an *observer*.

Elizabeth excused herself and went to the bathroom.

So he wouldn't forget, he picked up the little gift box and sat down in the overstuffed chair. He hadn't realized how big a hole there was in his life until he saw her at the door. His physical pain was hardly noticeable anymore. He wasn't sure how amorous he could be in his present condition, but he could think of nothing better than holding her.

Elizabeth came out of the bathroom with a mischievous grin… only to find Josh asleep in the overstuffed chair. She rolled her eyes, mimicking him quietly. "Pills don't have much effect on me." Taking the pillow and blanket from the bed, she tucked him into the chair. As she did, she saw the little beat-up gift box in his hand. She shook her head and smiled. There was no way she was going to wait another three months. Carefully slipping it out of his fingers, she leaned over and kissed him gently on the lips.

As she drove home, she knew Sheri was right. It was all just a dumb misunderstanding, and it was as much her fault as his. Sheri had confirmed that there wasn't, and hadn't been, any romantic relationship between him and Sheri. She smiled. Sheri had also told her, however, that if she ever got tired of him, to let her know.

There was still the question of who Josh really was. She was puzzled. He sure didn't sound like any prophet she'd ever read about. In fact, he seemed theologically challenged. Then a thought occurred to her. Maybe he was just helping her think through things to clarify them in her mind. She laughed. The whole thing seemed surreal.

It was well past midnight, but she had promised Sheri she'd call and tell her the outcome.

When Sheri answered, Elizabeth said, "You were right on both counts. Although brilliant, he *is* clueless and had no idea what he did. And yes, he lied about his injuries."

Sheri asked, "How bad?"

"Nothing fatal, but he's a mess. He's got two broken ribs, and probably fractured a couple more. He also has major bruising and lacerations covering 50 per cent of his torso. I gave him 800 milligrams of Motrin and 6 milligrams of melatonin."

Sheri asked, "Are you still with him?"

Elizabeth laughed. "No! By the time we finished talking and I came out of the bathroom, he was sound asleep."

Sheri laughed. "Men."

"Thank you, Sheri! I can't tell you how much I appreciate your calling me and getting this straightened out."

"Glad to help." There was a pause. "Elizabeth, would you mind if I gave your number to Carl Casey's wife?"

"Carl's the CIA guy, right?"

"Yeah. Scupino told me that Kelly had a similar situation to yours. She lost her husband in an aircraft accident after being married for only a year. I've met her and think you guys would hit it off and might be good for each other."

"Sure. I'd love to talk to her. Sheri, thanks again! You are such a life saver."

"No problem. Get some sleep, girl."

After Elizabeth got home, she opened the little gift box. Inside she found a painted Russian doll. Nested inside were seven progressively smaller dolls. As she opened the last one, she found a little wooden heart inside. Wrapped around it was a gold necklace. As she pulled it out, she saw a tiny handwritten note. *"Thank you for helping me find myself and believing in me. I love you. Josh."* She tried not to cry as she realized he'd written the note months ago.

30

PROBLEM

Lopez saw the limo pull up in front of her house. She grabbed her jacket and went outside. The driver held the door open for her. As she slid in, she leaned over and kissed Brandon on the cheek. "Hi, Edward. Sure you can't stay for dinner?"

"Would absolutely love to but I've got to be in Ecuador tomorrow morning." He gave her an appreciative up-and-down look. "Sheri, you're even more beautiful than when we met fifteen years ago." He frowned. "Why was it that we didn't work out again?"

She laughed. "You're kidding?" She shook her head. "We're the exact same personality. Highly motivated, task oriented… eventually we'd have to kill each other."

He laughed, shaking his head. "Oh yeah, I forgot. Regardless, you look great and it's good to be working with you again." He paused. "On to saving the world. On the phone, you said you had a solution. I assume you were referring to – how we're going to break this to the world?"

"Yes." Looking thoughtful, she started slowly. "We all have a fascination with the unknown. Did you know that the second biggest commercial holiday after Christmas is Halloween? People love mysteries and conspiracies."

Brandon nodded. "OK."

"Instead of telling people directly what's going to happen, we leak it, and then deny it. It's weird, but people are often more likely to accept something if they believe it's a secret. The beauty of a conspiracy is that it can't be proven wrong, because anyone who attacks it…"

Brandon finished, "Must be part of the conspiracy."

She nodded. "It also allows people to get used to an idea a little at a time. Just like people, societies can go into shock, causing very bad things to happen."

Brandon nodded. "Sounds good, but how do we do that so we get international exposure without ending up in the tabloids?"

She smiled. "That's where you come in. You've got a huge and reputable media division. We need *you* to start leaking some vague comet-danger information to your media people. Tell them it came from a high-level US government official on condition of anonymity. Coming from you, they'll accept it immediately. Then we have the US government deny it."

Brandon frowned. "Josh was OK with this?"

"Yeah, he said government denial wouldn't be a problem." She paused. "By the way, after spending time with Josh in Antarctica, what do you think of him?"

Brandon grinned. "He threw himself off a cliff; he's a complete lunatic."

Sheri nodded, smiling, "Yeah, I love him too." She shook her head. "Anyway, we can also put some key words in the leak. Words that people can google."

"Google?"

"After hearing a rumor, people often check things out on the Internet. We can use key words like 'Dark Comet' and 'Shiva Hypothesis' in the leak. That'll allow people to educate themselves and forward the information to others. The more it's looked up, the higher it's ranked in the search engines. The higher it's ranked, the easier it is to find, et cetera."

Brandon shrugged. "Makes sense."

She smiled, looking out the window. "I have to admit, it's kind of fun being in on a conspiracy."

Looking at her seriously, he said, "*In* on a conspiracy?... Sheri, you're creating it."

She laughed. "Got to be a couple books in here somewhere."

It was late October, seven months since Josh's return and five months before they had to start deflecting the comet. As usual, he and Scupino were the first in the conference room. Sheri arrived next. He hadn't seen her since their dinner in Kansas City. He gave her a quick hug and whispered in her ear, "Thank you, Sheri, you are a goddess!" She winked and hugged him back.

The meeting came to order. Scupino said, "Katori's still at Los Alamos, but he said work's going well on the Comet Asteroid Tracking and Projector Beam Deflector... dang, that's way too long. Hey, what's a good nickname for this thing?"

One of the Air Force engineers said, "Let's use the Navy's naming system and call it ComAstTraProBeaDef!"

Everyone laughed. The Navy's strange habit of using the first few letters of each word often ended in unpronounceable or comic results. Without missing a beat, Scupino fired back, "No, no, let's use the Air Force's superior acronym system. We'll call it – let's see, that would be – Cat Pee!" There were groans and more laughter. A lively discussion ensued. Finally, by adding "Laser" and ignoring order or grammar, they came up with "CAT Blaster."

Josh thought wryly, Schrödinger would've been proud.

Smiling, Scupino said, "OK, now that we've got the important work done, we can continue with the pesky technical details. Katori said they're building the first scale model for testing, and it appears to be ahead of schedule. How are we coming on the power source?"

Shepherd said, "We found the perfect small reactor. Made by a Los Alamos spin-off company called Hyperion, it's an easily transportable, sealed module about the size of a hot tub. With a small steam turbine, it can produce twenty-five megawatts of power and costs only 50 million."

Scupino said, "Awesome! When can we get it?"

Shepherd said, "The first ones are being built now and should be ready next year."

Scupino, obviously holding back irritation, said, "Dr. Shepherd, we need to be feeding power to this thing in six months."

Surprisingly, Bobinski jumped to Shepherd's defense. "Shepherd's right. They are perfect for our purpose and we should put in priority order as soon as possible. Even offer bonus for faster production."

Scupino frowned but nodded.

Bobinski continued, "Until then, there are two small graphite-moderated reactors in Chukokta, Russia. They've produced eleven megawatts each since 1976. They're upgrading to newer reactors. They will sell old ones to us with new uranium cores. They're big, heavy and need more assembly and monitoring, but they're robust and we can buy them now. They can fill gap until modular reactors are ready."

For the first time, Shepherd didn't have a rebuttal. Although still frowning, he actually nodded his head.

Scupino said, "How soon can we get these, and not that it really matters, but how much do they cost?"

Bobinski smiled. "We can have in one month. Negotiated special two-for-one price, 15 million for both reactors, but need additional 5 million in cash."

"Sounds great." He paused. "Do I really want to ask what the cash is for?"

Bobinski continued matter-of-factly, "Cash ensures reactors delivered in good working condition."

Scupino asked, "Five million?"

"Offered two-week trip to Disney World to all plant workers and managers if reactors delivered on time and stay operational for twelve months. We also buy new computers and patrol cars for local police." He smiled. "They help avoid unnecessary paperwork and escort reactors to airfield where C-17 picks them up. Also paid local – how do you say – mob?"

Scupino said, unnecessarily, "Mob?"

"Yes, we pay mob to protect shipment from criminals."

Smiling, Scupino shook his head. "Glad you're on our side."

Listening to the sums expended, Smith didn't feel bad about what he had charged for his services. The money would go directly into the anonymous trust fund for the children of Maria Chevalier... the woman he killed. She had three small children. The funds would provide for them as they grew up and cover their college education. The money from this job, combined with his savings and life insurance, should fill the fund, allowing him to retire. He'd carefully planned exactly how he was going to retire so that the insurance would go to the trust fund. He thought wryly, at least *retiring* people was one of his areas of expertise.

In a classified briefing room at the National Reconnaissance Office, Northrop Grumman briefed the program status of their newest spy satellite. Dr. Jackie Jones wrapped up her PowerPoint presentation. The last slide highlighted the program's recent and significant schedule slips. At the bottom, it simply read, "Lead Engineers Tasked with Higher Priority Program." She knew that would stir up discussion.

The Deputy Director of NRO said, "What higher priority program?"

Jones said, "We don't know, sir. It's black like ours but it's important enough that it pulled our lead engineer and most of his team away."

The Deputy Director shook his head. "We're a Defense Category One, Top Secret program. Who could have higher priority?"

She shrugged. "Just conjecture based on Dr. Cho's area of expertise…"

"Air Force?"

"That would be my guess. He did their airborne laser."

He sighed. "If this continues, it's going to kill our schedule. I'll talk to the Director."

Dr. Garrett Cho asked the test technician, "How much longer?"

"Capacitors will be at full charge in twenty minutes."

Just then, one of Cho's engineers came in with a boxful of Slurpees. Cho loved the frozen drinks and had corrupted his entire team. While waiting, his four young engineers and physicists sat around sucking Slurpees. Cho lifted his Slurpee and toasted, "Happy Thanksgiving." They returned his toast with grins.

The youngest, tallest and skinniest, Greg Langlois, was an electrical engineer and software wizard. He asked Cho, "You think this one will work?"

Cho said, "Absolutely."

Langlois smiled. "You always say that. What makes you so sure this time?"

Cho shrugged. "It has to. It's the last mirror."

Langlois said, "Uh oh."

Cho shook his head. "Relax, dude. We'll figure it out."

"No… it's not that. I just got a brain freeze."

Their optical engineer laughed. She said, "That's not good. Your brain can't afford to work any slower than it already does."

Their team physicist added, "Brain freeze is a simple heat-transfer problem. All we have to do is dunk your head in boiling water for a few minutes."

The optical engineer winked at Cho. Then she said, very seriously, "Greg, push your thumb against the roof of your mouth. The heat and pressure from your thumb is supposed to help."

As Langlois complied, the cell phones came out.

Knowing Greg's image would probably become a screen saver, Cho laughed hard enough to spit Slurpee.

He enjoyed working with his young team. They were irreverent and frequently dissed each other, but they worked well together and were creative, particularly Langlois. He might be gullible, but he was probably the brightest on the team.

The test technician finally reported, "Doctor, the capacitors are at full charge. Ready to fire when you are."

The chamber looked like a submarine with portholes. Heavily armored, the walls were high-strength steel, several inches thick. The "portholes" were even thicker bulletproof glass.

After the final checks, the technician counted down, "Five, four, three, two, one."

There was a loud bang like a shotgun blast.

"Dang it!" Cho said with real frustration. "There goes another one." He didn't have to see the test chamber to know what happened.

After it cooled, they opened it and Cho dutifully peered inside. He saw tiny beads of melted glass sprayed across the metal walls and windows. He pulled his head out and each of the others peered in. As Langlois pulled his head out, he asked, "Any other mirrors we could try?"

Cho shook his head, "No, this company has the best and most reflective mirrors in the world. This was their newest prototype."

The optical engineer said, "No mirrors can handle this much

energy. We're vaporizing them and we're not even running at full power."

The physicist said, "Yes, but you have to be impressed by our laser's power-conversion efficiency. We're cranking out some serious photons."

The optical engineer shook her head. "Unless we figure out how to get a tight beam out of the atmosphere, we're dead." She raised her eyebrows and added softly, "Maybe literally."

31

UNCOVERED

The Deputy Director of the CIA, Brian Davidson, rarely closed his office door. He wanted to make sure his people knew they had access to him in a world where access was tightly controlled. There was a knock on the doorframe. The Deputy looked up to see one of his directors.

"Sir, got a minute?"

"Sure, what's up?"

"Got a complaint from the Director of the NRO."

"A complaint?"

"Yeah, it appears our next-generation spy-satellite program is being delayed by some other super-secret program."

Davidson sighed. "What else is new? Do we know anything about the other program?"

"Well, NRO already checked with the Director of National Intelligence and she didn't know anything about it. DNI thought it might be Air Force, but the Air Force claims they don't know anything either. In fact, they're whining that one of their programs is affected too." He laughed. "Course, they immediately blamed the Navy." He smiled. "I think the Air Force/Navy football game must be coming up."

Looking back at his paperwork, Davidson said, "Black defense programs are usually the worst-kept secrets. What's the rumor mill say?"

"Well, that's the weird part. Rumors are hinting at extraterrestrial stuff and the South Pole."

Davidson sat up in his chair, interested for the first time. "Really?"

"Yeah, normally we'd dismiss it like all the other silly rumors, but this program's sucked up several big-name engineers and scientists."

Nodding, Davidson said, "Check your sources. If it still looks interesting, we'll take it to the boss."

It was early December. Josh noticed the meeting had ballooned to forty people.

Scupino started it with, "OK, we're T minus three and a half months to our first operational firing. Dr. Lopez, how's our cover story holding up?"

"So far, so good, but there's a simple law about secrets." She glanced meaningfully around the room. "The chances of a leak... go up exponentially with the number of people involved. It isn't a question of if... but when."

Scupino nodded. "Dr. Katori, how's our CAT Blaster coming?"

Katori looked concerned. "We have a serious technical hurdle with the beam correction. Cho's still at Los Alamos trying to figure out options."

"What's up?"

"The scale-model Blaster is performing beautifully. This thing has an incredible energy-conversion ratio. If we'd been able to do this a couple decades ago, we could've built an impenetrable missile defense. They still have to figure out how to scale it up and get the aiming system configured but I'm not worried about that right now. The problem is the beam correction. We're using a concept from optical astronomy. They've used it for years to take better pictures by correcting for a light beam's passage through the atmosphere."

Scupino said, "I understand the concept but can you explain the details?"

Katori said, "We're bouncing the laser beam off of a deformable mirror. Tiny servos in the back of the flexible mirror rapidly make minuscule changes to the mirror's shape. Those changes compensate for atmospheric distortion. A low-powered guide laser, fired up through the atmosphere, tells the computer how to manipulate the mirror's surface. It reshapes it hundreds of times a second. It's a tried and true system."

Scupino said, "Sounds good so far. What's the problem?"

"This system will keep the beam collimated – ah, focused – enough to burn the comet even at the huge distances involved. The problem is the power. In a matter of milliseconds, this mirror is trying to reflect a billion-watt beam."

"So...?"

"Captain, no mirror is perfect. I mean no mirror can reflect 100 per cent of incoming light. The best of the best are remarkable at over 99.99 per cent."

Scupino nodded. "Even if the mirror only absorbs a tiny fraction of a per cent, one hundredth of a per cent, times a billion watts would be..."

Katori finished, "Ten kilowatts. It's vaporized every mirror. Without correction, we can't focus the beam enough to hit the comet."

A discussion ensued among the engineers. The debate heated up. In each case, they discarded the ideas due to physics, technology, or time.

Finally, during a brief silence, Josh asked, "What causes thunder?"

Everyone stopped talking and someone said, "What?"

He repeated the question. "What causes thunder?"

All eyes turned toward him with expressions varying from confusion to irritation. Josh knew his question sounded like, "If a tree falls in the forest..."

With a slightly patronizing tone, one of the young engineers said what others were thinking. "Lightning?"

Josh smiled. "Really? The electric discharge generates the sound?"

The engineer looked a little less confident. "Well no, I think it's more like a... a sonic boom."

Not letting up, Josh said, "From?"

One of the senior physicists jumped in and said in a lecture tone, "It's caused when the electric discharge superheats the air to tens of thousands of degrees. The hot air expands faster than the speed of sound, creating a sonic boom, and then falls back into the vacuum..." His expression suddenly changed from lecture mode to interest. "A vacuum or *hole* in the air is created."

Chandra grinned as the scientists and engineers looked at each other with raised eyebrows. Several conversations began.

Scupino grinned at Josh and shook his head. Finally, he held up his hand for silence. When it quieted down, he tentatively asked, "Is it possible, instead of correcting our beam, we could punch a sort of pilot hole through the atmosphere, just before we fire the main beam?"

Chandra winked at Josh and clarified, "Fire the beam twice in rapid succession, with the first shot superheating the air and opening a vacuum tunnel for the second?"

The physicist who'd explained thunder said, "It won't be a pure vacuum, but it would be extremely low density. We'd have to optimize the laser frequency of the first shot for absorption by air molecules, but… it *might* create a hole for a few milliseconds."

Chandra smiled. "Light travels fast. That's all we need." She looked at Katori. "Is it possible to fire the beam in rapid succession with different frequencies?"

Katori scratched his head. "It's not impossible." He paused. "We'll have to think about how we could do it. But I do know we'll need more power." He paused again. "We planned on using one reactor as the primary and the second as a backup, but maybe with both online…"

Chandra raised her hand.

Scupino nodded.

"Can Kenny and I get excused from class? We need to go chase this idea down."

Scupino smiled. "Class dismissed. Let me know what you figure out."

As they broke up, Sheri smiled to herself. She had warned everyone about security leaks… while she was busy working with Josh on a press leak.

There was something else she needed to work on – Tim Smith. Catching him before he left, she asked, "Tim, may I talk to you for a moment?"

He nodded.

"I'd like to sit down with you, briefly, and compare notes on some of the team personnel. I may have some psychological insights that could be useful in protecting the program and people in it." She thought to herself, including you.

Smith frowned, but then nodded. "Actually, Dr. Lopez, there is an area where I could use your help." He paused, looking directly at her. "Of course, this would have to be kept very confidential."

"Call me Sheri. Tim, I'm a psychiatrist, we deal in secrets all the time. What can I help you with?"

He said slowly and quietly, "I'm having some challenges regarding the background of one of the members of this team."

"Which one?"

Looking around, he said, "I'd rather not discuss it here."

Davidson read the report and decided to visit his boss.

The Director of the CIA was talking on the phone with his feet propped up on his desk. Seeing his Deputy at the door, he motioned him in.

Davidson came in and sat down, accustomed to these waits. Director "Buster" Johnson earned his nickname honestly. Looking a little like George C. Scott in the movie *Dr. Strangelove*, he was a short, swarthy man with a strong handshake and a temper to match. Like the general in the movie, he also had an irritating tendency to chew bubblegum.

Although he wasn't a lot taller than his Director, Davidson was different in almost every other characteristic. He was trim with fine features and always dressed neatly with a tie. Even though he knew he'd never operate in the field again, he believed it was important to set the example. He was an avid runner and still competed in triathlons although well into his fifties. He was also a patient man, rarely got excited, and always enjoyed a good puzzle.

The Director finally got off the phone. "What's up?"

"Sir, we've got something a little odd going on and I wanted to bounce it off you."

Buster, chewing gum as usual, asked, "You mean that Iranian thing?"

"No sir, this is internal. Have you ever heard of a black program codenamed *Resurrect*?"

"Nope. What's it about or will you have to kill me?"

The Deputy smiled. "Well, that's the weird part. This appears to be a black program among black programs. It's been sucking up experts from other programs but we can't find any agency or military branch that claims it."

"Why should we care? Are they killing anyone or threatening to?"

"No. The reason we found out about it is that it's impacting our next-generation spy satellite. Their best and brightest engineers are being funneled into it."

Buster laughed. "So we're really talking about a black-program rice-bowl fight?"

"Possibly."

"Well, unless it threatens national security or we're given a direct mandate to investigate, let's just keep an eye on it. See what else you can find out... quietly. Don't want to look like idiots by investigating a pet program of this administration, like that NASA fiasco last year."

Josh knew the schedule would continue to slide until they fixed the beam-correction issue. Every day, the comet moved 3 million kilometers closer, making it that much harder to deflect. *These* issues, however, paled into insignificance in comparison to his latest challenge – Elizabeth had invited him to her parents' home for Christmas.

He didn't want to go, but she pointed out there was little he could accomplish on Christmas Eve or Christmas Day. Even those toiling to save the world had to have a breather. She was right. The team needed to spend some time with their families. It was a powerful reminder of what it was they were all trying to save.

Although he'd talked to Elizabeth frequently since Sheri brought them back together, he'd only managed to meet her twice since then, and only for a quick lunch in between events. He finally accepted Kelly's marriage, and his physical injuries had healed as well. He really did want to see Elizabeth. Actually, he wanted to do more than just see her... but her parents' house wasn't exactly what he had in mind.

32

CHRISTMAS

Two days before Christmas, Davidson was back in the Director's office. "Remember a couple weeks ago when I told you about that black program called *Resurrect*?"

Buster frowned as he stuffed papers into his briefcase. "Uh, yeah, I guess."

"My preliminary check shows a sizable program involving engineers and scientists from Boeing, Grumman, and NASA. There are rumors about operations in Los Alamos and even Antarctica. I've talked to all the major agencies and military branches and no one appears to know anything about it. It may be so highly classified that they aren't talking, but it's unusual to have something this big without an obvious sponsor. My instincts say we should check further. It's probably a genuine program but I'd like to confirm it with the President."

Buster nodded vaguely. "I'll ask him, but it'll have to wait." Smiling, he added, "I'm out of here. Short of DEFCON One, I don't plan to be back until well after Christmas." He slapped Davidson on the back. "Merry Christmas."

Josh flew to Austin on Christmas Eve. He didn't expect snow but stepping outside the terminal, the almost eighty-degree breeze caught him by surprise. Looking around, he immediately saw Elizabeth. She was leaning against her jeep wearing a light summer dress that fluttered softly in the breeze. He suddenly appreciated the warm weather.

After hugging her tightly, he threw his small bag in the back. Climbing into the passenger seat, he asked a little uncomfortably,

"What did you tell your parents?"

"I just told them you were a military officer working on a sensitive program in Kansas City. I also told them you didn't have any family, and I didn't want you to spend Christmas alone. They accepted it without question."

On the way to her parents, Elizabeth gave him a brief rundown on her family. He was happy just to sit and listen to her talk, but as they arrived, he began to second-guess himself. He was afraid it would be awkward and wanted to stay at a hotel. Elizabeth said that her parents had insisted he stay with them.

He found her parents to be very kind and open. He spent much of his time playing with four of Elizabeth's very young nieces and nephews. He decided that fighter pilots and small children played well together, probably because neither had grown up yet. He also discovered that his new body made an exceptionally effective jungle gym.

He also spent time talking to Elizabeth's mother. Very much like her daughter, she was a beautiful and gracious lady with old-world charm. He suspected that she was aware of his attraction to Elizabeth. Women had that knack, a mother even more so, but she was very kind and never asked any uncomfortable questions.

After dinner on Christmas Eve, Josh went for a walk to give Elizabeth time with her family. The dark tree-lined streets followed the rolling topography of the hills. It had cooled off after sunset and he enjoyed the exercise as he randomly followed the serpentine streets. There was no one out. Everyone was with their family tonight. He appreciated Elizabeth and her parents, but it was hard not to think about the family he lost. Out there, somewhere, were Kelly and Carl, celebrating their first Christmas with their daughter... *his* daughter. It still hurt to think about it but he no longer ran from the memories. Smiling sadly, he gave them all a silent toast, whispering, "Merry Christmas." Wiping his eyes, he extended his toast to Jesse. If it weren't for him, he wouldn't be here to make a toast. He wouldn't let pity sneak into his thoughts but feeling a little melancholy, he cleared his mind and asked, "Jesse, are you there?"

After a few seconds, he sensed his attention.

"Jesse, I know I've been a real pain to work with and I want to apologize. Thank you for all that you've done for me. You really are amazing." Not wanting to dwell on his past, he said, "The last session was a mind expander. Would it be all right to ask some more questions?"

He sensed permission.

"Based on our last conversation about the Big Bang and quantum physics' apparent need for an observer, could that 'observer' have been some type of… supreme being?" He thought this was an appropriate question, considering tomorrow was one of the holiest days of the world's largest religion. During his reading, he had been surprised to learn that the majority of the world's population believed in a god, and over half of the world believed in the same God.

What does your science say?

"I suspect many scientists would say that they can't exclude the possibility but believe that understanding the universe doesn't require a supreme being."

What do you think?

"I thought that too… until our 'observer' discussion. Now, I'm not so sure, but I have trouble imagining what a supreme being would be or do."

You've studied quantum mechanics, n-dimensional space, and multi-verses. How comfortable are you with these concepts?

Josh hadn't discussed n-dimensional space with Jesse. He suspected Jesse was aware of his thoughts even when they weren't communicating. It was both comforting and disturbing. He responded to the question. "I'm not comfortable with any of these ideas. They're hard for me to grasp."

These are tenets of your current science and yet they are not intuitive.

"OK."

The answers you seek are far beyond that.

"So, can't you explain them to me?"

Describe color to someone who's been blind from birth.

"That would be tough."

What if they were three years old and blind?

"That would be impossible." He paused. "You're saying I have no frame of reference that would allow me to understand."

Yes.

"Can you at least give me something, maybe a dumbed-down version?"

What is the universe made of?

"Matter and energy."

Simplify.

"Ultimately, matter and energy are interchangeable. You can convert matter into energy. We've done it with atomic bombs. And energy into matter. We've done it in particle accelerators."

Which came first?

"Well, if the Big Bang is correct, I guess the universe started with a huge blast of energy. As things expanded and cooled, matter sort of condensed out of all that energy. So I guess if you had to simplify it, the universe is made of energy, just in different forms."

Define Energy.

"You mean like energy with a capital 'E'? Uh, let's see. Through the Big Bang, it created the universe. It powers and defines the universe. It can change forms but can be neither created nor destroyed and will always be here... what does this have to do with my original question?"

How would you define a Supreme Being?

"I guess it would be an omnipotent power that created and controls the universe, is indestructible and is everywhere and always will be..." He paused. "OK, I see the similarity. So what are you saying? A Supreme Being is just Energy?"

Silence.

Finally, he asked, "Wrong question?"

Yes.

Josh said, "So, is Energy... God?"

Is red an apple?

He sensed that their conversation was over. That was OK. He needed time to think.

The President of the United States, Don Yager, was tired. He had worked right through Christmas again this year. He felt like he was constantly juggling – juggling marbles, bowling balls, and hand grenades.

As he finished the North Korea discussion with his Director of National Intelligence and the CIA Director, he looked down at his notebook and saw one more action he could check off. "Wait. Buster, you know that black program you asked me about a few weeks ago? The one that's messing with your spy-satellite program?"

"Resurrect?"

"Yes. I checked with the Cabinet, the Joint Chiefs, and NASA. They've all gotten back to me. No one appears to know anything about it."

Buster and the DNI both frowned.

Buster said, "I didn't expect that." He paused. "Then, we really need to get to the bottom of this ASAP."

The President caught a slightly raised eyebrow from the DNI. She'd been the CIA Deputy Director in the past and they both knew Buster's reputation. His appointment was the result of political realities. Buster was a lawyer and a strong leader but tended toward a "Ready, Fire, Aim" mentality.

Looking Buster in the eye, the President said, "Let's find out a little more about it before we start kicking in doors. Maybe it's a legacy project from a past administration. I'll check with them. If we don't get anything concrete, then you can go ahead with an investigation."

Buster said, "Yes, sir."

Buster told Davidson about his conversation with the President. "Let's go ahead and get a jump start on this. If the President finds out it's from a previous administration, we can always stop the investigation."

Davidson said, "I'll call Lafferty at the Bureau."

Buster said, "Wait a minute, this is our baby!"

He looked at Buster with some surprise. "What little we know suggests it's all based in the US."

"Brian, I know what our jurisdiction is but this is impacting our spy satellite and I hate telling the President I don't know about something in the black world. Besides, you mentioned Antarctica – that's not FBI jurisdiction."

Davidson thought, the South Pole wasn't anyone's jurisdiction.

He was used to the Director's outbursts and learned not to take them personally. "I'll broach the idea of keeping operational lead with Lafferty, but you may want to call the FBI Director yourself. I think Jay Jost will be more receptive if the request comes directly from you."

Buster nodded.

Davidson added, "We'll probably discover this is a genuine program." His instincts said the opposite. There was something strange here but he didn't want to spool up the Director, not yet. "We'll need to proceed with kid gloves on this."

Buster just said, "Yeah, whatever."

The intelligence world was painted in shades of gray, but Davidson knew Buster saw the world only in black and white.

33

INSIDE

Davidson met with the Deputy Director of the FBI, Bart Lafferty. He knew Lafferty well, having worked with him on past projects. Like Davidson, Lafferty was a career agent who started on the streets and worked his way up. He had a good reputation as a leader. A big man, he fit the classic Irish cop profile with a mop of reddish hair going rapidly gray. Brian knew that looks were deceiving: Lafferty was a Stanford grad, and a gentleman.

Davidson ran through everything they knew.

Lafferty had no problem with the CIA keeping operational lead, and they agreed that the first thing they needed was someone on the inside.

Lafferty said, "It'll be hard to spin-up an agent with enough technical background to pass 'em off as an expert."

Davidson agreed. "We'll have to find someone who's already in the program and 'turn' them."

"Brian, you guys have more experience in converting scientists and engineers to the dark side. What do you suggest?"

"Start at the top."

Lafferty raised his eyebrows in question.

Davidson said, "We need to befriend the program's office manager."

Lafferty laughed. "You're right, they do run the show."

Davidson added, "We've identified her. She's senior, very experienced, and highly respected."

Lafferty shook his head and said, "Despite political correctness, they are, to this day, almost always women, aren't they?" He paused. "Glass ceiling?"

Davidson smiled. "I think it's simply because men suck at multitasking. Women are more competent at running the complexities of an office populated with people."

"But will she have access to the classified information we need?"

Davidson said, "Many office managers are read into these programs because they have to handle the administration, but that's not why we go to them. Women are actually less likely to leak classified information. No, the reason we need her is that she can help us identify our mole. She has the most important information." He smiled. "She knows the office politics and where the skeletons are buried."

"So in the government and engineering world, who makes a good mole?"

"Human nature is the same, whether pipe fitter or PhD. We look for people who have either something to hide or an ax to grind."

Lafferty shook his head, "You guys are sneaky."

Davidson smiled. "Why, thank you."

A couple weeks later, Davidson told Buster, "We should have our informant soon. Apparently, it hasn't been easy. Most of those involved are fiercely loyal to the program and its leaders."

"How'd you do it?"

"We established a relationship with the office manager. She's been extremely helpful."

Buster winked, "A little 'undercovers' work?"

Davidson sighed. "Actually the office manager is a grandmother. All it took was inserting a young lady from the Bureau posing as a new office assistant. She made friends with the office matriarch and simply asked her who to watch out for. Never underestimate the power of women asking questions."

Buster looked a little disappointed.

Kevin Yankovic was the CIA agent assigned to find an informant. Working with the FBI, he had gone through the correct channels to ensure his visit looked official. Their cover story was that he was from the Government Accounting Office. It wasn't unusual for the GAO to take an interest in government-funded programs at contractor facilities. Yankovic had an intuitive ability to read people, with the possible exception of his teenage daughter. The young FBI agent they'd inserted supplied him with a description of the major team players. After studying their profiles, he believed he had two potential candidates.

To increase his credibility, they pulled some strings and borrowed the office of the local Defense Contract Management Agency's Commanding Officer. As his first candidate arrived, he opened with a low-threat approach. "Dr. Shepherd, thank you for seeing me on such short notice. I know you're a very busy man."

Shepherd nodded nervously.

"The reason I wanted to talk to you is that we are aware that you are part of a black program that we're concerned about. Along with the FBI, we are investigating funding irregularities. We need to determine if there is a need for a criminal investigation. As the program's logistics expert, we wanted to talk to you first." Yankovic knew very well that in the government and contractor world, a GAO visit to your program was like an IRS audit of your tax return.

Shepherd fidgeted and didn't make eye contact.

Yankovic liked this approach because it didn't automatically implicate anyone. It did, however, encourage the individual to separate himself from the program. Yankovic continued, "You know the program I'm speaking of?"

Shepherd said, "Yes. Yes, of course." He paused, looking around. "I knew there was something fishy going on."

Yankovic leaned forward. "And why is that?"

"I have three degrees, seventeen certifications and over thirty-five years of experience in my field, but they act like I don't know what I'm talking about. I told them their site was poor and their timeline preposterous, but did they listen to me? No. They bring in some Russki who has no degree and no certifications."

The reference to the Russian was very interesting, but he had to let the fish run with the line. "Yes, I can certainly understand your frustration." He listened sympathetically as Shepherd continued to complain. He had one more interview but he was sure he had his mole.

After twenty more minutes, Yankovic actually felt sorry for anyone who had to work with this guy. He called this type of personality the "all-knowing black cloud." They never quite understood that, even though they were knowledgeable, no one wanted to listen to them. They came across as negative about everything and superior to everyone.

Davidson stopped by Buster's office. "We've got our informant and we're already getting some interesting intel. We probably need to call a meeting."

Buster said, "Let's do it. Who's our mole?"

Agency policy was never to use names, even in closed meetings. To reduce the risk of compromising their identity, they referred to them generically or with code names.

Davidson clarified, "You mean, how did we choose him?"

Buster said, "Yeah, whatever."

"He's one of the team's experts and sits in on most key meetings. The office manager told our agent, no one likes him. Evidently, he believes that the leadership doesn't think he knows what he's doing…" Looking at Buster, Davidson suddenly felt uncomfortable as he finished, "… and it makes him look incompetent in front of his team."

Buster nodded, oblivious to the parallel.

Two months after discovering the beam-correction problem, Katori and Chandra called a meeting to discuss the progress. Smaller than usual, it included just the core engineers and physicists, Scupino, Smith, and Josh.

Chandra started. "Well, we tested Josh's crazy idea and it worked, at least in the lab. We figured out the correct frequency and power needed, and then passed it to Katori's team to do the hard stuff."

Josh noticed that Katori had bags under his eyes and looked like he'd been sleeping in his clothes. Cho, sitting next to him, didn't look much better.

"It's harder than we thought," Katori whispered, having lost his voice. "Two beams with different frequencies and power, fired from the same place within milliseconds," he paused for effect, "but we did it, or at least we think we did. It was our youngest engineer, Greg Langlois, that came up with the idea that finally worked."

Cho nodded. "It worked on our scale-model Blaster at low power. We think it will work full scale but it will require replacing components after each firing."

Scupino shook their hands. "Awesome! I'm impressed and very proud of you and your team." Continuing gently, "What does this mean as far as our timeline?"

Katori rubbed his eyes. "We need to talk about that. This redesign put us significantly behind schedule... about six weeks."

Scupino glanced at Chandra.

She said, "These guys have been working their butts off, living on a few hours of sleep, but every day that passes makes a comet that much harder to deflect."

Scupino said, "Dr. Katori, Dr. Cho, fantastic work! Please pass our congratulations to your team." Looking down at his program schedule sheet, he added, "That pushes the first firing at the Pole back to May 7th, three months from today." Looking back at them, he said quietly, "I have to ask you to look carefully at your timeline. See if there is anything we can do to pull the schedule forward... anything at all."

Davidson, sitting in Buster's office, said, "The informant is giving us excellent information. This thing's a lot bigger than we thought. They're trying to build the world's most powerful laser to deflect earth-impacting comets, and they're going to put it near the South Pole. Our agent says that by all appearances it looks like a genuine program. They have highly respected engineers, military officers, and astrophysicists on the team. They seem to have plenty of funding. Although we don't know the source, our accounting department doesn't see any illegal transfer of government funds or anything from offshore."

Buster nodded. "Sounds like a good program."

Davidson said, "Yes..."

Buster said, "But?"

"They're operating under a tight timeline due to a possible

comet impact in a little over a year."

Buster laughed. "A comet hitting the earth? That's Hollywood crazy."

"Actually, Chen from the Science Directorate says comets are a real threat." He paused. "What raises the warning flag is that the experts say there are no known comets that will come anywhere near the earth for the next 500 years."

Buster shrugged. "Could they have detected a new one?"

"Our people say that's possible, but if any observatory found a new one, everyone would know within hours. This project claims they've known about a possible threat for almost a year."

"Then where do they claim the information came from?"

"Our informant says no one knows. It's classified, even to them."

"Who's the ringleader?"

"Navy Captain Joe Scupino, former captain of the aircraft carrier USS *Ford*." Looking at his folder, he added, "He's a highly decorated officer with a good reputation. He'd be an admiral today if it hadn't been for a fire that destroyed some prototype fighters right after he assumed command. He works for NAVAIR, you know, Admiral Hendricks."

"Let me guess, Hendricks doesn't know anything about this."

"No, but that's not impossible. There are black programs that cross service and agency boundaries."

Buster said, "Could Scupino have been 'turned' by a foreign power because his career was ruined by that fire?"

"Anything's possible, but we have detailed background and personality profiles on him. He was a nuclear weapon delivery pilot, so he was in the PRP program."

"PRP?"

"Personnel Reliability Program. They continuously evaluate the stability of those who have particularly sensitive jobs, like carrying a live nuclear weapon in a single-seat fighter. Scupino's profile and career indicate he's about as stable and ethical as they get. If he were on the other side, we wouldn't even think about trying to turn him."

Buster frowned. "He has to report to someone. This isn't rocket science."

Davidson smiled. "Actually, it *is* rocket science."

Buster didn't smile.

Davidson continued, "Short of taking Scupino in for questioning, we can't be sure who he reports to. I don't think we want to do that yet. If we're investigating a genuine program, we risk compromising it, not to mention embarrassing ourselves. If it isn't genuine, then we tip our hand."

"Are there any other significant players?"

Davidson pushed several pictures across the desk to Buster. "Several, but they read like a *Who's Who* of science and engineering. NASA's Dr. Victoria Chandra, Boeing's Dr. Lee Katori, and the famous psychiatrist Sheri Lopez, to name a few. There are, however, two on the team who do have my interest. One is a Russian-born construction expert and the other guy is someone they appear to defer to on budget issues."

Looking at them, Buster said, "I don't care about the accountant. What the hell are Chinese and Russians doing on the program? What do we know about *them*?"

Davidson knew Buster was from a different era and had an inherent distrust of their old Cold War adversaries. "Sir, Lee Katori is third-generation American, and he's of Japanese, not Chinese, descent. The Russian is a naturalized American citizen and renowned construction expert. We actually have a dossier on him from the Cold War era. He had little use for the Communist party. We're doing more background work on him but he should be pretty easy to track." Davidson paused. "I'm more interested in the accountant. We've broken a lot of terrorist operations by following the money trail."

"Who is he?"

"His name is Josh Meadows."

"What do we have on him?"

"Nothing. That's the reason I'm interested."

34

PROPHET

Josh set the program schedule sheet down. He had to find a way to speed things up but he also needed to take a break. Sitting alone in his apartment, he tried to contact Jesse. He never got a straight answer about a Supreme Being, so he'd try a different tack.

After sensing Jesse's presence, Josh asked, "Is there life after death?"

Are you alive?

He laughed. "*Touché*. OK, *outside* of being given a new body, does our consciousness survive death or do we just dissipate?"

What do you think?

"Why do I bother asking?" He knew the drill. "Obviously, we'd like to believe there's some form of life after death. All religions believe it in one form or another. Christianity purports to have had an individual who came back to prove it. If it's true, where are all these consciousnesses now?"

Where do your religions say they are?

"Heaven?"

Where is heaven?

"That's my question. If it exists, where is it? Why don't we see any evidence of it?"

How many dimensions are there?

"Dimensions?" He sighed, thinking, here we go again. He said, "Four. Three spatial and one time."

Four?

"Yes." He paused. "Well... we're trying to create a Theory of Everything, something that will tie all the major forces together into one equation. According to String Theory and Supersymmetry, more dimensions are required to make the equations balance."

How many more?

"I think the leading theory is M-Theory. It contends that there must be eleven dimensions."

Where are they?

"You mean, where are the seven dimensions beyond the regular four?" He paused. "I don't know."

I see.

Slowly Josh said, "So what are you suggesting? Heaven is in the seven missing dimensions?"

You're comfortable with seven missing dimensions?

"Well, yeah, but that's the result of… an equation…" he finished weakly.

Silence.

"You know, Jesse, it's interesting, the Talmud, the Qur'an, and the Vedas all talk about seven heavens and even the Bible has a fascination with the number seven. And why are there seven days in a week?" He knew he was pulling a "Seinfeld," talking around Jesse's question. "I mean, it's easy to figure out where the day, month and year came from – earth's rotation, moon cycles and the seasons, but why seven days? Why not five or ten to match our fingers?"

Silence.

"OK, OK… you're right. If a physics equation suggests there are seven invisible dimensions – I'm good with it. If a minister suggests there's an invisible heaven – I have a problem. I'm a science chauvinist." He smiled. "I promise I'll try to keep a more open mind." He laughed, thinking it *would* be totally wild if physics and religion ended up intersecting in *seventh heaven.*

Davidson had several Middle Eastern operations in progress and a congressional hearing, but he continued to follow the developments in the strange comet program. It was late February before he brought the results back to Buster.

Davidson dropped a surveillance photo on Buster's desk. "No one knows who Josh Meadows is or where he came from. Most of his team assumes he's CIA."

Studying the picture, Buster said, "What do we have on him?"

"He doesn't have an office anywhere and lives in a small apartment in St. Louis. The only consistent thing we get is that he stays in the background, and everyone, including Scupino, respects him. He's probably early thirties and in excellent physical shape. No accent and knows both engineering and military lingo. We pulled his fingerprints off a glass but they've turned up absolutely nothing. Since 9/11 that's almost impossible, particularly for someone in the government or the military-industrial complex."

Buster shook his head, "He has to have a government clearance. Can't we track him through that?"

Davidson shook his head. "He has a Boeing access clearance that should be tied directly to a government clearance, but it dead ends. There's no background check or history linked to it. The computer system has it tied to some dead military officer. If I didn't know better, I'd swear he's one of ours."

Buster frowned. "Could he be?"

"Sir, we have highly sensitive programs with deep-cover agents, but I assure you, I'd know if this guy was on our payroll. He's not ours. I checked with the DNI and FBI. He doesn't belong to them either. Our informant says that the rumors suggest he's a former SEAL, but it's probably just because he looks like an athlete and saved an engineer from falling off a cliff."

"SEAL Team Six gets involved in some weird stuff."

Davidson shook his head. "It is possible his identity was erased but those programs almost always involve us, and the military isn't claiming him either."

Buster drummed his fingers on the table. "So you're telling me… we've got a bunch of high-level military, engineers, and scientists developing a powerful energy-beam weapon, *supposedly* to protect the world from an impending comet that no one should be able to predict. *And* one of the key players is a total mystery."

Davidson shrugged. "That pretty much sums it up."

Buster looked at his Deputy. "Could there be some super-secret government agency we're not aware of?"

Davidson said, "Sir, nothing's impossible but I've been in this business my entire life. I think I would have heard about an agency that could do all this. I suggest that we run this by the Administration one more time."

The President said, "Buster, I checked with the last two administrations. No one knows anything about it. How could someone infiltrate our military-industrial complex and create a fake program, for God's sake? Don't we have security checks and balances to prevent this?"

Buster glanced at Davidson.

Davidson said, "Mr. President, those checks and balances have been working against us. They're designed to keep information from being *extracted*, not inserted. If this thing isn't real, this guy's brilliant and knows our system inside out."

The President shook his head. "Get to the bottom of this, but," he looked Buster in the eye, "I don't want any cowboy coups. I want to know what they're really doing. If this is a genuine program, I want to know who's behind it. If it's not, I want to know who's behind it."

Buster said, "Yes, sir."

Davidson added, "Sir, they have operations in Antarctica. We'll need support from the military."

The President said, "Antarctica... I think that's under US Pacific Command."

Davidson nodded. "Yes, sir, I believe that's Admiral Carroll Rea."

"I'll tell the Sec Def and the Joint Chiefs this is a priority and to support you with whatever you need."

Buster said, "Thank you, sir."

As they left the White House, Buster said, "Brian, this becomes the top priority for this agency."

"Yes, sir." Davidson paused. "This is a very unusual situation. Whoever they are, they've breached our military-industrial complex. We have to assume they might be able to do the same with other government agencies."

Buster's eyes narrowed. "You mean, like ours. What are you suggesting?"

"I'd like to run this operation with extremely tight security and as few participants as possible. Use only senior personnel with top-level clearances and full compartmentalization. With your permission, I'll talk directly to the Directors of National Intelligence, Homeland Security, and the FBI. Ask them to do the same. I'd even like to have an internal cover story among our agencies and the White House. There've been too many leaks in the past with other programs."

"Good idea."

Davidson asked, "What do you want to call the operation?"

Buster frowned. "Well, everything points back to this Meadows character."

Davidson said wryly, "'The Jackal' is already taken."

Buster said, "He's predicting a comet's going to clobber the earth, a comet that can't be seen." He paused. "We'll call him the Prophet."

Davidson sighed. Operation codenames weren't supposed to give any hint about the operation or subject, that's why they were *codenames*, but he needed to pick his battles with Buster carefully.

35

DOUBTS

It was only two months to the first test firing of the Blaster. Chandra and Katori stopped Scupino and Josh after one of the technical meetings, and asked if they could talk privately. They went to Scupino's office. Smith was already there.

Chandra began, "Captain, we trust your leadership and we're all committed to this program but there are things that… well, there have been some questions." She glanced guiltily at Josh.

Josh knew where this was going.

Scupino asked, "Like what?"

"Our NASA accountants say they've never seen this 'color' of money before. I know for the Antarctic operation, we're routing money through a private company to hide government involvement." She frowned. "But the funds to NASA and Los Alamos are also coming from a private company. Our government accountants are having anxiety attacks."

Katori added, "My key engineers, like Cho, are getting heavy pressure because they're letting their other programs slide and can't tell their boss why. There are some seriously irritated program managers out there that will be gunning for us."

Chandra frowned and said, "Ultimately… our team leads are asking why this program remains classified." She paused. "If the threat to our world is real, why aren't we involving everyone to increase our resources?"

Scupino asked, "Are you having resource or funding challenges?"

Chandra said, "No. If we need something, we just buy it."

Katori nodded in agreement.

"So, we have a problem because…?"

Chandra and Katori looked at each other sheepishly.

Josh knew this wasn't Scupino's battle. Catching his eye, Scupino gave him a nod.

Josh said, "Dr. Chandra, Dr. Katori, I understand your team's concerns. How are you feeling about the project personally?"

Katori smiled. "Don't worry about me. I'm having a blast. This must be what it was like to be part of the Apollo program."

Chandra said, "I completely agree… it's just…"

Josh smiled. "Go ahead."

"Josh, I'd work on this project if you told me your fairy godmother gave you the tip, but we're a year from its arrival. It should be inside the orbit of Jupiter and beginning to outgas. I've been keeping a tab on the major observatories. No new comets have been detected. It sure would help our team to have something more concrete." She looked at Katori. "Particularly for those under the gun, like Cho."

Josh nodded and made a decision. "What if I can get you the coordinates and trajectory?"

"That would be fantastic! At this range, we should be able to find it if we know where to look."

Josh asked, "How will you handle the inevitable questions of where the information came from?"

Chandra said, "Most astrophysicists who specialize in asteroids and comets aren't involved with planetary probes. With my background, they'll probably assume it came from one of our deep-space probes. I doubt they'll question it as long as it's coming from me, but I don't really care what they think as long as we get search time on the big scopes." She frowned. "It's odd, but scientists and engineers like numbers. Give us some coordinates and we're happy. When can I get them?"

Smith observed the interplay silently. He was as curious and skeptical as Chandra. After his conversation with Lopez, he learned several things. He discovered that Lopez was very good at what she did. She was trying to analyze *him*, just as he was trying to get information from her on Meadows. Of course, he would never let her inside, but he had to admit, her motives seemed based out of genuine concern for him. She was an impressive woman. Despite his best efforts, it was hard not to like her. He, however, was equally good at subtle interrogation and was able to learn at least one rather surprising thing about Meadows. Unfortunately, instead of clearing things up, it deepened the mystery.

Davidson set up their first meeting in a special CIA conference room. He had checked that everyone on the team was a veteran with the highest security clearance. The internal cover story was a billion-dollar international drug cartel operating out of southern South America.

Buster started the first official meeting of the Prophet Operations team. "What do we have?"

Davidson, holding up several reports said, "Their Antarctic base is further along than we thought. The two Russian reactors are in place at the base of the mountain but aren't up and running yet. On top of the mountain, the structure that will house the energy-beam projector is almost finished."

Buster said, "Russian reactors?!"

Davidson nodded to the Deputy Director of the CIA's Science and Technology Directorate, Dan Chen.

"They're small industrial reactors and don't use weapons-grade uranium," Chen explained. "It's an old design. The Russian construction expert, Christoff Bobinski, procured them and is coordinating their installation."

Buster frowned. "Maybe, but I don't like Russian involvement, particularly with anything nuclear. Plus, we're going to have an international incident on our hands when the world learns we installed reactors at the South Pole." He shook his head. "Tell me about this comet deflection beam thing?"

Chen said, "They refer to it as the 'CAT Blaster.'"

Buster smiled. "Good name. I hate cats."

"It's based on the old strategic defense technology. It generates a tightly collimated, extremely high-power laser beam capable of vaporizing what it hits."

"So they're creating a powerful laser weapon?!"

Chen said, "Sir, the equipment is huge. It's not portable or effective against ground targets. It really appears to be designed to put a lot of energy on a target in space."

"Can it shoot down airplanes?"

Chen shrugged. "It's certainly powerful and accurate enough." Looking at some notes, he added, "But they don't have any search or tracking radar."

The CIA Associate Director for Military Affairs, Lieutenant General Norma Glosson added, "There isn't a lot to shoot at the South Pole, and there are faster, simpler ways to take out aircraft."

Buster nodded, chewing his gum vigorously. He suddenly said, "My God, they're going to use it to take out our space station and satellites. They could cripple us by hitting our imaging, GPS, and communication satellites. Bastards will probably take out our DirectTV too. We'll be blind and deaf."

Chen frowned and softly repeated, "DirectTV...?" Then louder, "Sir, since this is a laser, it's a line-of-sight weapon. If it can't see it, it can't hit it. The energy-beam could easily take out satellites above it, but most of our satellites and the Space Station are in low, equatorial orbits. We do have some imaging birds in polar orbit they could hit, along with southern-hemisphere geosynchronous satellites." He shuffled through several sheets and found what he was looking for. "However, our engineers say the system runs off capacitors which have to be charged between shots. They designed it for a single powerful shot with several hours of recharge time. He'd only be able to take out one satellite before we nailed him."

Still animated, Buster said, "I'm telling you, we may not know what the system can really do and putting it in Antarctica may be a ruse. We need to round these bastards up and sweat the information out of them."

Davidson jumped in. "Sir, this CAT Blaster is still in a government lab in Los Alamos, and our informant says they've got technical problems. We can round the players up and shut them down within hours. *But*, we still have no idea who the Prophet reports to. If we slam the door now, we may never know."

Buster sighed. "OK, but what contingency plan do we have if we guessed wrong?"

Davidson nodded at General Glosson.

Glosson said, "The Pole base is a geographically fixed and unarmored target. We can easily destroy it with a single bomb or missile. The issue is distance. Land-based aircraft would have to fly thousands of miles, but it is within the range of a ship-based Tomahawk cruise missile."

Buster, still chewing loudly, said, "Yeah. Now that's what I'm talking about."

Glosson continued, "As you know, they can be launched from a ship or sub off the Antarctic coast. We could blow anything off the top of that mountain within a few hours."

Buster said, "Norma, the President gave us authorization for full military support."

She nodded. "I'll call Admiral Rea and get a Tomahawk shooter assigned."

Once again, Davidson realized Buster didn't have the patience for intelligence work. He needed to bring him back from bombs to bugs. "Sir, I think the key to all this lies with the Prophet himself."

Buster asked, "Have we started surveillance yet?"

The FBI Deputy, Lafferty, said, "We just started. We're assuming we're watching an intelligence operative familiar with surveillance techniques. We're using the most subtle and least intrusive technology we have."

Buster grunted, "Let me know when you have something."

Josh had to get the comet's coordinates and trajectory. He went for an early-evening run around the park near his apartment. Based on Chandra and Katori's comments about their program's impact on other programs, he suspected – no, he actually sensed – his rogue program was no longer operating under the radar. Although he might be able to communicate with Jesse without speaking, it was easier and more comfortable to talk to him out loud.

Setting a steady running pace, he cleared his mind and very softly said, "Jesse, sorry to bother you, but I need to know everything you know about the comet. We have to have its location and trajectory."

A picture formed in Josh's mind – a poorly illuminated, large, black blob against a black background. He should have known Jesse wouldn't send him a picture on his cell phone. It looked like a giant charcoal briquette.

Along with the picture, he got the dimensions, coordinates, and trajectory. He stumbled and almost fell, yelling, "Fifteen kilometers!"

Another runner coming from the opposite direction heard him, smiled, and said, "Fifteen K, way to go!"

Stepping off the trail, Josh leaned over with his hands on his knees, catching his breath. He'd assumed the comet was no bigger than five kilometers, the size of Shoemaker-Levy. He shook his head, saying softly, "Jesse, a fifteen-kilometer mountain will erase mankind and exterminate practically all life on earth."

Yes.

He was very angry with Jesse... but he was angrier with himself. He replayed their conversations. Josh had assumed... but never asked.

36

THREAT

Josh called Scupino and asked for an immediate meeting with Chandra, Katori, and Lopez.

Scupino asked, "Smith?"

"Sure."

The six of them gathered around a small table in Scupino's office. As soon as Chandra sat down, Josh handed her a piece of paper. She looked at it, and then at him with raised eyebrows. Josh nodded. "That's it. That's the enemy."

Chandra pulled out her phone and began typing quickly, saying, "I'm passing these coordinates to one of my colleagues at the Keck observatory. Do we know its dimensions?"

Josh didn't say anything.

Chandra finally looked up from her phone.

Josh sighed. "It's fifteen kilometers in diameter."

Chandra and Katori spoke at the same time. "Fifteen kilometers?"

Chandra fired back, "Josh, a fifteen-kilometer comet is a planet killer! It's bigger than the asteroid that killed the dinosaurs. Its size combined with its higher velocity makes it about *three times* more destructive. The dinosaur killer wiped out 70 per cent of all life on earth. Imagine three of them hitting us at the same time… almost nothing will survive."

Josh said softly, "I know."

Scupino asked, "Josh, is it really fifteen kilometers?"

He sighed. "Yes, we just found out."

Chandra said, "I need to go. We need to run some calculations."

Scupino nodded.

They got up to leave, but Katori remained seated. They all stopped and looked at him questioningly. Katori, staring through the table, said with a flat, emotionless voice, "We designed the Blaster to deflect a five-kilometer comet."

Chandra added, "I'm sorry, Josh, since we didn't know how big it was, and you mentioned Shoemaker-Levy…"

Katori interrupted, "We can't deflect a fifteen-kilometer comet."

Scupino said, "Can't we scale up the CAT Blaster or build two more?"

Katori, looking up at Scupino, shook his head gently. Looking very tired, he said, "Joe, the *diameter* is three times larger… but the volume is the *cube* of the diameter. That means a fifteen-kilometer comet has *twenty-seven times* the mass of a five-kilometer comet." He continued softly, "Unfortunately, Newton's law applies. Increase the mass twenty-seven times…"

Scupino finished, "We'd need twenty-seven Blasters."

There was silence.

Josh hadn't really considered how much more mass was involved. But he'd never intended for this program to be the entire solution! It was just supposed to be the pilot program, the pump primer. No… no, that was an excuse. He never asked Jesse how big the comet was and when he found out, never thought through the implications. The devil was in the details, and he sucked at details. More accurately, he tended to ignore them. Didn't matter how good you were at seeing the forest, if you drove into a tree. His only solace was that there was no way he could have hidden a program big enough to produce twenty-seven Blasters.

Finally, Scupino said, "We probably don't need to share this with the rest of the team just yet. We need them thinking clearly." Turning to Katori, he said gently, "Lee, it's important to start figuring out what it'll take to scale up."

Katori nodded mechanically.

Scupino put both of his hands on the table and said quietly but with strength, "Our job is to prove we can hit a comet. Do that, and all the world's resources will be at our disposal. We'll be able to build dozens of these things."

Chandra looked up at Josh and Scupino. "I know this sounds strange, but… it just became real." She paused. "A year from now, we'll be successful and partying our brains out, or we'll be dead along with everyone we've ever known."

There was a moment of somber silence. Then Scupino broke it with, "I vote for the party. *However*, to do that, we *have* to accelerate this program. What can we do?"

That night, Josh paced in his small apartment. It was March 21st, the anniversary of his death and almost exactly one year to impact. To deflect the comet, they needed to be firing twenty-seven Blasters right now. Instead, they were still trying to produce one. He was frustrated and angry with himself. He needed to go for a walk.

It was a cold, clear, spring night with few people out. Under his breath he said, "Jesse, I could really use your help."

He was relieved to sense Jesse's presence.

"I've pushed the 'secret source' with my team as far as it'll go. I feel like the little Dutch boy with his finger in the dike. I may have an elevated sense of paranoia, but I also have elevated senses. Someone's watching me. I could sure use some close air support right now."

There will be a precursor to the comet.

He laughed. "I gotta be the only person who's actually relieved to hear voices in his head. What do you mean, 'precursor'?"

The comet is the debris from a massive collision. It has crossed earth's orbit in the distant past.

Josh said, "So the earth will pass through its debris trail? Good, a spectacular meteor shower will get people's attention and bolster our case. How soon?"

Twenty-five days.

It was one week since Josh had told them the size of the comet. He saw Katori was already in Scupino's office, sitting across the table from Scupino, doodling on a pad of paper.

After Chandra, Smith, and Lopez came in, they closed the door.

Scupino nodded to Katori.

Katori tapped his pencil on the table, set it down and looked up. Not looking happy, he said, "We need to skip the test firing at Los Alamos... do it at the Pole. It'll buy us back a few weeks. We'll fire it April 17th instead of May 7th. We'll need to ship it to the Pole a few days before that, to get it installed."

Scupino nodded. "We'll be going for broke."

Katori added, "We'll be testing everything at the same time: reactors, capacitors, tracking system, alignment system, software, and the Blaster. Something we'd never do on a regular program because the risk's too high. We have to prove this thing works as soon as possible to have any chance of scaling it up in time."

Sheri added softly, "It's important for another reason. When the comet is identified, it's critical that people have something to give them hope. Without hope, bad things can happen to societies."

Scupino said, "Like a stock-market crash?"

"And worse. With the stakes so high, government statements or promises carry little weight. Many will assume we're lying to them to prevent panic."

Chandra shook her head. "People would really believe the government would lie about something this important?"

Sheri raised her eyebrows. "Yes... and they'd be right." She paused. "I've been involved with several studies that asked the question, 'If there was nothing we could do about an apocalyptic disaster, would it cause more social damage and pain to tell people?' Guess what the answer was?" She paused again. "Regardless, a successful firing could be just the beacon that people can rally around."

Tim Smith cleared his throat. As usual, everyone had forgotten that he was present. All eyes went to him. He said quietly, "We may have another problem. I have indications that we're under surveillance."

Scupino looked surprised. "By who?"

Smith shook his head. "I don't know yet. They're extremely good and are keeping a very low profile."

"Terrorists?"

"I don't think so. They're too sophisticated and subtle."

Chandra said, "Who on earth could possibly be opposed to

what we're doing?"

Sheri frowned and said slowly, "Put yourself inside the head of an outside observer. What do you see?"

Smith nodded at Sheri but Chandra shook her head and said, "I don't understand."

Sheri said, "You might *see* the world's most powerful energy-beam weapon being developed."

Smith, glancing at Josh, added, "You might *assume* the comet is nothing but a cover story."

Chandra just said, "How twisted would that be?"

Scupino looked at Smith. "What should we do?"

"Nothing yet. I'm going to drop into the background and see if I can observe the observers. If I sense a threat, I'll bring in support. In the meantime, if you see anything out of the ordinary, *do not* call me. Text me using the security app I put on your phones. I'll find you."

Josh's brain was spinning. He felt like he was looking into one of those infinity mirrors that reflected back into itself forever. He was playing a game within a game. No, it wasn't a game. He was facing a powerful adversary. Like Jesse, it had no face.

He said to Scupino and Smith, "In light of this, I suggest that we don't tell anyone about our plan to move the schedule up. Let's operate as if we're going to do the test firing in Los Alamos, and ship the Blaster to the Pole at the last minute."

Smith agreed. "That might be prudent."

"OK." Scupino nodded. "Let's do it."

As they were breaking up, Josh said, "Oh, I almost forgot. We also found out there will be a precursor to the comet. We're expecting a large meteoroid, big enough to put on an impressive light show. On a similar trajectory, it should arrive within a month."

As Josh turned to leave, he noticed Smith watching him. In fact, it seemed like Tim's eyes were always on him. It was just paranoia – understandable, in light of Smith's announcement.

Davidson started the second meeting by dropping a newspaper on the table with the headline, "Earth Under Threat From Comet?"

Buster picked it up, as Davidson said, "It says the information came from a high-level but undisclosed government source. It's not a front-page story but it's in several major papers and, of course, the tabloids. We also got a message from the President's Chief of Staff, asking us what we know about it."

Buster slammed his hand on the table. "This is going to get rapidly out of control unless we shut them down."

The CIA Operations Director, Cindy Bishara said, "We also just found out from our informant that the Prophet's now predicting the arrival of a smaller comet fragment." She looked down at her iPad. "It's supposed to arrive in less than three weeks."

Buster said, "Don't tell me, it's too small and too dark to be easily detected."

"Yup."

Lafferty asked, "Why would he do that? He'll expose himself as a fraud in a few weeks when the fragment doesn't show up."

Davidson asked, "When are they planning on test-firing this thing?"

Bishara said, "The first full-power test is scheduled at Los Alamos in about two and half weeks."

Davidson raised an eyebrow.

Buster said, "Amazing coincidence! Don't you see? They're behind schedule. He's using this imaginary comet fragment to scare his people into working faster. We're onto his game."

Davidson said, "The informant also says Meadows is scheduled to go down to the Pole base before the first firing. Since all their logistics flights have to go through the Falklands for fuel, I recommend we let him get to the Falklands and arrest him there."

Buster frowned for a moment and then smiled. "Yes. The Falklands are perfect. Nowhere to run and outside the US we have more... options."

Davidson nodded. "I'll work through MI6 to get permission."

Buster added, "There may be hostiles at the Pole to protect or take the equipment."

"We can have commandos assigned to take the Pole base just in case," Davidson said, looking at Glosson.

She nodded, "I'll ask US Pacific Command to give us an Arctic-trained SEAL team."

Davidson asked Bishara, "What about communications when

we arrest the Prophet?"

"To prevent him from warning anyone, the Brits can jam everything in and out of the Falklands once the operation starts."

Lafferty added, "We'll round up all the others in the US at the same time."

The President said, "Buster, sounds like a good plan." He paused. "I have to tell you though, it still doesn't add up in my mind. Why would someone who's made these inroads into our system use such an elaborate ruse? Stealing nuclear or biological weapons would have been easier and more effective."

Buster retorted, "Don't you see? He's using fear and playing on everyone's desire to be a hero and save the world. It's a brilliant strategy that keeps otherwise smart men from asking too many questions. He's using our own capability against us. It will make me… make *us*… appear not only weak, but stupid, to the rest of the world."

"Maybe, but it just doesn't make sense… seems too much like a *Mission Impossible* plot."

A little too loud, Buster said, "If you know any agency that could be behind this, let me know!"

The President raised his eyebrows.

"I'm sorry, sir. No one's claiming this joker and I don't believe people understand what a threat he is."

The President said, "All right, you've got a green light, but if possible I want this Prophet alive. We need to know what's in his head."

As they left the White House, Davidson got a secure text. "Sir, it appears we got a fingerprint match on the Prophet."

37

IDENTIFY

Waiting in Buster's office, Bishara immediately reported, "The fingerprints match a John Doe, found on the side of a road almost a year ago. He was naked and unconscious. They brought him to Kansas City Medical Center, where he remained in a coma for several days and then," Bishara looked up at Buster, "he woke up, claiming amnesia."

Buster said, "I knew it! He's a plant." Frowning, he asked, "Why did it take so long to make the fingerprint connection?"

Bishara shook her head. "You're not going to like this. They fingerprinted him as a John Doe at the hospital but found no matches, so they contacted Homeland Security. The Bureau evaluated him as a potential threat. Guess who the evaluating psychiatrist was?"

Buster smiled. "Dr. Sheri Lopez."

"Yup. They kept him under surveillance for a while, but eventually closed the case…"

Buster finished, "… based on Lopez's assessment."

Bishara nodded. "The problem was that when all this was done he was still a John Doe. The computer made the fingerprint match but with no identity attached, it ignored it. It's a software glitch. They're fixing it now. We're bringing in the Homeland Security caseworker for questioning."

Buster said, "He's going to have a lot of explaining to do."

Bishara continued, "The medical report indicates the Prophet was remarkably healthy and is extremely intelligent. The surveillance report says," she looked up with raised eyebrows, "he lived with one of his nurses for several weeks. That explains some of the phone conversations we've tapped."

Buster matched her eyebrows. "Well, at least he's human. Bring her in when we pull the trigger." He smiled unpleasantly. "She may provide some *leverage*."

Elizabeth got a call from Josh. After some small talk, he said to her, "Things are going well but they're going to get a little crazy. I may not be able to talk to you for a while." There was a pause. "I don't want there to be any misunderstanding this time. I haven't been very good at showing it, but I *really* care about you."

She said, "Then why does this sound like an exit speech?"

"It's nothing of the kind." She heard some irritation in his voice and knew it was mostly because they couldn't talk openly on the phone. "In fact, I'm *really* looking forward to an intimate discussion on *certain* cosmology theories. It just would be *best* if you stayed there for now."

She smiled. So, he did finally catch on. She said, very positively, "You do whatever you need to do. I'll be fine here." It was easy to humor him, since she'd already formulated her plan.

As soon as she got off the phone, she called Lesia, told her there was a family emergency and she'd have to be gone a week. She threw some clothes in a bag and hopped into her jeep.

Davidson entered the conference room. Buster was already there. "Sir, this is Carl Casey, from the European directorate. He's one of our key international law experts. Carl, tell him what you just told me."

"Sir, I was just brought into the Prophet operation today, but I actually met this guy, Josh Meadows – the Prophet – almost a year ago."

"What?"

"Yes sir, he read me into his program."

Buster, looking incredulous, said, "Why didn't you tell someone?"

"Sir, I had no idea about *your* operation, I wasn't part of it. As for his program, I went through the normal paperwork channels. It was approved, and as you know…"

Davidson finished. "Can't talk about it once you're read into it."

Carl continued, "I assumed CIA leadership was already involved."

Davidson laughed. "*We are…* on the opposite side." He shook his head gently. "You've *got* to admire how this guy works."

Buster glared at him and turned back to Carl. "Out with it. What do you know about him?"

"Never met him before he contacted me a year ago. We shared a close friend. My wife and I have had dinner with him. He knew details and stories that confirmed it. I'm positive he is, or was, a military officer. He speaks the lingo."

Buster's eyes narrowed. "Let's get a hold of this common friend."

Carl shook his head. "He was killed in an F-18 crash a year ago."

Buster said, sarcastically, "How convenient."

Frowning, Davidson asked, "Carl, what's the name of the pilot who died?"

"Commander Josh Logan."

Davidson flipped through some papers. Finally finding it, he raised his eyebrows and said, "That's very interesting. In the computer, there's a link between the Prophet's security clearance and this deceased military officer. Could he be…?"

Carl frowned and shook his head. "Logan's dead. I was at the funeral. It was an open casket. Besides, this guy doesn't look anything like him."

Davidson continued, "Carl, what's your assessment of this man?"

Still frowning, Carl said, "He's very intelligent, eloquent, likable, but intense. He seems like someone you'd play golf with or follow into battle."

"Great! Can you tell us anything useful?" Buster said with a scowl.

Carl continued, "Sir, we're all skeptics by nature. If this guy's a fake, he's the best I've ever seen. Are we absolutely sure he's not for real?"

Buster's face got red. "This guy comes out of nowhere, fakes amnesia, and uses a dead pilot's security clearance. What the hell do *you* think?"

The Deputy jumped in. "Sir, Carl's worked both analysis and operations. He's been involved with many interrogations and is a good judge of character."

Buster continued in a loud voice, "Am I the only one who's not living in Disneyland? This guy has us building the most powerful energy-beam weapon on the face of the earth!"

Davidson nodded to Carl, signaling him to sit down.

Buster continued to look shocked while vigorously chewing his gum.

During the uncomfortable silence, Bishara jumped in. "Sir, would you like to go over the plan for securing the Pole base?"

"*Yes!* Let's talk about something *useful*."

"Sir?" Carl volunteered.

Buster gave him a "What now?" look.

"I assigned one of our people to his team to help with security. So, we have another operative inside his team."

Buster's eyebrows went up and he stopped frowning.

Davidson looked at Carl and said quietly, "A protector?"

Carl nodded.

Buster said, "Is this operative capable of taking the Prophet out?"

Carl nodded. "*More* than capable."

Buster said, "Finally, some good news." He turned to Bishara, signaling her to continue.

Bishara said, "As you know, the plan is to send in a C-17 with an Arctic-trained SEAL team and an AC-130 gunship."

Davidson added, "The last report said there are almost a dozen people down there, mostly PhDs and engineers."

Bishara continued, "The SEALs will have a nuclear expert with them to shut down the reactors."

Buster interrupted. "I want overkill on this op. I believe there are other players tied to the Prophet who intend to sweep in and take the technology, probably kidnap the technical people. We're not taking chances. I'd like to have fighters overhead just in case."

Davidson said, "Sir, we're using the AC-130 because it has the range." The AC-130 was a CIA favorite; he didn't need General

Glosson to explain its capability. "They carry twenty-five-millimeter Gatling guns that can fire almost a hundred half-pound, high-explosive rounds a second."

Buster smiled.

Glosson added, "The land-based fighters don't have the range, but we have an aircraft-carrier battle group, USS *Reagan*, on a port-call in Australia. They can deploy and be in striking range within a couple of days. Her battle group also has a good-sized marine contingent that can be inserted by V-22 Ospreys, if needed."

Buster chewed loudly. "Yeah, there you go."

Davidson knew that Buster loved aircraft carriers, or more accurately, the ability to *direct* them.

Glosson continued, "The only way any bad guys can get in or out of there is by air. We can requisition an Air Force AWACS. With its radar, if anything flies, we'll know."

Buster said, "Good. Do that! I want continuous coverage. After they finish testing the Blaster in Los Alamos, the Prophet could head down any time."

Carl cleared his throat. "Sir, the Blaster's on its way to the South Pole now."

All eyes turned toward him.

Buster said, "What?"

He looked at his watch. "It should be arriving shortly."

Davidson said very clearly and slowly, "Carl, are you sure?"

"Yes sir, they were behind schedule. I think they made a last-minute decision to skip the Los Alamos test and do the first live test-fire at the Pole."

Buster pounded the table. "Damn it, I was right! He used the fear of a meteor shower to push up the schedule. When it doesn't show up – he'll be uncovered as a fraud. That means he's got to make his move soon." He gave Davidson an "I told you so" look.

Davidson frowned. "This changes things." He turned to Glosson. "We need to put the C-130 and SEAL team on four-hour alert. Let's get the AWACS in theater now. Call US Pacific Command. Tell him we need to pull the carrier battle group out of Australia and send them south. If Admiral Rea needs presidential authorization, tell him it's on its way."

Glosson said, "Done."

He turned back to Buster. Shaking his head, he said, "I had hoped we'd know who was behind the Prophet by now." He paused. "But if the Blaster's down there, it could be fired," he glanced at Buster, "or taken, any time. I think we need to pick up the Prophet sooner than planned."

Buster nodded vigorously. "Absolutely, we need to slam this door shut now!"

Davidson looked around the room and said, "OK, let's figure out how to take the Prophet without giving him a chance to warn anyone." He turned to Carl, "Where's our protector operative?"

Carl said, "I'll confirm it, but I think he's at the Pole now."

Davidson nodded. "So is our mole. They'll be our insurance policy in case the Prophet somehow gets word to the Pole base before we pick him up."

Turning to Lafferty, he said, "How fast can you put together a plan to capture the Prophet?"

Lafferty said, "That depends on whether we have to arrest all the participants at the same time. Remember, we're talking Dr. Sheri Lopez and one of NASA's leading scientists. We'll need a couple of days to coordinate that."

Buster scowled. "No, we can't wait, I want him now. The others can wait."

Lafferty said, "We'll still need to get the warrants and coordinate the operation with local law enforcement. We can probably pull it together tonight and have him in custody early tomorrow morning. That's the best time to grab a suspect anyway."

Davidson asked, "When?"

"About 5:00 a.m., St. Louis time."

Buster looked a little disappointed. "If that's the best we can do." He paused. "Where's my Tomahawk shooter?"

Glosson said, "USS *Truxton* is off the coast of Chile." She looked at her watch. "She can be in launch range in about thirty-six hours."

Buster said, "Excellent."

After the meeting, Carl caught Davidson. "Brian, I understand the Director's frustration, and you know I'm as skeptical as they come, but something doesn't add up."

"Yeah, there's a puzzle piece missing, but it's hard to argue with the fact that no agency's claimed him."

Carl sighed. "I know." He added with a half smile, "Aiding and abetting an international terrorist probably isn't going to look good on my next evaluation."

Davidson gave him a half smile. "Get in line."

Carl added, "Oh, by the way, there's something else. I didn't want to say it in front of the Director. Our operative, the protector, is actually being funded by…"

Davidson finished, "By the Prophet?"

"'Fraid so."

Davidson shook his head. "So, the CIA's not only protecting the Prophet, we're on his payroll." He laughed. "It'll be a shame if we have to kill him before I get to meet him."

38

RENDEZVOUS

Scupino answered the phone. "Hi Victoria, how's it going down there?"

She laughed. "We're freezing, but the installation's going well. The reason I called is that I've been talking to my colleague at the Keck observatory. Jim, they didn't find anything at the coordinates Josh gave us."

There was a long pause, then Scupino asked, "What if it's a dark comet?"

"Keck has some of the most powerful telescopes on earth. It'd have to be awfully dark for them to miss it."

"What if its surface is similar to that Araki-Alcock comet?"

"Less than one percent reflectivity?" There was another pause. "Yeah… I guess it's possible they could miss it. Absorbing that much sunlight, it'll have a descent IR signature."

Scupino knew she was thinking out loud as she continued, "We really need an infrared space telescope." She sighed. "But we might be able to pick it up on the UK or IRTF infrared scopes on top of Mauna Kea. I'll make some calls."

There was another pause. "Jim, no offense to Josh… but at this point I'm kinda hoping he's nuts."

Scupino just said, "Keep me informed."

After hanging up, Scupino drummed his fingers on his desk for a several seconds. Then picked up his phone and dialed. "Sheri? Jim Scupino. Need to talk with you as soon as possible…"

Josh arrived back at his apartment to find Elizabeth on his laptop. She barely looked up, as she held up a small hand-written note. It said, "Your internet access has been compromised."

Both angry and happy, he said, "Elizabeth, you cannot…"

She interrupted him as she stood up. "Give me a hug and tell me how beautiful I am."

He shook his head, walked over and hugged her. Looking down into her face, he kissed her and said, "You *are* beautiful, inside and out."

"See, that wasn't so hard." She stepped back and became all business, "Josh, what's happening?"

"Let's go for a walk." They grabbed jackets and went outside to the small park nearby. Not well lit, it was usually quiet and empty at night. Josh knew being outside wasn't a guarantee they couldn't be overheard. Technology was such that few places were impervious to eavesdropping, but it would make it more difficult. Keeping his voice very low, he told her about the comet fragment.

She listened intently and became excited. "That's great news. In a few days, the whole world will be more open to the possibility of a comet."

Josh shook his head. "Sometimes I wish I could see the world the way you do."

She looked into his eyes. "You can." She paused. "Josh, have you ever had a challenge in front of you that was so big you knew you couldn't do it alone?"

He smiled. "You mean like trying to stop a comet from eradicating life on earth?"

She laughed. "Yeah, that wouldn't be a bad example. What do you do when you face overwhelming situations?"

He knew she was fishing. The best way to deflect was to answer a question with a question. Jesse certainly used it on him. "What do *you* do in those situations?"

"I focus on what I want and ask for help."

"From who?"

She cocked her head and smiled. "The little voice in my head."

His eyes got wide, and he almost asked, "Jesse?" Instead, he narrowed his eyes and asked, "What voice?"

She gave him a half smile and raised one eyebrow. "Josh, hello, it's called prayer."

He was both disappointed and glad. Part of him hoped he wasn't the only one talking to Jesse, but he was also relieved. He couldn't handle *another* schizophrenic right now.

WASHINGTON DC

It was almost midnight. Lafferty took an FBI jet from Dulles to St. Louis. With the sensitivity of the case, the Director of the FBI had asked him to oversee it personally. He had to admit, he enjoyed being in the field again. His team had worked all afternoon preparing for the arrest. It was overkill. Buster was a knucklehead and he felt sorry for his counterpart. On the other hand… this guy *had* hijacked the military-industrial complex.

They would cordon off several blocks around the Prophet's apartment, and shut down his Internet and cell phone before moving in. SWAT snipers would back up a crack FBI team. State and local police would lock down the outside perimeter. They'd also have a helicopter overhead. The Godfather wouldn't get more assets.

Before catching a nap on the two-hour flight, he checked in with the surveillance team. They'd bugged the Prophet's apartment with the latest and least detectable audio system, but they'd deemed video too risky. Instead, they had placed hidden cameras in the hall outside and around the apartment complex with an agent or camera watching every exit.

The surveillance team reported that Meadows left the Boeing Phantom Works after working late and drove to his apartment. The only unusual event was that his girlfriend arrived an hour earlier. They'd gone out for a short walk in the local park and then returned to the apartment.

It usually worked to their advantage when the target was *occupied* with a partner, but it could also complicate things. You never knew what men would do under pressure. The SWAT team was good. If he used her as a shield, he would die quickly. He'd seen pictures of Elizabeth Edvardsen. Knowing the Prophet's future, he toasted him with a cup of coffee. "Enjoy, it'll be your last."

ST. LOUIS

He watched Elizabeth disappear into the bathroom with her small travel bag. It was late but he needed to check a couple of reports on the computer. His guilt gone, his body healed, and with no parents in sight, he felt like a teenager waiting for his first kiss. He was having a hard time concentrating on the computer. She finally came out... but she wasn't wearing her usual negligee with the short silk bathrobe. Instead, she wore a pair of long flannel pajama bottoms and a T-shirt. He sighed.

He didn't have to be Dr. Ruth to know she was dressing for sleep, not play. As he watched her spread a blanket on the sofa, he noticed how the flannel pajama bottoms and T-shirt clung to her. She could make a burlap bag look sexy. Lost in his teenage fantasy, he realized he'd been totally unchivalrous. Standing up, he said, "Thanks for fixing this up for me. You're sleeping in my bedroom."

She frowned.

He said, "I often sleep on the sofa. Since I have to work late tonight, it works out well." He hadn't planned on working late.

She looked up at him and said, "I really don't mind."

"What type of cad would allow a beautiful woman to sleep on his sofa?" He added, "I'll change the sheets in the bedroom." He didn't want her sleeping out here simply because he knew he didn't have the discipline to watch her sleep without nibbling on her.

She said a little abruptly, "Don't worry about the sheets. I'll take care of it."

Lying on the couch, Josh had trouble falling asleep. After midnight, he slid into a nebulous intersection of consciousness and dream. He was partly aware of his surroundings, but his body felt like it was made of lead. The room closed in on him. The apartment, the city, the world, seemed to pulse in and out with his heartbeat, getting smaller and tighter with each beat. Then his perspective suddenly changed. He seemed to be outside himself, watching his body on the sofa. There were faint "threads" radiating out from him in all directions. Each tied to an action. Do this – and that happens. Do that – and this happens. It was similar to his experience with Kelly at the restaurant. It was fascinating and terrifying, like seeing the future, or many futures. He realized he'd seen these threads in his dreams before and had unconsciously used them to drive his strategy and actions. He even saw situations where acting prudently created the wrong path. What he sensed – actually felt – were forces closing in on him. He knew he was under surveillance, but now he sensed something more sinister.

He followed a thread that appeared to move him in the correct direction. His choices caused it to branch like a movie that had different endings. The further in the future it went, the more the threads overlapped. Like multiple TV channels interfering with each other, the correct path was harder and harder to distinguish. What he *could* see clearly was that staying where he was would result in failure. No, worse than that, staying would lead to death and destruction. He saw buildings and people on fire... but not from the comet and not a year from now. He couldn't tell why or when, but it was soon, very soon. Even the paths that seemed to lead to a successful firing of the Blaster had an ominous similarity. They faded to black like the credits at the end of a movie. He wasn't sure what that meant but had his suspicions. Regardless, he knew what he had to do.

He came fully awake. First, he contacted Greg Langlois, the young engineer who was good at improvising under pressure. Josh was certain he'd need that ability soon. It was 12:30 in the morning. He used the app that Smith loaded on his smart phone, to encrypt the text he sent.

Langlois answered immediately, saying that he was up, gaming.

Josh texted, "problem. pushing schedule up. need ur help. can u leave 4 pole asap?"

"yes"

"b at flight ops 1 hr?"

"k"

"pack warm. don't tell anyone."

Greg typed back, "cool." He was excited to be going with "James Bond," as the young engineers jokingly referred to Josh. A movie and gaming buff, he couldn't help but think this was like being a character in one of his favorite games. He didn't get out much.

Josh dressed quickly. He wrote and rewrote Elizabeth a short note and tiptoed into the bedroom. With the fade-to-black vision he'd seen, he suspected this would be the last time he'd see her. Unlike Kelly, at least he could tell her how he felt, how much he appreciated her and apologize. If they succeeded but he didn't survive, he hoped she wouldn't hate him. If he failed, he knew she wouldn't hate him for long. He slipped the tiny note under her hand. Leaning over, he kissed her gently on the lips, etching her face into his memory. He softly said, "I love you." She smiled in her sleep as he left.

Using his *memory* of the future, he moved quickly. He turned the TV on and the living-room lights off. The flickering of a late-night movie dimly illuminated the apartment. He smiled as he realized it was *Invasion of the Body Snatchers*.

He dressed in black cargo pants, topsiders, a dark-blue shirt, and a black baseball cap. Scooping up his laptop, he threw it in his small bag and went to the front door. He grabbed the door handle and froze.

He closed his eyes for a moment... then let go of the handle. He set the bag down. He sensed a rhythm. Silently, he walked to the sliding glass door that opened onto the tiny balcony. He inched it open. Glancing outside, he quickly slid through and closed it. He kept his body pressed against the wall next to the door. There were no buildings across the street from which to observe his apartment. With his excellent night vision, he looked down and scanned the dark parking lot. Looking closer, he noticed a van seemed to have a very slight red glow emanating from the side and part of the roof. He realized with amazement he was actually seeing a heat signature. He'd heard that there were people who had the ability to see very slightly into the infrared spectrum. Once again, he thanked Jesse for his genetically enhanced body. Without a doubt, inside that van sat his unnamed observers. Unfortunately, they probably had low-light and infrared cameras and could see as well as or better than him. He needed to move fast. He took a deep breath and climbed onto the balcony's metal handrail where it met the wall.

The agent was glad that they were finally going to arrest this guy. He was tired of sitting in the van all night. He had two giant monitors with nine separate video-camera feeds, and just like cable TV, there was nothing on. His partner sat next to him with headphones, monitoring the audio feed and playing solitaire. Even though they were both relieved every few hours, it got old continuously watching static video feeds. He started his umpty-millionth scan of his low-level-light cameras. Following a set pattern, he began with the hall and entrance cameras and then looked at all the exterior feeds. To the irritation of his partner, he always ran through them under his breath like a checklist. "Hall camera one and two, clear. Elevator camera, clear. Lobby entrance, clear."

Stretching, Josh was just able to get his fingers over the bottom edge of the balcony above. Doing a quick pull up, he peeked over the balcony deck. Through the sliding glass door, he could see the upstairs apartment was dark. As he started to pull himself up, the rotting deck-board under his left hand gave way. The end of the one-by-six broke off cleanly and fell. His body swung like a pendulum, hanging from the slipping fingertips of his right hand. Trying to hang on, he looked down. The piece of broken board hit the asphalt below.

The agent heard a noise outside. Standing up, he moved forward in the van and looked out the window. Rolling it down, he stuck his head out and looked around. Listening carefully, he scanned the parking lot and the entrance to the apartment.

Hanging from the balcony, it was hard to be inconspicuous. His old body would never have been able to hold on with his fingertips. His new body was amazing but it wouldn't survive a four-story fall. Straining to keep his grip, he quietly pulled himself up with one arm until he could reach the railing with his other hand. He grabbed the metal railing, pulled himself up, and then quickly climbed over. He pressed himself against the wall next to the sliding glass door and froze. He caught his breath as he listened intently for any activity below.

The agent saw nothing. To his partner, who was looking up with interest, he said, "Heard something in the parking lot. Probably just a dog or cat."

He went back to his video console and completed his scan. "Stairwell exit one and two, clear. Balcony, clear. Side entrance, clear. Alley, clear." As expected, he saw nothing.

Josh reached over to the sliding glass door. Thankful that it was unlocked, he opened it slowly. Hearing nothing, he slipped inside with all his senses straining. He heard regular snoring coming from down the hall. He silently glided around the dark furniture to the front door. Unlocking and opening it, he peered out. The hall was empty. Normally, he'd go to the left toward the elevator. Instead, he went right, to the stairwell.

He went down the stairwell as fast as he could, bypassing the ground-floor exit. The stairs continued down to a basement area. At the bottom, there was one locked door to an equipment/storage room. Sliding a credit card between the doorframe and door, he was able to open the simple lock. He entered a large, dim, windowless basement. It was dank, musty, and filled with boxes and rolls of carpet. Across the room was a small red exit sign. He went to it and slowly opened the door. It creaked loudly with lack of use.

Peering out, he saw he was in an outside stairwell, a walkout basement exit. He slipped out onto a set of concrete steps going up to ground level. Taking a few steps up, he poked his head up like a periscope. He was in an alley, illuminated by a single sodium-vapor streetlight. Obviously failing, it buzzed loudly and flickered. Every thirty seconds it would dim for a few seconds and then relight.

Across the narrow alley was a broken chain-link fence. A large dumpster next to the fence provided some cover. Timing the light, he dove across the alley as the streetlight blinked. He quickly wiggled through a hole in the fence and found himself in a dark, poorly maintained parking lot. The lot surrounded a squat industrial building. Skirting the side of the building and staying in the shadows, he climbed over a tall fence and jogged to the street. For the first time in months, he sensed no one watching him. He enjoyed the two-mile jog to the airport in the crisp night air.

It was 1:30 a.m. when he arrived at Boeing flight ops, only a half hour before the weekly C-17 left for the Falklands. Greg was already there. He sat with a small duffel bag and a "geek" cap.

Geek caps were new to the market and still quite the fashion risk. Ball caps covered in form-fitting, flexible solar cells, they had a thin antenna on top. The cap charged a smart-phone and provided better reception. Although the caps were clever and functional, the name was accurate. Greg also sported augmented reality glasses, a Bluetooth headset and keyboard-mouse gloves. This truly took computers to the street. Observers would see the users staring at nothing, wiggling their fingers in the air, and talking to themselves. Josh's sister worked with autistic children and he couldn't help but notice the similarity.

He clapped Greg on the shoulder and thanked him for coming on such short notice. As they walked out to board the C-17, Josh smiled at Greg's appearance. He was Josh's height but weighed maybe 140 pounds and had a knack for unusual clothing combinations. He obviously didn't care what others thought, or maybe wasn't aware. Josh suspected he was color blind, or at least hoped so. He was actually a good-looking kid, but Josh couldn't help but think his geek cap and tech gear were effective at several functions, including birth control. As they climbed onboard, Josh promised himself, if he lived through this, he'd talk to Greg about women.

IV
CONFRONTATION

39

CAPTURE

Elizabeth woke up suddenly, disoriented in the strange bed. It was early morning and still dark. As she got her bearings, her intuition said something was wrong. She turned on the bedside light and saw a small folded piece of paper lying on the blanket. Opening it, she read:

> *Elizabeth, I'm sorry I have to go. I had a premonition I can't ignore. I'm catching the early morning flight to the Falklands. I apologize for leaving suddenly, but where I go, I cannot protect you. Cooperate with the authorities. You are everything that's good and noble about the human race and, I believe, the most beautiful woman in the world. Your belief in me is greater than I am. You deserve much better and you will find it. I love you. Josh.*

Before she could react, the doorbell startled her. It was 5:20! Still clutching the note, she went to the door. Looking through the peephole, she saw a tall, dark-haired man with a dress shirt and black jacket. She asked, "Who is it?"

"FBI, we have some questions, ma'am."

"It's awfully early, can we talk later?" she asked, knowing full well that wasn't going to happen.

"No, ma'am, this cannot wait. Would you please open the door?"

"I need to see some ID."

He held it up to the peephole. She folded up the little note from

Josh, put it in her mouth, and swallowed it. Taking a deep breath, she opened the door to let her fate in.

He came in quickly followed closely by five others. They wore black windbreakers with "FBI" on the back, wielding automatic weapons. By their bulk, she guessed they had bulletproof vests underneath. The man who spoke to her held her near the wall as the others moved rapidly through the small apartment.

The other three came back quickly and said, "He's not here."

The lead agent holstered his pistol and turned to her. "Where is he?"

She shook her head and said honestly, "He was here when I went to sleep."

He watched her closely as she spoke. He didn't say anything but nodded to the female agent who had joined them.

She quickly frisked her, told her to put her hands behind her back, and handcuffed her.

The male agent said, "We have a warrant for your arrest on the grounds of National Security."

All Elizabeth could say was, "National Security? You're kidding."

He didn't respond but spoke into a microphone. "He's not here. Bring in forensics. We're taking her out now."

The female agent asked Elizabeth if she had shoes.

"In the bedroom."

As the female agent went to the bedroom, Elizabeth saw three more people come in with suitcases. One started taking pictures. Another picked up Josh's bag by the door and pulled out his laptop with a gloved hand.

The female agent returned, dropped sandals in front of her, and steadied her as she slipped them on. She wrapped a blanket around Elizabeth's shoulders and led her outside.

With an agent holding each arm, they took her down the stairwell and out the door. There were several large black SUVs outside and a helicopter overhead. Looking up, she saw it orbiting with a searchlight swinging back and forth. It was surreal. She felt like she was in a police drama. A few curious apartment dwellers peeked out from their balconies. Flanked by the two agents, she walked erect and kept her chin up as they put her in the backseat of an SUV. There were flashing blue lights everywhere. She almost said, "For me? You really shouldn't have." But thought better of it.

LANGLEY

Davidson was in Buster's office. It was 6:30 Eastern Time when they got the call.

They put Lafferty on the speakerphone. Davidson saw Buster's shock when they heard Lafferty say, "He wasn't in the apartment."

With Buster speechless, Davidson quickly asked, "His car is still there?"

"Yes."

Frowning, Davidson fired back, "When did the surveillance team see him last?"

"Surveillance video shows him returning from a walk in the park with Elizabeth Edvardsen. They were clearly ID'd going inside at 10:05 p.m. Inside audio confirms it."

Davidson persisted, "Could he have slipped out and taken another car?"

"We had the entire building, inside and out, under surveillance, and no cars left after 10 p.m. We're going through the video surveillance records now. If he slipped out, we have a cordon around several city blocks and a helicopter with IR sensors. We'll find him. Edvardsen's in custody and on her way downtown for interrogation. We'll report back as soon as we have anything."

As Lafferty hung up, Buster looked at his Deputy. "Where is he?"

ST. LOUIS

In silence, they drove to an office building. They took her to a small interrogation room, still wrapped in the blanket. The woman agent removed the handcuffs, sat her at a table across from two chairs and left.

With nothing else to do, she examined the room. It was about as nondescript as it could be. Maybe ten by ten, beige linoleum floor, beige paint, and white, acoustic ceiling tiles with industrial fluorescent lighting. The table was gray painted metal with no drawers and no sharp corners. There was a large mirror on the wall that faced her, probably a one-way mirror. She tried to sit casually, but it was difficult wearing nothing but a T-shirt and pajama bottoms. She pulled the blanket around her.

Then she thought, it was all a state of mind. She wasn't going to let her environment, which she couldn't control, affect her identity and belief, which she could. She sat upright. She'd pretend she was wearing a suit, and the blanket was a designer shawl. Still nervous but proud of what they were doing, she knew she was right; they were wrong.

LANGLEY

Davidson, tapping a pen against his leg, suddenly looked at Buster. "May I use your computer?"

Buster slid his chair to one side.

Davidson grabbed the keyboard. They had access to the most sophisticated, high-resolution satellite system in the world... but sometimes, you just didn't need it. Calling up Google Maps, he found the Prophet's apartment building and switched to satellite view. Slowly he zoomed out until he could see the airport.

"Dang." He grabbed the phone and asked Bishara to come up to Buster's office. As she came through the door, Davidson motioned her around so she could see the screen. He pointed at the airport. "What's the schedule for their logistics flights to the Falklands?"

She scrolled through her iPad. "Looks like they've been running them... every Thursday."

Davidson fired back, "That's today. What time?"

"Usually, it's early in the morning. It's a twelve-hour flight. Let me check." She pointed to Buster's phone.

Buster nodded.

After a few seconds, they heard her say, "Two o'clock. Are you sure?"

Before she could hang up, Davidson grabbed the phone. He looked at the clock as he waited for Lafferty to answer. It was almost

6:00 a.m. St. Louis time.

"Bart, was Boeing Flight Ops under surveillance?"

"No, we pulled everyone in for his capture."

Davidson shook his head and said with certainty, "He's on his way to the Falklands."

Lafferty said, "You sure?"

"I'd bet my retirement on it."

Buster said calmly, "Get the team together."

He glanced at Buster, surprised he hadn't exploded.

Buster, obviously reading Davidson's look, said, "If he's outside the US, he's no longer under FBI jurisdiction... or US law."

40

INTERROGATION

ST. LOUIS

After a few minutes, two men came into the room and sat across the table from Elizabeth. They didn't introduce themselves. The bigger of the two was at least six-four and twice her weight. He looked like he came out of a mafia movie. With a large broken nose and one bushy eyebrow, the word "testosterone" came to mind.

She sighed, whispering a quick prayer under her breath.

The big one asked, "Do you know Josh Meadows?"

"Of course I do."

"Where is he?"

"I don't know. Why do you want him?"

"Just answer the questions."

"I haven't done anything wrong."

He leaned forward menacingly. "You're about to be charged as an accomplice to treason, espionage and conspiracy to commit terrorist acts against the United States. These charges carry the death penalty."

They were trying to scare her. It was working pretty well. "Josh Meadows is a good man," she said defiantly.

"Josh Meadows is a threat to this country and if you don't answer the questions we'll assume you are too!"

She shook her head and matched his volume. "You don't know what you're talking about, and I have the right to a lawyer!" She was worried but also angry, and refused to get emotional in front of them.

The second man had been watching her intently. He turned to Mr. Testosterone and nodded slightly. Silently the big man got up and left. Elizabeth noted that the second guy was the opposite of the first. Smaller and well groomed, he looked more like a corporate vice president. As he spoke, his voice and manner were much softer. She guessed they were using the "good cop, bad cop" approach.

The big FBI agent entered the dimly lit room, joining two women in suits and a tall, intense-looking man wearing a sports jacket. Watching the interrogation through the one-way mirror, the big agent said quietly, "Looking at her file, I didn't think the intimidation approach would work."

One of the two women said softly, "She asked for a lawyer."

The tall man said, "Not yet. We need that information fast and you *know* we aren't worried about her Miranda rights."

The other woman looked at him with raised eyebrows, but said nothing.

Leaning forward, her interrogator said softly, "Elizabeth, Josh's in serious trouble. Time is of the essence. If you don't want to see him hurt or killed, we need you to tell us everything you know about him as soon as possible."

"Why, what are you trying to do to him?"

"Elizabeth, we need to stop him before he gets himself killed. You can help us prevent that."

She thought wryly, this wiped out any question about Josh having delusions of grandeur. Not only did the FBI think he was a national threat, they couldn't even catch him. She didn't doubt he was in trouble but he was much more than they knew. "I don't believe that."

"Elizabeth, it's often those who are closest who don't see what's happening."

Elizabeth remembered her earlier pledge. They were not going to control her belief. She decided it was time to take the offensive. "You're making a huge mistake. He's trying to prevent a comet from wiping out all life on earth and if you interfere with him, you put yourself, your families, and the entire human race at risk!"

Leaning back, he said, "Elizabeth, what do you really know about Josh?"

She knew… it was going to be a long night, but she also knew her rights. "I'm not afraid of what you can do to me, and I know Josh is doing the right thing. I also know I have a right to a lawyer."

The tall man behind the one-way mirror shook his head and said quietly, "It's safe to say her relationship with the Prophet is real, at least from her perspective. Tony will stay in the 'what's good for Josh' mode. It's time to play our last card." He nodded at one of the women. "Counselor, you know what's at stake. We don't want her. We want him."

Both women nodded.

As they left, the big agent said, "She's not a bimbo. She's very intelligent, yet she believes all this crap."

The tall man said, "The Prophet's fooled senior military officers, leading scientists and Sir Edward Brandon." Looking through the mirror, he shook his head. "About the *only* thing I am certain of at this point, is that the Prophet has good taste."

Elizabeth looked up as the door opened. Two women in suits entered. The first woman was medium height, slim with an athletic build and short, light-brown hair. She was about Elizabeth's age and attractive but looked like she was all business. She came directly to Elizabeth and introduced herself as Rachel Eisenbeck, her appointed Federal Defender. She pulled one of the chairs around to Elizabeth's side of the table and sat down next to her.

The second woman was a little shorter with long, beautiful, auburn hair and fair skin. Like the Defender, she was impeccably dressed. Elizabeth's first impression was that she was very cute and young, maybe mid twenties. As she sat down across from her, however, Elizabeth realized she was closer to her own age. She surmised that her beauty and apparent youth had probably caused more than one attorney to underestimate her.

Her newly appointed lawyer began by saying, "Elizabeth," she gestured across the table, "this is Amy Sobrero from the Federal DA's office. She's agreed to offer you immunity from prosecution *if* you will help the FBI with their investigation and tell them everything you know."

The DA had a disarming smile and said softly, "Ms. Edvardsen, we know that you wouldn't do anything to harm your country, and understand that you are an innocent victim in this case. All the FBI is trying to do is avert disaster. Your information may be critical to that effort *and* saving the life of Josh Meadows. We will grant you full and total immunity from prosecution regarding anything involved with this case." She slid a sheet of paper across to Elizabeth's attorney.

Her Defender, picking up the sheet, added, "The charges are very serious, and this is an unusually generous offer. As your attorney, I would strongly recommend you accept it."

Elizabeth remembered the note, now resting in her stomach. Josh had told her to cooperate.

She would do just as he said... kinda like when he told her to stay in Kansas City. Ignoring the paper and pen her attorney slid in front of her, she said, "I haven't done anything wrong, and Josh not only hasn't done anything wrong, he's trying to save the world. This is a terrible mix-up. I will cooperate fully in an effort to help unscramble this insane situation."

She knew Josh created the "mix-up" intentionally, but it was still a mix-up. She'd "help" them understand that they were interfering in something they didn't grasp. She wouldn't tell them what she *really* believed. That would just solidify their belief that both of them were nuts, eliminating her ability to put doubt in their minds.

She decided to look at this as a game. Their job was to wear her down with doubt, while pulling out information they could use against Josh. Her self-appointed job was to paint a picture that would make them question themselves.

LANGLEY

The entire team assembled by 7:00 a.m. Lafferty, on a speakerphone, said, "You were right. I talked to the Flight Ops personnel at Boeing. He arrived at 1:30 this morning along with a young software engineer named Greg Langlois. They took off at 2:05 a.m. and are scheduled to arrive in the Falklands about 2:00 p.m. our time."

General Glosson said, "The C-17 pilots are Air Force test pilots. We can contact them by radio and have them diverted to wherever you want."

Buster asked, "Where are they now?"

Glosson looked at the ceiling as she did some quick calculations. "Probably over the Gulf of Mexico, but I can get their exact location in a few minutes."

Davidson looked at Buster and said, "Recommend we go with the original plan to capture him in the Falklands. Keep him isolated on an island where we have the upper hand. We're a little behind but we can have our team landing right behind him."

Buster said, "What if he doesn't go to the Falklands?"

Davidson nodded and turned to Glosson. "We need a tight watch on that aircraft. If it deviates from its planned route *at all*, we need to know and contact the pilot ASAP."

Buster nodded at Davidson. Davidson took that for approval and continued, "Otherwise, we let them proceed." Looking at Glosson, he asked, "How soon can we have our aircraft headed south?"

"We called in the aircraft crews and SEAL team as soon as we heard what happened in St. Louis." She looked at her watch. "They should be launching within the hour. They're out of Hurlburt AFB in Florida. So, they're closer to the Falklands and can be there an hour or so after the Prophet arrives."

Bishara looked at the Deputy and said, "We have two of our people in the Falklands right now. Do you want them to capture the Prophet when he arrives?"

Davidson asked, "Are they experienced operatives?"

Bishara shook her head. "No. Their job was to coordinate the administrative side and act as a liaison with the locals."

Davidson said, "Can't risk it. Have them stay back. This guy's got eyes in the back of his head. Their only mission is to ensure the Prophet's C-17 stays put after it lands. We'll wait until we have the CIA/SEAL team in place before taking him."

Buster asked, "Do we have clearance to operate in country?"

Davidson said, "Yes, I've been working closely with Tony Collins the MI6 Deputy Chief."

Buster asked, "Do they understand how dangerous this situation is?"

Davidson nodded. "They know everything we know and have already coordinated with Scotland Yard and the British military in the Falklands. We have a closer working relationship with them than we do with many US agencies."

Buster nodded. "Good."

From the speakerphone, Lafferty said, "When do you want to round up the rest of the players in St. Louis and Los Alamos?"

Davidson looked at Buster. "We know his girlfriend didn't contact anyone before we arrested her. No sense tipping our hand until we have him."

Buster nodded.

Davidson said, "Bishara, as soon as our team lands in the Falklands, start jamming their cell phones. Bart, at the same time, let's take everyone else into custody."

Lafferty said, "Our operatives know that the scientists and engineers are innocent pawns. When we pick them up, they'll be told they're being taken into *protective* custody."

Buster said, "What about Lopez and Chandra?"

Lafferty said, "We have all the legal warrants. We'll emphasize it's for their own protection."

Glosson added, "We have presidential authority to use the carrier battle group. They'll be pulling out of Australia shortly and heading south. They should be within strike range in thirty-six hours."

Someone knocked and came into the room. He handed a note to the Deputy and left. As Davidson read the note, his eyebrows went up. "Sir, just got word from the Keck Observatory in Hawaii. They think their infrared telescope may have detected something at the coordinates the Prophet supplied. It's too early to plot a trajectory."

You could hear a pin drop as all eyes went to the Director.

Buster's face started turning red and his veins began to pop out. He released a string of expletives that would've made a sailor proud. Finally, winding down, he looked around the table and said in a controlled voice, "This guy's kept one step ahead of us the whole way. He's obviously planted the information."

Davidson said, very softly, "It's a Caltech and NASA observatory."

Barely keeping his temper in check, Buster said, "The Prophet's an expert at manipulating government agencies." He pointed at Carl Casey, almost smiling. "For God's sake, he's had us working for him!" He took a breath. "I want everyone from the observatory who knows about this picked up immediately for questioning. If there are any leaks, I want them discredited."

Davidson paused.

Buster slapped the table. "I mean right now! Do you understand me? This jerk is *not* going to make a jackass out of me or this agency!"

Davidson said quietly, "Yes, sir." He turned to the team and said, "All right, we know what to do, let's move."

As they broke up, Davidson saw Buster signal him to stay behind. He assumed it was for a butt chewing, but Buster looked unusually thoughtful.

"I'm sorry, Brian, I know you're just doing your job, trying to dot the 'i's' and cross the 't's.'" He paused. "I've decided… I want you to personally take charge of the operation down in the Falklands. It's just too critical and I want my most experienced man on the scene."

Davidson was surprised. It was unusual for a Director or Deputy Director to leave the country except on official state business, and then only with full protection. The information in their heads was too valuable to risk. It was even more unusual for the Director to apologize. On the other hand, he'd love to get out of DC and back into the field. He also had to admit he wanted to be there personally when they captured and interrogated the Prophet. "Yes, sir."

"Great." Buster paused. "There's something else I'd like you to do. After they finish interrogating his girlfriend, I want her down in the Falklands." He smiled, looking down at a sheet of paper. "The forensic team found a notepad in his apartment. They were able to reconstruct part of a message he wrote her before he left. *Apparently*, he has some feelings for her." He looked back up. "He's managed to stay ahead of us at every turn." His smile turned unpleasant. "I want to use her pretty little body as a negotiating chip in case something goes wrong."

Davidson frowned but nodded slowly. He didn't like what he was hearing and wasn't sure it was legal to take her out of country, but he needed to have all his ducks in a row before he dared challenge the Director again.

As Buster left and Davidson headed toward his office, Carl Casey caught up with him.

Casey quietly asked, "Would you mind if I ran the observatory investigation? I'm not as vocal as the Director, but I'm not any fonder about being duped."

Davidson nodded. "Go ahead. Let me know what you find."

Returning to his office, Davidson called Lafferty. He explained that Buster wanted Edvardsen in the Falklands for leverage. "Bart, this is outside my area of expertise. Can we legally take a suspect, who's a US citizen, out of the country?"

Lafferty said slowly, "I guess I don't understand why we would *want* to. Brian, you've seen her dossier. She's never even had a speeding ticket. Her only crime was falling for her patient."

Davidson said, "I'm with you. If you tell me it's illegal, I'll tell him and we'll be done with it."

Lafferty sighed. "It's not *illegal,* but it's complicated." He paused. "The plan was simply to scare her into cooperating. We haven't officially charged her with anything." He paused again. "Actually… that could work to our advantage."

Davidson said, "I'm not following you."

"Brian, we don't have to arrest her and transport her. All we have to do is *ask* her."

Davidson said, "OK…?"

"Look, she obviously cares for this guy. She's not a wimp and she's aware of their Antarctic operation. If you thought your significant other was in danger and someone offered to take you to where they were…?"

"Got it," said Davidson. "Can you make that happen?"

"I can, but I'd like to know what the plan is for her." There was a pause. "Brian, I don't want to lead an innocent lamb to slaughter."

Davidson said, "Buster wants me down in the Falklands. I'll be there with her."

Lafferty said, "Enough said. I'll take care of it."

41

FALKLANDS

They arrived in the Falklands just before 3:00 p.m. local time. Although relieved that there wasn't anyone to meet them, Josh felt unusually anxious. They had to wait for the C-17's aircrew to get crew rest before they could continue to Brown Cow base. Borrowing one of the Boeing cars, they headed toward town to get a hotel. As they drove through the base, Josh was impressed. Mount Pleasant Royal Air Force Base was a serious installation, equipped with state-of-the-art facilities.

Leaving the base, they drove toward Port Stanley. He decided he liked the Falklands. It was beautiful in its cool, windy desolation. Other than occasional sheep, he saw little sign of civilization as they drove through wide-open tracts of treeless, rolling hills and windswept slopes.

LANGLEY

Bishara said, "Our on-site agent just reported that the Prophet's C-17 arrived. The pilot and crew are still with the aircraft. The Prophet and the young engineer left to get a hotel."

Buster asked, "Where are they going?"

Bishara said, "The only hotels are in Port Stanley. It's about thirty miles from the base. As an insurance policy, we closed the Prophet's aviation fuel account so they won't be able to refuel their C-17. *Our* C-17s will be landing in about twenty minutes."

Davidson said, "Good. Make sure our two agents don't try anything heroic. Have them stay at the airport and contact us immediately if the Prophet returns to the aircraft."

FALKLANDS

Josh thought the sky looked desolate and foreboding, with an angry, dark-gray overcast. Or maybe he was just projecting his mood. He couldn't shake the anxiousness. The further he drove, the stronger it became. Finally, he was about to stop the car, when his cell phone buzzed. He looked down and saw a text message coming in. It was accessing the encryption app, so he pulled over and waited for it to decipher the text.

There was no sender or address. It simply read, "ok, they'll meet u @ airport with budweisers. want 2 go cow tipping later. got 2 go, will b tied up, Godspeed."

He understood immediately. It was Scupino. His signature "ok" authenticated it. "Budweiser" was clearly a SEAL team, either at the airport or inbound. "Cow tipping" must mean they were going to shut down or destroy Brown Cow base. "Tied up" was self-explanatory. The charade was over. They were coming to collect or eliminate him, and stop all they had done. Josh closed his eyes.

"Sir, are you OK?"

"Just give me a second to think."

From his thread visions, he knew what happened in the next few minutes could stop them in their tracks or allow them to move to the next critical juncture. He cleared his mind and thought of Jesse. Suddenly, an idea formed. He knew what to do, or at least try. He opened his eyes. "Change of plans."

"What is it?"

Josh did a wheel-spinning U-turn, as he handed his phone to Greg. "It's a warning message from Captain Scupino. Our program's been compromised. Believe it or not, there are forces trying to destroy it. I could use your help but I have to warn you, from here on out I'll be cutting corners and it could be dangerous, possibly very dangerous. If you want, I can drop you off at the base."

"No, sir, I eat danger for breakfast." He smiled. "Sorry, movie line. What can I do to help?"

"You sure?"

He nodded.

"Greg, I don't suppose you have internet access down here?"

Greg, still wearing his geek cap, whipped out his glasses and gloves. "Of course. If there's a tower, I can tap it."

After a few seconds he said, "I'm online."

"Log into the program site. We need to send a message to our team at Brown Cow base right away." Josh dictated, "'Resurrect has been compromised by elements inside our own bureaucracy. They have access to our communications system. Ignore any command that doesn't have proper authentication. If approached in person by government agents, confirm their identity.' Sign it with my authentication code, 'Jesse.'"

Greg repeated it back to Josh and then sent it.

"Greg, I also need to look up some information online." He explained what he needed to google.

After a few seconds, Greg handed him his glasses. Josh was surprised he could read while seeing the road through glasses. He quickly found what he needed. Josh gave the glasses back and did several quick calculations in his head. He finally sighed and said, "This should be interesting." He drove as fast as the sedan would go back toward the airport.

Muttering in frustration, Greg took off the video glasses. "Just lost the internet connection and phone signal."

LANGLEY

Glosson said, "Sir, our first C-17's on final approach. The second one is five minutes behind it."

Bishara added, "Our agents report that the Prophet's C-17 hasn't been refueled, and the Brits are jamming all voice and data transmissions in or out of the Falklands. We've also taken over the satellite communication link to the Pole base. They can't send or receive anything without going through us."

Buster exclaimed quietly, "We've got him."

FALKLANDS

As Josh and Greg approached the airport, they saw a C-17 taxiing in. They were still a mile and a half from the airport entrance but with his exceptional vision, he saw another C-17 already parked... next to theirs. Game on.

LANGLEY

Bishara said, "Sir, our SEAL team and British Army Special Forces from the Falkland garrison have taken control of the Prophet's C-17 and rounded up the crew and Boeing reps. The Capture Team is headed out now. Working with local law enforcement, they're also putting up roadblocks on all roads around Port Stanley just to be on the safe side. There's one other small civilian airport and they've got that covered too."

Buster asked, "Do they have the Prophet's picture?"

"We're circulating it now, but on an island of 3,000 people it's pretty easy to find 'Waldo.'"

Buster frowned, not getting it.

Bishara explained more seriously, "He'll be easy to identify. He's the one they don't recognize."

Buster nodded.

Davidson said, "Let's flip the switch on the US portion of the operation."

Buster said, "Do it."

Lafferty, back from St. Louis, picked up his phone, and said, "Execute."

42

THEFT

FALKLANDS

Just before reaching the main terminal, where the C-17s were parked, Josh turned at a military hangar. There was a small guard gate at the entrance. As they approached, Josh said, "Not only could this be dangerous, but it could also get you in serious trouble." He smiled. "I won't hold it against you if you want to back out."

Greg swallowed. "No, sir, I'm in."

"OK. Greg, do you have your Boeing badge?"

"Yes, sir."

"Put it on and follow my lead." As they pulled up, Josh showed the guard the access badge they used in the US.

The guard looked puzzled. "You'll need to get a base badge."

Josh said, "We've been called in for an emergency aircraft repair and need to get to the maintenance area immediately." While he said that he focused on "knowing" the guard would let them pass.

Just then, three military vehicles with lights flashing and sirens blaring drove past the gate, behind them. They were coming from the main terminal, undoubtedly headed toward Port Stanley. Josh didn't turn around but caught a glimpse of US military fatigues in his rearview mirror as they went by.

The guard looked up with interest, then turned back to Josh and waved them through. "Move along."

Josh looked at Greg, and Greg grinned back. "That was like the scene where Obi-Wan Kenobi uses the force on the Storm Troopers."

Josh laughed. He hated to admit it, but he was thinking the exact same thing.

They parked outside the hangar. As they walked toward the entrance, he looked at the six F-18 Super Hornets sitting on the tarmac, and committed their tail numbers to memory. Just before he walked in the door, he turned to Greg who was looking distinctly uncomfortable and said, "Greg, this is one of those rare times when the ends do justify the means. What I'm about to do could get both of us in trouble." Then Josh continued in a TV commentator voice, "And although rare, side-effects may include bullet holes."

Greg's eyes got wide. Then he started laughing. "This is like playing *Splinter Cell Seven* on Xbox."

Josh just shook his head. "The single most important thing you can do is say nothing and look like you know what you're doing. Ready?" As they went in the entrance, Josh looked at the plaque on the wall that identified the RAAF Number 1 Squadron, Wing Commander Bob Gulick. They went straight to the Commanding Officer's office. With urgency, he asked if the Wing Commander was in. The airman said, "Sir, he left for the day. Do you need to reach him?"

"No, we'll run down to maintenance and talk to the Flight Sergeant… uh…"

"You mean Sergeant Laura Hawkins?"

"Yeah, Hawkins, thanks."

They headed down to the maintenance department and asked for Flight Sergeant Hawkins. A tall, serious-looking woman said, "That's me."

Josh introduced them. "We're the tiger team from Boeing. Wing Commander Gulick told us to get our butts here ASAP. You probably just got the maintenance bulletin about the emergency software configuration issue."

The Flight Sergeant shook her head. "Crap."

Josh knew the lingo. A software configuration error was a rare but scary problem in a fly-by-wire aircraft with dozens of interconnected computers. Josh added, "Luckily it only affects a few aircraft. The ones that might have the problem are bureau numbers 5124637 and 5124644."

She said, "Yup, those are ours, but I haven't seen the bulletin."

Josh smiled. "For once we're moving faster than the paper pushers."

She didn't smile. "Will this take them out of flight status?"

"Not if they pass a quick software check. Just need to do a power-on cockpit test. Can you give me the maintenance books on them?"

Without a thought, she handed them to him.

"There's a chance none of 'em will be affected, and I'll go away and not bother you again."

She finally smiled back, nodding her head.

He went through the first book for show. He studied the second aircraft's book carefully, noting flight status, maintenance gripes, and fuel. It was a two-seater configured as a tanker, with a refueling store hanging from the belly and two large drop-tanks on each wing. This allowed it to refuel other Hornets while airborne. With 30,000 pounds of gas onboard, it carried more than its own weight in fuel. He said, "We'll start with the tanker."

The Flight Sergeant said, "I'll see who I can pull off one of the birds to help you."

"That would be great but Greg here is a qualified Plane Captain."

Greg looked up at Josh with wide eyes.

She looked at their badges and said, "OK."

"Is there a place we can change into some coveralls?"

"There's a men's room down the hall on the right."

LANGLEY

Bishara reported, "Our team just hit the hotel. They weren't there. They never checked in. They're searching for the car now."

Buster frowned but said, "We've got him bottled up on an island. No matter how good he is, he can't hide for long. I want more assets on the ground as soon as possible."

Davidson said, "We'll shut down the civilian airport and cover the seaports. I'm more concerned about the Blaster at the South Pole. Can we go ahead and send the SEAL team onto the Antarctic base?"

Buster said, "Absolutely."

Glosson nodded, "The second they're refueled, we'll have 'em airborne."

FALKLANDS

Josh went down the hall with Greg in tow. Glancing back to make sure no one was looking, they walked past the men's room until he found the pilot locker-room. There were no flight ops going on, so it was empty. "Greg, watch me and do as I do." Josh found and tried on several torso harnesses. With the survival vest integrated into them, they were bulky and hard to get into. He found one that was close. "Find one that fits and put it on like I did."

Greg said, "You're going to jack an airplane!"

Josh said, "No… *we're* going to jack an airplane."

Frowning, Greg said, "This wasn't in the job description."

"Greg, if we live through this, I'll show you how to successfully meet women."

Greg grinned. "OK."

Josh found helmets that would fit. Helping Greg get his legs into the correct loops in the harness, he thought, Greg was an amazing kid. Most people would've freaked out by now.

"Now put your coat on over the outside to hide the torso harness."

They put their helmets, oxygen masks, and gloves in a bag.

"Sir, I know you're a genius and all, and everybody thinks the world of you but… can you really fly one of these?"

"Greg, these are some of the most advanced fighters in the world." He turned and headed out the door, adding over his shoulder, "But it's OK… I got an Xbox."

Greg, still frowning, shrugged and followed him.

The two-seat F-18 was easy to spot on the tarmac. It was the only Hornet with five large tanks hanging from its wings and belly. They walked out briskly but casually. They were in luck; no one was around the aircraft. Josh pushed the button that electrically opened the canopy. Then he released a latch that dropped a small, rickety-looking boarding ladder from under the wing's leading edge extension. "Greg, climb up and get into the back seat." Josh followed him up. While glancing around the tarmac, he connected Greg's torso harness to the ejection seat and hooked up his oxygen mask.

"Don't put your helmet on yet."

From his perspective on top of the aircraft, he looked around and saw a couple of airmen working on another aircraft. They were a hundred yards away and showed no interest. So far, what Josh and Greg were doing would look normal.

He climbed back down, and with a quick check to make sure no one was watching, pulled out all the flight-safety pins and covers, and kicked the chocks away from the wheels. Climbing back up the ladder, he noticed Greg was beginning to look a little panicky. Josh knew he had to be firm. As he armed Greg's ejection seat, he said, "Look, Greg, I do know what I'm doing. Don't touch anything unless I tell you to, and definitely stay away from anything with yellow-and-black stripes on it. Got it?"

Greg swallowed and nodded.

Leaning across Greg, he quickly checked all the switch positions and set Greg's intercom to Hot Mic. "Greg, when you see me put my helmet on, put yours on." He patted him on the shoulder and smiled. "This is going to be fun."

Greg, already wide-eyed, raised his eyebrows further.

Josh slipped into the front cockpit and strapped in. He was smart enough to know that he was dangerous without a checklist. As he lowered the canopy, he closed his eyes. With his IMAX memory, he was able to recall in detail the last time he started a Super Hornet. He turned the battery power on and started initializing the navigation system. He plugged the Pole base coordinates into the computer. No one would notice them until he started the Auxiliary Power Unit. The small APU turbine provided the "air" to start the engines but it was almost as loud as the engines themselves. Finally, he put his helmet on and flipped the APU switch. In his rearview mirrors, he could see Greg donning his helmet.

The APU cranked up with its usual, and unfortunately, very characteristic howl. As soon as the ready light came on, he routed the APU's high-pressure air to crank the number-two engine. As the engine slowly spun up, he listened to the radio, monitoring the ground-control frequency. He saw one airman, a hundred yards away, watching them. He just stood there looking at them curiously.

As soon as the engine reached idle, he released the parking brake, pushed the throttle forward, and began taxiing. He noticed the airman was now running back toward the hangar. The Australians used the squadron call sign "Phoenix." Appropriate.

He switched the high-pressure air over to start the other engine. Doing his best Australian accent, he called himself Phoenix Seven, and requested taxi clearance. They cleared him to taxi, but then came back and said they didn't have a flight plan on him. It wasn't that uncommon to have late submissions or mix-ups. As he continued to taxi, he just said, "Sorry, mate. I'll get it straightened out on the squadron frequency, call you right back."

As soon as he said that, he switched to the tower frequency and listened. He taxied as fast as he could. Unfortunately, thirty tons, perched high atop three small wheels, made the fighter handle on the ground like a three-legged pig on valium. He was almost to the runway when he saw a truck with flashing lights headed their way.

As he reached the runway, he did just like his mom taught him. He looked both ways for traffic. He saw a large cargo jet on final approach a couple miles out. He knew they'd have to scramble to abort their approach. As he rolled onto the runway without a takeoff clearance, he keyed the mic and said "Sorry." Skipping the engine run-up checks, he pushed the throttles forward to full power. The tower, excitedly, said, "Phoenix Seven, you haven't been cleared for takeoff! There's an aircraft on approach, clear the runway immediately!"

Unlike his last takeoff, he couldn't afford to use the afterburners. They needed every drop of fuel. As his heavily loaded fighter lumbered down the runway, the truck with the flashing lights caught up to him. It ran parallel to him on the taxiway. He hoped the driver hadn't seen too many Rambo movies.

He heard a cockpit warning tone. Glancing down, he saw a "Ladder" warning on his display. He *totally* forgot that the little boarding ladder was still down. It could only be raised from the ground. As they took off, the increasing airspeed would rip it out of the aircraft. He just hoped it wouldn't go down an engine intake.

He was a little clumsy on the controls as he lifted the fighter into the air but it came back fast. It felt good to be back in the cockpit. As soon as he had his landing gear up, he turned south and accelerated to the optimum climb-out speed, which the Hornet calculated for him. He loved these jets. They took care of all the boring but important details, so he didn't have to. He hated to admit it, but if it weren't for GPS, navigation computers and fuel calculators, he would have been lost at sea a long time ago.

He heard a loud thump. The boarding ladder ripping off the aircraft and bouncing off the fuselage was an audible reminder of his aversion to detail. He checked his left engine indicators. Whew. Probably left a few dings but missed the intake. It did remind him to turn his IFF (Identify Friend or Foe) off. Without his radar repeater highlighting his position, he knew he would quickly disappear from the ground-based radar screens.

He keyed the intercom. "Greg, you all right?"

"Yes, sir, this is totally wild. It's almost like *Microsoft Flight Simulator 12.0.*"

Josh released his oxygen mask and let it hang by one bayonet fitting. Smiling, he replied, "Yes, they did a great job making these fighters feel as close to that game as possible."

Oblivious to the satire, Greg asked, "Do you think they noticed that we jacked a jet?"

43

ESCAPE

Bishara received a phone call during the meeting. After a few seconds, they heard her say, "Oh no! Are you sure?… How long ago?… Is there any chance?… OK, keep me informed."

Seeing her expression, Buster said, "What is it, Cindy?"

"Someone just stole an F-18 Super Hornet from the Australians."

Buster yelled, "It's him, it's got to be! What the hell are Super Hornets doing in the Falklands?"

Davidson shook his head. "Remember, the UK asked the Aussies to deploy them as a warning after Argentina bought the Russian SU-27s."

Buster said, "Tell them to shoot him down!"

Bishara said, "Too late. By the time they figured out what was going on, he was outside their surface-to-air missile range, but they're scrambling another Hornet to intercept."

Buster continued to rant. "This is insane! How could he fly one? Where does he think he's going? He can't make it to the South Pole in a fighter!"

Bishara squinted her eyes and said quietly, "Well… actually, there *is* a chance…"

Buster pointed a finger at his Deputy. "*You* told me that *we're* not using fighters because they don't have the range."

Bishara came to Davidson's defense. "That's true, but this Super Hornet was fitted out as a tanker with extra drop tanks. Our Navy guys are running the numbers now, but there is a slight chance that if he flies a perfect flight profile…"

Buster yelled, "Oh my God! Launch the C-17s and gunships.

Where's the Tomahawk shooter and the carrier?"

Davidson, trying to spin Buster back down, said, "We've already given the command to launch the C-17s with the SEAL team. They're taking off now."

Glosson added, "We've downloaded the target coordinates to the USS *Truxton*'s launch computer. They're programmed and ready to fire on our command. The USS *Reagan* is preparing a strike package with tankers, just in case. She can have fighters overhead shortly after the C-17s arrive at the Pole. They can also insert a Marine team by V-22, shortly after."

Buster was beginning to sweat. "We need to launch the Tomahawks now and be done with this."

There was silence in the room. Davidson said, "Sir, we can't do that. Most of the people down there are innocent civilians. Some are high-profile American scientists..."

Buster interrupted, "If they're stupid enough to be duped into building this thing for him..." His voice trailed off as all eyes were on him. He looked at Davidson angrily. "Then tell the SEAL team they're authorized to use deadly force. I want a termination order on the Prophet right now!"

Davidson continued in a quiet voice, "Sir, the Prophet's head of security is one of our contract agents. If, by some miracle, he survives the flight, our man can immobilize him quickly. The only guns down there are under his control, but he doesn't need a weapon. He is a weapon. We've got him."

Buster sounded almost plaintive. "That's what we always think. Don't you see? At every turn he's made fools of us!" In a more controlled voice, he continued, "I'm not taking any chances this time. I want a termination order on him, and I want it now!" He slammed his hand on the table.

Davidson glanced around and said quietly, "Yes, sir. The President is involved with this operation, so we'll need Presidential authority for a termination order."

"Give the termination order to our agent on *my* authority. I'll get approval from the President." Buster's eyes narrowed. "I also want a one-million-dollar bounty on his head."

Davidson said softly, "We'll have to go through the Attorney

General and State Department to authorize that."

Buster said, "No we don't." Sarcastically he added, "I'm a lawyer, remember?" Continuing as though completing a closing argument at a trial, he said, "We've ascertained that the Prophet has no identity. Therefore, he's not an American citizen *and* he's now outside the US. Even so, we don't need a *public* bounty." He turned to Carl. "We simply offer *our* contract employee a large bonus."

Davidson knew targeting a foreign terrorist outside the US was well within their authority, as was granting incentives for anti-terrorist operations.

Carl looked at Davidson for confirmation.

Davidson nodded.

Buster slapped his hand on the table again, "*And* I want that Tomahawk shooter ready to fire the second I give the word!"

"Yes, sir."

FALKLANDS

The SEAL team commander, Lieutenant Commander DeVries, was getting his men back together for the final leg to the Pole base, when the call came in on the C-17's encrypted satellite communication link.

He turned to his Senior Chief and told him about the stolen Hornet.

Shaking his head, the Chief responded, "Who're we chasing, Jason Bourne? Should we tell the Aussies who he is?"

"We don't even know who he is. Hopefully they'll shoot him down, but regardless, we've been ordered to press on to the South Pole ASAP. *And*, we've been given unlimited Rules of Engagement."

The Chief frowned. "Unlimited ROE? So we can shoot anybody and everybody." He shrugged. "Makes the job easier but I don't understand. Aren't there American engineers and scientists down there?"

DeVries nodded. "There has to be a lot at stake. Something down there is incredibly dangerous." As the Chief ran off to round up the team, DeVries continued to himself, "Or, it's personal… or both." He wouldn't shoot anyone unless required, but he'd pull the trigger without hesitation or remorse to complete the mission.

44

INTERCEPT

SOUTHERN OCEAN

"Won't they try and shoot us down or something?"

"By the time they get clearance to shoot a ground-to-air missile, we'll be outside their range," Josh said optimistically.

"What about sending another fighter after us?"

"Well… that is a possibility."

"But we can outrun them, right?" Greg said enthusiastically.

"We could if we weren't flying a Bingo profile."

"What's a Bingo profile?"

"Bingo means minimum fuel. We're flying the perfect climb, cruise, and descent speeds to give us the maximum range."

"So the speed for maximum range isn't really fast?"

"Greg, it's like when you're running out of gas in your car. You know going faster will just reduce your mileage."

"But… a jet chasing us won't have that limit?"

Greg was sharp. "Nope. Another Hornet in burner could catch us. Not only are we flying a slower profile, we're also configured as a tanker."

"What does that mean?"

"Greg, look at the wings. See all the tanks hanging under them?"

"Yeah."

"This fighter is set up to refuel other fighters. That gives us a lot more gas but also a lot more weight and drag. We're slower and less maneuverable until they're empty and we jettison them."

"So they *can* catch us."

"Yeah, but it'll take a while to scramble another jet, and we have two advantages. Super Hornets are stealthy – hard to find on radar. Plus, we're running away from them. That shrinks the range of their AMRAAM missiles. They'll have to get pretty close to shoot. I'm less worried about burning than freezing."

"Freezing?"

"Do you know how far our South Pole base is from the Falklands?"

"2,000 miles?"

"Actually, it's almost 2,800."

"I didn't know fighters could fly that far."

"Me neither."

There was silence from the back seat.

"Greg, normally they can't, but with the five extra fuel tanks, it should give us a range of about 2,500 miles. We're also going to jettison them as soon as they're empty. That'll buy us another 100, or so."

Greg said quietly, "That's still 200 short."

"Well, those numbers assume some fuel left for approach and landing."

"So we'll be almost empty when we land?"

Josh hesitated. "Yeah… well, we probably need to talk about that." He paused. "Greg, do you like extreme sports?"

"Yeah, love to watch them on the Internet."

"Ever wanted to try any of them, like bungee jumping or… skydiving?"

"No, I'm more of a gamer."

He decided to bring it up later. "By the way, Greg, we've got another small challenge. The same guys who were trying to intercept us in the Falklands are almost certainly headed to the polar base right now."

"I don't understand. We're trying to save the world. Are they terrorists?"

"No, I'm afraid it's much worse. They're from the government and they're here to help."

With obvious confusion, he said, "But you're from the government."

"In the government, the left hand doesn't always talk to the right hand. Normally, we could work this out with some emails and a couple conference calls, but we're a little short on time."

ST. LOUIS

Elizabeth refused to sign the immunity from prosecution agreement.

After almost ten hours of interrogation, they put her in a locked room. There were no windows, one cot, a toilet, and a sink. She was still wearing her pajamas with her blanket around her. She thought it was late afternoon and realized she had had nothing to eat, but she wasn't hungry.

She paced around the room for a while, and then, emotionally exhausted, she sat down on the cot. She wanted to cry but she knew they were watching and wouldn't give them the satisfaction.

SOUTHERN OCEAN

Australian Flight Lieutenant Tommy Harper climbed in afterburner. He followed the ground-based vector from the airport's radar, but they'd lost contact with the rogue Super Hornet shortly after it took off. Using his jet's powerful radar, Harper picked up a faint target moving due south at 35,000 feet. He was still about 80 nautical miles away but closing fast. Looking down at his fuel gauge, he realized it was going to be close. He called back to base on an encrypted frequency. "Boss, I got him painted. He's headed due south, angels 35, doing about 500 knots."

Wing Commander Gulick replied, "Roger. How's your fuel?"

"I'll have to jettison my drops." He paused. "If I don't get within range in ten minutes, I'll have to turn back or we'll lose another jet."

"Keep pressing, you're cleared to jettison."

As he blew his drops off, he asked, "What's my ROE…what do you want me to do with him?"

"Tommy, we're trying to figure that out now. Just be ready and try to get him on the radio."

"Roger that." Again, he thought, who am I chasing? As he

manned-up, they told him it was two guys posing as Boeing technicians. Before the attack on the World Trade Center, he'd never have thought terrorists had the sophistication to steal and fly an aircraft. He shook his head. He had to either get them to turn around, or make sure no one could ever use their own fighter against them.

Josh heard a low-pitched warbling tone. Greg said, "What's that?"

"We have company."

"The bad guys?"

"No, just some seriously irritated Aussies."

"What are we going to do?"

"How do you feel about prayer?"

Two of his drop tanks were empty. He happily jettisoned them into the ocean. With the new flight configuration, the computer recalculated his maximum range profile, allowing him to speed up a little and climb another 1,000 feet.

Loud and clear on Guard, the emergency radio frequency, he heard, "Super Hornet flying south, we're intercepting you. If you return to base, you won't be harmed."

Josh didn't respond. Their confusion about who was in the cockpit might still be an advantage.

Greg asked, "Have they launched a missile at us?"

"No, you'll hear a high-pitched warbling tone when they lock us up for missile launch."

"Can't we just outrun them with afterburner, like in *HAWX* on Xbox?"

"With our burners lit, we'd go through ten tons of fuel in twelve minutes. Unfortunately, they forgot to install a game-reset button in this crazy plane. Not only wouldn't we make the base, we wouldn't even make it to Antarctica."

Greg volunteered, "We'd retain consciousness for fifteen minutes in freezing water."

Josh shook his head. "Discovery Channel?"

"*Titanic.*"

Flight Lieutenant Harper radioed back to base. "He's not responding to the radio calls. I don't have enough fuel to join on him, but I'll be in missile range in a couple of minutes." He looked at his fuel gauge. "I'll have just enough time to squeeze off a missile before I'm on emergency fuel. I need to know what you want me to do."

At the base, Wing Commander Gulick said to himself, "Where the hell could he be going? He's heading south! There's nothing there…" He shook his head in frustration.

"Boss, I'm at the edge of radio range. Can barely hear you. Need the ROE."

Gulick sighed. He had to make the call. His career was already over for losing the jet. "Haven't heard anything back from Command. On my authority, if they don't return, splash 'em."

Harper replied, "Roger." Then to himself he said, "Root me!" Like all fighter pilots, he looked forward to testing himself in combat, but shooting one of his own bloody jets in the clacker wasn't what he had in mind.

He had a radar lock and selected his AMRAAM missile. The HUD immediately showed the range circle, indicating he was still out of range but closing. He flipped the Master Arm switch on. The missile-launch button on his stick was now hot.

Josh heard the warning tone shift to a higher-pitched warble no pilot wanted to hear. The Aussie had locked him up in preparation for missile launch. He once again pictured in his head the course of action needed, and hoped Jesse was "listening." At the same time, he heard another transmission. "Super Hornet headed south, this is your last chance. Return or I'm going to splash you."

Josh came up on the radio. "Aircraft in pursuit, break off your attack. I'm a US government agent on a critical mission. Please contact the United States government immediately and they'll explain the situation. Really apologize for borrowing your aircraft; we'll replace it."

Harper used his other radio. "Boss, did you hear that transmission?"

He heard nothing but static. It was going to be his call. If they were just crazy Boeing reps, they'd crash or eject in the ocean and freeze to death. Blowing them out of the sky would be merciful. But this guy didn't sound crazy, and he couldn't imagine any situation that would require stealing a fighter without a US government heads-up. The transmission had to be a ploy to give 'em time to escape. In either case, the answer was clear. He came up on the Guard frequency and said, "Mate, that's bull and you know it. There's no way I can confirm that before I have to launch."

The computer determined the missile was now in range. In his HUD, he had a "Shoot" cue. Harper, with his thumb over the launch button, thought to himself, this sucks. He keyed his mic. "Give me one good reason why I shouldn't put this AMRAAM up your arse?"

Josh had a flash of illogical insight. When he was an F-18 instructor, he flew with an Australian foreign-exchange pilot. They'd become friends. The Australian Hornet community was tight and there was a chance this pilot might know his friend.

Josh replied, "I've been pinched on the butt by Mel Gordon's wife, Vivian."

There was a moment of silence, then laughter on the radio. "Fair dinkum? Vivian pinches everyone! That's how she says g'day."

The radar warning tone ceased.

Josh said, "Yeah, I know. She's an amazing lady, probably smarter than both of us combined."

"Ain't that the truth? Don't know what you're doing, mate, but I hope you packed long underwear. Gotta go. Good luck and Godspeed."

Josh breathed a sigh of relief, adding, "Thanks. When we get back, I'll buy you a pint."

"You're on."

Greg said, "We made it!"

Josh said wryly, "Yup, all downhill from here." He checked the distance to Brown Cow base. They were still almost four hours away. With their current fuel, the navigation computer was telling him they weren't going to make it.

"Greg, how much time do you need to get the tracking-system software online?"

"About two hours."

"Can you do it faster?"

"Maybe cut an hour off, but it'll take a few hours to charge up the capacitors from the reactor anyway."

Josh said, "It's going to be really close. Tell you what, why don't you review anything you can. We still have a ways to go."

"I'll be ready when we get there."

"Good. By the way, can your computer fit inside one of your coat pockets just in case we have to move quickly?"

"Sure."

"When you're finished with it, why don't you go ahead and put it in there and button it up. Then see if you can get some sleep."

"OK."

He jettisoned another tank. Their predicted range improved, but the computer was still coming up way short.

MOUNT HOWE

Tim Smith had been down at the Pole base for several days in preparation for the arrival of the rest of the team. He went back to his bunk for a quick nap. When he got there, he saw his Iridium satellite phone blinking, indicating a missed call. The phone was more than twice the size and weight of a normal cell phone but guaranteed connection anywhere on the planet. It even worked fairly well at the South Pole. He put on his headset and checked voicemail. It was Carl. He wanted him to call back ASAP.

45

METEOROID

Jesse hadn't responded to Josh's calls in several days. He wondered if Jesse had other operatives like him. He was relieved when he finally responded. "Thank God you're back again, but it may be too late. My house of cards is collapsing. I used up my last disappearing act. No place left to run." He paused. "Isn't that comet fragment supposed to arrive soon?"

It enters the atmosphere in ten hours.

"Any distractions would be welcome right now. Where's it headed?"

The coordinates and trajectory appeared in Josh's mind. He plugged them into the Hornet's navigation computer. Expecting it to be over the ocean by statistical odds, he was surprised when the display put the coordinates almost on top of London. "Well, they're not going to be able to miss this. By the way, how big is it?"

Like the comet, he suddenly saw it in his mind – it looked like a slowly rotating, lumpy, black boulder. He immediately sensed it was fifty meters across.

Startled, he said, "Fifty meters? That's the size of a small building!" His photographic memory allowed him to recall anything he read, but he hadn't studied the impact of anything smaller than a kilometer. Still, he was sure fifty meters was bad. "Could it do damage or kill people?"

Yes.

"Yes?! We need to get the word out. We may need to evacuate London!"

He tried his UHF and VHF radios but got no response. He tried different frequencies and the emergency Guard channel, but knew he was in one of the few places in the world where there was no one in radio range. "This is a nightmare! You knew this thing was coming in over a city but didn't tell me. Why are you giving me this information now when there's nothing we can do about it?"

Can't you?

Josh paused and thought. "Are you suggesting… we can deflect it?"

Can you?

"I have no idea. They haven't finished installing the Blaster, much less testing it! The tracking scope may not be able to see something this small, and the beam's probably not powerful enough. Even if it works, they'll shut us down or blow us up before we can fire it. Thousands will die. We'll lose all credibility and never have time to stop the comet."

Is this the outcome you wish?

"Of course not!"

Then why are you rehearsing it?

Josh stopped his mental death spiral. He took a deep breath and tried to slow his breathing and anger. As he thought about it, he realized it was no one's fault but his own. He'd never asked Jesse the size of either the comet or the comet fragment – absurdly obvious questions. It dawned on him: his stubborn analytical nature prevented him from accepting guidance. He only wanted *suggestions*, and then, only when he asked for them. Jesse had honored that. The result was that he was playing catch-up, with the survival of mankind hanging in the balance.

He actually envied Elizabeth, who could believe with conviction on nothing but faith. Maybe he could learn from her, but even as he thought that, he knew it wasn't ever going to happen. She'd been open, kind, and trusting. He'd repaid her by withholding the truth and keeping her at arm's length. In retrospect, it was fortunate they'd never consummated their relationship. She had lost her first husband, and if his "fade to black" future were accurate… Even if he survived, she'd soon learn he wasn't what she thought he was. Her feelings would die with her belief in him. She might even hate him for deceiving her. Great, one love thought him dead, and another who'd soon wish him dead… it'd make a great Country song.

It was a bit late to ask Jesse for relationship advice, but he had nothing else to do until he was within radio range of the base. Sensing Jesse's attention, he asked, "What do you do when someone loves you because they think you're something you're not? Or, more specifically, what do you do when they see through that, to what you really are?"

Have you claimed to be something you're not?

"I lied by omission. By not confronting her, I let her believe I was something I'm not."

What does she think you are?

He frowned. "Uh... I'm not really sure."

What are you?

"Well, I'm... uh..."

Then how do you know you're not what she thinks you are?

He laughed out loud, realizing the absurdity of the situation. He was flying over Antarctica in a stolen Hornet without enough fuel to land, chased by a C-17 full of SEALs who were almost certainly going to kill him. Even Dr. Ruth wouldn't have wasted her time giving him relationship advice.

MOUNT HOWE

Smith didn't like what he was about to do next but after talking to Carl, he didn't see any option. He just kept his mind on the primary goal – take care of the three children he'd orphaned. As head of security, he knew this program's personnel and equipment vulnerabilities. With that knowledge, what he was about to do would be childishly easy, but like everything else he did, he would be thorough and leave nothing to chance. Picking up a satchel of tools, and making sure no one was around to observe, he headed outside to commit sabotage.

ANTARCTICA

Bitching Betty disturbed his thoughts with the casual announcement, "Bingo. Bingo." He checked their distance to Mount Howe. The navigation computer was indicating about 320 miles. Engineers erred on the conservative side… he hoped. As he reset the Bingo fuel warning to 2,500 pounds, Greg woke up and said, "Did you say something?"

Josh said, "No. Did you get any sleep?"

"Yeah, but I had weird dreams. I was flying without an airplane."

"Interesting… Greg, got some new information while you were sleeping. Turns out that one of the comet fragments is going to strike near London in about nine hours."

Greg asked, "Is it big enough to cause damage?"

"I think so, but Chandra will know for sure."

"Snap! Can we deflect it?"

"Don't know but it's going to be that much more critical that our test firing be done at full power."

Greg said, "It's going to be risky pushing full power through it on its first shot."

"Just make sure you're ready to go when we get there."

For several minutes, Josh tried the radios on various frequencies but still heard nothing.

Then Betty repeated, "Bingo. Bingo."

Greg asked, "Are we out of gas?"

"No, Betty's an alarmist. We still have 2,500 pounds left."

"How long will that last?"

"Another twenty minutes or so."

Greg asked, "Why is the computer warning system a female voice?"

Josh thought his question was a bit of a non sequitur, but realized Greg was a computer wizard. Explaining it would delay having to worry him about their impending method of debarkation. "Years ago, before there were female fighter pilots, they did studies, and discovered men respond better to women's voices."

"Why didn't they change it when women started flying fighters?"

"Hate to break it to you, but the studies showed that women *didn't* respond any better to men's voices."

"Well, *that's* not fair."

Josh laughed. "I agree."

He tried again to reach the Pole base on his UHF. "Brown Cow base, this is Josh Meadows, over." He repeated his call several times. Finally, he got a static-filled but understandable reply. "Commander Meadows, this is Major Crowley, we weren't expecting you."

"I know. Change of plans. Is Chandra there?"

"She's on top of the mountain."

"Please patch me through. This is an emergency."

A minute later Chandra's voice came on the radio. "This is Chandra. Is that you, Josh?"

"Yes. Victoria, I just learned that the comet fragment we're expecting is fifty meters across and will enter the earth's atmosphere in less than nine hours."

Chandra said, "Fifty meters? Josh, large meteoroids heat up and explode in the upper atmosphere, but this one's big enough to be another Tunguska."

Josh said, "Is that likely?"

"I'm afraid so. The Tunguska object was probably similar in size. It created a blast of around ten megatons that flattened everything in a forty-kilometer radius." She paused. "Where's it headed?"

"London."

She said, "Oh my God, we have to evacuate London!"

Josh said, "Let me give you the coordinates so the observatories can back this up."

After he gave her the coordinates and trajectory, she said, "I can't reach the observatories. We're having communication problems." There was a pause. Then she said, "If these coordinates are right, the shockwave could level and set fire to much of the city. It could kill tens or hundreds of thousands. Josh, your source has informed the authorities already, right?"

Josh said, "No! We have the same problem you do. You've got to get this information out somehow."

"Josh, we got word that the program's been compromised. Shortly after that, we received strange communications from people claiming to be from the government. They told us to stand down, but they didn't have the correct authentication passwords. We knew they weren't real and ignored them. Unfortunately, they killed our satellite link. We have no way to communicate!"

Josh said, "Keep trying. See if anyone has a satellite phone that's working. Broadcast in the blind if necessary. Give as much technical detail as possible. Victoria… *can we deflect it?*"

"Deflect it?"

He heard Katori in the background: "We don't even know if it will fire." There was a pause, and then Katori said, "Cho, what do you think?"

Cho said, "Well, at this close range the beam will still be incredibly tight. I think it's powerful enough to vaporize a nice divot into it, and create a decent jet plume."

Josh repeated, "Dr. Chandra, is it possible?" There was a longer pause. He knew she was running calculations on her laptop. It took sixty long seconds before she replied.

"No, no, Josh, I'm sorry. We can't. It's just not physically possible this late. Even if everything worked perfectly, the impulse from the gas jet isn't enough. It's just too close, too fast and the earth's too big to miss. I'm… I'm sorry."

"It doesn't have to miss the *earth*, just London."

She replied immediately with excitement in her voice, "You're absolutely right! We only have to nudge it enough to get it over the ocean. If we can slow it enough to shift its impact 500 kilometers…" There was another pause. "Yes, yes, there is a slight chance, if we hit it with everything we've got as soon as possible. This all depends on the coordinates being accurate and it being reflective enough that we can track it. Sorry, Josh, I don't have time to talk; gotta run some calculations."

Katori jumped on the radio. "Josh, we weren't even supposed to do the test firing for a couple of days; we just finished installing it. We haven't checked out any of the circuits or even tried to charge the capacitors yet. If something goes wrong, it could destroy the Blaster, possibly blowing us up in the process."

Josh said softly, "I know, but there's too much at stake. You and Cho are the best there is. Even if we *can* get the word out, you know they can't evacuate everyone from a city in eight hours."

He could actually hear Katori sigh over the radio. Josh added, "I have Greg Langlois with me for the software interface stuff."

Katori, sounding very tired, said, "Good. We'll need him. Josh, I have to go. I need to find Bobinski and get the reactors online."

Josh said, "Judy, are you still there?"

"Yes, sir."

"Can you send a snowcat out about two miles due west of the base? We're going to need a ride."

"Did you say two miles *west* of the base?"

"Yes, we'll be arriving rather abruptly and we're not dressed appropriately."

Crowley said, "I don't understand."

"I'll explain when we're on the ground."

WASHINGTON DC

It was 9:30 p.m. Davidson boarded the specially equipped Gulfstream G650 for the twelve-hour flight from DC to the Falklands. It was the fastest, longest-range, executive jet on the market. They'd also specially modified it with extensive satellite communication and defensive systems. He'd only flown on it a few times, preferring to travel by more conventional and economical means. Buster had no such reluctance, using it as his personal airliner.

He had serious reservations about not being in the Ops Center when the SEAL teams arrived at the South Pole, but Buster had been very firm. All he could do before he left was talk to a couple of the key team members. As concerned as he was, his job was to be the Director's Deputy. As long as he was giving legal directives, Davidson would support him, whether he agreed with him or not.

46

EJECT

Greg asked, "Why aren't they meeting us at the airfield?"

Bitching Betty chose that time to say, "Fuel Low. Fuel Low."

Josh said, "That's why."

"We're out of gas?"

"No, we have another ten minutes."

"How far are we from the base?"

Josh said, "About twenty minutes."

"Then how are we going to land?"

"We're not. Greg, trying to land a fighter with no engines is tough under the best of conditions. Add darkness, insufficient altitude and an unlit ice runway; it's just too risky."

"What are we going to do?"

"We're still at 37,000 feet. We can glide there, but eventually we're going to have to step outside."

"We're going to eject?!"

"Yup, just like in *Top Gun*." Remembering the movie, he realized that was probably a bad choice for illustrating an ejection.

"But I don't know how to eject."

Josh, speaking slowly and calmly, said, "Don't have to. It's set for Command eject. When I go, you go. Listen carefully, Greg. We still have plenty of time, but when I say get ready, I want you to put your head back against the headrest with your chin slightly elevated. Put your hands in your lap and extend your feet so that your thighs are touching the seat cushion. I'll do the rest."

"Why didn't you tell me this earlier?"

"Would have ruined your nap."

"But how do I use the parachute?"

313

"It'll open by itself, and you'll come down just fine. Just look at the horizon. Don't look down. Keep your feet together, knees slightly bent. When you hit the ground, just roll with it. Make sure your jacket's zipped up and your helmet and gloves are on tight. Also, make sure you have that little computer zipped in as tightly as you can. The departure's a bit of a rush."

"You've done this before?"

"Yup."

"So it's really not so bad?"

"Actually, I died."

"That's not funny." Greg's voice was rising with panic.

Josh said in his calmest voice, "I'm sorry, Greg. Don't worry; we'll be ejecting under perfect conditions. You'll be fine. This will be a great story to tell your kids and grandkids some day."

For the first time, Greg sounded plaintive and scared. "Commander Meadows, why is all this happening? It isn't fair! They can't be doing this to us. The government needs to do something about these people. Someone needs to… sue someone!"

Josh stifled a laugh. Greg had been a real trooper but the pressure was catching up. He decided to try to take Greg's mind off the ejection by engaging him in a philosophical discussion. He knew where to start.

Greg's comment about suing was funny but indicative of Greg's, and even Josh's, generation. Many were raised by "helicopter parents." They hovered around their children, believing that their job was to make sure everything was fair and controlled. Understandable, but, unfortunately, the world was neither fair nor controlled. When these kids got into the real world, they were in for a shock. They assumed that when something went wrong, it must be someone else's fault or a lawsuit was required.

"Greg, how do you think unfairness in our country can be better addressed?"

"What?!"

"Greg, if you were king, what would you do to fix things?"

"Commander Meadows, you're just trying to take my mind off ejecting."

"Yup."

There was a pause. "Good idea." After another pause, Greg said, "I think too many people get to do anything they want and in the process hurt others. Everyone needs to operate under the same rules so no one has an unfair advantage."

Josh scanned his fuel gauge – it read zero. "Can you give me an example?"

"Yeah, when I was going to high school and college, jocks were treated differently. The academic standards didn't apply to them. Winning a stupid athletic event was more important than learning. Some slept through classes and flaunted it. No one should be able to do that."

Betty cheerfully said, "Engine Left. Engine Left." Josh watched as the RPMs on the left engine started to drop.

Greg asked the obvious. "Are we out of gas now?"

"No, still have the right engine."

Betty corrected him. "Engine Right. Engine Right."

Josh said, "Now we're out of gas, but we'll glide for another ten minutes." As the engines wound down, it was unnaturally quiet in the fighter's cockpit.

Greg, the consummate computer engineer, asked, "Will the flight-control computers remain powered without the engines?"

Josh said, "No worries. The engines are still windmilling with the air running down their intakes. That's enough to spin the generators and supply power. Even if they weren't, we have backup batteries." He shut down the radar and all unnecessary electronics to reduce the load on the generators.

"Greg, do you understand that no matter how hard we try to make things fair… the universe isn't fair? It's not fair that a comet is on a collision course with earth. It's not fair that we respond better to women's voices, than they do to ours. How do we regulate that?"

"I understand that, but we can control the unfair actions of *people*."

Passing 25,000 feet, he checked the navigation computer and refined their heading. "OK. As king, what would you do to make sure all students are treated fairly?"

"I don't know… I guess I might have the teachers keep a closer watch on what was happening both in and out of the classroom, and give them the power to take action."

"OK. Let's say they assign someone to every student. They could follow you all day and make sure no one broke any rules or did anything unfair." Josh checked the distance to the base. With no drag-inducing tanks, they'd glide about seven feet forward for every foot they dropped, but they still had fifty miles to go. It would be *very* close.

Greg finally said, "That would suck. You'd always have someone looking over your shoulder. You'd have no freedom."

Josh smiled. "Bingo. Reducing unfairness requires more control. The way to eliminate *all* unfairness would be with total control. There's your tradeoff – control versus freedom."

Greg added, "Besides, what if the person following you didn't like you?"

"Good point. Who gets to decide what's fair? Puts a lot of power in the hands of the regulators and enforcers, doesn't it? That's the paradox of government. If we seek security above all else, we achieve maximum security, which also happens to be the name for the tightest cell in a prison."

Greg said, "Guess it has to be a balance."

"That's something governments have struggled with since the beginning of time. Figure out that perfect balance and I'll vote for you."

ST. LOUIS

Elizabeth had been there for three hours. Sitting on the cot, head in hands, she replayed every conversation she'd ever had with Josh. She'd maintained her position throughout the interrogation but it took a toll. They couldn't be right… could they? She wasn't just some gullible mark. No, she couldn't, she wouldn't, believe that… but it was so hard to hear what they kept saying about Josh.

She heard the door open and looked up. The female FBI agent who'd handcuffed her introduced herself politely and asked Elizabeth to accompany her. Still holding onto her blanket, she followed mutely.

They went up in an elevator to what looked like a hotel suite. Inside, she was surprised to see they had a nice dinner waiting for her. She saw that they also had her purse, makeup bag, toiletries and clothes from Josh's apartment. The woman agent then surprised her by asking her if she'd accompany them on a flight to the Falklands.

It sounded like a request, but it didn't matter. Josh was at the South Pole base and they staged out of the Falklands.

"I'm ready to go whenever you are." She stopped eating and started changing clothes as fast as she could.

Ten minutes later, she was on her way to the airport. They rode in another black, unmarked SUV with a police escort. It took them right onto the airport tarmac where she saw a large, sleek business jet with subdued US government markings. Climbing the stairs and entering the executive jet, she realized it was several steps up from first class. In addition to her FBI escort, who followed her inside, there were two people already onboard. One was obviously a flight attendant, who welcomed her and asked her what she'd like to drink. The attendant also told her there was a bed and bathroom in the back she could use after they were airborne.

The other individual was a tall, dark, serious-looking man. He wasn't wearing an FBI windbreaker but she could see a holster under his sports jacket. He introduced himself and called her "ma'am" but never smiled. She really wasn't sure if they were escorts or guards. She didn't care. She was going to see Josh.

LANGLEY

The Prophet Operations team started to assemble in the Operations Center. Carl knew nothing could happen until the Prophet and the SEAL team arrived at the Pole. By 10:00 p.m., the entire team was present, minus the Deputy Director.

Carl initiated a STU-III encrypted call from the Ops Center to Davidson, who was now over the Atlantic. Davidson thanked Carl, and said he'd like to stay on the line during the entire operation if possible. He asked if Lafferty was there.

"Yes, sir."

"Can you have Bart pick up, but stay on the line."

Carl brought Lafferty over and gave him another phone.

Davidson asked, "Bart, anything useful from the interrogation of Edvardsen?"

Lafferty said, "Just got off the phone with our chief interrogator. Not much concrete we didn't already know." He paused. "Brian, I have to tell you, my guys are some of the best. Edvardsen made a strong case for this crazy comet thing. Our chief interrogator said, and I quote, 'She's not just the Prophet's play toy. She's very intelligent and made compelling arguments that we're messing in something we don't understand.'"

"Dang it, Bart, I've felt the same, but as much as I hate to admit it, Buster's right. If the Prophet was for real, the responsible agency would have come forward and slapped our hand by now."

Lafferty sighed. "I know, just wanted to pass that on, for what it's worth."

"Thanks, Bart. Carl, you still there?"

"Yes, sir?"

"What have you found out about the observatory's claim?"

"We squelched the information and put FBI personnel at the observatory to ensure it isn't leaked. As suspected, they were given the tip on where to look by Dr. Chandra."

"Figures."

Carl continued, "The astrophysicist I talked to swore they found *something* out there, but he admitted the image was barely detectable above atmospheric noise. That makes it hard to determine distance or trajectory. I hope you don't mind but I took their data and passed it, through back channels, to other observatories." Carl added, "If it's not independently confirmed, we'll know it's nothing."

Someone handed Carl a paper. "Sir, can you hang on a second, I just got something in." After reading it, he said, "This is interesting. Even though we cut off the satellite communication to the Pole, Dr. Chandra is transmitting coordinates for that smaller meteoroid. She's claiming it's going to hit London in about eight hours with catastrophic consequences."

Davidson said, "Yeah, right. What are the odds that it would just *happen* to hit a major city? It's more of the same, intended to cause panic and confusion." He paused, remembering Lafferty's comments about Edvardsen. "Uh… just in case… why don't you forward that information to the observatories you sent the other data to."

MOUNT HOWE

It'd been six months since Josh had been here on the survey visit. Instead of spring with perpetual sunrise, it was now fall, with perpetual sunset. The sun had set three weeks earlier. It was much darker than his last visit, with only a little twilight in one corner of the sky. He could just make out the lights of the base camp with the mountain range silhouetted behind it. He put the Hornet into a gentle turn that would fly them over the top of the mountain and then outbound over the base.

As they descended and got closer, he could clearly see the faint lights on the mountaintop. With no engines, they'd be unaware of the silent Hornet as it glided overhead. He looked at the outside-temperature indicator. They weren't dressed for thirty degrees below zero. He needed to be as close to the base as possible, so they wouldn't freeze, but far enough that the jet wouldn't hit anything.

"Greg, it's almost time. Remember what I told you. Make sure your coat, gloves, and helmet are on tight and your visor is down. Head back firmly against the headrest, chin slightly elevated, with your feet resting on the rudder pedals. Keep your hands in your lap. I'll tell you before we eject."

After crossing the mountaintop, he pushed the nose down. With the bitter cold, he didn't want them spending much time in a parachute. As the radar altimeter indicated 2,000 feet, he raised the fighter's nose to slow the descent. His navigation computer indicated they were a mile west of the base. At 1,500 feet above the ground, he leveled off, slowing the jet into the heart of the ejection envelope. He set the autopilot, told Greg, "Here we go," and pulled the handle.

The Plexiglas canopy blew off the jet as the back seat, with Greg, fired first. Josh didn't realize how loud it would be, but didn't have time to think about it as his seat followed a fraction of a second later. The ejection charge slapped him into the seat as rocket motors accelerated him into the frigid night sky. Hitting the 140 mph subzero air was beyond cold. It was like a belly flop off a high-dive into ice-water. At the apex of the seat's trajectory, the parachute deployed, ripping him out of the seat. What a rush! It was a new experience, since he remembered little of his last rocket ride. Shaking off the shock, he looked up to check his parachute canopy. It was good. He kept his oxygen mask on to keep his face warm, but with his helmet visor fogging up with ice, he lifted it and looked around for Greg in the weak twilight. He couldn't see him anywhere and felt a pang of panic. Greg was here because of him!

Looking to his right, he saw the Hornet's faint green formation lights. The autopilot was still trying to carry out his last command and maintain altitude, but as the airspeed decayed, the fighter stalled. It rolled over like a submissive dog, becoming nothing more than twenty tons of expensive alloys and composites. A bright flash lit the darkness, followed by a screeching boom. The residual fuel vapor in the tanks created a small orange fireball, punctuated by the detonation of the air-to-air missiles. Reflecting beautifully off the icy white plain, it provided just enough illumination to locate Greg's parachute, just below and to his left.

It was cold and still as they drifted with the light wind. Looking at Mount Howe with his exceptional dark-adapted vision, the twilight-illuminated mountain looked like a breathtaking but underexposed postcard. On the very top, he saw the silver dome that housed the Blaster. Looking at the bottom of the mountain, he could see the lights of the base camp. He also saw headlights, a mile off, headed their way. He enjoyed the few seconds of serene solitude, realizing they might be his last.

Landing on the hard ice-pack jolted him back to reality. He popped his parachute release fittings and headed toward Greg's chute about a quarter mile away. From his survival vest, he pulled out a Velcro-wrapped emergency strobe light. He switched it on and stuck it to a matching Velcro patch on the top of his helmet. It would make it easy for the snowcat to see them in the dark.

He jogged the remaining distance to Greg. In the eerie strobe illumination, he saw Greg still buried under his chute. Josh clawed through the canopy. Uncovering him, he saw that he had gotten his oxygen mask off and was smiling. All he said when he saw Josh was, "Wait till the other gamers hear about this! But I forgot to look at the horizon and roll. I think I broke my ankle."

Josh released Greg's parachute fittings, bent over, loosened his shoe, and felt his ankle. "Don't think it's broken, but it's probably badly sprained. Ride will be here in a minute." He noticed Greg was shivering violently. Wrapping him in the chute, Josh sat down next to him with his arm around Greg's shoulder and waited.

A couple minutes later, the snowcat pulled up and a man climbed out. It was hard to identify anyone in Arctic gear. Without saying a word, he came over and helped Josh get Greg on his feet and into the back seat. Josh realized it was Tim Smith. As they climbed into the front seat, Josh turned around and asked Greg how he was doing.

Greg, still shivering violently, said, "Wwwwicked! My fffirst ride in a fighter, first ejection, and ffirst parachute landing! Now we're going to fffire the bbbaddest laser in the world!"

Josh knew Greg's adrenaline was still pumping. There was nothing like facing death and winning to change your perspective. Smiling, he turned back and saw Smith looking at him seriously. He noticed Smith was wearing a holster with a nine-millimeter automatic. He had worked with him for almost a year but Smith *was* a CIA operative. Josh felt stupid. Still another detail he hadn't really thought through. His only chance was if they hadn't contacted him, or if Smith didn't believe the contact was authentic.

47

BLASTER

As soon as they got into the main Quonset hut, all eyes were on him. They also had a video link with the mountaintop. It was the proverbial "locker-room talk" before the big game. Before he could start, one of the young engineers asked, "Did you really fly a fighter here?"

Josh couldn't help but smile. Before he could answer, Greg jumped in. "It was awesome!"

"Where is it?"

Greg said, "Dude, it *totally* blew up."

"Sweet!"

Chandra, overhearing it on the video feed, just shook her head.

Josh, trying to put his serious face back on, said, "OK, this is it. This is what we've all been working for. We have to do it a lot faster than planned but we have the chance to save thousands, maybe hundreds of thousands, of lives. As you know, we also have another challenge. Our program's been compromised."

The same young engineer asked, "By who?"

"It's too complicated to explain right now but there are some elements in our own government" – he thought to himself, minor elements like the CIA and the military – "who want to shut us down."

Major Crowley asked, "Why on earth would anyone want to do that?"

Josh shook his head, "I'm really not sure." His intuition told him why. "I believe someone thinks we're going to use it to shoot down satellites. All I *am* sure of is that they're very serious and probably on their way. With the meteoroid inbound, we don't have time to unravel the insanity."

Crowley said, "This is *the* most powerful laser in the world, but it would be incredibly stupid to put a satellite killer at the South Pole."

Josh said emphatically, "I know! We have to prove this thing does exactly what it's supposed to do. But to do that, we *have* to fire it the second the capacitors are charged. We won't have a second chance. We're going to prove it works *and* save a city at the same time." He paused. "If we're visited, it will be by US commandos with guns. Don't try to be a hero. They don't understand and probably won't want to hear your explanations."

"How do we know they're not terrorists?"

He thought to himself, define "terrorist," but said, "You'll have to trust me on this one. They're from the government, and they *think* they're here to help. Do whatever you can to give us a chance to take out that meteoroid but don't get yourself killed. Do you understand?"

Most of them gave nervous nods.

"OK, what's the status?"

Bobinski appeared very relaxed. Josh knew he was an adrenaline junky and worked best under pressure. "Reactors coming up to full power and charging capacitors. One reactor is being cranky but we'll fix it. We're three hours from full charge."

With raised eyebrows, Wooldridge said calmly, "Our biggest challenge is that we haven't been able to locate the comet fragment."

Katori on the video link said, "We also have an issue with the integration software between the tracking and the beam-aiming system."

Josh said, "Meaning?"

"We're dead in the water unless we can get the software talking to the targeting servos."

Josh looked at Greg. "Can you fix it?"

"Yeah, but I have to be at the control console on the mountaintop."

"Then let's get you up there ASAP."

Crowley said, "One of the helicopters is up there idling. I'll call them down to pick you up."

Josh nodded. "Can someone help Greg? He needs some warmer clothes and boots, and he's got a sprained ankle." To the rest he said, "It's show time!"

As the young optics engineer helped Greg hobble out the door, Josh heard her quietly ask, "James Bond can fly fighters too?"

Greg said, "Absolutely! But…" he glanced back and added quietly, "I'm not sure he knows how to land them."

Smiling, Josh put on a borrowed jacket and sat down on a stool to put on boots.

As everyone bundled up and left, he realized he was alone in the Quonset hut with Tim Smith. Smith remained seated in a chair eight feet away, facing him. As Josh looked up, he saw that Smith was watching him again. He also saw an Iridium satellite phone attached to his belt. Josh raised his eyebrows and looked at him questioningly, as he slipped on a boot.

Smith said softly, with no emotion, "The program was bound to be compromised… eventually."

Josh just nodded. He felt sweat begin to run down his back.

In the same calm voice, Smith said, "If you don't mind my asking… how *do* you know the things you know?"

Josh quickly assessed his options. Despite his enhanced reflexes and martial-arts training, his seated position and distance from Smith made him a sitting duck. A physical confrontation represented a low probability of living, much less succeeding. It would be his last resort. He went through a series of possible responses. None sounded persuasive, even to him. Too late, he realized he'd come to depend too much on his premonitions. They'd totally failed him here.

He needed to know what Smith knew. As he finished fastening one boot and slipped on the other, he said, "The agency's contacted you, haven't they?"

Smith nodded.

"They're having trouble figuring out who I'm working for."

Smith nodded again.

"They don't understand or believe in what we're doing."

Smith said softly, "*That* would be an understatement."

He noticed Smith was sitting with his right hand on his thigh near the holster.

Josh sighed. Starting slowly, he said, "Tim, I…"

Before he could finish, he heard the door behind him open and glanced back. He'd never been so happy to see the scowling face of Winston Shepherd. Behind Shepherd was Drake Wooldridge.

Shepherd said, "Josh, the helicopter's landing now."

Josh hoped Smith wouldn't shoot him in front of Shepherd and Wooldridge. Standing up, with one boot still unfastened, he looked back at Smith… to see him holding his nine millimeter.

Checkmate. He'd have to make his move. At least from a standing position with his boots on, he had a tiny chance.

Still facing Smith, Josh heard, from behind, the unmistakable metallic double click of a slide drawn back on an automatic pistol. Slowly looking over his shoulder, he saw Shepherd scowling… but his arms were at his side and he was looking sideways at Wooldridge. Wooldridge held a forty-five automatic pointed directly at Josh.

Shepherd said to Wooldridge, "You can't be serious."

Without looking at Shepherd, Wooldridge said, "Shut up, Shepherd, you're a moron." To Josh he said, "I am one of the world's leading experts in comets. Did you really think you could pull the wool over my eyes and treat me like an idiot?" Wooldridge smiled smugly. "I've been working with the authorities for over two months now, and I'm putting an end to this ridiculous charade." He gestured toward Smith, "We've been offered a very nice bonus for bringing you to justice, dead or alive."

Josh's heart sank. There was no way he could take both of them. He didn't see this coming. How stupid could he be? The hints had been there with Wooldridge, and Smith… Smith worked for the CIA!

He had to focus and come up with a plan, but he was drawing a complete blank.

Smith stood up and casually walked around Josh toward Wooldridge. He kept his distance and his nine millimeter stayed up and in front of him.

Josh slowly rotated to continue facing Smith as he moved to Wooldridge's side. Totally blindsided, he realized his visions were probably nothing more than dreams after all.

Stopping next to Wooldridge and his smug smile, Smith said quietly to Josh, "You were saying?"

Josh sighed and said, "Tim, the meteoroid is real and…"

Before he could finish, Smith casually but quickly pushed the barrel of Wooldridge's pistol up and away from Josh. With an amazing flick of the wrist, Smith snatched Wooldridge's gun out of his hand, saying, "Give me that before you accidentally shoot yourself."

Wooldridge, startled, said, "I captured him. He's mine and so is the bonus, no one…"

With the same calm voice, Smith added, "And shut up before *I* accidentally shoot you."

Josh was genuinely surprised.

Smith popped the clip out of Wooldridge's gun and handed the clip back to him.

Wooldridge looked at the clip with confusion. "It's empty."

Smith winked at Shepherd and said, "Thanks for the heads up. You were right."

Josh wasn't sure what transpired behind the scenes but it was the first time he'd *ever* seen Shepherd smile.

Smith holstered his pistol and said to Josh, "You've got a helicopter to catch. I'll join you in a second. Shepherd and I are going to introduce *Wooldridge* here to some duct tape."

Josh realized he'd been holding his breath. He released it with a "Whew." As Smith started pushing a silent Wooldridge toward the back of the Quonset hut, Josh tentatively said, "Tim…?"

Smith, without emotion, said, "I'm retiring anyway. Guess Carl must be thinking about a career change too."

Speechless, Josh slapped him on the back as he headed to the helicopter.

Josh and Greg strapped in with Smith joining them a minute later. Bundled up, they sat three across on a web seat. The helicopter had heat but it couldn't keep out the Antarctic cold. As the H-60 lifted off, Josh glanced at Greg, whose head was bobbing in time to the helicopter's vibration. All helos felt like parts could vibrate off at any moment. As an engineer and pilot, Josh suspected helicopters were really just a collection of parts flying in loose formation.

It was a short flight to the top. Reviewing what just happened, he had a lightbulb moment. He never had a premonition about the confrontation with Smith because it *never was*. As he closed his eyes to think through the next step, he had another prescient moment. In addition to the flash of the Blaster, he saw another flash, a muzzle flash. He opened his eyes just as the helicopter made its approach to the small mountaintop landing pad.

Josh had seen pictures, but he'd never been to the finished facility. There were two structures, a control-room building, and a dome housing the Blaster. The control room looked like a cross between a couple of mobile homes and one of his childhood Lego creations. Twenty feet wide by forty feet long, it had seams every five feet. It sat on concrete blocks with steel cables anchoring it to the ground. A fat umbilical cord, thirty feet long, attached the control room to an observatory-like aluminum dome. About twenty-five feet in diameter, the dome was open on one side and he could see a dimly lit interior.

After they landed, the helicopter copilot caught Josh's eye and winked. It was Brandon! Before Josh could say anything, Brandon held up a finger to his lips. Of course, Brandon, the adrenaline junky, angel investor, and pilot, wasn't going to miss the first firing. He must have worked something out with Scupino and Smith so he could be here incognito. Josh just shook his head as he got out of the helicopter.

Walking toward the control room, he stopped to peer inside the dome. He saw someone in a parka crouched over a giant metal box with dozens of thumb-sized wires coming out. There was no heat in the dome. The Blaster and its tracking scope had to be at ambient temperature. Although it was impossible to see a face, from the man's size Josh was sure it was Cho.

He'd seen pictures of all the Blaster's components, but never assembled. He wasn't sure what he'd been expecting... probably Marvin the Martian's Giant Disintegrator. The reality was a bit different. The first thing he noticed was the noise. Right next to the entrance was a refrigerator-sized heat pump. He knew it kept the mercury-cuprate superconductors at an Antarctic-embarrassing minus 170 degrees. Following the thick metal hoses to the Blaster, he saw an imposing structure. A cylindrical aluminum core, eight feet in diameter and twenty feet tall, pointed at the sky with what looked like beer-kegs strapped around the perimeter. Thin metal cooling fins sprouted from the bottom and sides like a bad haircut. Attached to it with metal struts were two large optical telescopes with video feeds. A plethora of flexible tubes and wires came out of the back. They had mounted all of it on a massive but rather standard-looking telescope mount. He knew the mount could rotate the Blaster 360 degrees, and elevate it in hair-thin, ten-thousandth-of-a-degree increments. In reality, it looked more like a giant, mutant hair dryer on life support, than the salvation of humanity… but to Josh, it was a thing of beauty.

They entered the control room through the only door. He immediately saw several giant computer monitors mounted on one wall. Facing the monitors were two rows of plastic folding tables and chairs, like you'd rent for a wedding reception. On the tables sat a dozen laptops that controlled all the Blaster's many systems. Katori and Chandra were working intently on two of them. Cables went everywhere. The room was on the dim side to make the monitors easier to see. There were no windows except a small porthole in the door. It looked less like an energy-beam control center, than a laptop repair shop.

The back of the room had a massive metal wall that looked armored. On the other side, he knew, sat a dozen giant capacitors. The size of washing machines, they were like huge batteries, charged by the nuclear reactors at the foot of the mountain. Each could hold the equivalent of a lightning-bolt's worth of energy. More importantly, they could release all of that power to the Blaster in a millisecond.

The control room had a constant background noise. It was a combination of laptop fans, electric heaters, intercom static, and a high-pitched hum from the capacitors on the other side of the wall. He also noticed the aroma of hot electronics mixed with stale coffee and a dash of "wet dog."

Katori and Chandra looked up as they entered. Josh just raised his eyebrows in question.

Chandra pointed at one of the large monitors and smiled.

"There she is!"

Josh, squinting, tried to make something out on the screen. All he really saw was some dark shapes and an occasional glint among the static.

"It's right where you said it would be, but the dang thing's like a lump of coal. It's so dark I can't keep the tracking scope locked. It's this stupid twilight. It's creating too much ambient light for the telescope to be effective. We'll have to wait until it gets closer."

Josh looked at the digital clock on the wall and said, "It's going to enter the earth's atmosphere in less than seven hours."

Chandra sighed and rubbed her eyes. "I know, I know… but you have to understand, this thing's still very far out. It won't even cross the moon's orbit for another four hours."

Katori said, "One of the reactors is kicking an over-temperature fault and dropping offline. They have to keep resetting it, so we're not charging as fast as we should. The capacitors are up to about 60 per cent but at this rate it could take four more hours."

Josh asked, "Can we fire it with less than 100 per cent charge?"

Katori said, "Yes, but…"

Chandra interrupted. "We'd have to fire it more than once. We don't have time."

Katori shook his head. "We'll be lucky if it fires once."

Chandra added, "We need every erg of energy we've got. With each minute that passes, the chances of moving it get smaller."

Josh turned back to Katori. "Can we override the over-temp shutoff on the reactor?"

Katori looked up and said, "Maybe, but if the warning is real, the reactor could go critical and melt down."

Josh just looked at him.

Katori nodded. "Yeah, right, London." Katori got Bobinski on the intercom. "Chris, we won't have enough power to pull this off unless we can keep that second reactor online. Can you override the over-temp fault?"

Bobinski said, "Dah, we take all overrides off."

Katori frowned and looked back at Josh with raised eyebrows, then continued, "The software interface between the tracking system and the aiming servos is still out of commission. Without that, we can't point the Blaster."

Greg, already on a laptop, said, "I'm on it."

Josh said, "Where's Cho?"

Without looking up, Katori said, "Outside getting frostbite. He's trying to align the Blaster to the tracking system and check the power-circuit continuity."

Josh asked, "How much time until we can fire it?"

Katori said, "Assuming we get the reactor back online, the interface bug worked out, and Chandra can hold a visual lock, the capacitors should be up to full power in about two hours."

"Can we do anything to speed that up?"

Katori shook his head. "Sorry, Josh, we're still limited by the laws of physics."

Josh wondered about that, but said, "OK, can you run through the firing sequence with me? We need everything ready, so the second we're charged, we can fire."

Katori said, "I'm overriding all the procedure safety checklists and transferring the control to the main panel over there." He pointed at the panel in front of the largest screen. Josh looked up at the central display screen. It was broken into three "windows" with various graphs and indicator boxes. They were all red.

Katori pointed to the first window on the left side of the screen. "Once the tracking system has a stable lock, this box will turn green. The middle window shows that the Blaster is actually moving to align with the tracking system's input. When it syncs, it will also turn green. The last section on the right is the bar graph of the capacitors' charge. When it hits 100 per cent, and the other systems are green, it will be ready to initiate the firing command."

They all heard it at the same time. It was the unmistakable sound of a C-17 on approach. They looked at Josh.

Josh ignored it. "Can you set it so it'll fire automatically when the capacitors hit full charge?"

Katori said, "We can set the tracking-scope lock and the projector's aiming system to fully automatic, but there's still one manual intervention required for safety. When the capacitors are at full power, someone *must* hit the interlock safety switch or the firing will be aborted."

Josh asked, "Where's that?"

"It's the big red button on the main console."

Josh laughed. "You're kidding. To fire this thing we really have to push a big red button?"

Katori smiled sheepishly. "Yeah well, it's actually a go-no-go button. The firing sequence is automatic but we have to push the button to *allow* the firing sequence to continue. If we don't press it within ten seconds after the capacitors reach full charge, the system aborts and discharges the capacitors. But once it's pushed, it's impossible to stop the firing sequence."

Frowning, Josh said, "Shouldn't it be green…" He shook his head. "Never mind. Can we push it now?

"No. For safety, it requires human intervention to fire, and it can't be pressed until we hit 100 per cent charge."

48

SEALS

Carl looked at the clock. It was 11:20 p.m. The Op Center received confirmation that the C-17 had just landed. They had excellent intelligence and knew where everything was. The plan was for the SEALs to break into three groups. The first would secure the other C-17. They'd also commandeer the helicopter and use it to get to the top of the mountain. The second team would shut down the nuclear reactors. The third would secure the snowcats and the Quonset hut where the rest of the staff was located.

They were getting a live video feed from the C-17. The flight crews were pointing several cameras at each of the base buildings and one at the top of the mountain. The cameras had zoom lenses and low-light capability. Due to the angle, they could only see the top of the dome that housed the Blaster. They could also monitor all radio communications between the SEAL teams. The first objective was to cut off any possible escape and shut down the power, without which the Blaster would be useless.

MOUNT HOWE

Bobinski reported, "Second reactor running a little hot but it's back online and putting out 110 per cent power." There was a pause. "I think we will have company down here."

Josh said to Bobinski and the others, "Obviously, things didn't get straightened out back at home. These guys are here to shut us down. Chris, try to keep us powered as long as you can, but be careful. They're dangerous… they know not what they do."

"*Dah.*"

Josh looked at Katori. "How much longer?"

Katori looked at his laptop. "Another hour and a half to full charge." He asked quietly, "Won't we have *visitors* up here before then?"

Smith, who was standing silently at the back of the room with the H-60 pilot and Brandon, cleared his throat. "I'm afraid someone may have disconnected the second helicopter's transmission-oil heater."

The pilot looked at Smith and shook his head with a half smile.

Katori nodded. "They'll have to use one of the snowcats… unless… they also have issues?"

Smith added, "Regrettably."

Josh knew that SEALs never showed up unprepared. They'd have their own vehicles and would know exactly how to get up here. Normally, it took a couple hours, but these were SEALs. He looked at the capacitor charge. The real question was how on earth could they keep the reactors online?

LANGLEY

After less than five minutes, the first SEAL team reported that they had taken control of the other C-17 and the helicopter without any resistance and were putting their pilot into the H-60 to take the team to the mountaintop.

MOUNT HOWE

The second SEAL team had the nuclear reactor expert. They came through the reactor-building doors in a rush with guns up. Bobinski and his men were sitting with their feet propped up on the consoles, drinking coffee. The SEALs yelled for them to get on the floor. Searching them, they found them unarmed. The SEAL leader reported that they'd secured the reactor building without any resistance and were going to shut it down.

LANGLEY

The third and last team reported the same. They had secured everything without resistance or casualties, accounted for all the snowcats, and reported that the engineers were mad but cooperating. Buster and the rest of the team watched the screens and listened to the radio reports, thinking it all rather anti-climactic. Although they still had to secure the mountaintop, they now controlled the power, rendering the Blaster useless. Stuck on the top of a mountain, surrounded by 300 kilometers of polar ice, there was no place for the Prophet to run.

MOUNT HOWE

The Navy helicopter pilot that accompanied the SEAL team was in the cockpit going through the start-up procedures. Six SEALs were onboard and fully armed. They carried the compact but deadly MP5 submachine-guns for close-quarters work.

The pilot had the engines up and running but when he tried to engage the rotors, nothing happened. The transmission refused to cooperate. Finally, he gave the "cut" signal to the SEAL Commander in the back. On the intercom, he said, "Sorry, guys, this bird ain't going anywhere; transmission's frozen."

The SEAL Team Commander simply said to his team, "Plan B." He reported the problem via radio as they headed toward the snowcats.

LANGLEY

Carl heard the report from the SEAL Commander. They would go up the mountain using the snowcats. Buster, frowning, began to pace, chewing his gum loudly. Carl relayed the situation to Davidson.

MOUNT HOWE

"Which one of you is Christoff Bobinski?"

Bobinski, from the floor, raised his hand.

The SEAL Team Leader said, "Get up, but don't make any sudden moves."

Bobinski stood up slowly. Having served in the Russian army, he knew he was facing a Navy SEAL. He also recognized the rank insignia, Senior Chief Petty Officer.

The Senior Chief said, "We have a nuclear engineer and reactor expert with us. I need you to shut down the reactors and kill the power to the mountaintop right now. Do you understand?"

Bobinski said, "Sure, but if we kill reactors, it will get very dark and cold."

The Senior Chief looked at his expert. The young engineer said, "There's a backup generator. If we need to, we can turn the reactors back on later."

Bobinski nodded and casually went over to the main control panel with the engineer. One SEAL went with them. The Senior Chief and the other SEAL stayed back, where they could cover everyone. He told Bobinski, "Shut it down but don't touch anything on that control panel without telling him." He pointed to his young engineer. To the engineer he said, "Check every step."

Bobinski picked up a clipboard in Russian and referring to it said, "First we increase the cooling and make sure SCRAM interlocks are ready." The young engineer nodded as Bobinski leaned forward to comply.

After ten minutes of the slow step-by-step process, the Senior Chief interrupted, "How long's this going to take?"

Bobinski stopped and turned around slowly. "To shut down safely by procedure, about hour and a half."

The young engineer nodded. "That's probably about right for a normal shutdown."

The SEAL Team Leader said, "That's not acceptable! We need this thing offline now. I know these things can be shut down in an emergency faster than that."

The engineer said, "Yes, we can SCRAM the reactor. That

drops graphite control rods into the core, absorbing the neutrons and stopping the reaction, but we might not be able to get it started again."

The Senior Chief said, "I don't care. SCRAM it!"

The engineer raised an eyebrow but turned to Bobinski. Bobinski shrugged his shoulders, "OK." He pointed at the large red button at the top of the control panel. The young engineer reached out to it. He looked back at the Senior Chief, who nodded. He pushed it. A very loud alarm startled all of them.

After a few seconds the SEAL asked, "Is it shut down?"

The engineer, looking carefully at the control-panel indicators, said, "No. The rods failed to drop. The alarm is indicating a SCRAM failure. If I'm reading this right, this reactor is at full power *and* it's over-temping!"

Bobinski, shutting the alarm off, said with a half smile, "*Dah*, she's like Russian woman, hard to turn on, but once on, very hard to turn off."

The young engineer and Senior Chief weren't amused.

Bobinski continued more seriously, "We have trouble with reactors. Damaged during transport. Cold weather hasn't helped."

The SEAL Team Leader said to both of them, "I don't care what you have to do, shut it down and shut it down now!"

The engineer looked at Bobinski almost pleadingly. Bobinski glanced quickly at one of the repeater monitors that showed the capacitors at 89 per cent. "We must do emergency manual shutdown."

The young engineer said, "I assume the SCRAM button on the other reactor is also *malfunctioning*?"

Bobinski shrugged. "We can try it."

The Senior Chief leaned over to the engineer and said quietly, "Are they stringing us along?"

Frowning, he whispered back, "Maybe, but the Russians really don't seem to worry that much about fail-safes. This thing appears to have *none*."

The SEAL said to Bobinski, "How long will the emergency manual shutdown take?"

Bobinski turned around slowly and said, "If you quit asking

questions and pointing guns at us, we can have it down in about twenty minutes." Bobinski thought wryly, twenty *maintenance* minutes – which were *very* different than SEAL minutes.

LANGLEY

As the SEALs' radio report came in about the reactors and the dead snowcats, Carl heard Buster swear and spit out his gum. Looking around the room, Buster walked over to the control console where a Navy liaison officer sat. Gesturing, Buster talked to him quietly.

MOUNT HOWE

It had been a half hour since they heard the C-17 land. They had lost all contact with the base camp. Josh hated standing around waiting. Trying to be useful, he got everyone a fresh cup of coffee. Tasting it, he realized *fresh* was a relative term.

Chandra, finishing the trajectory simulation on her laptop, pushed her chair back and announced, "That's it! All we have to do is slow the meteoroid a tiny bit. That will delay its entry into the atmosphere, allowing the earth to rotate London out from under it."

Katori asked, "Does that mean we can just hit it head-on with the beam?"

"Yes! That simplifies the targeting." Standing up, she rubbed her eyes and stretched.

Josh came over and stood beside her as she drank her millionth cup of coffee. "Victoria, I can't tell you how much I appreciate your trust. I know it's been tough keeping the faith without concrete evidence, not to mention government agents telling you to cease and desist."

She turned to Josh with raised eyebrows. "Actually, they said, and I quote, 'Josh Meadows is a threat to national security.'" She smiled. "This is the weirdest program I've ever been a part of. I mean, with people like Bobinski and," she whispered, nodding toward the back of the room, "Sir Edward Brandon?" She smiled. "Josh, I've been in the government my entire career. I *know* things can go terribly wrong in a bureaucracy." She tapped her finger against her lips as if thinking. "Let's see… listen to a faceless bureaucrat on a satellite link, *or* believe a combat-decorated carrier captain and a madman who throws himself off cliffs to save people." With feigned concentration, she said, "That's a tough one."

Josh smiled. "You and Katori are amazing, and the way you work under pressure…"

"Pressure?" She shook her head dismissively as she sat back down. "Josh, I have three teenagers at home."

SOUTHERN OCEAN

In the twilight off the Antarctic coast, the bow of the guided-missile destroyer crashed through twenty-five-foot swells. The Captain of the USS *Truxton* was standing in the ship's Combat Information Center when the message came in. As he read it, his body automatically swayed to compensate for the ship's pitch and roll. They were in the middle of one of the polar cyclones that frequented the Southern Ocean. The storm's wind and waves were within the ship's launch parameters, but it made for a rough ride.

He checked and rechecked the authorization code and coordinates. Then he gave the order. The keys were turned and two Tomahawk Block IV cruise missiles exploded out of the destroyer's deck cells. They climbed out of an orange cloud of fire into the cold night sky, temporarily illuminating the ship and the dark, rolling sea. As the missiles jettisoned their rocket boosters, small wings popped out and their turbine engines spun up. They turned to the south and accelerated.

The Captain sent back the launch confirmation and went to the Tomahawk console. He grabbed a cup of coffee and sat down to watch the missiles' progress on the big display. They had positioned themselves as close to the Antarctic coast as possible, but the missiles still had a 700-mile journey. It would take them – he looked at the countdown timer – one hour and twenty minutes to reach their target. They would then promptly deliver two 1,000-pound high-explosive warheads with an accuracy measured in inches. He had a hard time imagining what they needed to blow up that close to the South Pole, but the CIA must know what they're doing.

He looked up as his Executive Officer entered CIC.

His XO said, "Check this out. We're going to be joined by friends in this God-forsaken place." He handed the Captain a clipboard.

Reading it, the Captain raised his eyebrows, "*Reagan* and her entire carrier battle group?"

MOUNT HOWE

Twenty minutes had elapsed. The Senior Chief was angry. "Forget about the reactors! I want the power to the mountaintop cut off!"

Bobinski said, "We can do that but it wouldn't be wise before we shut reactor down."

"And why is that?"

"Reactors are putting out eleven megawatts of power. If we don't shut down reactor first, where will that heat go?"

The engineer chimed in, "He's actually right. This thing's running in the red. It's over-temping at full power. It should have already shut itself down. If we pull the load suddenly, without any way to SCRAM it, it could go critical and melt the core."

The Senior Chief said, "What's the worst that can happen?"

The engineer looked at him incredulously. "Ever heard of Chernobyl? We'll have a core meltdown with an explosive release of radioactive uranium. If the explosion doesn't kill us, we'll die of radiation poisoning before they can get us out of here. There's no place to run."

Frustrated, the Senior Chief let loose with a long string of expletives, finally ending with, "Just finish what you're doing!"

Bobinski smiled to himself. He actually started life as a language major and was impressed. He hadn't realized the grammatical versatility of the worst word in the English language. The SEAL had used it as an interjection, noun, verb, adjective, and adverb, all in one sentence.

Bobinski overheard the Senior Chief call his Commander. He reported that they had to shut the reactors down before they could cut the power. Bobinski was close enough that he also heard the reply. "We're on our way to the top. I don't care what you have to do.

The power *will be* off before we get there. Is that understood?"

"Yes, sir."

ATLANTIC

Elizabeth tried to stay awake but the combination of emotions, no sleep and hours of interrogation took its toll. No matter how hard she fought it, the drone of the jet engines finally lulled her into a deep sleep, torn by nightmares.

49

STANDOFF

It had been over an hour since the C-17 landed. Josh was startled when the door opened. Cho came inside, accompanied by a blast of bone-chilling air. He closed the door and pulled his parka hood back. Shivering, he said, "I aligned that sucker and she looks good but I didn't have time to check the continuity of all the power circuits."

Katori nodded.

Josh watched Cho pick his way back toward his laptop. He gingerly squeezed his large frame between consoles and stepped over cables. As he sat down, he said to no one in particular, "It's definitely going to work!" Then, glancing around furtively, he made a quick sign of the cross.

MOUNT HOWE

The Senior Chief glanced at his watch and with a calm but deadly voice said to Bobinski, "It's been over thirty-five minutes, why isn't it off?"

Before Bobinski could respond, the Senior Chief said, "I think you're lying." He looked at the engineer and said, "Kill the power."

The engineer shook his head and started to say, "That would be extremely dangerous…"

Before he could finish, the Senior Chief walked over to Oleg, who was sitting in front of the power distribution panel. He asked, "Do you understand me?"

Oleg nodded and said, "Yes."

Slowly and clearly, he said, "You will shut the power off now."

Oleg shook his head.

The Senior Chief took his pistol out, pulled the slide back, and put it to Oleg's head. Calmly, but with steel in his voice, he said, "Shut the power off now, or die."

Oleg saw the capacitor charge at 97 per cent. Keeping eye contact with the SEAL, he slowly reached up on his control panel and flipped a breaker.

The lights in the control room immediately went out.

In the dark, Bobinski flipped the SCRAM alarm override switch. As the ear-splitting alarm began to howl, Bobinski yelled, "Oh my God! Reactor's going critical! She's melting down! Everyone to get out, now!"

MOUNT HOWE

Josh, suddenly feeling restless, moved toward the door. The heaters and the fans of the electronics made a lot of background noise, but he thought he heard a sound outside. They were out of time. Instinctively, he moved to the wall on the hinge side of the door. With his sensitive hearing and a little more, he knew a split second before...

The door burst open and two SEAL commandos rushed in with submachine-guns in front of them. One went left, one right. Josh, flat against the wall, was able to move with blinding speed behind the first SEAL. With superhuman agility, he unlatched and pulled the SEAL's pistol from its holster. As the commando started to spin to his right, he felt his own nine-millimeter pressed against his neck.

Smith, almost as fast, dropped to the floor. In a jujitsu move, he came up under the second commando, with his pistol barrel just inside the bottom of the SEAL's bulletproof vest.

Three more commandos spilled in.

Josh positioned himself carefully behind his SEAL to prevent them from getting a clean shot at him. As the SEALs saw the situation, everyone froze.

Knowing the deadly accuracy of these commandos, Josh knew that if Smith hadn't engaged, they would have shot right by the man Josh was holding. SEALs are never held hostage. Quickly, Josh spoke. "I'm the man you're looking for. I'm going to return this pistol to its owner. We are American citizens on a critical and highly classified mission that you are endangering. I ask that we all take a deep breath, and that you lower the barrels of your weapons from my people so we can talk." He slowly rotated the pistol barrel up and away from the commando's neck. He turned it toward himself, offering it handle-first to the SEAL. Smith did the same as he slowly stood up. The explosive tension in the room dropped.

While he was acting, Josh's mind worked at phenomenal speed. There was no way they'd win a firefight against heavily armed SEALs. He only realized why he had done what he did, after the fact. Making a physical move that was almost impossible, and then identifying himself as their target, earned their respect, and he hoped, a few precious seconds.

Bobinski and the technicians scrambled out of the building into the frigid cold with the SEALs. The last out was the Senior Chief. He looked around and saw that all the building lights were out. The only illumination came from the C-17.

Josh put his hands up. The SEAL he returned the gun to frisked him and stepped back. The SEAL Commander lowered his weapon slightly, and the other SEALs followed his lead.

As the SEALs frisked the others, Josh watched the monitor out of the corner of his eye. It showed that the tracking system had finally locked on to the meteoroid. It also indicated that the Blaster's aiming system should be moving the Blaster into its firing position. The power board was at 98 per cent.

The officer said to Josh, "You are Josh Meadows?"

Josh said, "Yes."

"My orders are to take you into custody immediately and shut down your operation. We are authorized to use deadly force."

Josh read the insignia on his uniform. He was a Lieutenant Commander. Josh said quietly, "On whose authority, Commander?" Josh doubted they knew where their orders came from, nor was it relevant, but he needed time.

The SEAL Commander said, "I am acting on orders authorized by National Command Authority. I appreciate the fact that you didn't put up a fight or attempt to flee, and took responsibility, but my orders stand. As long as your people continue to cooperate, I give you my word they will not be harmed. We'll let the experts sort this out."

Josh said, "Thank you." He was dealing with an honorable warrior. He continued, "This operation is highly classified and intended to deflect a large incoming meteoroid. If we don't initiate the beam in the next few minutes, the meteoroid will destroy London. It's critical that you contact your command authority immediately."

"I will do that but my orders are to secure this facility and take you into custody and back to the US where you can plead your case. I was told specifically to stop *all* operations immediately."

Josh saw that the tracking scope had just synced. The aiming system was now showing green. If everything was working, the Blaster should be pointed in the right direction and slowly tracking the meteoroid. Three down, one more "green" to go. All they needed was full charge. He saw the indicator change to 99 per cent. Just a couple minutes, that's all they needed.

Josh continued in a calm voice, "Doing that will result in the destruction of a major city. Your unit and command may take the blame. I know you're following orders but you're an officer in the United States Navy… as was I. You swore an oath to defend the constitution of the United States against all enemies foreign and domestic. The US and the world are facing a hugely powerful enemy. It's closing at forty kilometers per second. Every minute we waste, reduces the chance of our success. I'm asking you to exercise your authority as on-scene commander. Please contact your command and ask for an immediate review. You know as well as I, blue-on-blue engagements occur, and the government's right hand doesn't always talk to the left. Tens or hundreds of thousands could die."

He could see the conflict in the officer's eyes but the man shook his head and said, "I'm sorry. My orders are very clear. I promise to contact my command as soon as we've shut your operation down." He signaled to start rounding up the control staff.

This man was not going to bend. The capacitors were still at 99 per cent. Josh just needed a few more seconds. He'd try one last stall tactic. "We can shut it down but we have extremely high-voltage capacitors with tens of thousands of amps of power. If we don't shut them down properly, they could explode. Your people and mine could be seriously injured."

The SEAL Commander paused and then said, "We're shutting down the reactors now and have experts coming in behind us." He motioned with his gun for Josh to move toward the door.

He knew the SEAL respected him but it was clear that he was finished listening to Josh's monolog. He assessed the situation. Fifteen feet from the panel with the red button, two tables in between, and four SEALs with their weapons pointed in his direction. He had no choice – when it hit 100 per cent, he'd run for the button and hope he could hit it before they cut him down.

Bobinski and his men had no coats. The Senior Chief told his team to move their shivering captives to the C-17 quickly. Bobinski noticed the Senior Chief looking nervously over his shoulder at the reactor building, as he hustled them toward the aircraft. He heard him report over the radio that the power was finally off but the reactor could melt down. Bobinski couldn't hear the response, but the Senior Chief suddenly stopped, turned around, and looked up. Seeing lights on the mountaintop, he swore loudly, pulled his pistol, and ran toward Oleg.

MAUNA KEA

The Keck observatory, after receiving a tip from an unidentified government source, was the first to detect the meteoroid. They immediately sent messages to twelve other observatories and NORAD to confirm the detection and plot the impact point.

MOUNT HOWE

The charge indicator hit 100 per cent and the display turned green. A buzzer went off and several lights changed color. Chandra, on the far side of the room, gave him the distraction he needed. Pointing to the display, she said loudly, "Oh my God. Look at the capacitor board!" All eyes turned to her and the board.

Before Josh could launch himself, Smith pushed the SEAL nearest him off balance. Closer to the red button, Josh knew Smith was going for it. Once again, Josh's mind sped up and everything appeared to move in slow motion. In a flash, he calculated that the SEAL Smith pushed wouldn't recover fast enough to stop him. The other two SEALs were still looking toward Chandra, but the SEAL Commander saw what was happening. He was already swinging the barrel of his submachine-gun toward Smith. Josh wasn't close enough to hit the Commander before he fired. Their only chance was for him to intercede. He pushed off the wall behind him with all his strength. The submachine-gun, aimed directly at Smith, fired… just as Josh crossed between them.

Two bullets caught Josh in the stomach and spun him around, just as Smith hit the red button. A third bullet grazed Josh's right arm, as he crashed into a table with computers. Smith continued to the floor, as a fourth bullet just missed his head, ricocheting off the armored metal wall.

The SEAL Commander yelled, "Hold your fire! Hold your fire!"

Josh, lying on the floor amongst a tangle of computer cables, heard the warning siren begin and the sound of the capacitor primers releasing.

One SEAL ran to Smith, shoving him to the floor with his boot and pushing the gun barrel to his head. Another pointed his weapon at Josh. The warning siren continued as the electronic hum got louder and higher pitched. The Commander grabbed Greg Langlois. Holding his gun on him, he yelled, "Shut it down! Shut it down!"

Greg looked pale but yelled back, "There's nothing I can do! We can't stop it once it's started!"

As if on cue, the giant capacitors discharged simultaneously, sounding like a fireworks grand finale. A brilliant flash, from the tiny porthole window, lit up the control room. A high-pitched scream ended in a wall-shaking, bone-rattling boom. It felt like a lightning-bolt striking inside the control room.

In less than a blink of an eye, millions of amps of power excited trillions of photons into coherent, perfectly collimated lockstep. As they reached their exit threshold, they departed the Blaster at the speed of light. First, at a frequency absorbed by air molecules, the two-meter-wide beam superheated the air to incandescence. As the frenzied molecules bounced off each other, they forced the atmosphere out of the way, creating a vacuum tunnel. A few milliseconds later, the second, more powerful train of photons followed the tunnel created by the first, at a frequency tailored to heat ice and rock instead of air. The double beam was a beautiful, brilliant blue-green, so intense that even stray reflections could damage an unprotected eye. As the second beam left the atmosphere, the vacuum tunnel collapsed with a sonic boom. The photons crossed the distance to the incoming meteoroid in less than a second.

As the Senior Chief dragged the shivering Oleg back toward the reactor building, the landscape lit up with a blinding blue-green light, followed seconds later by a double thunderclap. Oleg smiled.

LANGLEY

Someone yelled, "Look!"

On the video monitor, fed by one of the C-17's cameras, they saw a bright, blue-green beam. It blinked and then dimmed. Never completely fading, the laser's path permanently burned the camera's sensor. They also heard a double boom on the SEALs' open mics.

MOUNT HOWE

In the control room on top of the mountain, all sound stopped. Only the ringing in their ears remained, along with a smoky haze and a growing smell of black powder and burning insulation. The light coming through the small window faded to a green glow.

On the video feed from the dome's interior, they saw the Blaster's liquid tellurium/sapphire core had exploded. The superconducting mercury cooling lines had burst, adding to the colorful fire from the melted electrical cables. An exterior camera, pointed above the dome, showed the sky. Disrupted air molecules along the beam's path fluoresced with a bright-green glow. The long, narrow artificial aurora pointed toward the deadly meteoroid, like an accusatory finger.

Into the silence, the SEAL Commander said, "What happened?!"

Greg, with a crack in his voice, said, "You butthead! You just killed the best man I've ever known." With tears in his eyes, he said, "He was telling the truth. The beam fired like it was supposed to… if it wasn't too late."

Still lying on the floor, Josh whispered to himself with a Monty Python accent, "I'm not quite dead yet."

The Commander shook his head and nodded to one of his men. He went to Josh and bent down. Checking his pulse and looking at the wound and spreading pool of blood, he said, "He's alive," he shook his head, "but it doesn't look good."

The Commander, in a softer voice, said, "Do what you can."

Josh felt pain but it seemed distant. He felt the blood soaking through his shirt. The bullets obviously missed his heart but he wasn't sure what they did to his other organs.

Smith and Brandon, daring the SEAL holding the gun to do anything, slid over to where Josh was lying. Josh felt Smith put pressure on the wound to slow the bleeding.

The SEAL said, "I'll be right back with a medic bag."

GLOBAL OBSERVATORIES

Dozens of observatories were now tracking the comet fragment. All of them recorded a brief but intense flash from its surface.

LANGLEY

Carl noticed that Buster had stopped biting his nail and was watching the main screen with apparent calm. Suspicious, Carl walked over to the console with the Navy operator and asked how things were going.

The operator said, "Four minutes to missile impact."

Carl grabbed the phone next to the operator and switched the line to Davidson, praying he would still be online.

Davidson answered.

"Buster has Tomahawks inbound, four minutes out!"

Davidson said, "Give me the Navy guy!"

Carl handed the phone to the operator and said, "This is Deputy Director Davidson."

50

DEFLECT

As the SEAL Commander was trying to reach his Command for further orders, they all heard the sound of a high-pitched jet engine getting rapidly louder. It had the unmistakable rising Doppler pitch that indicated rapid closure. The SEAL Commander recognized it and yelled, "Incoming! Hit the deck!" He threw himself on the floor and the others followed his lead. The missile's whine escalated. Within seconds, it sounded like it was in the room with them. When it couldn't get any louder… the Doppler pitch suddenly dropped. The sound began to recede, followed by the sound of a second engine. After a few more seconds, they picked themselves up off the floor. Two deep reverberating booms sounded in the distance.

Greg was the first to ask, "What was that!?"

With a frown, the SEAL Commander shook his head gently, "I think that was plan C."

Katori, standing up, said, "*Those* were Tomahawk cruise missiles."

The SEAL Commander gave him a raised eyebrow.

Katori said, "Before Boeing, I worked for Raytheon, the maker of those things. That's closer than I ever want to get."

The SEALs nodded.

SOUTHERN OCEAN

The Captain of the *Truxton* looked at the display and confirmed that the missiles had received the command. This was the first *operational* test of the new Block IV Tomahawk's redirect-in-flight capability. He was surprised the missile's receivers could pick up the satellite signal this close to the South Pole. The Tomahawks probably bypassed their target by a matter of feet, detonating less than a mile beyond.

The operator who sent the redirect command said, "Wow! They *really* cut that close."

The Captain nodded. He wondered if they'd ever know what was going on. He sent the confirmation of a successful abort back to Langley.

LANGLEY

Still holding the phone and his breath, Carl reported to Davidson that they'd been able to redirect the missiles. Davidson asked him to patch him through to the Director of National Intelligence.

Carl said, "I can do better than that. The DNI came into the Ops Center a few minutes ago. She's standing against the back wall. Buster doesn't even know she's here."

"Put her on."

After a short telephone conversation between Davidson and the DNI, Carl watched her walk up behind Buster and say, "That was an incredibly dangerous backup plan!"

Buster spun around with irritation until he realized who was talking to him.

She continued, "Did you know that Sir Edward Brandon was on the mountaintop?"

His silence said it all.

She continued coldly, "You took a huge risk that the new Tomahawks could be redirected that close to the South Pole."

Without thinking, Buster said, "They can be redirected?"

Her eyes narrowed and she tilted her head sideways. She lifted her right hand and motioned to two agents.

As Buster turned to look at the security agents, she said softly, "Please escort Mr. Johnson out of the Ops Center, and pull his access on my authority." The men didn't even blink as they flanked the now silent Buster.

As they were escorting him out, a CIA analyst burst into the room, almost knocking Buster over. He yelled, "NORAD and NATO just announced an evacuation order for London. They're predicting a meteoroid impact in five hours!"

The DNI announced loudly, "This operation is now under my personal control. I'm ordering all forces to stand down and render assistance to the Pole base staff *immediately*!"

MOUNT HOWE

The SEAL Commander received a command communication. It had the correct authorization codes. It immediately rescinded the use of deadly force and told them they were to assist the personnel at the base in any way they could. And, oh by the way, one of the helicopter pilots they were holding at gunpoint was actually Sir Edward Brandon! He shook his head, swearing. He could have used that information ten minutes ago.

Chandra, who had been staring at one of the monitors, suddenly pointed at her laptop screen, exclaiming, "We hit it! We actually hit the dang thing dead on!" She added, "The question is… was it enough?" She started to move over to her laptop but a SEAL restrained her. She looked at the Commander like a mother ready to discipline an unruly child.

The Commander immediately told his team, "We've just been ordered to stand down and assist these people in any way possible." He realized that whatever they were supposed to have stopped, they didn't, and it was probably a good thing. He had read the dossier and knew who Dr. Victoria Chandra was. "I'm sorry, Dr. Chandra. Is there anything we can do to help?"

She ignored him and moved to one of the laptops. Studying several tables of numbers and graphs, her fingers whizzed across the keyboard.

Cho, looking at the remote video feed from the dome, said, "Blaster's slagged."

Just then, the power and overhead lights went out and red emergency lights came on.

Katori said, unnecessarily, "There go the reactors."

The overhead monitors went dark. The laptops, on battery, remained active.

Katori turned to Chandra. "Did you get enough trajectory

information before they cut the power?"

Chandra didn't answer but kept working. She stood up suddenly, startling the SEAL behind her, who raised his gun instinctively. Oblivious, she said, "It's impossible to be sure this early. Trajectory changes are so tiny, but there's a chance."

Cho blurted out, "You mean it actually worked?!"

Greg said, "Yeah, but it blew itself to bits."

"Who cares, we can build another. I can't believe it actually worked!"

Chandra and Katori both turned and looked at Cho with some surprise.

Cho looked amazed. "You don't understand. These things *never* work the first time and certainly not when you test them at full power!" He did a little NFL touchdown victory spike. Then stopped, looking apologetically toward Smith and Brandon, kneeling next to Josh.

CHEYENNE MOUNTAIN

NORAD was the first to notice the trajectory change. They recalculated and published the new impact point, checking and rechecking with the observatories. They didn't rescind the evacuation order for London. Instead, they added a new one for low-lying areas on the southern coast of Ireland and the western coasts of England, France and Spain. In addition to grounding all air traffic in Western Europe, a new order went out to ships in the Eastern Atlantic. They were to move away from the impact area as fast as possible and prepare for an atmospheric explosion with hurricane-force winds and seas.

MOUNT HOWE

Smith, still holding pressure on Josh's wound, leaned over and said quietly and with uncharacteristic emotion, "Josh, I'm… I'm sorry."

Josh whispered back weakly, "Are you serious? Chandra said you just *protected* hundreds of thousands of people. It was someone else's turn to protect you." He knew Tim's so-called "retirement" was his planned "accidental" death. He whispered, "Tim, you've paid your debt. This could never have happened if you retired yourself." He thought he actually saw Tim's eyes get glassy. He was beginning to feel lightheaded but needed to tell Tim one last thing. With his hand, he weakly motioned Tim toward him, whispering, "Tim."

Tim bent closer.

"This is important."

Tim leaned closer still.

"… Lopez thinks you're hot."

Surprised, he leaned back smiling and shook his head.

Josh could hear the SEAL Commander saying on the radio that they were sending a critical casualty down by helicopter. The SEAL medic came back and took over. He sprayed the wound, put on a pressure bandage and gave him some type of shot.

Josh had a metallic taste in his mouth. He knew it was his own blood – probably not a good sign. He started feeling fuzzy and disconnected. He'd been here before. For him, the mission was done. He felt completely at peace for the first time since his return. He could finally let go…

As the SEALs loaded the stretcher into the helicopter, it was too loud to talk over the turbine engines. The SEAL Commander caught the medic's eye. The medic understood the unspoken question. Glancing briefly at the body on the stretcher, he shook his head.

51

IMPACT

Three hours after the Blaster fired, a Marine V-22 Osprey landed on the ice near the C-17. It offloaded a small Marine recon team. Twenty minutes later, it was airborne again, flying at its maximum speed through the frigid Antarctic night. After taking on needed fuel from an airborne tanker, it continued on to a stormy ocean rendezvous.

EUROPE, NOON

A few hours' warning shouldn't be sufficient to notify a continent. In the modern world, however, with twenty-four-hour news networks, social Internet sites and pervasive smartphones, few in Europe weren't looking skyward.

Entering the upper atmosphere, over Hannover, Germany, the meteoroid created a beautiful white-orange streak almost as bright as the sun. It crossed Germany and the Netherlands in thirty seconds. Traveling thirty times faster than a rifle bullet, it penetrated deep into the atmosphere before the intense heat and violent deceleration overcame the building-sized meteoroid. At 25,000 feet, 500 kilometers west of London, it finally exploded with the power of a seven-megaton bomb, raining red-hot pieces of rock into the Atlantic. The glowing fragments, some the size of softballs, looked like large raindrops hitting hot asphalt.

The Tunguska-sized explosion damaged the ships that couldn't move fast enough, or got the word too late. The shockwave pushed the giant vessels around like sailboats in a gale-force wind, tipping many to the point of capsize. Those who stayed inside survived with mostly minor injuries. Those sailors who were unaware or ventured out to see the meteor, perished. The blast created a ten-foot tsunami that struck the coastline.

The waves inundated low-lying areas from Ireland to Spain, and crossed the Atlantic to the United States. There were billions of euros in property damage, but the advanced warning saved tens of thousands of lives. The explosion echoed across Europe with a trail of ionized gas that remained visible long into the night.

NETHERWORLD

Josh was back in Jesse's netherworld. He wasn't frightened. Sensing Jesse's presence, he immediately asked, "Did we do it? Did we deflect the meteoroid?"

Yes.

"Awesome!" Then more contritely, "I imagine you're getting tired of meeting me like this."

Jesse's voice felt like a warm presence. *You've done well. There is no higher expression of love for your fellow man than to offer your life.*

It meant the world to have his approval. "Thank you, Jesse." He needed to thank Jesse for far more than the compliment. "And thank *you* for listening to my pleas and whining, and saving our collective butts!"

ATLANTIC

She awoke, and found herself lying in a small bed in a tiny but nicely trimmed cabin. Someone must have carried her here. She had no recollection but it wasn't surprising, considering her condition. She got up, peered out the window, and saw nothing but ocean through the clouds far below. A clock on the wall said nine-thirty. She went to the door that she thought pointed to the front of the jet, and cracked it slightly. Peeking out, she saw the two agents sitting in chairs. The woman was working on a laptop, and the man was talking quietly on a phone connected to the wall. The flight attendant was working in the forward galley. She went to the back door of the cabin and found a small, well-equipped bathroom. It even had a little shower. She remembered the flight attendant saying it was a twelve-hour flight, so she had time before they landed. She now understood the term "sweating the information out of someone." She felt very grubby and the mirror confirmed it. She smiled to herself. In all of her travel fantasies, she never dreamed of showering at 40,000 feet.

They had placed her bag and clothes in the cabin. After showering, dressing, and putting on some basic make-up, she felt much better and realized she was starving. Tentatively, she opened the door to the main cabin and came out. The woman agent smiled and called to the flight attendant, who asked her what she wanted for breakfast.

"Whatever's easiest and fastest to fix. I'm starving."

The flight attendant winked, as she handed her a large, warm sticky bun and a cup of coffee.

Elizabeth sat down at one of the small tables.

The woman agent came over and said very politely, "Ms. Edvardsen, I think you may want to check out the news." She swiveled one of the flat-screen monitors toward her and gave her the remote control.

Elizabeth scanned through to find a news channel. It wasn't hard. It appeared this TV only carried news. Then she realized that breaking news had preempted every channel. She stopped at the news network she usually watched. The flight attendant put a large, hot omelet in front of her. She said a quick prayer and dug in. She realized that between the interrogation and sleep, she lost an entire day. Apparently, she was coming in late to something everyone else already knew about.

As it began to sink in, she clapped her hands over her mouth in excitement, tears in her eyes. Someone deflected a meteoroid bound for London. It landed in the Atlantic, saving hundreds of thousands of lives. Details were still coming in, but it was clear that a secret base at the South Pole had hit the comet with some type of energy beam. As if that wasn't enough, there was a bigger story. There was a "mother" to this meteoroid. Detected much further out, it also appeared to be on a collision course with the earth.

Elizabeth asked how soon they'd be landing.

The female agent said, "In about two hours, ma'am... but there's been a slight change of plans. We'll be transferring you to another aircraft for the final flight."

"Final flight, where to? Is that where Josh is?"

Elizabeth saw the two agents exchange a quick glance. Both looked uncomfortable. The male agent said quickly, "I'm sorry, ma'am; they'll explain it all to you when you arrive." He changed the subject to the weather in the Falklands.

She could tell there was something they weren't telling her but decided not to press it. She was elated that she and Josh had been totally vindicated. She wanted to do a victory dance and yell repeatedly, "I told you so!" But she would be a gracious winner. They probably already felt bad enough.

SOUTHERN OCEAN

In the heavy rain and late-morning twilight, the V-22 transitioned to vertical landing mode. With limited visibility and large ocean swells, the tired Marine pilot struggled to match his aircraft to the motion of the pitching deck. As he skillfully and firmly set the aircraft down, a crew rushed out in the driving rain to take the critical cargo.

FALKLANDS

Elizabeth watched through the window as they landed. Heavily overcast, it was windy and cool as she stepped through the jet's door. They gave her an FBI windbreaker to wear. As she came down the steps, directly in front of her was a stubby, gray, twin-engine turboprop. It looked like a caricature of an airliner. An airliner designed by a committee, and considering its size, a committee that ran out of money. It was truly an ugly duckling compared to the sleek business jet. On its side, it proudly wore "United States Navy" with "VRC-30" on the tail. The male agent, seeing her expression, reassured her. He said that although the Cod looked funny, it was only because it landed on aircraft carriers.

"Aircraft carriers?" This was getting stranger and stranger.

Misunderstanding her question, he told her it was one of the safest carrier-capable airplanes.

She suspected "safe" and "carrier" was an oxymoron but didn't care as long as it was taking her to Josh. The male agent – she still couldn't remember his name – accompanied her onboard the Navy aircraft. She sat in a rather makeshift-looking seat. A young woman in a flight suit gave her a quick safety brief and handed her a vest and a soft helmet with a headset. The vest, with its integrated inflatable life-preserver, didn't instill a lot of confidence. They told her it would be a three-hour flight. As the engines started, she understood why she wore the helmet.

WASHINGTON DC

The press grilled the world's leading astrophysicists in a huge video conference. The scientists reinforced each other, telling similar stories. They confirmed the comet's existence and estimated its size and trajectory. Without intervention, the world was scheduled to end in eleven months on March 21st at 10:00 a.m. Greenwich Mean Time.

SOUTHERN OCEAN

The surgical suite was located near the center of the ship, both to protect from battle damage and because the ship's motion was muted near its center of gravity. Despite the ship's size and the Captain's attempts to maneuver it to reduce motion, the raging cyclone rocked the operating room like a cradle. The surgeon, however, had years of experience treating combat casualties, from Iraq to Los Angeles inner-city hospitals.

They had been in surgery for five hours. In this case, however, the surgeon knew that too much time had elapsed before they could operate. The medics had attempted to chill his body during the long transport, but with the severity of the wounds, on top of the extreme sea state, her patient's survival prospects were basically zero.

The anesthesiologist said, "His blood pressure's dropping again."

The surgeon said, "We're almost finished."

"He's sixty over forty. I've already pushed five units. He's not responding to the drugs anymore."

"I can't stop here. Do what you can."

They both heard the cardiac-monitor tone change.

The anesthesiologist shook his head. "He's tachycardic… we're losing him."

The aircraft was small enough that she could see into the cockpit and out the aircraft's windshield. As they descended, it was easy to identify the aircraft carrier, even in the late-afternoon twilight. It was the largest ship of a small flotilla, all headed in the same direction. As they made their approach, all she could think was, there's no way they're going to get this thing… on that. Getting closer, she could actually see the ship moving in the rough seas, and began to realize how big the carrier really was… but still not big enough to land on.

Suddenly she felt very anxious, but it wasn't the impending landing. It was for Josh. She didn't know why but she was suddenly very afraid for him. She closed her eyes and prayed as they landed.

The little turboprop touched down firmly and snagged the third cable with its arresting hook. It went from over 100 miles per hour to a dead stop in 200 feet.

NETHERWORLD

Tentatively, Josh said, "Jesse, I hate to ask… I toasted another body, didn't I?"

Yes. Your body is dying.

"I'm not going to get another one, am I?"

No.

"I guess this is the end of our journey together."

Our journey is just beginning.

His shadowy world faded for the last time.

SOUTHERN OCEAN

To Elizabeth, it felt more like a crash than a landing. As the engines shut down, a Petty Officer from the ship came onboard to escort her. Over the jet noise, he yelled, "Please follow me very closely until we're off the flight deck and inside the ship."

As she stepped off the aircraft and glanced around, she understood why. It was total chaos, or at least appeared that way. There were dozens of jets all around her. Some were parked literally inches apart, while others taxied. She saw one jet catapulted off the deck with another sitting at full power right next to it. She was impressed and mystified how they kept from running into each other. It was also loud. No, it was beyond loud. Her stomach and spine felt the rumble of afterburners from a fighter seventy feet away. There was a pervasive smell of jet exhaust, tinged with sea air. The steel deck she walked on looked like the skin of an avocado, dark and rough with a bit of an oily sheen. What amazed her was that all of these sights, sounds, and smells were taking place in the middle of the Antarctic Ocean in an area the size of a Walmart parking lot.

As she tried to follow her Navy escort, she felt the motion of the ship and had to compensate constantly just to walk. The thirty-knot wind added to the challenge, and her light clothes and windbreaker did little to stop the Antarctic air.

Once inside, with the large metal hatch closed, it was like stepping into another world. She removed her helmet and vest, and along with her FBI escort, followed a Navy Commander in khakis. They walked through a metal maze of passageways, hatches, and ladder wells. She had a good sense of direction but knew she'd never find her way back without help. They finally brought her to a nicer-looking part of the ship with wider passageways and shiny blue linoleum with stars. Her Navy escort took her to a locked door, entered a button combination in a small box on the wall, and opened it. Inside was a small conventional-looking conference room. Her escort motioned her to enter but stayed outside. He said, "Would you please wait here, ma'am. There's coffee on the table and someone will be joining you shortly."

She nodded and went inside. She could still feel the ship gently rocking and rolling. It had to be rough out there to move something this big. She carefully poured herself a cup of coffee and sat down to wait, feeling surprisingly calm.

52

DÉJÀ VU

He tried to focus his eyes. It took a while but when he could finally see clearly, it was white acoustic ceiling tiles – again. Unlike last time, he felt a rocking motion and smelled the faint background odor of hydraulic fluid and jet fuel mixed with a tinge of methane. Josh recognized it instantly. It was like being home. He was onboard a ship, almost certainly an aircraft carrier.

He looked sideways and saw the familiar IV bag and EKG leads. He could also feel a small plastic tube blowing oxygen in his nose. He started to prop himself up but his stomach immediately let him know... bad idea. He felt like someone ran over him with a truck and punched him in the stomach for good measure. His head pounded and he was very queasy. Despite that, he was in a great mood. He was alive and they had proved it was possible to deflect a comet!

The biggest challenge was ahead but the secret was out and his part was over. It really didn't matter what happened to him now. He suspected his best prospect was life in prison, but that wouldn't be so bad. *Life* in prison would mean he succeeded.

A doctor came in to check his vitals and look at the wound, asking the usual questions about how he was feeling and if he needed any more pain medication. He felt pain but it was bearable and he didn't want to cloud his mind. He was just savoring being alive. Josh noticed the doctor's nametag. He was a Lieutenant Commander. Appropriate, he thought wryly. Shot by a SEAL Lieutenant Commander, and now another one had to fix him up. He also noticed the command pin on the nametag was USS *Reagan*. He'd done carrier qualifications onboard the *Reagan*.

The doctors and medical corpsman were polite and attentive

but left quickly and didn't talk. He also noticed an armed Marine in fatigues standing outside his room.

Less than fifteen minutes after he woke, he had visitors. While he was recruiting his team, Josh had done his homework on who was who at the major federal agencies. He immediately recognized the Deputy Director of the CIA. Two serious-looking, plain-clothed agents flanked him a few paces behind. They kept Josh in their view. He wondered if they thought he'd try to attack them with an IV bag.

The Deputy started by saying, "Sorry about shooting you, but it looks like you're doing remarkably well."

Josh smiled. "Apology accepted."

"Do you know who I am?"

"Deputy Director of the CIA, Brian Davidson."

"Actually, Acting Director."

Josh frowned. "What happened to the Director?"

Davidson gave him a half smile and said quietly, "You did." He turned to the agents behind him and asked if they would please wait outside. They looked a little surprised but complied. He continued, "Buster is retiring due to… health issues brought on by… job stress."

Josh looked sheepish. "Sorry about that."

Davidson didn't smile. "Don't be. He wasn't cut out for the job. Now that we've established who I am, do you mind telling me who you are?"

"Who do you think I am?"

"Please don't answer my question with questions. Who do you work for?"

"You wouldn't believe me if I told you."

"What," he smiled, "extraterrestrials?"

"Do you believe in extraterrestrials?"

Davidson smiled. "There you go again." He paused. "Josh… is that really your name?"

"Yes, actually it is."

"Josh, I've seen the data. That thing you built near the South Pole did in fact give the meteoroid enough of a nudge. It missed London and hit the Atlantic – *spectacularly* – but with few lives lost.

We need to thank you for saving a city and hundreds of thousands of lives. I'm just glad it's over."

Josh said, "It's just beginning."

"Yeah, we know. They've identified the fragment's mother and plotted her trajectory. It looks like we're right in the crosshairs, as you predicted. The entire world knows now." He paused. "That doesn't answer the question of who *you* are, or who you work for. There's no record of you existing prior to Kansas City Medical Center. We've looked hard, very hard. After 9/11, it's almost impossible to escape detection. Almost everything we do is recorded somewhere. All we can say for sure is who you're not. You don't belong to any government organization… and yet you have the knowledge of several."

"Kind of bold to say you know the membership of every government organization."

Davidson continued matter-of-factly, "Not really, that's my job. The only organizations that can make someone invisible, I'm a member of or in close contact with." He frowned. "It's not just that. You have information that shouldn't be possible. According to our experts, nothing can detect a comet as far out as you did. On top of that, your medical records from Kansas say you have perfect health… too perfect. They've never come across a specimen like you – no fillings, inoculations, or scars."

Looking down at his stomach, Josh said meaningfully, "No scars?" Looking back up, he said, "So, you think I'm an alien?"

"No. While in surgery, they poked around inside enough to know you're human… not that they wouldn't have wanted to dissect you if you hadn't made it."

Josh raised his eyebrows at that comment. "So, what's your theory?"

"I don't know. That's why I'm asking. If you told me you were psychic or working for little green men, I'm not sure I'd question it."

"Does it matter?"

"Of course it does!"

"Why?"

"How are we to handle you?"

"You think I need to be handled?"

Davidson frowned but didn't answer.

Josh continued, "Do you trust me?"

"What?"

"Do you trust me?"

"It's my job *not* to trust."

"You didn't answer the question."

Davidson just shook his head. "It appears you just saved our butts despite our best efforts to stop you. You hijacked the whole military-industrial complex and had it doing your bidding, while holding the most powerful government agencies at bay." He stopped and looked behind him and added, "Very impressive, by the way." He continued, "The people who worked for you trust you completely. In fact, we heard the story about the cliff rescue. I'd have discounted it as exaggeration, but we got the same story from several eyewitnesses." He shook his head. "Frankly, I'd love to see you working for us… but I'm not entirely sure we shouldn't be working for you."

Josh smiled. "Why did you make the CIA your career?"

"What?" Davidson sighed and shook his head. "I'm going to have to go back to remedial interrogation school." He pulled a chair up next to the bed and sat down. Smiling, he said, "What the heck. Josh, I was a history major. I remember it like it was yesterday. It was the day I discovered that World War I happened largely due to wrong assumptions and miscommunications. I believed, and still believe, that if we can ferret out the truth, if all the parties know what's really happening and why, we might prevent governments from making stupid mistakes, mistakes that cost thousands of lives. Maybe even stop wars that don't need to happen."

Josh said, "You're an idealist."

Davidson looked genuinely surprised. "I've been called a lot of things during my career, but it's been a very, very long time since anyone called me an *idealist*." He smiled and shrugged. "Thank you."

Josh nodded. "We're not that different, you and I. If you have to *define* me, think of me as another cynical, idealistic soldier. Like you, I have discretion to operate autonomously, but still have to report to a higher authority. The human race has a huge challenge ahead. It's going to take the best that we can be to survive. I helped, but I'm not Superman."

"You did a pretty good imitation."

Josh shook his head, "Superman wouldn't be sporting an IV."

Davidson became serious. "You asked me if I trusted you, but trust goes both ways. Can you give me something, anything, to anchor you into… my world?"

Josh understood exactly what Davidson was asking. He needed something to make Josh appear human. Josh sighed. "I can't tell you much but I can tell you that I grew up in the United States. I was educated as an engineer in an Ivy League school." He knew Davidson was a Yale graduate. "And I was a Navy pilot."

"Yeah, we kinda figured that out after you stole the Hornet. By the way, your landing sucked. The Australians are already asking when we're going to replace it."

Josh frowned, shaking his head. "A gallon just doesn't go as far as it used to."

Davidson laughed. "OK, you asked me if I trust you. I believe actions speak louder than words. Based on that, as hard as it is for me to say this, and it better never be repeated," he sighed, "yes, I do trust you."

"Thank you. I know *exactly* how hard that is to do."

Davidson asked, "So where do we go from here?"

"I was nothing more than a catalyst. All the cards are on the table now. There's nothing more I can add."

Davidson nodded.

Josh continued, "Ultimately, the next step is your call. I have no identity. No one will miss me. I've broken enough serious laws that no one would blame you if I were to suffer *complications* from the operation."

Davidson said, "You're not a very good poker player, are you? You're not supposed to show all your cards."

"No, but I *am* a good judge of character."

Davidson smiled. "Yeah, you probably also realize that there's no way we could ever prosecute. To do that would require showing what you actually did. It would be *awkward* delaying the trial for a Medal of Honor ceremony." Continuing more seriously, "The problem is that you can't just fade into the shadows. There are people out there who know you and know what you did. There will be too many questions."

Josh responded, "Actually, not many people *do* know me or what role I played. Between your agency and the administration, I bet you can come up with a great story to explain all this."

Davidson raised his eyebrows. "You're willing to let others take the credit for this?"

"Absolutely."

Davidson smiled. "Well, *that* won't be a problem."

Josh added, "I think this is an opportunity to share some of that credit, help smooth the international effort ahead."

Davidson said, "Don't worry, that's something that we and the State Department are experts at." He paused. "On another note, I noticed you didn't exactly live lavishly. You had a cheap one-bedroom apartment and drove a used Ford. I assume your finances aren't superhuman?"

Josh realized his "slush fund" from Brandon would cease. He smiled and shook his head.

"Tell you what. I'll create an account for $175,000 per year that you can draw on any time. By the way, that's what I make. Consider it a pension from the federal government for services rendered. If you don't deserve it, no one does."

Josh smiled. "A pension… or a retainer fee?"

Davidson shrugged with a slight smile. "Whatever."

"I imagine, use of that account might be… traceable?"

"Yeah, I figured you might think of that." He continued more seriously, "Josh, I can promise you as long as I'm around, that information will go to no one but me, but yes, I would like to be able to contact you."

"Thanks, I'll think about it." Josh realized there was one other thing he needed to do. Carl not only acted as a filter to protect them; he *had* to have been the source of the text warning from Scupino. "Brian, none of this could have happened without Carl Casey and Tim Smith. I don't know what happened behind the scenes but I'm sure without Carl, I'd be sitting in a prison cell and London would be burning. Tim Smith actually *fired* the Blaster, knowing he would almost certainly be killed in the process."

Davidson added, "As I understood it, he *would* have been killed, if *you* hadn't gotten in the way."

Josh continued, "Both of these men risked everything to make this work."

Davidson nodded. "They're good men. I'll make sure they receive the Distinguished Intelligence Cross. It's actually the fun part of my job." Looking at his watch, he said, "I've got to go. I have to brief the President." He frowned. "But first I have to figure out what I'm going to say. You've created quite a challenge… and opportunity for us." He put a card on the table next to Josh. It had nothing but a telephone number on it. "This is my direct line." As he turned to leave, he said, "Oh, we're assigning medical personnel to supervise your recovery."

"Thanks, but that won't be necessary."

Davidson said, as he left, "It's the least we can do."

After waiting almost an hour, Elizabeth saw the door open. A slim man in his fifties entered, flanked by two men. Smiling, he walked over with his hand out, saying, "Ms. Edvardsen, it's a pleasure to meet you. I'm Brian Davidson." He said to the two men with him, "Will you please excuse us for a moment?"

As they left the room and closed the door, she shook his hand, not knowing what to expect. She assumed he was a government official but didn't know who he represented.

As if reading her mind, he said, "Ms. Edvardsen, I'm the Acting Director of the CIA and I want to sincerely apologize to you for your incarceration and interrogation. We didn't understand what Josh was doing. We had good intentions but, as much as I hate to admit it, we were operating under some major misconceptions. I'm so sorry. Can you ever forgive us?"

This took her by surprise, but she was nothing if not adaptable. He looked as if he was prepared to take a verbal beating. "Mr. Davidson, Josh is… unique. I can imagine your situation quite easily. No apology necessary, officially or personally." She already liked this man.

With a look of relief, he smiled and said, "Please, call me Brian. Elizabeth, we also owe you a huge debt of gratitude."

Surprised, she asked, "Me… why me?"

"You put sufficient doubt in your interrogators that we forwarded the meteoroid trajectory information to observatories and NORAD. The early warnings saved countless lives at sea and along the coast." He paused. "Would you like to see the Prophet... I'm sorry, I mean Josh?"

She cocked her head to the side and looked at him carefully. "Did you say... the Prophet?"

"Sorry, slip of the tongue. That was just a codename we used." Continuing with a slightly apprehensive look, "I don't know if anyone told you, but Josh was... injured during the South Pole operation."

"What happened?!"

Davidson frowned. "He's fine, but he was accidentally shot."

Her eyes got wide. "Shot!"

Speaking quickly, he added, "The bullets have been removed and he's doing well. I've already been in to talk to him. He seems to have an unusually strong..."

She interrupted him. "Can I see him?"

"Yes. Yes, of course."

Davidson accompanied her to the ship's sickbay. As they followed a Navy commander on a several-minute walk through the metal maze, he continued to talk to her. They finally reached sickbay. It was a small but fully equipped hospital. She recognized most of the equipment and was impressed. It made sense if you had to handle serious combat casualties. At a private room with a Marine guard, Davidson stopped outside and waved her in.

Josh heard someone outside and looked up. He was shocked to see Elizabeth. She ran to his bed and gently grabbed his face in her hands. With tears in her eyes, she said, "Are you all right?"

Smiling and trying not to get emotional himself, he said, "I'm doing great, really."

She gave a small laugh but her voice quavered as she said, "What is it with you? Do I need to buy you Kevlar underwear?"

He laughed and then winced. "I can't believe you're here!"

She leaned forward and kissed him on the forehead. "How and where did you get shot?" She was already peeking under his sheet.

"I haven't seen it myself but I think I have an extra belly button or two."

With anger, she said, "Who did this to you?"

Josh said, "It's not important and please don't hold it against anyone. Brian Davidson is a good guy. You can trust him."

He realized he needed to come clean. It wouldn't get any easier with time. He'd rather have a root canal than what he was about to do, but they were alone. He didn't know if they would let him see her again and he needed to be the one to tell her. He said softly, "Elizabeth... I need to tell you something. It's something I should have told you long ago."

She took his hand and with a little smile said, "You really don't know anything about plumbing, do you?"

He couldn't help but smile. It was true; sprinkler systems and faucets never worked the same after he "fixed" them.

He started and then stopped. Finally, he sighed. "Elizabeth, I'm so sorry... I'm not what you think I am." There it was, finally out in the open.

She frowned and said slowly, "What do I think you are?"

He frowned. "I... I'm not exactly sure."

She gave him a compassionate smile. "Then how do you know you're not what I think you are?"

A chill went down his spine at still another parallel Jesse conversation.

She shook her head, laughing softly. "Josh, you *really* don't get it, do you? You're cute but you are soooo dense. I would love you, even if you turned out to be a raging schizophrenic with delusions of grandeur. Don't you understand, it doesn't matter to me who you are or who you *think* you are or aren't." Looking around conspiratorially, she smiled, adding, "But we might be able to set aside the *delusions* of grandeur diagnosis." She continued, "You know, my Uncle Jess always used to say, never underestimate a woman's intuition."

Speechless, he just stared at her.

She leaned over and kissed him gently. While he was still trying to process, she added, "I'm going to be sticking around until you're fully recovered."

Finally grasping at a subject he could comprehend, he asked weakly, "They'll let you take that much time off work?"

She grinned. "Brian – probably as a way to make amends –

offered me a contract to be your personal nurse through your recovery… to the tune of $250,000."

"Wow."

Looking mischievous, she said, "Look, it's not as though I really want to be around you, I just need the money to fix the plumbing in my condo." She winked. "The contract says that I must supervise your full medical recovery and ensure you reestablish all your physical abilities." She gave him an innocent look. "Course, I'm not entirely sure what *all* your physical abilities are."

Saving Josh from responding, a corpsman came in and said he'd have to check the wound and change the dressings. Josh watched Elizabeth, as she watched the corpsman examine him. He wasn't impulsive, but came to a sudden decision. As the corpsman left and Elizabeth came back over to his bed, he asked, "Elizabeth, you really aren't mad at me? I mean, you're not just being nice because you feel sorry for the situation I put myself in?"

She didn't say anything. She just smiled and shook her head and held his hand.

He decided to forge ahead. "Then, Elizabeth, could you do me a favor?"

She said, "Sure."

"If I survive and don't do life in prison, will you marry me?"

Her eyes got big. He'd accomplished something rare. He'd rendered her speechless. Finally, tilting her head slightly, she said with a large smile and damp eyes, "Let me think about it. Yes."

Just then, one of the agents came in and asked if he could speak to her. She leaned over and gave Josh a big kiss, and then left with the agent, saying she'd be back.

As they left Josh's room, the agent said to her, "I'll escort you back to the Director and then show you to your stateroom. You can return here any time you wish." He handed her a plastic ID on a neck strap, and said, "Ms. Edvardsen, this will take care of you while you're on the ship." Then he handed her a manila envelope and explained. "There's a State Department passport and a government credit card for any expenses." As they walked, she took the maroon passport out, opened it, and looked inside. She was thankful for the passport… but couldn't they have found a better picture?

He brought her back to the small conference room. Several people surrounded Davidson, but as soon as he saw her, he disengaged and came over. "Elizabeth, is there anything we can do for you?"

She said, "You've been great and I really appreciate your honesty. I don't hold what happened to Josh against you. I can't, because he doesn't. In fact, he said you were a good guy and to trust you." She paused. "But if you don't mind my asking, how did he get shot?"

Davidson, surprised, said, "He didn't tell you?"

"No," she shook her head in disbelief. "He said it wasn't important."

Davidson started slowly, "Let's just say, the individual responsible won't cause any more trouble. He's currently under sedation."

Elizabeth looked at him closely. "You introduced yourself as *Acting* Director."

Davidson gave her a half smile.

Raising an eyebrow, she asked, "What will happen to the… ah… individual responsible?"

Davidson thought she'd make a great agent. "Nothing *dramatic*, unfortunately. He's been removed from his position and will retire from government service… under supervision."

She nodded silently.

He looked her in the eye. "Elizabeth, may I ask *you* a question?"

She nodded again.

Glancing around to make sure no one was listening, he quietly asked, "Who is he and how was he able to come up with a plan to find and move a fifteen-kilometer mountain?"

She raised her eyebrows and tilted her head slightly. With a half smile, she said, "I tell you the truth. If you have the faith of a mustard seed, you can say to this mountain, move from here to there and it will move. Nothing will be impossible for you." She winked.

He frowned, but his eyes automatically glanced upward for a fraction of a second. Then, gently shaking his head, he said, "Ah… yeah, OK," and changed the subject. "Well, I better be going. I've got a lot of creative explaining to do." He smiled as he took her hand. "Take good care of him, Elizabeth. We may need his help again."

EPILOGUE

Headlines:

Australians Sacrifice Super Hornet to Save the Queen… Squadron Commander and pilot to be knighted…

CIA Director Buster Johnson Resigns over Health Issues… President Yager says it's a great loss but respects Johnson's decision. Acting Director Brian Davidson has President's complete confidence…

Millennium Comet Officially Named Chandra-Wooldridge… With humility, Dr. Wooldridge stated, "I certainly don't want to take all the credit. It was a team effort…"

Strategic Defense Initiative Cover Story for Secret Comet Deflection Program? Department of Defense spokesman refused to confirm or deny…

Admiral Joe Scupino Appointed Director of new UN Planetary Defense Directorate… Admiral Scupino earned his second star, as the 10th Blaster became operational on top of Mount Howe…

Sir Edward Brandon Asked to Run for Prime Minister…

NEXT

In a dream, Josh said, "We're successfully deflecting the comet!"

Yes.

"Are there more challenges ahead?"

Yes.

"Another comet?"

No.

"Then what?"

Something much more dangerous.

"What could be more dangerous than a fifteen-kilometer comet?"

Mankind and that which mankind creates.

The conversation faded as he slipped back into a peaceful sleep. He wouldn't worry or remember for another year.

CHAPTER 1 OF *CONCEIVE*, THE SEQUEL TO *RESURRECT*

MOUNT HOWE, MARCH 21ST, 8:15 GMT

"If there are any changes to the projections, I'll contact you immediately. And thank you, Mr. President, I'll pass that on to the team."

Admiral Joe Scupino hung up the phone and looked out over his Antarctic base, a base with only one purpose – to deflect the Millennium Comet. The C-5 on approach was the last jet scheduled to arrive today… maybe forever. He glanced at the countdown timer on his desktop screen – less than two hours to the comet's arrival.

It was almost time to go down to the Fire Control Center. He knew having the boss present made some of his people nervous, so he usually slipped in just before a firing… but not today. This was their final and most critical shot.

His office sat directly under the airfield's control tower, thirty meters above the ground. Wrapped in heavily insulated windows, the panoramic view was reminiscent of the bridge of a ship. Fifty-below-zero, fifty-knot winds howled outside, as he watched the huge cargo jet struggling to land on the blue-ice runway. The sun was just below the horizon but wouldn't rise for another six months. In the perpetual twilight, the runway and taxi lights reflected off the ice they were embedded in, giving the airport a beautifully surreal character.

As the C-5 safely touched down, he looked directly below at an An-225 Antonov. Floodlights illuminated blowing snow, swirling around the giant Russian jet as they towed it to a huge, heated hangar under the tower. This international bucket brigade of jets had built a nuclear-powered base of 15,000 engineers, scientists, and construction workers.

Pouring a hot cup of coffee, he looked out the windows facing east. Mount Howe dominated the view, towering 1,700 feet above the plain. On the northwestern slope, his eyes followed the headlights of the snowcats winding their way to the top. He could just make out the silver domes dotting the mountaintop like mushrooms. Inside each of the ninety domes sat the world's most powerful and accurate lasers.

The elevator "dinged." He turned to see his highly efficient taskmaster, also known as his Flag Aide, bounding out. Lieutenant Molly Cardoso was dark, wiry, and always in motion. Studying her smartphone intently, she answered his unasked question. "We still have a few minutes, sir."

Looking back out the window, he put both his hands around his warm coffee cup. "You'd think after ten months, we'd get used to the cold."

"I'll have them check the heating system."

He shook his head. "It's fine." He nodded toward the three-story, windowless building, nestled at the base of the mountain. "The nuclear reactors are putting out plenty of power and heat. In fact, they're starting to melt the ice." He paused. "It's probably just the 8,000-foot elevation." The reflection of his face in the window contradicted him. Months of crushing responsibility and little sleep had taken their toll. Did he really look that tired? The reflection of genuine concern on the face of his young aide confirmed it.

He turned to her, smiling. "Molly, you keep up with the news. How's the world reacting?"

"Well, let's see. The conspiracy theorists don't believe there's a comet or Antarctic base and we're just actors in a studio. There are some people that are convinced the world's ending and are partying their brains out." She smiled. "But I think the majority accept the situation with cautious hope. There's been a major resurgence in science and religion." She paused – unusual for her – and added, "Things once important become trivial. Things trivial become important."

"Why Molly, you have the heart of a poet."

"Doubt it, sir. I hate poetry." She looked at her watch.

Getting the hint, Scupino took a last look at the mountain and followed her to the elevator.

As the doors closed, she said, "Sir, you're scheduled for a short talk to the team as soon as we arrive at the Control Center. It'll be televised across the base, and," she looked at him meaningfully, "it'll be picked up by the press and probably broadcast around the world."

He gave her a tired grin. "I promise, Molly, I won't tell anymore sea stories." He paused. "Have you talked to your folks recently?"

"I talked to my dad in LA yesterday. He's fine." She hesitated. "I wasn't able to talk to Mom… she flew back to Rio de Janeiro to be with my grandparents."

Scupino looked at her with concern.

She sighed. "I know. I've seen the trajectory simulations. I told her if things don't go according to plan…" She looked down. "She said it's where she was needed."

Scupino gently squeezed her shoulder.

As the elevator doors opened and they walked to the Fire Control Center, she attached a wireless lapel mic and snatched his coffee cup.

Looking like NASA's Mission Control, the front wall was a giant display with status information and live views of the mountaintop. Facing it were rows of occupied monitoring stations, and above and behind, a glassed-in press gallery. There was a subdued but constant buzz of voices and keyboard clicks.

As Scupino moved toward the front of the room, he saw his Deputy Director and Chief Scientist, Dr. Victoria Chandra, near the back, talking to the Control Center Director.

Over the loud speaker, a calm voice said, *"T-minus thirty minutes."*

That was his cue. As he stepped up in front of the main display, the room quieted.

"I'll make this fast. You have more important things to do than listen to speeches. After ten months of backbreaking work, we've delayed the Millennium Comet three and a half minutes. Doesn't sound like much, but it will allow the earth to move 6,000 kilometers in its orbit… and out of the comet's crosshairs. Although it *will* still graze the atmosphere, you and the millions who've supported us, have prevented a direct impact that would have erased humanity and most life on earth. Congratulations. I'm incredibly proud of each and every one of you."

There was a round of spirited applause.

He glanced at the display behind him. "We're twenty-eight minutes from our final salvo… the most critical to date. You're about to rotate a fifteen-kilometer mountain to ensure it holds together as it crosses the atmosphere. Nothing must stop us."

He paused. "Just got off the phone with the Secretary General of the United Nations and the President of the United States. They, along with all the world's leaders and citizens, send their heartfelt thanks and prayers for your success.

"We're a truly international team and come from many different belief sets, but at this point, I don't think any of us would believe it unreasonable to request supernatural help. Please join me in a quiet prayer."

After the prayer, Scupino moved through the Control Center, patting backs and shaking hands. He knew everyone by name. Finally working his way to the back, he smiled at Chandra and said, "Graduation day."

"*T-minus fifteen minutes.*"

After getting both of them a cup of coffee, Scupino asked the same question he'd asked her almost every day for the past ten months. "So… how are we looking?"

She took a sip. "Latest projections have it penetrating fifty kilometers into the atmosphere and coming within seventy kilometers of the surface. Computer models still show multiple earthquakes, tsunamis, major meteoroid damage, and a very powerful electromagnetic pulse… but it's all stuff we're expecting and hopefully prepared for."

Scupino asked, "Rotation?"

"We're close to having our potato-shaped comet's skinny face forward. Just need to hit it *hard* enough to stop the rotation and stabilize it in that orientation."

Scupino nodded and then quietly asked, "What are the odds it'll hold together when it hits the atmosphere?"

"With the correct orientation and no rotation, it'll have 15 per cent less drag."

He said nothing.

She continued, "Do you know how many times NASA has used atmospheric braking for planetary missions?"

He finally said, "Optimistic press releases aside…"

She sighed and looked him in the eye. "Joe, we just don't know. We're dealing with a lumpy, fifteen-kilometer mountain. Even if we do everything right… it has to hold together through hundreds of Gs of deceleration at 3,000 degrees."

"T-minus ten minutes. Target data upload complete."

"And if it doesn't?"

Looking past him, eyes unfocused, she said, "You've seen the simulations. If even part of it breaks up and explodes in the atmosphere… we're talking a 100 million megaton bomb."

Scupino shrugged. "Better than the 2 *billion* megatons of a direct impact."

Chandra nodded but very quietly added, "Yeah, but 100 million megatons is still ten times more powerful than all the nuclear weapons in the world combined."

Before Scupino could respond, the Control Center Director, Colonel Carlos Comulada, interrupted. "We got a problem." He pointed at the display. It showed a schematic of the ninety Blasters, but two branches of ten Blasters were blinking red. "We just lost the power conduit to twenty Blasters. Probably wind damage. We're clocking seventy knots on the mountaintop. I just sent in the emergency team."

"T-minus eight minutes. Targeting servos aligned."

Scupino asked, "Can we re-aim the other Blasters to compensate?"

Chandra said, "Yes, but seventy Blasters aren't enough." Calling up data on her tablet, she said, "We've *got* to get at least fifteen of them back online, or we won't be able to stop the comet's rotation."

As Comulada returned to his desk, he said, "They have six minutes to evaluate, repair, and evacuate."

Scupino noticed the press had sensed something and were pointing cameras their way. Chandra leaned over and whispered, "If it hits the atmosphere with *any* angular momentum, it'll tear itself apart."

"T-minus six minutes. Capacitors at 100 per cent charge."

One of the mountaintop cameras was now displaying a damaged dome, ripped apart by the wind. Next to it, they could just make out shadowy figures in the twilight. Struggling against the subzero, hurricane-force winds, they were hunched over a damaged power-junction box.

"T-minus four minutes. Computer-controlled tracking initiated."

Comulada turned back to Chandra, "We've got to re-aim the remaining Blasters before the automated firing sequence locks them out."

Chandra closed her eyes. When she opened them, she said, rapidly, "Re-target, assuming we have *eighty* Blasters online."

Comulada's eyes narrowed. "You sure? If we end up with only seventy, re-targeting for eighty will make things worse."

Chandra snapped, "Do it!" Then stepping forward so only Comulada and Scupino could hear, she added, "Carlos, if it's spinning at all when it hits the atmosphere, we're toast. We've got to go for broke."

"T-minus two minutes. Targeting coordinates locked in."

On the screen, they saw metal debris rip off the dome and just miss the heads of the repair team. Scupino knew it all hinged on the frostbitten crew, and they were running out of time.

"T-minus one minute. Capacitor initiators armed."

Chandra began to pace.

Comulada pointed excitedly at the screen. "They got one circuit working. That's ten Blasters back online!"

Scupino shook his head. "Still not enough."

Chandra said, "Re-route the power intended for the dead Blasters to all the others!"

Comulada frowned. "They can't handle that much power. We'll melt their cores."

Chandra said, "We have to compensate for the missing Blasters. They only have to fire one more time. Melt 'em!"

Comulada nodded. "Re-routing power."

"T-minus twenty seconds. Target locked. Fire commit."

At the front of the Control Room, the display of the Blaster's status changed. Ten Blasters went black. The remaining eighty changed from green to yellow, with a flashing "112% Power" next to each. There was a buzz around the room and in the press gallery. Scupino yelled to Comulada, "At that power, some of them may explode. Tell the repair team to take cover inside the dome of one of the dead Blasters!"

Comulada nodded, speaking quickly into his headset.

"T-minus fifteen seconds. Abort disabled."

They saw, on screen, the last shadowy figure dive into one of the domes. As the door to the dome closed, they heard, *"T-minus ten, nine…"*

Shaking his head, Scupino clinked his coffee cup to Chandra's. "Whatever the outcome, it's been an honor and privilege to serve with you."

"Five, four…"

She whispered back, "Honor's all mine." She paused. "Just wish Josh had lived to see this."

"Two, one…"

Blindingly beautiful blue-green lasers lit the Antarctic plain like a flash photograph. All eighty beams stabbed at the comet in what might be humanity's last act of defiance.

SOUTH AMERICA, MARCH 21ST, 9:45 GMT

On the northeast coast of South America, Josh Meadows stood on a cliff overlooking the Pacific. His new bride stood beside him, her blonde, wind-tousled hair illuminated by the setting sun. The muted sound of pounding surf rose from hundreds of feet below as they looked across the ocean. Just above the horizon, tiny pinpoint lights, sparkled briefly like fireflies in the distance.

Josh said, "That was it… our last shot."

She nodded. "How close will it get?"

Still staring at the horizon, he said, "It'll cut through the atmosphere for a thousand miles and come within forty miles of the surface."

"No, I mean how close will it get to us?"

He pulled his eyes from the horizon and gave her a half smile. "Got your sunglasses?"

She gave him the look.

"Sorry. It'll enter the atmosphere 400 miles east of here. Moving 120 times faster than the speed of sound, it'll cross this coastline twenty seconds later." He smiled. "We have ringside seats."

"Is it safe?"

He shrugged. "As long as it doesn't break up."

"And if it does?"

Josh raised his eyebrows and looked back at the horizon. "We'll be the lucky ones. We won't be crushed, drowned, choked, or starve to death."

"Let me guess… because we'll be incinerated?"

"Along with everyone in South America."

Looking back at the horizon with a smile, she said softly, "Kind of a buzz kill on the ringside seats."

AUTHOR'S NOTE

Although this is a work of fiction, the science behind the story, particularly regarding comets, is not fiction. Thanks to the work of a dedicated cadre of astronomers (often on shoestring budgets), the chance of a large asteroid sneaking up on us decreases each year. Not so of comets. It's still almost impossible to detect a new comet on a collision course until it's too late. Recent research indicates that the chance of a comet impact may be hundreds of times greater than originally believed. All we know with absolute certainty is that impacts have happened and will again. The time to the next impact could be millions of years... or weeks. With a year or less to respond, humanity's survival depends on having a plan in place that we can quickly activate. Currently, we have no such plan.

Quantum physics and cosmology are even stranger than portrayed. Basic human intuition breaks down when we consider the tiniest of scales (subatomic), and the greatest of scales (the universe). Following quantum mechanics and cosmology to their conclusion ultimately leads to the spiritual... or a migraine.

We will back up our beliefs by contributing a portion of the proceeds from this book to non-profits that support humanity's future. We'd love to have your input – your vote will decide where a portion of the contributions will go. If you'd like more discussion on real-world threats, the intersection of physics and the spiritual, or a sneak preview of the second book of the trilogy, please join us at www.resurrecttrilogy.com/next.html